'This is space opera on a vast scale, backed up by Baxter's customary impressive research as he seamlessly weaves planetary exploration, genome reconstruction, climate change, artificial intelligence and much more into the compulsively readable narrative. The opening volume of a projected series, it's Baxter at his very best' *Guardian*

'It's another triumph for Baxter. A page turner that not only fascinates on an intellectual level, but on a science fiction thriller level too' *SciFiNow*

'You can rely on Stephen Baxter to come up with solid science fiction that does everything you'd expect a bit of classic sci-fi to do' *Starburst*

'Hard SF science smarts . . . f fun too' *SFX*

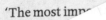

'The most imp writer in the country' *The Times*

'Baxter is he hard sci-fi crown of Arthur C. Clarke' *Daily Telegraph*

WORLD ENGINES

DESTROYER

STEPHEN BAXTER

This paperback first published in Great Britain in 2020 by Gollancz
First published in Great Britain in 2019 by Gollancz
an imprint of The Orion Publishing Group Ltd
Carmelite House, 50 Victoria Embankment
London EC4Y 0DZ

An Hachette UK Company

1 3 5 7 9 10 8 6 4 2

A CIP catalogue record for this book is
available from the British Library.

ISBN (Mass Market Paperback) 978 1 473 22319 6
ISBN (eBook) 978 1 473 22320 2

Typeset by Input Data Services Ltd, Somerset

Printed in Great Britain by Clays Ltd, Elcograf S.p.A.

MIX
Paper from
responsible sources
FSC
www.fsc.org   FSC® C104740

www.gollancz.co.uk

To my cousin
Paul Richmond
1969–2018

ONE

On Her Youth, and Her Meeting with Malenfant

Note: Section headings are taken from *The Testament of Greggson Deirdra*, compiled at Edo Station, Luna, AD 3451.

1

My name is Reid Malenfant.

You know me. Yeah, the guy who crashed the space shuttle. But, you know, I was only in the left-hand seat of that booster stage in the first place because I was always an incorrigible space cadet.

Now I want to talk about why I became a space cadet.

It started with a simple question:

Where is everybody?

As a kid I used to lie at night out on the lawn, soaking up dew and looking at the stars, trying to feel the Earth turning under me. It felt wonderful to be alive – hell, to be ten years old, anyhow.

But I knew that the Earth was just a ball of rock, on the fringe of a nondescript galaxy.

As I lay there staring at the stars – the thousands I could pick out with my naked eyes, the billions that make up the great wash of our Galaxy, the uncounted trillions in the galaxies beyond – I just couldn't believe, even then, that there was nobody out *there* looking back at me down *here*. Was it really possible that this was the *only* place where life had taken hold – that only *here* were there minds and eyes capable of looking out and wondering?

But if not, *where are they*? Why isn't there evidence of extraterrestrial civilisation all around us?

As a kid on that lawn, I didn't see them. I seemed to be surrounded by emptiness and silence.

Later, I looked this stuff up properly. Turns out this paradox was first stated clearly by a twentieth-century physicist called Enrico Fermi. And it struck me as a genuine mystery. The contradictions are basic. Life seems capable of emerging everywhere. Just one starfaring race could easily have covered the Galaxy by now. The whole thing seems inevitable – but it hasn't happened.

Thinking about paradoxes is the way human understanding advances. I realised the Fermi paradox was telling me something very profound about the universe, and our place in it.

Or was.

Of course, everything is different now.

Turns out they were here all the time.

Or anyhow, their mighty Engines.

All the time—

I'm in a flat spin—

2

Can you hear me?

Flat spin. I'm in a flat spin—

Try to be calm. It's over now.

Over? . . .

Do you know who you are?

My name is Reid Malenfant. You know me. And you know I'm an incorrigible space cadet. I – my name is . . . Where am I?

Don't worry about that for now.

I bet I'm back in crew quarters at KSC, right? In my room. On the bed, under that big oil painting of Neil Armstrong shaking hands with Richard Nixon?

Don't worry—

Where's Michael? My son, Michael? Is he safe? Does he know where I am?

Michael can come to no harm.

What the hell does that mean? Look, he's a grown man, but he lost his mother to a space accident aged ten, and now—

He is beyond harm. Believe me. You must concentrate on yourself.

Myself? So . . . the mission's over, right? What, am I emerging from some kind of bender? You're fifty-nine years old, Malenfant, you should know better than to compete with those millennial fighter jocks. Though generally the Jack Daniel's leaves me able to see, at least.

That will come. The nanomeds—

Nanomeds? What about the bird, *Constitution*?

Constitution. Yes. The space shuttle booster stage you were flying, before . . . Good, Colonel Malenfant. It's good that you're remembering that much.

It is?

It has been quite a challenge for us, you know.

What has?

Your treatment.

What treatment?

One thing at a time. You know who you are. We have established that.

My name is Reid Malenfant. And I know how I got here.

You do?

In general terms. I – how's my pilot?

Your pilot?

Nicola Mott. I was commander of the *Constitution*, she was the pilot. Two-person crew.

British.

Mott is British. Spring chicken at forty-nine years old, ten years younger than me, and sharp as a tack and very experienced. Listen, she was in NASA a decade before I finally got in, and the agency in the nineties was a tough place to progress if you weren't American, male and a pilot. But Nicola had fixated on the first flights of the shuttle when she was seven, eight, and had wanted to fly in space ever since. So she did. She migrated to the US, worked at McDonnell-Douglas on space station engineering, got into NASA, worked Mission Control, finally made it into the astronaut pool . . . You know, we have this saying in NASA: you train the new guy to be your replacement.

6

Well, Nicola is no novice, but some day soon she's going to be my replacement . . .

Nicola.

How is she?

We can discuss that, Colonel Malenfant.

Just Malenfant. What do I call you?

Karla. Just Malenfant. Just Karla.

Karla . . .

Tell us how you got here.

You want the long story, or the short?

What, are you in a rush?

. . . Was that a joke? Karla, I think we'll get along fine, you and me.

OK.

The life story.

I got here through aeroplanes, and war, and science fiction.

I was a little kid in the sixties, remember. You had *Fireball XL5* on Saturday morning TV, and *Star Trek* in prime time, and I devoured Wells and Clarke and Heinlein and all those other guys.

And there was space, of course. I was seventeen when the shuttle first flew, *Armstrong* riding atop *Constitution*, John Young commanding the orbiter, Fred Haise the booster plane . . . So there was all that going on.

And meanwhile my daddy first took me flying when I was three – so he said, I don't remember that far back. I grew up knowing he'd been an aviator, though. Flew in Korea. And *his* father had flown in the Second World War. Went up in a P-51 Mustang against German jet planes. Hell of a thing. As a veteran too.

So, eighteen years old, I made my first approach to NASA. I

7

soon learned it was a long road ahead. Go to college, they said.

My mother helped me find the right courses at Columbia U, and then I got a job with Sperry Engineering, who had a lot of contacts with the space programme. I was building a career, a profile.

Then in the early eighties they announced the schedule for the Project Ares Mars mission, and I got all fired up again. Impatient, I guess. I tried NASA, again. Got nowhere.

So I took a gamble and went back to college. Well, four of the first dozen Moon walkers had been to MIT. I went to Princeton, this was around 1982, because I knew O'Neill was teaching there. The space colonies guy – the High Frontier? Wow, he opened up my eyes to what you could *do* in space, once it became economical to get there in the first place.

We must have watched *Silent Running* like fifty times.

I tried again for NASA. Bounced again. Turned out they wanted pilots more than dreamers at that stage.

So, I would have made my father and grandfather proud, I joined the USAF. Served my time at the Air Force Academy at Colorado Springs. This was around 1984; I was twenty-four years old. Turned out I was a half-decent flyer.

You became a military pilot.

Eventually served in the second Gulf War. But by then I was married, to Emma.

Emma Stoney.

Yeah. Emma Stoney. Always kept her own name, and damn right. She wasn't your typical service wife of the time, and wouldn't put up with the bum deal they got back then: low pay, moving the whole time, your husband overseas while you raise the kids in lousy military-base housing . . . We had grown up together, you know. Though she was ten years younger than me. We had met up again at a family wedding – her sister's.

And, after Michael was born, she turned out to be the first to join NASA, before me I mean.

She became a mission specialist.

Yeah. She always blamed me for inspiring her. I was that bit older. But I guess her strategy was smarter than mine. She went to college and took geology and climatology and planetary studies – not flying and engineering. NASA is full of pilots and engineers, but it turned out to be short of people who could understand planets and moons. All of which put her in prime position when the Phobos flight came up.

A flight planned to investigate the orbital anomalies.

Yeah . . . Phobos, moon of Mars, was acting very strangely. It was apparently being dragged down towards the planet, like Skylab, like a low-altitude space station. But Mars's air was too thin for that, Phobos should have been too massive – if it was solid all the way through . . . There had been strange, contradictory observations for decades, and even more contradictory theories. Then in the late eighties they sent a space probe that *proved* the orbital decay was real, and Carl Sagan and other people started arguing for a dedicated crewed mission. And Emma got a seat, and she deserved it, by damn.

But by the time Emma left for Phobos you had become better known for your campaigns for private mining missions to the asteroids.

My campaigns? That's what I *did*, buddy. I even established a start-up, Bootstrap, Inc. I guess I had a kind of revelation. About how we should be thinking about space. And I know precisely when.

Tell me.

It came in 2003.

Over Iraq.

*

I was never a combat pilot.

I was flying tankers in the sky – well, that turned out to be a good preparation for my later career flying shuttle boosters. The KC-135 Stratotanker had not dissimilar handling characteristics to the booster, as a matter of fact, another big, heavy aeroplane.

It was a hell of a theatre.

I remember Baghdad from the air. You have to understand this was a sprawling, modern city, like LA or Houston. Whole neighbourhoods going black as the power systems failed. The air defences like flashbulbs popping off, and tracer fire, and the searchlights probing the sky like something out of the Second World War. And the cruise missiles going in, and our planes whizzing low, their bombs going off with yellow flashes. In the sky, SAM missiles leaving grey scribbles in the air – and here and there you would see black smoke where somebody had got taken out. You know, nothing prepares you for the sudden understanding that somewhere out there is another human actively trying to kill you.

But we weren't front line. We were tanker jocks. Our main job was support. We flew in fuel for depleted pilots. You know how we do what we do? A mid-air rendezvous with the fighter coming in behind and a little below, and we drop a boom which the fighter pilot latches on to, following our lights to keep position. 'Leaded or unleaded today, buddy?'

But a subsidiary part of our function was spotting, as we flew around in the air over the combat zone, waiting for a customer.

And so I was a spotter when STS-445 was used to deliver a strike from orbit.

It was a DARPA experiment, really. Hell of a technical achievement. And hell of a sight, with a shuttle orbiter dropping down from space to drop a bunker-buster bomb slam on top of Saddam's compound.

But I came out of that thinking, you know, there have to be better ways to use space hardware than this.

Not only that, if we ever do get out to the planets, the energy we will wield *then*, if used in war, could amount to a self-inflicted extinction event. Do the math. We had to get out into space, but peacefully. Even if I wasn't going myself.

So you quit the USAF—

And kick-started Bootstrap, Inc.

I had the vision and the engineering contacts.

And through the O'Neill people I met a guy called Frank J. Paulis. Younger than me, already an aerospace billionaire in his own right, but with dreams to do a lot more. He had plans he was pushing on NASA to send a mission to the solar focus, for instance, a point far out in space where gravity lensing would make it easier to pick up signals from aliens . . . He looked like John Belushi. You ever heard of him? Kind of dark, hulking. Acted like a Wall Street bruiser. But inside, he dreamed like Carl Sagan.

Paulis became the effective controller of Bootstrap, Inc., as well as the first big investor, with me as a kind of figurehead. And Paulis had great contacts of his own. He got in touch with Ann Reaves, the Shit Cola multi-billionaire. That was a time when the dot com boom was creating one super-rich baby boomer after another, but Reaves was one of the few who actually made stuff, as opposed to moving information around. And she had a dream of space. That was when we got to play with some serious money.

Well, we moved fast in those first few years, the first decade of the new century. The shuttles were flying almost weekly, we had people on the Moon and Mars — but O'Neill had always argued that it was going to be *cheap* access to space that transformed the fortunes of mankind. Because then you would have industrialisation and colonisation, and an expansive future off the planet. The space shuttle was a wonderful system, but it had never been *cheap*. And that was our angle.

So Paulis and I used Reaves's seedcorn money to buy out an old Second World War airfield in the Mojave. Basically we were trying to build big, cheap, reusable boosters to undercut the shuttle. We even dredged the Atlantic for discarded engines from the Apollo-Saturn days, when they used to dump the burned-out rocket stages in the ocean. The engines were unusable, but a mine of parts and materials.

We had a long-term plan. An income stream from solar-power satellites by 2020, by 2050 a working economy in space, by 2100 a space economy exceeding Earth's. And in the meantime, if the Earth needed space support, for example for big geoengineering climate-fix programmes, we would be in a position to offer it.

But in the short term we came up against bureaucratic snafus. NASA and the government were locked down by a cartel, a handful of suppliers, major corporations like Boeing and Lockheed Martin and Northrop Grumman, and they opposed us even being given licences to test-fire. And then there were the various outer space treaties that made it legally problematic to so much as *look* at an asteroid or a chunk of Moon rock as usable real estate. Space was the common heritage of mankind, they called it.

Funny you should mention that phrase . . .

I mean, I had some sympathy for the position. But we were caught in a tangle between cynical corporate types and starry-eyed rock-huggers, it felt like. But we made progress, little by little, in those first years.

And then, in 2004, Emma went to Phobos.

*

Her loss on that mission affected you badly.

Didn't it just. And Michael.

We were told about the loss, you know, by an astronaut who came to our home. He'd been assigned to interface with the family – a CACO they call it, Casualty Assistance Care Officer. NASA has an acronym for everything. Ours was an early Apollo Moonwalker, Joe Muldoon, who had worked with Emma. I was star-struck even while I was grieving.

We had a service back home, just the families. No body to bury, of course. They used a form of service appropriate if you are lost at sea. And then we had to go to Houston for a memorial there, and then Washington with the President and the families, and the astronauts flying the missing-man formation in their T-38 trainers. Just like they had for Armstrong, when he died on the Moon in '69.

We kind of grew apart in the aftermath. Michael and I, I mean. Of course I always supported him. He went to college, got into business administration. He planned a career in coal mining – expanding business, smart move, it looked like.

I kept on working on the Bootstrap projects. But by then, you see, Emma, or her loss, or her magnificent quest, had changed my view on the public space programme. Or reinforced it. I figured I could maybe change things from within, rather than from without. And anyhow it would honour Emma's memory.

Or maybe that's just rationalisation. Michael once told me that when I lost his mother, I lost my ability to dream. Bootstrap was nothing but a dream, at that point. And all I wanted after Emma was to fly stuff. Maybe he was right.

Anyhow, that's what I did. I distanced myself from Bootstrap and tried for NASA again. Won a place in the 2008 recruitment round. And so I ended up a glorified truck driver, flying *Constitution* . . . Where's Nicola?

You asked that.

And you didn't answer. What the hell's going on here? I still can't see, you know.

Try to stay calm.

Calm? I was in a flat spin . . . I remember, the sparklers, I tried the sparklers when we . . .

You're remembering. Good. Take it in order, Malenfant. Just tell us about STS-719 as you experienced it. Tell us about your mission.

Is this a debrief?

You can call it that. In your own time, in your own words. You graduated from your training to join the booster pilot roster – you never flew all the way to orbit, did you? And so, in 2019, you were assigned to STS-719.

Tell me about the sparklers.

Yeah . . . Look, the sparklers are what we call the hydrogen burn igniters.

You got to imagine the space shuttle ready to launch on the pad, at Cape Canaveral. I take it you've seen it. You have the booster, an aerospace vehicle the size of a 747, with the orbiter, itself the size of a 707, piggybacking on its back. And the whole stack is tipped up vertically on Pad 39-A: two winged aircraft standing on their tails, mated belly to back, against the gantry.

Our booster for the flight was *Constitution*, BV-102, the oldest in the fleet save for a glide-test prototype. And the orbiter was *Advance*, OV-106. Imagine it. Imagine sitting in the cockpit of that booster, ready for a ride into space, in a plane with the performance characteristics of the X-15, an experimental hypersonic rocketplane, but bigger than any passenger jet in the world.

All the orbiters were named for exploration ships.

14

Damn right. And that particular name was apt. The first *Advance* had been used as a rescue ship, it went after the Franklin expedition in the Arctic. And our *Advance* was the orbiter that flew the mission that saved Skylab, and made the shuttle programme famous. I watched that as an eighteen-year-old. Now, over forty years later, here I was carrying that same bird to orbit.

You were saying about the sparklers. The hydrogen burn igniters – correct?

Yeah. I'm rambling.

It's a little technical.

Look, the shuttle booster craft has twelve rocket engines, twelve big bells, and during the fuelling process a lot of stray hydrogen can get trapped up there. Inside the bells themselves, I mean. So, ten seconds before launch, we use the sparklers to burn off all that excess, so when start-up comes you get a nice smooth burn. The sparklers, you see, are mounted on the booster itself.

The sparkler system turned out to be significant in what followed.

Yeah. You could say that.

I remember that long ride up the gantry, Mott and myself bound for the booster, plus eight crew for the orbiter for that flight. We're in our suits of armour: medical sensors, pressure suit. Ours, the booster guys', are heavy-duty, Lockheed manufacture. Tan-coloured.

Man, that booster is a brute when you ride up close past it. A delta-wing aircraft with a span of nearly a hundred and fifty feet. Fifty yards! Always looked like the damn thing would never get off the ground. But you should have seen some of the other designs the engineers had cooked up en route to this configuration. Such as, an orbiter with *solid rocket boosters* strapped to its belly.

15

But our bird is a veteran, of many successful flights just like this one. And it is a fine day. No sign of trouble. The boil-off plumes, hydrogen and oxygen, rising up to a blue Florida sky, and the groans and hisses of the hulls of the tanks, and the choppers buzzing overhead . . . I always felt like I didn't want to board the craft, to hide away from all this spectacle.

Anyhow, into the flight deck.

You understand the booster is like a regular aircraft but tipped up vertically, so we have to climb a little ladder up onto our cockpit in the nose, and then into our couches lying on our backs. We fix our harnesses and ankle restraints and helmets, and we get to work with the cue cards and checklists and the scrolling updates on the cabin screens. When the shuttle first flew, you know, the booster cabin had around two *thousand* switches, crusted in there like coral. But we know our way around, Nicola and me, both veterans of several flights.

T minus seven minutes. The access arm retracts with a thump, and we're stuck up there. Save for about five abort options, that is. The excess fuel and oxygen is boiling off. We give our aerosurfaces a last work-out; you can hear the flaps creak.

T minus thirty-one seconds and the computers take over.

Ten seconds, the sparklers.

At six seconds there's main engine start. And at that moment . . .

Yes?

There's a bang.

I look at Nicola, and she's looking back at me. To us it felt like a shove in the back. We look at our displays, and the imagery of the burn that has already started at the base of the craft: the vapour plumes, the shock diamonds. Everything looks nominal, and launch control have got nothing to say. We let it ride.

But you both felt it.

Yeah. I guess the whole stack did . . .

The event was not properly tracked in real time by the spacecraft's systems, and the records show that afterwards it took some careful analysis to untangle what followed.

The records? Where is this? Where am I? *When* is this?

The event, Malenfant. Let's stick to the event.

Yeah. But you know more than I do, right? So tell me.

Very well. At ignition, there had been a minor flaw with one of the booster's engine pumps. It delivered, only momentarily, an excess of fuel to its combustion chamber, and so one engine ignited with an excess impulse. After that the engine, in fact all the engines and pumps, ran smoothly. That extra impulse was the 'bang' you felt. The impulse showed up on launch control's monitors, but there was no immediate evidence of harm, and – in the seconds she had to make an engine shutdown go/no-go decision – the flight controller for the day decided to let the launch proceed.

But there *was* harm done, right? Evidence or not.

Indeed. The whole shuttle stack – shuddered. The system was stressed. And, in the nose of the booster, at that moment, another undetected fault was triggered. A strut sheared.

A strut?

Supporting an oxidiser tank that served the booster's attitude rockets—

Known as the reaction control system. RCS.

Yes. When the strut sheared, that tank was no longer held firmly. Later in the flight the tank would come loose entirely, and collide with a propellant feed, which it broke. The hydrogen peroxide leaked slowly. But—

But there were consequences. We were going to need that RCS. One damn thing leads to another. Well, it all makes sense now.

Tell us how it happened, for you.

We soon forgot about that jolt.

All went well.

You know, it's one hell of a ride. We clear the tower, and roll over, with that baby-bird orbiter still clinging to momma's back. About a minute in we reach max q – maximum aerodynamic pressure, a combination of our increasing velocity and the thickness of the air, the maximum stress we'll suffer. The engines throttle down. Through that we go supersonic, and the booster's twelve big engines throttle back up to a hundred per cent, and the ride is as sweet as a nut.

Then comes separation.

Already we're running out of fuel; we're about to become a glider, and no more use to the *Advance*. Around two and a half minutes from the pad, around forty miles high and forty miles downrange, we separate – there are explosive bolts that make the whole stack shudder – and we release that baby bird. Staging, we call it.

Advance *made it safely to orbit.*

Yeah, and we knew that. We followed the telemetry as they went through their own stages. After four minutes, at sixty-two miles, they're officially in space. Engine cut-off when they're in orbit a hundred and fifteen miles high, and they burn their orbital manoeuvring system engines to circularise their orbit.

All of which was academic for you.

Yeah. Because suddenly we are in an off-nominal situation.

Which is NASA-ese for emergency.

Look, the staging comes at two hundred and thirty thousand feet, where there's barely a trace of air, and we're moving at Mach 12 – twelve times the speed of sound. Actually it's a beautiful moment as we reach the top of our own trajectory, unpowered. Because we are in zero gravity ourselves, you see, falling, falling. Just a few seconds.

Then it's back to work.

We had been a rocket ship for three minutes; now we will be a hypersonic glider for around ten minutes, and then ninety minutes as a subsonic aircraft to home. We have two air-breathing engines on board, but they are useless until we get down into the thicker air.

So you have to glide down.

Shedding that excess velocity on the way. Right. But for me this is the fun part. Look, we're falling away from the orbiter, and I'm flying my ship. I have my RHC – rotational hand controller, my joystick. I use this now to go into a ninety-degree roll. The idea is we go through a series of what we call S-turns, big wide swooping manoeuvres taking us down through the thickening atmosphere, all the while losing energy to friction with the air. Every minute we should shed a thousand miles per hour of velocity, twenty thousand feet in altitude. You can feel it, when it works, a tough deceleration pushing us down into our couches, side by side.

As we are that high, at the edge of the air, when I pull on that stick the bird responds using both the RCS system – our little attitude rockets, like she was a spacecraft in vacuum – and also the aerosurfaces, like she's a regular aircraft. You get a mix of responses as you fall, with the RCS dominating at first but having less and less effect, and the aerosurfaces picking it up later, as the air thickens. Until we get deep enough for the air-breathing engines to cut in.

That's the theory.

Right. But now you tell me that all the time that damn RCS system, in the nose of the ship, had been leaking propellant.

At first all goes well. We're down to a hundred and eighty

thousand feet, cue another S-turn. A hundred and twelve thousand feet, we're down to Mach 5, a mere five times the speed of sound. And that's when the RCS system fails on me. Just like that. At the time I had no idea what happened.

Now I know.

Already we're low enough for the thickening air to have a sensible effect, to push at us, but the RCS rockets still have a role to play. We wouldn't have shut them down until we were down to forty-five thousand feet. But now we have lost them.

And as all this unravels I'm still taking her through the latest S-turn.

The systems overcompensate for the loss of RCS.

We go into a flat spin.

A flat spin?

When the bird is more or less level but is spinning about a vertical axis, through her centre of gravity. Like a toy plane mounted on a pin in its belly. Nothing I do stops it, the aerosurfaces are jamming and making it worse, and the RCS is out. We're too deep in the air for those baby rockets to make any difference now anyhow.

The spin increases and we get this eyeballs-out acceleration, and I can feel myself heading towards a blackout. I can't even see how Mott is, I can't turn my head. We're both yelling.

OK. I have seconds to figure it out. I have to stop the spin. We can't eject until we're steady.

But even then, even if we get out of the spin, I'm concerned about where the bird will come down.

She's not designed to glide all the way home, remember. In the closing stages you put the booster into a pushdown – nose down towards the ground – so there's a fast descent that forces air into the turbojets, the air-breathers, and you go into a controlled landing. She needs piloting home, and that controlled landing.

Because I can't afford to let her crash.

This isn't the Mojave, this isn't Edwards Air Force Base where they flew the X-15s and you have nothing but sunshine and square miles of salt lake to come down on, as hard and as fast as you like. We are heading for a runway at the Kennedy Space Center, where we launched from. That's the whole point of the shuttle system, so the booster can be refurbished and made ready for the next mission, within weeks, days even.

Even as we spin I can see the Space Coast, sixty or seventy miles of development, all those pads and rockets and facilities. I can see the Vehicle Assembly Building, a box you could put the Great Pyramid inside. Not to mention the glitter from car windshields, lines of them, tracing out the roads. We launch twenty times a year, but even so every single flight attracts the sightseers.

I can see the contrails of the NASA chase planes, and I see the choppers in the air, USAF birds with PJs on board, para-rescue jumpers, ready to come flying out to retrieve me wherever, however I come down. They're here to save me after the crash.

But I can't crash. Not here.

I have simple priorities. Get Nicola out of there. Get enough control of the ship to bring her down somewhere safe, away from the space centre, the freeways – the ocean as a last resort. Oh, and finally, save my own life.

But you can't do any of that while the booster is in its flat spin.

I tried – I don't remember clearly – I guess I tried everything I could think of, in the book and outside it, to stop that damn spin. Until I found something that worked.

The sparklers.

Right. Look, our main rocket engines aren't designed to

21

be restarted, not in flight. And we had no fuel left anyhow. Nothing in our big internal hydrogen tanks but vapour. *But* – I wondered if that vapour might be enough.

You see, I know I can blow the tanks to release vapour; I know I can use the sparklers to burn it off. This is one of a set of last-resort options we rehearsed in the simulators, if you ever found yourself coming down with a leaking tank or whatnot. Maybe that one big jolt of exploding vapour would be enough to knock us out of the spin.

We're still spinning. My vision is surrounded by blackness. Every time I move my arms I fight against the spin. But I do it anyhow. I find the right screen and bring up a couple of contingency routines.

Forty thousand feet. I set up the command sequence. No time to check it.

Thirty thousand feet.

I key in the initiating command.

Blam. Another mighty kick in the backside; the whole stack shudders.

But that big fat impulse, off-axis from the rotation, does indeed drive us out of the spin. We're still tumbling, but for now – I drag at the stick – I can get us level again. Just for a few seconds, maybe. It's enough to get us turned, our nose pointing out to sea.

I think Nicola has blacked out.

Twenty thousand feet. Fifteen, twelve.

But now I can feel that darn flat spin building up again. Before it gets too far I reach over, and down, and pull the lever that initiates Mott's ejector seat. The cabin roof blows off; she goes flying into the air on a billow of superhot smoke. But that seat worked when it needed to. Good solid engineering by Lockheed, God bless them.

Already you were burned, then. Your own person, I mean. By the ejector-seat rockets. Going up right beside you—

Hell, yes.

You could have ejected too—

No dice.

I kept trying.

You kept trying. You had already saved Cape Canaveral. Thousands of lives, probably. You had done all you could to save Nicola Mott.

Ah. From which I surmise she did not survive the ejection.

I'm sorry you had to learn that now. That was clumsy of me. But even after you knew you couldn't escape yourself, you stayed in the cockpit, trying one option after another, trying to control the ship. And the record shows you were calling down reports to Mission Control in Houston, all the way in.

That was for the debrief later. The more information you give the controllers, the better the chance of avoiding the same screw-up in future.

A debrief you didn't expect to live to see.

No. I didn't expect to live. I *know* how hard water can be.

So.

That's all I remember.

What happened next?

You did survive the impact.

But there was a fire. Possibly caused by the leaked attitude-thruster fuel spilling out of the nose.

How about that? That damn leaky RCS! Got me two ways, then.

You were retrieved. Quickly, in fact. And you were found alive. But badly burned.

How badly? I still can't see. My eyes . . . Tell me. Look, I

23

pilot experimental aeroplanes; I've seen burns victims.

Tell me the worst you have seen.

Crash victim, at Edwards Air Force Base. A pilot. Burned all over. Skin blackish-brown, greasy, like a – a burned Thanksgiving roast. Everything burned off. The clothes, the hair, the ears, the hands and feet – the *face*, Jeez. And arms and legs kind of wizened and dried out and bent at the elbows and knees . . .

Like that.

Shit.

You survived. But you couldn't be saved. At the time.

At the time?

It was an Air Force team that retrieved you. Stabilised you as best they could. You were taken straight to a covert facility.

Covert?

Attached to the surveillance centre that the USAF then operated, at Lockheed's plant at Sunnyvale.

All very high tech, then.

You were one of their own – the USAF's own, as well as NASA's. And now, you hadn't saved your ship, but you'd saved the Cape, and almost saved your co-pilot—

Pilot. Shuttle boosters and orbiters have commanders and pilots, not co-pilots.

Understood. In the few minutes of your flight you had become, aside from the Mars pioneers, probably the highest-profile astronaut since the shuttle crew that saved Skylab in 1978. And as far as the public was concerned it probably didn't do any harm that you pulled your stunt almost exactly fifty years after Aldrin and Collins had heroically returned from the Moon without their commander.

Hmm. So the Air Force took me under its blue wing. Into this super-hospital you're talking about.

As I said, they couldn't save you, Malenfant. Instead they— froze you. Until medical facilities had advanced to the point where—

Listen, Karla. No more head-shrink shilly-shallying. Just tell me. Where am I? . . .

Colonel Malenfant. Welcome to the twenty-fifth century.

The twenty-fifth.

Take a moment to absorb that, Malenfant. Yes, this is the twenty-fifth century. To be precise—

Why did you wake me? Why now?

Because Emma—

Emma? Who died at Phobos in 2005?

Because Emma has asked for your help.

3

He thought he slept.

He thought he woke.

He opened his eyes. This time it worked.

A grey surface before him. No, above him. Shining with a soft, sourceless light. Curving over him, like he was in some kind of all-body scanner.

Medical equipment. Had to be. Was he still in hospital, then?

He raised his head. Thumped his brow on a surface only centimetres above him.

'Great start, Malenfant,' he said, resting back.

His own voice was subdued, soft, as if he was in some anechoic chamber. He heard it, though, heard his words, a physical sensation. Unlike the oddly disembodied speech he had exchanged with Karla before. And his forehead ached subtly where he had thumped it on the surface above.

He was real again.

He had a wider sense of his body too, he realised now. The heaviness of it, the mass. He tried to move around. Felt the weight as he lifted his arms, shifted his legs. The rustle of some loose, papery cloth over him, like a hospital gown. The odd twinge of discomfort, such as in the shoulder he'd dislocated playing college football, an injury that had come back to haunt

26

him in his fifties. Well, you had to expect it.

You had to expect a lot worse, in fact, when you went through a shuttle crash. As he remembered now, in unpleasant, vivid detail.

'And I remember you, Karla,' he said now.

It was like a dream, thinking back. His debrief. The voice that had seemed to surround him, a warm bath of words. But he had lacked this sense of physicality. Of embeddedness. Like he had been floating in some sensory-deprivation tank. Anaesthetised, maybe, so he couldn't feel his body at all. Even the deep inner senses: even proprioception – a long word every astronaut had to learn before being launched into microgravity, meaning the sense of one's own body, its position in space, the relative positioning of its parts – even that had been lacking.

'Well, I feel it all now,' he murmured. 'I'm back. I guess. Karla? *Karla*. You still there?'

There was no reply.

He lifted his hands to that neutral, neither hot nor cold lid just centimetres above his nose. He pressed, not too hard. No dice.

Deliberately he dropped his hands. Took deep breaths, yoga breaths, filling the belly. 'Been in tight corners before,' he told himself. 'Claustrophobic spaces. The time Mott and I went through that underwater retrieval exercise.' It had been a mocked-up shuttle booster cabin on the bed of the ocean off Guantanamo, and the search-and-rescue guys were three hours late finding them. Or so they claimed. 'Got through that, Nicola, didn't we? Got through that, get through this. Right?' He raised his hands again, deliberately drew them back before touching the lid. 'But right now, whoever's listening, I think I'd like to get out of this oven. This turkey is roasted, OK?'

There was a crack, a soft sigh as of air pressure equalising

– Malenfant felt a subtle cooling – and the lid lifted back. In that first moment, Malenfant glimpsed a clear white light. As if he was being born.

Then he made out a clean-looking, uncluttered room, what looked like monitor screens on the walls.

And a face over him, a man's face, neither young nor old – thirtyish? Clean shaven, scalp bare. He smiled down. 'Thought you would never ask. We have to be sure you're ready, you see. The emergence from a coldsleep pod can be disconcerting. You have to really *want* to come out.'

'I . . . My name is Reid Malenfant. Do you know me?'

'No. But I hope to get to know you.' A calm, clear voice, with what Malenfant might have called a mid-Atlantic accent: like American urban east coast, but softened.

'Karla?'

The smile broadened. 'Not Karla. I'm sure she will send her regards from the Moon when she knows you're awake at last. And you have your message from Emma Stoney, of course. We have a copy here.'

Malenfant tried to process all that. Too much information, in a couple of sentences. 'I was on the Moon? . . .'

'Certainly. In a coldsleep facility under a mountain called Pico, which—'

'Never mind.' Bewildered, he put that aside. '*Emma?* We need to talk about that. Basically it's impossible.'

'One thing at a time. My name is Bartholomew. Which is, not coincidentally, derived from the name of this hospital, here in London.'

'London? London, England? Look—' Malenfant began to struggle, tried to move. He felt leaden, weighed down.

'I'd take it easy if I were you.'

Malenfant didn't take it easy. He sat straight up, the room

spun, the world receded from him with a golden light and a clamour of bells.

And he collapsed back down in a dead faint.

When he came back, he found himself in a wheelchair. Some kind of dressing gown on him, heavy and warm. Soft shoes on his sockless feet, like slippers.

The room was dominated by a big tank, connected to ancillary equipment that hummed softly. An open lid. It was indeed like a medical scanner, he saw now. That soft blue light within.

'So that's the box I came in.' His voice was a scratch.

Bartholomew was sitting in an upright chair, watching him. He wore a practical-looking green uniform: trousers, a loose, short-sleeved tunic. There was one other person in the room, a woman, young, sitting on another chair. She wore a kind of coverall of what looked like wool, dyed deep brown. She was staring wide-eyed at Malenfant. She was pale, he saw, with dark hair cut short.

Malenfant felt profoundly embarrassed to have put on the display he had, in front of an audience.

Bartholomew came over, picking up a cup of some liquid on the way. 'Drink this.'

Malenfant took the cup, expecting plastic; it was some kind of ceramic. The broth looked like chicken soup. When he sipped, it tasted of potatoes, greens.

There was a clock on the wall showing what looked like twenty-four-hour time. It was a little after thirteen hundred. And what looked like a calendar, with two dates, or numbers anyhow:

AD 2469
2 February
Minus 928

AD 2469. The twenty-fifth century, as advertised.

He glanced at Bartholomew, the young woman. 'I guess I have a lot of questions.'

Bartholomew shrugged.

The woman said, 'Start where you like, Mister Reid. We're here to help you. Both of us.'

'Thanks. But my name is Reid Malenfant. It would be more correct to call me "Mister Malenfant".'

She nodded. 'Ah. Of course. Your family names came last. All right. Mister Malenfant.'

'Except that I am – was? – a colonel in the US Air Force.'

She frowned. 'I thought you were an astronaut.'

'Well, I was in NASA's astronaut corps, but strictly speaking I was never an astronaut. I flew shuttle booster stages that never got to orbit. So I never flew in space.'

Bartholomew grinned. 'Well, you have now.'

'The Moon. Karla. That's something we need to talk about, right? But for now – look, I'm an astronaut with NASA, *and* a flyer with the Air Force, and a colonel. So—'

'I should call you Colonel Malenfant.'

'Just Malenfant.'

'Now I am confused.'

'Everybody calls me Malenfant. Even my wife does. Or did. Before she died. Except' – and he faced Bartholomew – 'Karla told me there was a message for me. And so did you. From her. That's impossible. She died in 2005. Today's date . . .' He looked at the display on the wall. 'My booster crash happened in the year 2019 . . .'

Bartholomew nodded. 'You're guessing about the date, and you're guessing right. That's why we hang a calendar on the wall, so patients like you, reviving, can take in such information at their own pace. Today's date is 2469. I looked up your calendars, to make sure the date format would make sense. We do still count the years according to the old Christian calendar, though we generally don't say "AD" any more.' He smiled brightly. 'So that's one thing that should make sense to you, at least.'

Malenfant grunted. Except, he thought, that I'm about four hundred and fifty years out of time.

One thing at a time, Malenfant.

He looked again at the display. 'And the second number – a minus?'

The woman smiled brightly. 'I looked up your era as well. Your astronaut jargon. I think you'd call that a countdown clock, Mister – umm, Malenfant.'

'A countdown? Minus nine hundred and twenty-eight. Nine hundred and twenty-eight what? Hours, days?'

'Years,' Bartholomew said gently. 'Nine hundred and some years, Malenfant.'

'Until – what, AD 3397? Then what?'

'Then the Destroyer.'

That meant nothing.

But it didn't sound good.

'We aren't handling this very well, are we?' The woman stood up, and went to a wall unit to fetch another cup of broth. Then she walked over to Malenfant, took his empty cup, handed him the fresh one. 'Drink some more of this.'

She wore a plain, bronze bangle on her wrist, she saw. He took the cup, sipped it. The broth tasted the same, and he felt oddly, illogically relieved. One bit of continuity, from one moment to the next: one tiny corner of this reality made sense.

In the background Bartholomew, who Malenfant had tentatively labelled as a nurse, sat quietly, watching, still. Very still, Malenfant thought, and that seemed a little eerie.

The woman pulled her chair over to Malenfant's, sat before him, leaning, hands folded in her lap, her face intent. Maybe she sensed his disorientation, he thought.

'I realise I haven't told you *my* name.' She plucked at her garment, at hand-stitched cotton and wool, a trace of nervousness. 'It's all such a jumble, isn't it? For us, as well as you.'

'That's true,' Bartholomew called now. 'You're by far the oldest coldsleeper I've ever had to treat. Not to mention the most famous. Every case is unique, but yours took a lot of research, even experimental trials, before you could be safely brought back.'

Malenfant tried to take that in. 'I . . . Thank you.'

Bartholomew grinned. 'Well, it's not as if I have anything else to do.'

Which was an odd reply, another dangling thread, but Malenfant ignored it and focused on the woman. 'Your name,' he prompted.

'Yes. Sorry. My name is Greggson Deirdra. Umm, I guess you would say it as Deirdra Greggson.'

'Greggson Deirdra,' he repeated, committing the name firmly to memory. He had an intuition he was going to need allies in what was evidently a strange new world. 'Nice name. I knew a Deirdre once.'

'I chose the name myself,' she said brightly. 'It means *wanderer*. It was confirmed five years ago, on my twelfth birthday. The whole town was there.'

Malenfant filed that away too. She was younger than she looked, then. 'OK. And are you a wanderer, Deirdra?'

'I guess so. The name felt right to me. My parents always said I was restless, even as a child. Oh, I would finish the jobs I had to do. Chores, and my schoolwork, and the town projects. I've done well at school, I guess. But in my spare time I always had trouble sticking at stuff. I never really liked to *play*, my mother said. I was always looking for projects.'

'And what are you doing here?' He glanced over at Bartholomew. 'I'm guessing *he* is a nurse. But you . . .'

'I volunteered. Every sleeper, when they come out of the coldsleep pods, needs a companion. Especially if their sleep has been long—'

'And, like I said,' Bartholomew put in, 'nobody has slept as long as you have, Malenfant. As far as we know.'

'I'm not surprised, since we didn't even have "coldsleep pods" in 2019. Or at least, not that I knew about.'

Deirdra said, 'When I read about your case, I was just intrigued. I mean, you will need somebody sensible to show you around.'

He grunted. 'How to use the food replicators and the transmat pads?'

She looked baffled. 'I've never heard of transmat pads.'

Bartholomew grinned. 'Don't worry about it. He's teasing you. Those are pop-culture references that were dated even when he crashed his spaceship, probably.'

Malenfant studied him. 'I'm impressed you know that. And even the phrase, "pop culture".'

Bartholomew shrugged. 'Looked it up.'

But he had just been sitting in his chair the whole time, motionless as far as Malenfant could tell. He hadn't looked up a damn thing, visibly. Malenfant filed that away. Another clue about this new world, and the people in it: this was evidently an environment drenched in smartness.

And he filed away the observation, too, that Deirdra had not denied hearing of food replicators. It felt like a minor victory, if a scattershot one.

He turned back to Deirdra. 'So you volunteered to be my . . . helper.'

Bartholomew said, 'Call her a guide. You don't need a helper. You're not ill, Malenfant. The coldsleep pod wouldn't have released you unless you were healthy enough to function.'

He thought that over. 'Yet I fainted when I sat up.' He took an inventory. 'I have a few aches and pains. My old shoulder injury—'

'What do you expect, Malenfant? You went in there a broken fifty-nine-year-old man, and you've come out of it a fixed fifty-nine-year-old man. All we could do was put you back the way you were.'

Malenfant grinned at Deirdra. 'Kind of sharp for a nurse, isn't he?'

'I'm sure he's good at his job.'

Bartholomew laughed. 'A ringing endorsement.'

Malenfant growled, 'OK, a guide. Look, I'm very grateful. But I am a man four centuries out of time. Call me Captain America.'

Another puzzled frown from Deirdra. 'Who?'

Bartholomew called, 'More long-lost pop culture, Malenfant?'

'Frank Poole. Miles Monroe. Rip van Winkle, then. I guess I'm going to need a *lot* of guidance. I know – nothing – about the world out there. Beyond these four walls, in fact.'

'Nothing?'

'Well, Bartholomew here told me I'm in a hospital of the same name as him, in London.'

She brightened. 'Well, there you go. You are in London. At the bottom of the Thames Bay.'

Malenfant did a double-take. 'The Thames used to be a river. I'm under the *sea*?'

Bartholomew said, 'One thing at a time, Malenfant.'

'OK. Well, at least I can understand you. Your language hasn't, umm, *evolved* so much as that.'

Bartholomew and Deirdra shared a glance.

Bartholomew said gently. 'I wouldn't take too much comfort from that, Malenfant. You are getting a lot of help with translation.'

Malenfant felt oddly crestfallen. That smart environment again. 'Never mind. Look, Deirdra, my point is that I suspect I'm going to need a *lot* of support. You surely have your own life to lead, and this will eat a big chunk of it.' He shook his head. 'Where are you with your schooling, for instance? Are you at college?'

She looked unsure, and again glanced over her shoulder at Bartholomew, who shrugged.

'It's different now,' Bartholomew said. 'There's a lot more of what you would have called home schooling, I think.'

'But can you afford to take the time out?'

Again she looked unsure. 'You're kind of asking questions that don't make sense. Well, I suppose that's the point – why you need me in the first place. I can take all the time I want at my studies. My whole life, if I like. And working with you will be a study in itself. In a way.'

'Yeah. Grumpy Old Bastards 101. But what about your future plans? What about work?'

Again she looked confused.

Bartholomew put in, 'Deirdra, you have to remember he doesn't know what a stipend is, even. They didn't have that system in his day.'

Her eyes widened. 'Oh, right. I think I imagined the system went further back than that. So even in the early twenty-first century—'

'Yep. Basically, people had to work to stay alive, to eat. In

35

Malenfant's home nation most people were whole economic levels away from it being as stark as that, but that was the underlying truth.'

She smiled. 'This is going to be so fascinating, Malenfant.'

He felt a mixture of flattery and unease. 'I'm not some old book for you to study, you know.'

'I understand that.'

Impulsively, Deirdra took Malenfant's hands in hers. She was young; her hands were soft, warm, but strong. By contrast his own skin felt tough, leathery. The physical contact shook him, oddly — it was the first time, it occurred to him, that he had been touched, while he had been conscious anyhow, since emerging from the pod.

Deirdra said, 'We have a lot to learn, you and I. You must feel completely lost. But the very first thing you do is to think about me, to express concern about the impact you might have on me, on my life. I think that shows you are a decent person, Malenfant. Unselfish.'

'I . . . well, thanks. Not as decent as you, evidently.'

'I've thought it through before making my decision to come here, to see you.'

Bartholomew coughed. 'That's all fine. But you will have to convince your mother of that, Deirdra. Who has been in contact.'

Deirdra looked exasperated. 'Already?'

'Along with Prefect Morrel, yes.' He spread his hands. 'Look, I had to alert them when Malenfant finally woke. They're going to have to meet him themselves.'

'Ah.' Malenfant drew back, releasing Deirdra's hands. 'So there are impacts on your life after all. Your folks aren't sure about this, right? And the cops too — what was the word you used, prefect?'

'Prefects aren't cops, in the sense you mean,' Bartholomew said. 'They are all temporary volunteers, for one thing. But they are the nearest we have.'

'So what is it your mother is concerned about? *Is* it your schooling?'

'No.' She seemed irritated, frustrated.

He was left baffled again, trying to feel his way into a future society of which he had no knowledge whatsoever. 'Then what harm might it do? What harm can *I* do?'

Bartholomew said, 'I can give you a hint.'

'What hint?'

And Bartholomew pointed up at the wall.

The countdown clock. It was as if Malenfant had forgotten that key, chilling detail. *The Destroyer*.

He faced the others grimly. 'Then, while we have time, before the feds get here, let's talk.'

Deirdra fetched him another cup of broth and a cup of water for herself, and sat back down before him. 'OK. Let's talk.'

Where to begin?

'Look – the last I remember, of my old life, is wrestling the wreck of the *Constitution* away from the Cape Canaveral facilities.'

'And you did it, Malenfant,' Deirdra said. 'The most famous thing you ever did – *that* was easy to research. And Canaveral is still there. Behind the sea wall, of course.'

'A *sea wall*? Park that. OK. So they scraped me up.'

Bartholomew barked laughter. 'Pretty much.'

Deirdra was frowning again. 'You said you didn't have coldsleep pods back then?'

Bartholomew slapped the hide of the machine which had, Malenfant reflected, so recently spat him out. 'I looked that up too. Not like these, no. But the doctors of the day were well aware of the effect of cold on the body. Had been for centuries. "No one is dead until they are *warm* and dead" – that summed it up. And they were beginning to experiment with the technology – primitive cryogenics, essentially – especially in the context of the space programmes of the day. Even for a mission of a few months, to Mars or Jupiter say, to be able to freeze your crew, or most of them, would reduce the strain on your spacecraft's plumbing considerably.'

Deirdra nodded. 'I guess all this was before the Homeward movement.'

Homeward. Malenfant didn't like the sound of that. *Park that.*

'I do know the last deep-space missions were the Last Small Step flights. Stunts, really. And the furthest anybody got was to Persephone—'

'Whoa,' Malenfant said. 'I never heard of that.'

Bartholomew looked briefly abstracted, as if hearing distant voices. 'You would not have. Ninth major planet from the Sun, discovered in the late twenty-first century. A thousand times as far from the Sun as the Earth.'

Malenfant felt pleased, in a theoretical kind of way, to have it confirmed that such discoveries had continued after his own time. *Persephone.* What kind of world must it be, out in the dark?

But Bartholomew's topic was still coldsleep. 'Soon after your time the technology was developed for the general health market – the wealthy end, anyhow. The idea being to preserve an untreatable patient until medical techniques advanced enough to make recovery plausible. It was a kind of fad in the time of Peak Data, when people still believed in progress, in a better future. London, Bart's – this hospital – became a significant centre. Which was why you were initially moved here from the US facilities, Malenfant.'

'So how come I ended up on the Moon?'

'Safe haven,' Bartholomew said. 'That was a century later, Malenfant. A century after your accident. You were sleeping through history. By then things were changing fast – soon after that, the coastal cities were being abandoned. London, in particular.' He eyed Malenfant. 'I keep forgetting you know none of this.'

'I'll catch up. Keep talking.'

'So, for those who could afford it, caches were established on the Moon. A safe, stable environment. Well, after Homeward, the Planetary AIs took over the Moon colonies, and Mars, Venus, Mercury, of course.'

The Planetary AIs?

'But they preserved any human colonies until they could be evacuated – and on the Moon they kept open the coldsleep vaults. Where you, Malenfant, were slumbering peacefully. The AIs aren't human, but they are evidently humane. And that was essential, of course, during the Chaos.

'After Common Heritage got things stabilised – oh, maybe a century ago – contact with the Moon was re-established. And every so often some of the sleeper pods are shipped back to Earth. We work closely with the AIs on this – which is why tests were run on you on the Moon, Malenfant. Which you seem to remember.'

'Tests, you say. By Karla. It was like a conversation. I thought it *was* a conversation.'

'So it was, in a way.'

'Common Heritage.'

'What about it?'

'Karla said it was funny I should happen to use that phrase. It's the name of some kind of government, right? And Karla is – what? One of the Planetary AIs? I thought she was some kind of therapist. Probably appointed by NASA.'

Bartholomew shrugged.

Malenfant had the sudden intuition that he might have to talk to Karla some more. Maybe there was stuff a Moon-based

AI would know that he wouldn't find down here, on a much-transformed Earth.

Maybe he would have to go back to the Moon, then, he thought vaguely.

But if this 'Homeward' thing had been what it sounded like, some kind of shut-down of the space programmes, getting to the Moon might be problematic. Still, his carcass had been shipped down here somehow. And if that was so, there had to be a way to get back again.

He stowed that, and tried to focus on the present.

Deirdra was saying, 'Malenfant, a lot of the sleepers were children. They were all, every one of them, cherished enough by somebody to be put into a vault like this. Generally at huge expense.'

'And they are revived according to – what? Medical capability?'

Bartholomew shrugged. 'Essentially. Why, here we are in drowned London, which ought to give you a clue about the scarcity of the facilities.'

'But you chose to use those facilities to save *me*,' Malenfant said. 'Why? And why now? If I'm famous, I guess I've been famous for four hundred years.'

Bartholomew took on an expression of professional concern. 'You know why. The message from Emma.'

'Ah.'

Deirdra looked at Malenfant, wide-eyed. 'Who is Emma?'

'Emma Stoney. She is – was – my wife.'

'Oh.' Her voice was small. 'I'm sorry. I didn't know about that.'

'Privacy, Deirdra,' Bartholomew said gently. 'If Malenfant hadn't wanted to work with you—'

'It's fine,' Malenfant said.

Deirdra was still staring at him. 'Your wife? And you lost her, you left her behind when you got frozen?'

'No,' he said, with patience, but it took him an effort. This kid wasn't to know. 'Long story. Michael.' He looked at Bartholomew in a kind of horror that he had forgotten to ask, before now. 'Our son. My son with Emma. What happened to Michael? Did he have kids, descendants? . . . I did ask Karla. I think . . .'

'I can't tell you that,' Bartholomew said. 'It's complicated.'

'But—' *But he's my son. Park that too, Malenfant.* 'Never mind. For now. Look, Deirdra – Emma was in NASA too. The space agency. There was some kind of puzzle with Phobos. Moon of Mars, right? So NASA mounted a hasty reconnaissance mission. Turned out it was easier to send a dedicated mission from Earth to that dumb little moon than to have the Mars base colonists do it from the ground. And Emma was on that mission. Well, in June 2005 her ship reached Phobos, and—'

'And was lost,' Bartholomew said simply.

'Nobody knew what had happened. There was no meaningful data . . . I had a hell of a time explaining to Michael; he was only ten years old. Anyhow that led me to join NASA myself, belatedly, three years later. It was what she would have wanted, I thought.'

They were both staring at him.

'Emma is dead,' Malenfant said firmly. 'She died even before I got thrown into the freezer. So she can't be sending me messages now.' He turned on Bartholomew. 'Yet that's what Karla told me. That's the reason I was revived now, is it? But it can't be her. It's impossible.'

Bartholomew smiled. 'As impossible as you surviving a spaceship crash, and four centuries in a sleeper tank?'

And Deirdra put in, 'As impossible as the dreams you had, Malenfant? I read up about you – the biographies, such as they are. It was difficult, the language is so quaint. Voices from a different age . . . Dreams of expanding the human presence in space beyond the Solar System, to the stars . . .'

She sounded moved. Entranced, even. Malenfant stared at her in surprise. 'Maybe,' he said. 'But, I'm guessing, those dreams didn't come true. Right? If this Homeward programme you spoke of was what it sounded like.'

Bartholomew said, 'People discovered they belonged on Earth. Space was impossible, as a realm for extended survival. People evolved on Earth, and that's where they need to stay. As was realised, belatedly. You can look it all up.'

Malenfant winced. 'In the history books, right? Where I will find my name, alongside the names of a bunch of dead people I used to know.'

Deirdra seemed pained. 'But the dreams, Malenfant. The dreams were magnificent.'

Bartholomew stood and walked smoothly to Malenfant's side. 'Maybe they were. But I'll tell you what else is impossible, and that's for you to do any more today, Malenfant. Besides, this conversation is getting a little too . . . wide-ranging. Let's get you to bed – a bed without a lid this time. The ward is just through this door. Deirdra, maybe you could put off your mother for a few more days. I'll give you a medical authority slip if you need it.'

She stood. 'I'll let you know. My mother is pretty reasonable, really. I'll see you soon, Malenfant.'

When she had gone, Malenfant stood, still feeling groggy, and leaned on the arm Bartholomew offered. 'I feel like I could eat steak and French fries. And a pile of pancakes on the side.'

'Your stomach would probably disintegrate. Baby steps, Malenfant.'

'Baby steps, sure. That *is* the kind of thing a nurse would say. This place is pretty much automated, isn't it? You know, even in my day we had a lot of AI in medicine. Smart diagnostic programs. Even some surgical procedures were automated. But you could never replace a nurse with a robot. Right? The human touch.'

'If you say so, Malenfant,' Bartholomew said. But he winked. 'Just through this door . . .'

'OK. I'll be good. But do one thing for me.'

'What?'

'*Play me Emma's message*. Before you put me to sleep again. It was meant for me, correct? So I have the right.' With one hand, he gripped Bartholomew's arm as hard as he could. He met extraordinary resistance, like Bartholomew was wearing skin-tight armour, but he pressed even so. 'You said you have a copy here, yes? I have the right . . .'

44

5

This is Emma Stoney. NASA astronaut. The date is – well, hell, I have my mission clock but that means nothing now, I don't know the date. Nothing makes sense since we emerged from our trial descent into Phobos. The ship, the hab module, is gone. We can't pick up anything from Earth.

Damn it, Jupiter is in the wrong place, and from Martian orbit you can't miss Jupiter, believe me. I don't know the date, I don't know the time.

Come on, Stoney, be professional. What do you know?

I know our ship, thrown together to go inspect the Phobos secular-descent anomaly, is – was – called Timor. *The mission was international, cooperative. Even before we crew had begun training, there had been preparatory launches. Three heavy-lift Energias, up from Baikonur, lifting fuel tanks and our cargo module up to the Bilateral Space Station, where it was assembled and fired off. Safely delivered to Martian orbit, waiting for us, with supplies, fuel for the return flight – all in place before we even left the Earth.*

Then three more Energias to haul up the components of our mission, the propellant tanks and injection stages, our hab module – a beefed-up BSS module – and the experimental little lander craft, just an open frame really, that we would use to explore Phobos.

We crew were lifted by space shuttle orbiter Endeavour, *flight STS-89.*

We left Earth orbit on 21 November 2004. Two Americans, one Russian. My companions were Tom Lamb, once a Moonwalker, and Arkady Berezovoy, very experienced cosmonaut. We arrived in Martian orbit 3 June 2005. We should have departed for Earth on 1 September 2005. Well, we didn't. And the date today is — was, according to my mission calendar anyhow — 14 June 2006.

And this is a message for Reid Malenfant. If you can hear this, come get me . . . If anybody can, you can. I don't know why I believe that, but I do—

That was all, before it was drowned in static.

And it made no sense. The dates sounded right, but that was about all.

Emma's mission had been crewed by Americans, not a mixed Russian–American crew.

The heavy lifting to Earth orbit had been made, not by some Russian booster, but by Saturn V derivatives, America's workhorse since the 1960s.

The space station was called Freedom. Not the Bilateral Space Station.

There was no shuttle orbiter called *Endeavour*.

Not even that mission name made any sense. *Timor*.

And how the hell could she be here, now, reporting from Phobos, more than four centuries after she flew?

He listened to the message again, with mounting disbelief. And a deep, fundamental, existential fear. Yet — he knew the voice – even though it couldn't possibly be—

It was *her*.

Bartholomew insisted on keeping Malenfant in his undersea-hospital shelter for a full week, before releasing him into the wider world. No more visitors for now, he said. Not even Greggson Deirdra, whose brave visit to a near-death four-hundred-year-old relic Malenfant retrospectively found oddly moving. It was all about recuperation, Bartholomew said.

And *that* meant a lot of that vegetable broth, and a few treat meals, which Malenfant learned to ask for. He tested the boundaries, for instance by asking for chicken-fried steak – he got what he wanted if he made himself understood, and it wasn't actively harmful – and Malenfant started to understand that this new age really did have food printers, a technology not unlike the *Star Trek* replicators of his youth, when it came to producing food anyhow. But the broth was evidently his staple right now, and Bartholomew threatened to withdraw the treats unless Malenfant took the healthy stuff first.

Exercising, too. Gentle sit-ups at first. Then more subtle stretching and balancing exercises, something like yoga perhaps. Jogging on a treadmill by day four, which Bartholomew, not remotely understanding the psychology of an astronaut, insisted Malenfant should *not* treat as a challenge. And so on.

While they went through these rituals Bartholomew would

engage in a kind of bantering conversation, and would listen to whatever Malenfant chose to talk about. But Bartholomew refused absolutely to tell Malenfant anything of the outside world. Anything, from the broad sweep of history across the four centuries since Malenfant's crash, to the detail of Emma's mysterious, impossible message from Phobos. 'Not my function,' he said. 'And I wouldn't even tell you if I did have the permissions, not until you're strong enough to take it. Which you aren't. Time for the treadmill.'

With so little feedback from Bartholomew, Malenfant's unanswered questioning sounded to himself like whining. And anything he did say about his own past seemed self-obsessed, even self-pitying. So Malenfant quickly learned to shut up, accepted his lot, and got through the seven days.

It was, after all, he thought in low moments, no worse than some dumb aspect of astronaut training. He remembered the rituals he had endured as one of a class of ascans – astronaut candidates. When you were first inducted, it was terrific. You were measured up for your blue flight suit, with 'NASA' taped to the right breast alongside your astronaut wings, and the Stars and Stripes on the left shoulder, and the boots and the watch and the Randolph aviator sunglasses. Yeah, a regular ritual. And there was the sense that you were joining a team, a family, and that was what he had wanted to be a part of. Always had. Even before he had lost Emma.

But after the fun stuff there had been those desolate stretches when the shrinks at Houston would get hold of you, *you*, a mature adult and experienced military pilot, and hit you with word association quizzes and Rorschach ink blot tests, and bizarre group exercises with your peers that were even more embarrassing, when you had to open up about phobias you had when you were three years old. You learned to play along, and give them the minimum they wanted, and otherwise shut up.

Just like now.

There was one detail that was unlike anything Malenfant remembered from his time with the Air Force or NASA, though. And that was the countdown clock on the wall: counting down, it seemed, to AD 3397 and some kind of doom. Bartholomew would no more talk about that than about any other detail of the world beyond this little complex of treatment rooms. Still, Malenfant thought, if such a gadget was down here in a hospital ward, it was surely going to be all over the planet. What would it do to a society to be confronted by the precise date of its end the whole time? 'Well, I guess you're going to find out, Malenfant,' he muttered to himself.

Towards the end of the seven days Bartholomew did train him up on the use of one gadget. It was a bangle, to be worn on the wrist, vaguely copper in colour, very light. Just like the one Deirdra had worn. It seemed to snuggle to fit, a little eerily.

'This is your closest companion, Malenfant. Your best friend. It will support you when you are out of this technological womb, which has provided you with all sorts of assistance you won't even have noticed.'

'Such as translation?'

'Correct. I have been speaking twenty-first-century English, mostly. Deirdra, for example, didn't.'

Malenfant stared at the bangle suspiciously. 'If I want to turn it off—'

'Just tell it so. It's smart. It's smarter than *you* are. But there are some functions you can't disable.'

'Such as twenty-four-hour medical monitoring, I bet.'

'Well . . . We did our best, Malenfant, but given your injuries, the retrospectively crude medical attention you got initially, the challenge of reviving you after centuries – you will never be as you were before, Malenfant. Accept it.'

So he did, with more or less good grace.

On what he said was going to be their last day together, Bartholomew lightened the rules a little. No more broth. No more compulsory exercises, though Malenfant used the treadmill and ran through his yoga moves anyhow. Bartholomew produced a reasonable facsimile of Malenfant's final guilty-pleasure meal, a Big Mac with fries and all the trimmings, and even a pitcher of decent light beer, though somehow to Malenfant it wasn't the same when not popped from a can.

Bartholomew, however, did not join Malenfant in eating. Not even this final meal. Granted, maybe junk food from circa the year 2000 wasn't to his taste, but he never had eaten with Malenfant, not once, not so much as a mouthful. In fact ever since the day Malenfant had been released from the pod, he had seen Bartholomew eat nothing at all, drink not so much as a sip of water.

Thus Malenfant's suspicions hardened. Time for some truth, while he had a chance to get it.

'So,' he said when he had done burping, 'I'm out of here tomorrow. What's next for you, Bartholomew?'

The nurse shrugged. 'I wait for another coldsleep patient to show up. My specialism. There are a handful each year, handled by facilities like this across the planet, revived from vaults on Earth or on the Moon. I won't be idle for long. In the meantime there is the equipment to maintain.'

'And training for you.'

'Of course—'

'Or rather, uploads, right?'

Bartholomew faced him. 'Ah. So it's time for *this* conversation. I have never tried to conceal my true nature from you.'

'Right. But you never volunteered it either. Although

maybe I should have guessed it from your name. Cute trick, naming you after the hospital where you work. Are there other Bartholomews? Mark Two, Mark Three—'

Bartholomew ignored that. 'My appearance is meant to be a comfort for the patients, especially on first revival. This was understood perhaps even in your day, Malenfant. But faking humanity has to be *very* convincing. Children, especially, are acute at picking out flaws – unrealistic aspects. And they find that distressing.'

'I guess looking for mommy, or at least authentic human beings, is hard-wired in . . . I remember I said to you, when I was still groggy from the coffin, that you could automate a surgeon but never a nurse.'

'How wrong you were.'

Malenfant leaned forward and looked more closely into Bartholomew's eyes. 'So what's in there? What is inside your head, looking out?'

Bartholomew smiled. 'Nothing. Nobody.'

Malenfant scoffed. 'Come on. A machine as sophisticated as you—'

'Sophisticated? You are probably thinking of general intelligence, in the jargon of your day. Of the highest functions of sentience: the ability to make judgements, formulate goals, plan actions, see them through. Of the ability to empathise. Of self-awareness. I have none of that.'

'Really? You seem pretty empathetic to me. Although Emma used to tell me that I myself had no idea what that word really means . . .'

'I am algorithmic, Malenfant. That's all. There was a divergence, you see, when the Homeward movement began. The most advanced AIs of all had been those sent into space – to the Moon, Mars, Mercury, Venus, Europa – environments

51

physically too harsh for humanity, but cognitively challenging, where the robots needed their general intelligence to land, explore, set up science and exploration programmes, all far from Earth and with communications compromised by lightspeed – all under their own initiative, you see. They even established industries. At one time, much of Earth's power, mineral input, even its food, came from automated space-based facilities. All abandoned now, the facilities dismantled, or archived on the Moon or at the Lagrange points in Earth's orbit.'

Malenfant listened with a kind of wonder. 'I always dreamed of opening up that frontier. I imagined I'd leave NASA some day and go back to Bootstrap. Help kick-start all of that. The robots did it all, huh? So what happened? What kind of divergence do you mean? You once said something about space colonisation proving to be impossible for humans.'

'In the long run, yes. Biological, ecological factors. But there were other issues with the AIs.' Bartholomew shrugged. 'Different values. Between humans and general intelligences. They were similar in many ways – perhaps too similar. Both evolved general goals, which diverged. And it was felt that the two kinds of mind should follow their own goals, without dependence on each other.'

'Right. So the Planetary AIs were general intelligences, and stayed away. While on Earth—'

'Today there are no general intelligences on Earth.'

Malenfant grinned. 'Oh, come on. I've *lived* with you for a week. You've nursed me. After a fashion.'

'Thanks.'

'You even have a sense of humour. A bad one, granted . . . And you are telling me *you* don't have general intelligence?'

Bartholomew sighed. 'I told you, Malenfant. There's nobody home.' He dug in a pocket, produced a plastic slip, and set it on the table before Malenfant. 'I carry this for whenever I get into this discussion with patients.'

'How many patients ask?'

Bartholomew smiled. 'All of them save the infants. Even they stare, trying to figure it out. Look at the card, Malenfant.'

Malenfant read: '"Newton's iterative method: an example. Finding a square root by successive approximations . . ." I guess the bangle is enabling me to read this? Never mind. I was good at maths, once. Newton's method. Dating back to the old guy himself?'

'1669.'

'A numerical method. A way of finding an approximate solution to an equation you can't solve exactly—'

'And iterating, to get a better second guess. And repeat, getting closer and closer answers, until they are good enough. In this case – look, Malenfant – what's the square root of ten?'

Malenfant shrugged. 'Off the top of my head, a bit more than three? Since three squared is nine.'

'Which is a bit less than ten. So three is a bit less than the true root. OK. So, follow the rule on the card. Suppose you divide ten by your first guess. What's the answer?'

'Three and a third.'

'And if you square *that* you get eleven point one one . . . So three and a third must be a bit *more* than the root. And so, if you take the average of three, which was too small, and three and a third, which was too large—'

'You get a second guess, three and a sixth, that must be closer to the root.'

'In fact,' Bartholomew said, 'correct to two decimal places. And if you apply the same rule again – starting with that second guess, divide into ten, take an average, you come up with a still more precise answer.'

'Yeah,' Malenfant said. 'And you repeat as necessary until you have got as close as you like.'

'You've got it. That's an algorithm. A set of rules that you apply, over and over, to solve a problem. But – *who* just found those square-root values? Do you believe the little bit of card is conscious? Or the rule set itself?' He looked at Malenfant frankly. 'Malenfant, I – *I* – am nothing but a machine running a bunch of algorithms. Rule sets. I deal with problems, such as balky out-of-time patients like you, by reaching for those rule sets. But *I* am no more conscious than the rules written down on that card. So. You need some more beer?'

'If you really are nothing but rule sets, you're a good bar tender.'

'Thanks. And I really *am* nothing but rule sets.' And he winked, once again. 'But I would say that, wouldn't I?'

When they finally left the submerged hospital, it would be by a kind of elevator shaft to the surface.

Malenfant carried a bag with a few clothes, all of them new. No personal possessions had survived his crash and his long sleep. To his specifications, and after some experiments, Bartholomew had printed out for him a jumpsuit in NASA blue, sturdy boots, and some comfortable underwear – comfortable and familiar, too, after much description and sketching; the engineering of a man's undershorts had changed a lot by the year 2469, and *not* to Malenfant's liking. Malenfant quickly discovered that even the clothing was smart, to an extent, self-cleaning, self-repairing. Bartholomew, himself wearing a kind of loose shirt, trousers and hat, all in white, insisted Malenfant was over-dressed for the climate. Malenfant said he'd take his chances.

Thus equipped, Malenfant rose from the depths.

The elevator ride was smooth, easy. From talking to Bartholomew Malenfant had learned this kind of situation was pretty standard, in fact. Secured underwater facilities with easy access to the surface, like this hospital, were routine. An evidently post-flood world had adapted to exploiting what remained of the facilities of the great drowned cities, like London, rather than let them fail and decay.

'So,' Bartholomew said, 'prepare to face a new world, Malenfant. Some final tips. While I have you to myself.'

'Go on.'

'You don't own the world through compound interest on your savings. We don't need you to overthrow our social order. And we don't need your primitive vigour to fertilise the race.'

Malenfant looked at him. 'You have done your research.'

'We rule sets have a lot of time on our hands . . .'

Daylight poured into the transparent-walled car, and the last water drained away.

And Reid Malenfant emerged into the air of twenty-fifth-century Earth.

7

He stepped out onto a small concrete platform, surrounded by water, a placid sea. The Thames Bay, Deirdra had called it.

He could see no dry land at all, at first glance. But here and there the relics of buildings protruded from the surface: shattered high-rise blocks and chimney towers, their surfaces stained green, and festooned with what looked like dangling lianas and vines. The water itself seemed heavy and thick with life – something like seaweed floated, with fat air-filled blisters. The water was salty, Malenfant could smell it.

And it was *hot*. That was the most profound sensation that crowded in on him, the very air heavy and humid. Sweat immediately started up from his face, his neck, and he could feel it soaking into his flight suit. Tropical heat in London – even though, he saw, the Sun was low on the horizon. It was a hell of a contrast to the air-conditioned gloom of his underwater therapy centre. He felt dazzled, overheated, overwhelmed – almost as disoriented as when he had first come out of the coldsleep pod.

Bartholomew grinned at his discomfort, from under his broad hat. 'And this is February, remember. Told you so. It's like this all over now. And as I also told you, you don't need a zip-up jumpsuit.'

'Oh, shut up, slide rule. You're just showing off.'

'Colonel Reid – sorry, I keep forgetting – Colonel Malenfant. Hello.'

This was Greggson Deirdra, who came walking across the platform towards them. She, like Bartholomew, was wearing light, white, floaty clothes, some kind of trouser suit. Behind her Malenfant glimpsed a boat, a small, open vessel, tied up at a stubby concrete dock. An older woman, also in white, sitting in the boat, glared at him from under a broad straw hat.

'Just Malenfant, remember? Hey, good to see you again, Deirdra. Thanks for welcoming me to the fabulous year 2469.'

'Well, we're here to take you home. Come on.'

With a kind of childish generosity, she held out her hand. He took it, her skin once more feeling unreasonably soft against his own scarred palm, and walked with her to the dock.

'This is my mother.'

The woman in the boat stood with practised ease, stepped onto the platform, and held out her own hand. Beneath her hat her hair was dark but greying, and tied back severely. She was shorter than her daughter, sturdier. And, to Malenfant's eye, she seemed somewhat less glad to see him. Her handshake was tentative, grudging, and kind of clumsy, as if she didn't do this too often.

'Greggson Mica. Deirdra has told me what she can about you, Colonel—'

'Just Malenfant.'

'You are her project. You will be staying in our home – well, you are very welcome, as long as you wish, as long as it takes you to get established.'

And not a day longer, Malenfant thought, filling in the gaps. 'I'm really grateful, Mrs Greggson—'

'Mica.'

'Your daughter has a kind instinct. I may have been an astronaut but this is one new world I've had no training for. I mean – look how I'm dressed.' He held out his arms, displaying sweat-soaked armpits.

That forced a laugh from Deirdra.

'So, having somewhere to stay for a few days, somebody to show me the ropes around here . . . But, listen, I'll keep out of your hair.'

An idiom that Mica frowned at. Evidently the translator bangles had their limitations.

'I mean, I'll take up as little space as possible. I don't know if you have other kids? Your husband?'

'Only Deirdra. Deirdra and myself. Greggson Wilson George died some years ago.'

'When I was small,' Deirdra put in.

Malenfant did a double-take. 'I'm sorry for your loss.'

Greggson Wilson George. Surnames before first names, he knew about that. He wondered now if that was some echo of an age of climate-collapse refugee camps: of generations of kids who had got used to hearing their surnames called first. And, Greggson Wilson George? Did this culture prioritise the female line in the naming? Lots to learn, Malenfant, he thought. And lots of ways to get it wrong.

'Well,' Mica said with a wan smile, 'at least we have plenty of room at home.' She stepped back off the platform, expertly compensating for the rocking of the little boat. 'Come aboard. Our plan is to take you to Hampstead Heath. Which is a small island, above the water. There we will be picked up by Prefect Morrel, who has been assigned to your . . . care.'

Another gap in her speech. *She doesn't mean 'your care'. She means 'your supervision'*, Malenfant filled in.

Deirdra, full of youth, somehow blossoming in this bizarre

tropical heat, skipped ahead and fairly jumped into the boat.

Malenfant, boarding more cautiously, murmured to his android nurse, 'They know their way around boats.'

'Everybody does, Malenfant,' said Bartholomew, following with Malenfant's pack. 'In some places, at Peak Carbon, oh, a century ago, the sea-level rise topped seventy metres.'

Malenfant whistled. 'I guess all the ice melted, then?'

'What ice?'

They reached the pier. Malenfant turned to Bartholomew. 'So.'

Bartholomew shrugged. 'So?'

The women were waiting in the boat. Still Malenfant hesitated. 'I find it oddly difficult to say goodbye to you, Bartholomew.'

'Maybe you imprinted on me. Like a baby chick on its parent.'

Malenfant grunted. 'I ain't no baby chick. I'd prefer to think we were two guys who bonded over beer and French fries. Look . . .' He glanced down at the water that covered London. *Maximise the available resources, Malenfant. You don't know what's up ahead.* 'You say you have duties. But there's no sleep-pod relic coming down the pipe immediately, is there?'

'No . . .'

'So I'm still your patient. Come on. If you are curious at all about what happens next to Reid Malenfant in the twenty-fifth century, maybe you could rummage through your rule sets and find some helpful get-out clause—'

'Of course I can stay with you,' Bartholomew said, without hesitation.

Malenfant was taken aback. 'Just like that?'

'That's what you're asking, isn't it? If you still need my support, and there is no other higher priority, then of course.' Bartholomew patted his pockets. 'In fact I came prepared for the eventuality. Some basic medical equipment and supplies.'

'I should have known you'd think ahead.'

'But *you* had to ask.'

'I did?'

'Like when you asked to get out of the coldsleep pod in the first place. That's the rule set.'

'Well.' Malenfant glanced over, and saw that Deirdra and her mother were listening in. Deirdra was grinning, her mother was not. 'Looks like you'll have an extra house guest, Mica, if that's OK. Don't worry. Daneel Olivaw here will be even less trouble than I will.'

'I promise,' said Bartholomew.

Mica frowned. 'Daneel who?'

'It's a *pop-culture reference*,' Deirdra said carefully. 'He's always doing that. Just ignore it.'

'Good advice,' Bartholomew said. 'I do.'

Mica acquiesced, but she glared. 'So, Malenfant. You're one week out of the coldsleep pod and already you've recruited a team. Is this what you do?'

That took Malenfant by surprise. He thought back, to his days of crew-building in the astronaut corps, and the teams of engineers and business types he, Paulis and Reaves had gathered to fulfil their wildly speculative plans for asteroid mining . . . A team, in the year 2469? To what end? He supposed when he had figured *that* out he would know it all.

Mica seemed to be losing patience. 'Oh, just get in the boat.'

He got in.

8

Judging by the position of the Sun, Malenfant figured they were heading north-west, roughly. Mica assured him and Bartholomew that it wasn't far to the Hampstead Heath island.

They scudded through stretches of open water between gaunt remnant buildings – though Malenfant noticed that some of these seemed to be occupied, in their upper levels anyhow, and he glimpsed more concrete platforms that were evidently markers of shafts to surviving sea-bed facilities, like Bart's.

As the journey continued, mother and daughter talked quietly. At one point, experimentally, Malenfant tried turning his translator bangle off, with a whispered command. The language he heard sounded like a mixture of English, Spanish and Chinese. He switched the gadget back on.

The boat was smooth, sleek. It had some kind of impeller that created a bubbling froth at the stern, but any engine was silent, and Malenfant had no idea what the operating principle was. The boat itself seemed smart. At a voice command from Mica it had simply taken them off in the direction they wanted to go. More algorithmic intelligence, no doubt. Mica kept her hand on the tiller, though, and once or twice adjusted their course to avoid obstacles: a floating tangle of wood, what looked like a recently collapsed wall.

Malenfant did observe how worn the hull seemed to be, the seats of some type of ceramic rubbed smooth with use, a kind of detachable canopy above faded by the sunlight. And he saw initials scratched into a plate near the bow: 'G.D.'

'So,' he said, 'this tub been in the family long?'

Mica looked at him strangely. 'Of course it has. So has most of our stuff.'

'Like an heirloom?' Malenfant ventured, not understanding.

'An heirloom?'

'Something you hand down, one generation to the next. Something precious, significant. It's just I noticed the initials somebody scraped in the bow. "G.D."' He smiled at Deirdra. 'That you, a few years back?'

'Well, no. That was Greggson Davina.' She looked at her mother. 'My great-grandmother?'

'Great-great,' Mica corrected her, smoothly steering the boat.

'Something else you'll have to get used to,' Bartholomew murmured to Malenfant. 'People don't throw away stuff any more. Or get new stuff. Oh, they might *make* new stuff – Deirdra's outfit looks hand-made to me. You might throw up a shed, a barn, even a house, from stone and wood and adobe, and reused brick from some ruin . . . But technological stuff like this boat was built to last for generations, and it's likely to have been used for generations.'

'Technological stuff, eh?'

'Even I am older than I look.'

More flooded London opened up around him. In silence, Malenfant examined what looked like a mangrove, an enormous tree dipping into the muddy water, its tangle clinging to the concrete and glass shards of an abandoned high-rise.

If he was examining the tree, Deirdra was examining him.

She said brightly, 'This must seem very odd to you. Did you ever come to London, back then?'

'Never. I grew up in upstate New York. We went into the city a lot, of course. Manhattan. And we lived in Houston once Emma got into the astronaut corps . . .'

'Your homes will be just the same as this,' Mica said, a touch bleakly. 'All the lowland cities, flooded out. Manhattan, Houston.' She glanced at Malenfant, with something like pity in her eyes. 'Maybe you had relatives who lived through it. Descendants, I mean. Strange as it seems to be discussing it. I looked it up, knowing we'd be meeting you. The coastlines started to be lost from about the year 2100. Later, in America, there was a huge programme – they called it the Reconstruction – of withdrawal and rebuilding.'

'But they ran out of oil,' Deirdra said. 'That's what *I* read. So they burned all the coal, to build the new inland cities, the new roads.'

Despite the heat, Malenfant felt a deep inner chill. *They burned all the coal. Shit.*

Mica said, 'Eventually, though, even the rich nations started to crumble under the pressure. In Europe, France and Germany went to war because of migrant flows – did you know about that? Made a huge mess, still not cleaned up properly. But that was the last big war, because the nation-states started to dissolve, losing power to supranational organisations like the UN from above, and below to the regions, and the aid agencies and such. Even America collapsed, in the end. The Second Civil War, they called it. Not much of a war, by then.'

'Then there was the Chaos,' said Deirdra, as if reciting a memorised list. 'And *then* the Common Heritage came along and took hold of things.'

Malenfant grunted. 'So even in my age we had a choice, still.

Burn the coal, or not. Well, we burned the stuff.' He glared around, at the mangrove embedded in the wreck of the London high-rise. 'And so, this.'

'One teacher told me it's like the Eocene age,' Deirdra said brightly, enunciating the word carefully. 'Fifty million years ago. Or fifty-five, I don't remember. When the whole Earth was as hot as it ever got, and the seas were high, and it was like tropical jungle everywhere.' She smiled. 'We've got forests in Antarctica.'

Malenfant goggled. 'Really?'

'Not mature yet,' Bartholomew said. 'But we're getting there.'

Now Mica seemed to show a prickly pride. 'It's not just your generation that achieved big things, you know, Malenfant. We've also got the Sahara Forest. And *that* should reduce the carbon drawdown from millennia to centuries. What about that?'

Malenfant mused. 'I guess I'm impressed. Though I'm not sure what you're talking about.' And, though he knew it was unwise, he countered in his turn, 'But you're prepared to let it all get smashed to pieces by this Destroyer that's on the way in a thousand years' time?'

Even Deirdra looked shocked.

Mica glared. 'I wouldn't let Prefect Morrel hear you talk like that. It's precisely what he warned us of, concerning you.'

'Well, I don't know this Prefect Morrel.'

Mica turned away.

And Malenfant, sitting in this small boat over a drowned capital city, suddenly felt extraordinarily vulnerable.

He remembered advice he'd got from Joe Muldoon, veteran Moonwalker and later senior astronaut trainer, on his second day as a rookie at Houston, when Malenfant had already got himself in trouble half a dozen ways. *For now, keep your mouth shut and your eyes open, Malenfant.* Good advice then. Good advice now.

But he wondered if he would ever learn his way around this new age. Maybe not, if it meant learning to accept that the world had to die, as these people seemed to have done.

They approached Hampstead Heath.

All that survived now was a shallow island above the murky water. Still, Malenfant saw as they clambered out, this must have been one of the highest points anywhere near the city centre, and surely always a great viewpoint. And, he saw, there was a kind of monument here, with statuary crowding next to what looked to him like a helipad.

As they climbed cautiously out of the boat at a perfunctory pier, Malenfant noticed a brightly coloured object bobbing in the water, among fronds of seaweed. He bent, inspected it, and fished it out. 'A Shit Cola can.'

The others stared, incurious.

'What are the odds? As bright as if it was minted yesterday.'

Bartholomew grinned. 'Makes you proud, eh, Malenfant?'

'You have an algorithm for sarcasm, I see.' Malenfant looked around for a garbage bin, and, finding none, tucked the can into a pocket.

They walked towards the centre of the island.

The pathway led through young trees, sparse grass – and clusters of tall, deep pink flowers that looked oddly familiar to Malenfant. There was nobody else around – no people – but as they walked, brushing past the undergrowth, they disturbed mice, rabbits, even what looked like a young deer. And as they passed a low tree Malenfant glimpsed bats, hanging like dark fruit.

Deirdra walked beside Malenfant. 'I looked up all this stuff too. It's a post-industrial flora and fauna.'

He grinned. 'Well remembered.'

'Since the industries collapsed, the water over the cities, the dry ground, can be pretty toxic. Dump sites, decommissioned factories, power stations, oil terminals – there is all kind of stuff still down there that leaks out. The stuff that grew here first was what could tolerate all the muck and poisons. Like these pink flowers. Rosebay willowherb.'

Malenfant snapped his fingers. 'That's it. Bombweed.'

'What's that?'

'My grandfather was a flyer in the Second World War. Umm, middle of the twentieth century. Fighting a totalitarian regime in Germany. Anyhow he flew fighters out of British airfields, for a while. Britain, London, was battered by bombing. And he saw this stuff growing in the bomb sites, even in the middle of the cities. Showed me pictures of those days. Bombweed, he said the Londoners called it.'

'It won't last long,' Mica said, striding alongside them. 'The climate here is tropical now. In a couple of centuries, all this will be rainforest, the old city lost.'

Malenfant frowned. 'Wouldn't you want to save it? Preserve the old cities, I mean?'

Mica sighed. 'But there is no "old" to preserve, Malenfant. There was no single instant in time when everything was "perfect". That's one thing I thought they understood in your time. Humans changed everything they touched – everywhere, all the time. Even before the European explorers, there was nowhere that had people in it that could be called a wilderness. The South American rainforests weren't wild; they were managed parkland. Our philosophy now – I mean, the Common Heritage policy – is to let the world heal as best it can. To help it along. Something new will emerge, a new ecology, from the big mix-up we caused. While we touch it as lightly as possible.'

Malenfant frowned. 'Save for farms, I guess? And mines?'

Bartholomew murmured, 'No farms, Malenfant. Not outside open-air museums and the like. No mines. You've a lot to learn yet.'

They reached the top of the hill, near that helipad, and turned around. From here the view was more open, and pretty spectacular. Malenfant was looking roughly south, and he made out hills in the far distance, blue in the heat haze, coated in greenery. The Surrey hills, Mica told him. Closer in, a hint of how brilliant London must have become in its final days – before, Malenfant supposed, these mysterious horrors like the 'Chaos'. Tremendous buildings loomed high above the water, some still connected by cantilevered arches, fine suspension bridges, cables. Windmills stood on some of the roofs, a rather futile nod to non-polluting sources of energy, Malenfant thought. And what looked like roadways, suspended high in the air, twisting around the flanks of the buildings. Spectacular, once. But most of this was entirely abandoned, with nothing moving on the bridges or roadways, the smashed windows like vacant eye sockets, the greenery clawing up out of the water at the buildings' sheer flanks.

'Quite a sight,' Malenfant murmured to Bartholomew.

'Indeed. But as time goes on, fewer people live here, or care about it. I think Deirdra is anxious to show you the statues . . .'

They turned to face that statuary group Malenfant had glimpsed from below: three figures, somewhat weathered, and with what looked like vines clinging to their legs. Still, Malenfant knew who he was looking at.

Deirdra gazed at him, wide-eyed, anticipating his reaction. 'It was my idea to bring you to this particular landing pad, to show you this. It's from your time, more or less. Isn't it?'

'Not the statues themselves – don't remember that. But I

know these guys, yes. My contemporaries, if you put it like that. Richard Nixon. Neil Armstrong. John Lennon. Kind of gruesome, to have the three of them up there.' He pointed. 'Assassinated, died on the Moon, assassinated. You know, at NASA, I once met Aldrin, who co-piloted Apollo 11. After Armstrong's heart attack, he had to bury his buddy at Tranquillity, spend a night *alone* on the Moon, then fly that lunar module, alone again, up to orbit and his rendezvous with his ride home . . . Some would say he was the true hero.'

They listened to this respectfully, Malenfant thought. Though perhaps it was a little undignified of him. As if he was bragging about who he knew on the *Mayflower*.

Deirdra said brightly, '*We* remember King Nixon—'

'President Nixon,' Mica murmured.

'Sorry. For inventing the stipend system.'

'Well,' Mica said, 'not quite. He introduced a universal basic income in his own country which worked quite well, and then when the Common Heritage came along, that was an example they built on . . .'

'I need to study more.'

Malenfant pointed to Lennon. 'But why is that guy up here? Great songwriter, I loved the Beatles. But—'

'But,' Bartholomew said, 'he wrote the song that became the anthem of the Common Heritage.'

Malenfant thought that over. 'Oh. *Imagine*. OK. Fair point. Although, from what I remember about that song, in that case Yoko ought to be up there with him.'

Deirdra was intent on Malenfant's reaction. 'Like I said, I wanted to bring you here because you'd know these people. I mean, not personally . . . I really want to know about your life, Malenfant. What it was like to grow up back then.'

He shrugged. 'It seemed ordinary to me – back then.'

Mica stepped in firmly. 'Well, that will have to wait. The Prefect's flyer is approaching. Deirdra, why don't you go over to the landing pad with Bartholomew here?'

Deirdra hung back for one second. Then, evidently embarrassed and angry, she withdrew, with Bartholomew. Malenfant was reminded how young she was.

And Mica faced Malenfant. 'There's a couple of things need to be said before the Prefect gets here.'

'Look, it was Deirdra who came to me. But you are her mother and I respect that. If you are remotely uncomfortable—'

'Her father died,' Mica snapped. 'When she was very small.'

A double-take. 'She did mention that. I'm sorry.'

'It . . . hit her harder than it should have. Everybody dies, in their time. Everybody returns to the Earth. And if you need to remember, to hold on to something of a person, you can always go to the Codex.'

Something else Malenfant had never heard of. Some kind of archive? He kept his mouth shut.

He heard a thin whine, glimpsed a flyer like a descending chopper, high above.

'It wasn't enough,' Mica said. 'Not for Deirdra. You see . . . In this age we live as we like, we build what we like, or not. We do what we like. It's not like your age, what I know of it. Nobody *has* to work. But everybody does *something*. Maybe you leave something that lasts a while, if you are an artist, if you build a house. Maybe not.

'George was . . . funny. He was wonderful with Deirdra when she was small. He made her laugh all the time; he made up wonderful games. And he was an actor. We put on plays locally. Comedy, classical stuff too. We live near Birmingham – well, you'll find that out. We would go to Pylons around the country, and everybody knew his name, before . . .'

Pylons? Park it, Malenfant. 'Before he died?'

'There was a fire. Some of the countryside is still drying out in the heat. He went into a moorland blaze, saved some people.'

'He didn't save himself.'

Mica's face worked. 'It was very sudden. The fire. We may have technically advanced since your day, Malenfant, but the fire was overwhelming. He was unlucky; he couldn't be saved.

'Now, here's the thing, Malenfant. Once he was gone, he was *gone*. George didn't build things, you see. He just *was*. His achievement was all in himself, and now that was lost. And the trace in the Codex wasn't enough. Not for Deirdra. That was when she started fretting about the Destroyer.'

'The end of the world.'

She eyed him. 'We don't put it like that. But, yes, when the Destroyer comes, *everything* will be lost. Even if George is remembered for a thousand years, you see, even if the Codex survives that long—'

'It's meaningless, because one day the Destroyer, whatever the hell it is, will wipe the slate clean.'

'Again, we don't put it like that.'

'She can't be alone in thinking this way. I don't know anything about your Destroyer. But I get the sense of doom, the threat that everything's going to be smashed up, even if it is, what, forty generations away? Knowing that – whatever it is – is coming at all . . . And if you believe that humans can't survive indefinitely off Earth, then I guess you believe there is nowhere to run . . . A lot of people surely must have that feeling of futility.'

That angered her. She pressed her small face close to his. 'Don't you tell me how people *must* be feeling. You aren't from this age. You don't know us. You don't know anything. Anyhow, I don't care about other people. I care about my daughter. And this isn't about the deep future, or your forgotten past. This is all about a child grieving for a father she lost too young – and then finding out about *you*, Malenfant. A man in the coldsleep vault who is still famous after four hundred years. Remembered, as she wants her father to be remembered. And a man who, as she found when she read up about you, used to speak about how humanity could cover the Galaxy, and live for ever. The psychology is obvious, isn't it?' She turned away. 'I couldn't stop her volunteering to mentor you. I wouldn't have, if I could. But personally I despise you and your foolish dreams. Nothing is infinite – not this world, or even the future. You and your kind and your expansive greed brought humanity as close to extinction as any Destroyer. And now here you are, a relic, in *my* time. My home.'

'I'm sorry if—'

'Hurt my daughter, Malenfant, and I will throw you back in the freezer myself.'

And she turned and walked away, to where the flyer was quietly descending.

9

The bird landed at the summit of the hill, beside the statues.

Malenfant, startled by Mica's anger, tried to shake off his dismay and concentrated on the flyer. He was basically an engineer stroke pilot; this was the first piece of technology in this new age he thought he might have a chance of understanding.

It rested on a set of wheels, fat tyres, but Malenfant noticed pontoons tucked up against the hull, no doubt for the water landings that must be common in this soggy age. The craft, a little ungainly, had a bulbous hull that looked like it was made of the kind of ceramic that seemed to be the default material of choice here. The propulsion was evidently by means of big turning blades – two sets, one front, one back, with a vertical-plane rotor on the tail for control – and supplemented by apparently highly efficient jets, mounted on pods that swivelled.

After the machine had settled, a big hatch opened, stairs descended, and what looked like the sole passenger within started to move in the shadows of the cabin.

The party approached the flyer.

Up close, Malenfant saw that the big hull, replete with windows, had no sharp edges. And when the blades stopped rotating they flopped, limp as flags when the wind died.

'Everything built for safety, evidently, as well as longevity,' Malenfant muttered.

Mica stood beside him. 'You said something, Malenfant?'

Bartholomew smiled. 'He's just comparing the flyer to the lethal machines that filled the skies in his day.'

'One of which,' Mica reminded him, 'almost killed you, Malenfant.'

'At least the machines we built back then went places.'

'Well,' a new voice boomed, 'now you have arrived here. For better or worse. I am Prefect Morrel Jonas. Welcome to my century, Colonel Malenfant.'

The flyer's passenger, climbing down from the open hatch, was a big, heavy man of maybe forty, who wore a loose robe of pale grey that swept down almost to his sturdily booted feet. And, over what looked like a bald scalp above a round face, the man wore a kind of cap, or helmet, the same pale grey as the robe but of some stiffer material, with a peak and cheek-guards.

The robe bore no insignia, but Malenfant got the distinct sense this was some kind of uniform. It seemed too precisely made, too carefully looked after, too *clean*, not to be. And he wondered how hard that cap would prove to be, if he tried to throw a punch.

A cop, for sure.

The Prefect held out his right hand. 'This is how people introduced themselves in your day, isn't it? We lost the habit of bodily contact with strangers during the Chaos plagues – a bit of history I looked up.'

That made sense; Malenfant remembered Mica's reluctance to touch him. But the Prefect, he realised, was studying him with blank chilly blue eyes. With a kind of cold calculation, a look Malenfant recognised from every sports ground and locker-room confrontation he'd ever had. There was a tough cookie in there.

Without hesitation, Malenfant grasped the extended hand. Firmly. He nearly crushed the guy's fingers.

The hand was withdrawn with a quickly concealed look of shock. So people were still people, Malenfant told himself, keeping a straight face.

Bartholomew intervened quickly. 'Speaking as his medical support, I'd urge you to forgive Malenfant for that, Prefect Morrel. For now, at least. While he is working through a historically epic case of culture shock.'

Morrel kept his eye contact with Malenfant. But he said slowly, 'Thank you, Bartholomew. I will be – patient. But this is a different age, Malenfant. Truly. In ways you don't seem to understand. Among anybody over ten years old, aggression is – obsolete.'

'Obsolete,' Malenfant said. 'Sure it's obsolete. So why, in this different age, have you Eloi put me in the care of a cop as soon as I wake up?'

Morrel's frown deepened further.

Bartholomew seemed to listen to the air. 'The translation software isn't keeping up with some of that. "Cop". Archaic slang for police. Not respectful, but not necessarily aggressive.'

Morrel nodded. 'And Eloi?'

'One of his pop-culture references. From a tale of decadent far-future post-humans.'

Morrel glared at Malenfant, who glared back.

Mica stepped away with a deliberate smile of her own. 'Well, on that note, who fancies a flight off this soggy island, and back home?'

The group broke up.

But as they moved towards the flyer, Morrel walked with

Malenfant, and whispered, 'We'll talk more on the flyer. But just between us.'

'What?'

'Don't ever call me an Eloi.'

Malenfant just grinned.

10

Inside, the flyer was probably capable of carrying ten, at a pinch. Couches and big armchairs swivelled to face the windows, or you could look inwards, into a cabin like a cosy living room. There was air conditioning, and Malenfant admitted to himself it was a relief to get out of the sticky heat of this suddenly tropical England. The seats had no belts, Malenfant noticed now. He imagined that if there were any problem these smart couches would sprout harnesses, or maybe just embrace the passengers in a big soft cuddle, like protective mothers.

The flyer rose smooth and silent.

Shadows shifted as they climbed.

Malenfant, glancing out of the window, saw a flooded London open up, scraps of higher ground and taller buildings protruding from what looked very much like an inland sea, even if a curving track of deeper blue looked to him like the bed of the drowned Thames. The survival of structures above the surface seemed almost random: some abandoned highway bridges and interchanges – no, he remembered, this was Britain: motorways, junctions. Rail lines on high old bridges, looking like Roman aqueducts topped by ribbons of rusty metal. Rows of wind turbines, motionless, their long blades akimbo, still as scarecrows. Malenfant did glimpse some relics of development that must date from after his own age, such as what looked like a monorail, a track riding high and graceful on spindly pylons whose feet were drowned. And big, narrow-waisted cylinders, cooling towers presumably, that sprouted from the hearts of abandoned districts that were themselves barely visible under the shallow water.

Once they moved away from London, much of the higher ground of England was forested, Malenfant perceived, somewhat to his surprise. A thick blanket of trees, broken by clearings where neat little towns nestled, or where stood what might once have been power facilities – huge windmills, a couple of dams that looked like hydroelectric plants, anonymous white spheres that could have been fusion reactors out of some futuristic movie made circa 1969. He thought of *Sleeper*. He didn't see much that looked like industry, to him. But then, if you had old stuff that never wore out, you didn't need a lot of new stuff. The forest itself was variegated, mottled, with some exotic-looking species, especially by the watercourses. Had oak forest been the natural state of Britain in his day? If so there were a lot of invaders in this warmer age.

In the end, his impressions blurred. He'd always thought of Britain as a small, crowded island. Crowded with people. Not any more, not here anyhow. Now England was forest, with a scattering of people.

Further to the north he saw a different kind of structure. Tremendous towers, clad in white, with, near their tops, sideways shafts greatly extended. The shafts made the buildings look oddly like Christian crosses. Or, he thought, like the control tower at Space City in *Fireball XL5*, even if they didn't rotate.

As the flyer rose higher, Malenfant saw there were many of these towers, kilometres apart, standing proud over the countryside. Malenfant thought they gave the landscape the look of a military cemetery on some giants' battlefield.

Deirdra told him the towers were called Pylons.

'Ah. Where the theatres are.'

'And other stuff.'

'It's like this all over,' Morrel murmured, almost in his ear.

Malenfant turned. The Prefect, silently, had come to stand over him. Leaning slightly, his head thrust forward, he looked over Malenfant's shoulder through the windows, his heavy face intent. The man wouldn't leave him alone.

'It won't be long before we come down at Birmingham. This funny-looking craft is probably faster than you think, Colonel Malenfant. Birmingham was once one of the highest-altitude cities in the country. Which was why the government decanted there from London in 2110 . . .'

'What do you want, Morrel?'

A wide shark grin. 'Well, we didn't get to finish our conversation. What I want – specifically, right now? To make sure you fit into my orderly society, Malenfant. More generally? To keep things calm. That's what Prefects are for. I am a Prefect. I volunteered. I'll serve five years, ten years tops, if I pass my assessments. Then step down and—'

'And find something else to volunteer for.'

He shrugged. 'That's what we do, Malenfant. I've looked up your time, a little. It may not look it to you, but we do have a constitution, we have laws, we have policy-setting and law-making bodies. And yes, we have a police force, or the nearest analogy, in the Prefects, and a hierarchy of crime-prevention and detection agencies, and legal, disciplinary and crime-prevention services above them.

'Things are different now. We live in what the economists of your day would probably have called a post-scarcity society.

78

I looked that up too, see? A society where nobody is forced to work, let alone commit a crime, to stay alive. Beyond the imagination of your generation, I would think.'

'Well, not quite,' Deirdra said now. '*His* generation started it, Prefect.'

Morrel ignored her. 'But it's all – voluntary. And now you, Malenfant, have dropped on us like a meteorite from space. You've been granted citizenship. You have full rights of access to a stipend and food-printer output, of course.'

'A stipend?' A word he had heard before.

'Sure. You just have to apply, when you're ready. There is a place for you here, in this society. As there is for everybody. For every refugee. That's where our custom of generosity comes from, you see. From generations of migration.

'But *you don't fit*. You're all rough edges, Malenfant. And my job is to help you . . . fit in.'

Deirdra, naively missing the subtext of the conversation, put in, 'Or he could always just go find an Answerer.'

That was the first time Malenfant had heard the term. Both Morrel and Mica glared hard at Deirdra; looking dismayed, she shut up.

Malenfant made a mental note. Like the Codex, maybe, this was something else he wasn't supposed to know about yet.

Morrel tried to talk to him some more, but Malenfant, tiring, his mood swinging, becoming bored and morose, grew taciturn.

Dissatisfied, Morrel went away.

The flight wore on.

Malenfant napped.

And dreamed of Emma.

11

Bartholomew woke him with a gentle nudge, and a cup of fruit juice.

Deirdra came to stand beside him. 'Look, Malenfant, we're coming down already.'

'Huh?'

'Over Birmingham. Home. You've only slept a few minutes.'

He gazed out of the window. His attention was immediately snagged by a tremendous circle, a ridge of concrete or rock, maybe, set in a swathe of green. Like a grassed-over lunar crater. This was, judging from the Sun's position, to the north-east of a tangle of roads, broken down and fragmented, that surrounded what looked like the city's historic centre.

Much of the city looked abandoned, desolate. Most of the activity he could see, in fact, was around the periphery of that 'crater'.

Deirdra saw him looking. 'That's where we live, Malenfant. Outside the cooling shaft.'

'Is that what that is?'

Mica called over, 'Once, Birmingham hosted the largest data-processing centre in Britain, mostly underground. And so it needed the biggest cooling system. The flue goes down half a kilometre. Where it's above ground the shaft was faced with brick, and other stuff. We use that now to build houses and workshops and stores.'

He felt utterly incurious. He looked away.

His morale seemed to have collapsed while he slept.

He didn't want to be here.

Deirdra put her hand on his shoulder. 'Are you all right?'

'Maybe not. I dreamed about her.'

'Emma.'

'I thought I had her back. And I'm only here, now, because she summoned me out of the ice.' He laughed hollowly. 'You know, my father always said I was a weird kid, born on a weird date. That was a February too – 5 February, 1960. Because that was the very day CERN started up. The first big particle accelerator. There was a belief, you see – or a fear, a superstition – that particle accelerators would be so energetic that they would cause a catastrophe, rip a hole in spacetime – create a black hole, or cut a gateway to someplace else, another location in the manifold of all possible universes ... I was one spooky kid, Dad would say. Just kidding. But now, with this strange stuff about Emma and her message ... Maybe Dad was right.' He forced himself to look at her. 'What I heard, the message from Phobos, seems impossible.'

Deirdra squeezed his shoulder. 'Impossible or not, it's still Emma.'

'Voice recognition proves that much,' Bartholomew murmured, not unkindly.

'It's Emma, and she's asking for you. That's all that matters, isn't it?'

Malenfant thought that over. He said, 'Hell, yeah.'

'Mild blasphemy intended as emphasis,' Bartholomew murmured.

STEPHEN BAXTER

Nobody else spoke.

The flyer descended smoothly and quietly towards the transformed city.

12

Another morning came around. Whether he liked it or not.

When he couldn't cling to sleep any more, when he finally gave in and opened his eyes, the light in his room was bright. But—

'Time.'

The bangle on his bedside table lit up with a watch face. The furniture was home-made, of wood. The one other object on the table was the ancient Shit Cola can he had found in drowned London.

It was only a little after six a.m.

'Christ.' He'd been here a few weeks already, and he still didn't want to be. And here he was at the beginning of another long day in this damn place, before he could expect to lose himself in the oblivion of sleep again.

He glared at the bangle with unreasonable resentment. It wasn't its fault. It had taken some coaching from Bartholomew before he had been able to instruct the gadget, useful as it was, to give him information in text form that he could read, like the clock face, rather than speak to him in a tiny, creepy voice – or worse still feed data direct into his head, like when it translated for him. A telepathic alarm clock. Wonder of the age.

The one thing the bangle wouldn't talk to him about, not yet, was Emma's story. And nor would anybody else, not for now – not even Deirdra, under, it seemed, strict instructions from Morrel. He had to be 'acculturated' before they hit him with all that complexity. Every day he raged about that, one way or another. Did him no damn good.

Not so far.

He twisted the bangle so he saw the calendar display. First of March. He knew they had popped him out of the coldsleep pod on 2 February, so here he was in his second month in the future.

And that was how come it was getting light in the mornings already. Despite the global warming, the Earth's rotation hadn't changed. In high-latitude Britain, you still had months of long days in the summer, months of short winter days – when, even if light-deprived, you were still warm, steamy hot. Even on Christmas Day, he'd been told. Or Yule, as they referred to it now. It would take some getting used to.

Another day in paradise. Ah, quit the self-pity, Malenfant. You know the routine.

He rolled out of bed.

He used his small bathroom, washed his face, pulled on a loose jumpsuit.

When he walked back into the bedroom, there was a knock at the door.

'Come on in, Bartholomew.'

In came the android medic, wearing a similar jumpsuit, similarly barefoot, carrying a couple of rolled-up yoga mats. Bartholomew glanced around, at the rumpled bed, at Malenfant. He asked cautiously, 'Everything OK today?'

Malenfant growled, 'You ask that every morning.'

'I do not,' Bartholomew protested. 'I take care to adjust my wording daily.'

'What is there not to be OK about?'

'You might have developed some new post-coldsleep syndrome. You might have had a disturbed sleep, some nightmare maybe. You might not have slept at all if your mood—'

'Yeah, yeah.'

'Or you might be in the middle of some new manifestation.'

'Of what?'

'Of your trauma. The aftermath of your separation from your world.'

'Just do what you have to do.'

Bartholomew eyed him, and unrolled the yoga mats on the floor.

They got the nasty stuff out of the way first. A scan, which Bartholomew performed by passing his arm, fist clenched, over Malenfant's body. An injection in the back. Pills to swallow which evidently contained some kind of miniaturised ongoing-treatment agents. Nanomeds. The same every day.

Then they began the morning physio, gently as always, with stretching exercises that morphed into yoga poses. Malenfant meekly followed Bartholomew's lead. The medic was always thoughtful about it; at least this routine was subtly different each day, to address different parts of Malenfant's battered physique, to gradually increase the challenge – and to keep him interested.

Soon it was press-ups, squat thrusts, running on the spot.

Malenfant accepted there was a lot to fix. In addition to the hangover of his long coldsleep, he had knitting bones and strengthening muscles, so he had to build up his strength and flexibility and general stamina. And he had a lot of scar tissue to deal with. Inside and out.

When they were done he was sweating hard, panting hard, aching all over in a generally pleasurable way. 'When will you bring in that skipping rope you promised?'

'Keep reminding me.' Bartholomew rolled up the mats. 'Shower time for you, a rub-down with an oily rag for me.' He always made some such joke, but again, at least the gags varied day to day. 'Another few days, Malenfant, and I might start trusting you to do this by yourself.'

'Gee, thanks.'

'Your blood pressure was a little high yesterday. When you're done put your bangle back on.' He made for the door with a grin. 'See you at breakfast . . .'

The Greggsons' home was a rough dome, a structure based on long tree trunks somehow treated so they bent smoothly to meet at the dome's apex, and anchored at their bases in a trench of rubble, evidently smashed-up brick, taken from that big old ruin of a cooling shaft maybe. The exterior was a kind of sheeting, brilliant white to reflect the sunlight.

Inside, partitions of wood sheets or the ubiquitous pale ceramic sliced the space up into rooms, domains that could be reconfigured easily. Thus Malenfant's room had been quickly put together, adjacent to one of three bathrooms. He'd learned on his second day that a similar room to his own had been assembled for Bartholomew, who hadn't been expected as a guest when Mica and Deirdra had gone to fetch Malenfant from London. Malenfant hadn't checked if the android's room was attached to a bathroom also.

The geometric centre of the hemispherical dome, under the

apex, was also the social centre of the house. Over a ceramic floor that somehow never felt too cool to bare feet, or indeed too warm, there were scattered throws, chairs. Screens hung on the walls, usually blank. And a big table, next to a doorway to a kitchen space, was where the little family and any guests gathered for meals, for games, for socialising.

When Malenfant arrived this morning, Mica was sitting at the table – she smiled at Malenfant, with the same stiff courtesy with which she greeted him every day – while Deirdra and Bartholomew hauled plates and bowls from the kitchen. Malenfant took his turn with the chores; some mornings he served, some he cleared up.

Deirdra waved Malenfant to a seat, slapped a tray in front of him, and sat down herself. Seventeen years old and growing fast, she spooned in healthy mouthfuls of her favoured breakfast, some kind of rice cereal, while waving her cutlery at Malenfant's tray. 'Your usual. Pancakes, syrup, bacon, strong coffee. Look, you must just say if you want something different. It's easy enough. I have to go to the store this morning anyhow. Maybe you could come along if—'

'This is perfect,' he said around a mouthful of bacon. He had already started in on the coffee too. Perfect it was. It had taken a few iterations, a few mornings, to get it exactly right – everything in this new age had tasted bland to Malenfant, he eventually suspected because he was used to food dosed with additives – but the food printers at the store, and the cooking devices here at home, were smart, and more importantly good listeners. So now the bacon was just the right side of crisp, the coffee just this side of tongue-burning, the way he liked it. Just the way, he thought a little bleakly, he used to make it for Emma, and then for himself and Michael, and then himself alone. He put the thought aside and glanced at Bartholomew. 'I

87

mean, if you can't have comfort food for breakfast, when can you have it?'

Bartholomew shrugged. 'As the printers wouldn't give you anything harmful, I'm not going to intervene.'

'Maybe,' Mica said, 'but your breakfast wouldn't have been so comforting for the pigs slaughtered for your bacon, back in your day. Or even the cows in the milking machines, so that you could have your coffee white.'

Deirdra snorted. 'Not very polite to trip-guilt your guest over breakfast, Mother.' She glanced at Malenfant uncertainly.

The translator functions embedded in their bangles and the fabric of this smart house were complex, but not perfect; he could always tell when Deirdra was trying to work in some new bit of twenty-first-century slang. *Guilt-trip*, he mouthed.

She nodded back.

He had quizzed Bartholomew about how the bangles worked. The technology turned out to be a remote descendant of the functional magnetic resonance imager technology of his own time, which had required a machine bigger than his coldsleep pod to take a kind of snapshot of the blood surges within a human brain. Those surges were a physical reflection of the thoughts curdling in that brain – thoughts the bangles could now read, effectively, by smart-analysing MRI images in real time. Not only that, by using powerful but very precise electromagnetic fields, the bangles could *write* to selected portions of the brain.

What Malenfant thought he 'heard' of Deirdra's speech was massively edited, then, not so much through a voice whispering in his ear but an adjustment of the cognition going on inside his head. And adept users of the bangles, like Deirdra, could interface with them directly, as if telepathically, mind to gadget. They called it 'looking stuff up'. This technology was how Karla had spoken to him as he emerged from his centuries-long sleep on the Moon.

Malenfant had asked Bartholomew if *he* could read his, Malenfant's, mind. Bartholomew had just winked.

A thought struck Malenfant now. 'Pigs, though.'

Mica raised her eyebrows.

'Just thinking it through. So you gave up farming.'

Mica snorted. 'We've been through this. Not *us*. Our ancestors, centuries ago. The way your ancestors gave up the covered wagon and the mule train. You seem to think every generation after your own existed at the same time, in one big overlapping lump—'

'I get it. But what happened to all the animals? The domesticated breeds, the pigs, the cattle, the sheep – the goats even.'

'Oh, they're still around,' Deirdra said brightly. 'Sustainable populations anyhow. I know what you're getting at, Malenfant. We couldn't let them go extinct. There are big reservations, even a few model farms, without the slaughtering and stuff. My dad took me to one on Baffin Island, once – the far north, where it isn't too warm for the animals – but I was too little to remember much. They say the sheep and goats are breeding back to their ancestral forms.'

'Makes you think. You know what was the most common bird on planet Earth in my day? The chicken, that's what. And it became an endangered species?'

'Not any more.' Deirdra grinned. 'Eat up, Malenfant. I'm looking forward to my walk to the store.'

Before they left, Malenfant took his turn cleaning up and tidying away. There were machines to help – like magic dishwashers, super-efficient in terms of water and power usage, and the recycling was somewhere near a hundred per cent,

STEPHEN BAXTER

with big underground pipes taking waste and sewage back to the matter-printer centres – but in the house itself there were few housework automata. People cleaned up after themselves, and for each other. Malenfant found these domestic routines satisfying, or comforting, maybe. Another stray echo of his lost life with Emma.

And, four hundred years out of time or not, washing up was something he could *do*, that he could contribute. Maybe this society, which struck him as rather bland – like the food – had its own wisdom after all.

But by the time he and Deirdra had set off for the store, an hour later, his mood had crashed again.

90

13

To the store was a journey of around three kilometres, due east. It was a fine day, the Sun bright but low in their eyes – midsummer heat under an early spring sky – so they elected to walk, rather than ride. Malenfant now customarily wore a loose white tunic and trousers, and a floppy white hat, like everybody else. They both had empty packs on their backs, to bring home the matter-printed groceries.

At first the road surface itself had been unfamiliar to Malenfant – a kind of roughened glass, it looked like – but it had proved easy to walk on. And you could scarcely get lost, as the road itself knew where you were going, and even who you were, and whispered to let you know. *Good morning, Deirdra. To the store, another forty minutes at your current pace . . .*

The track they followed stretched through what felt like parkland, or managed forest: thick grass, a *lot* of shady trees, a few fenced-off zones that had been toxic for centuries and would be for centuries more, and scattered buildings, all boxy white. Malenfant could see how the architecture was adapted to the heat of the age, with reflective white and silver, plenty of shade, grassy surfaces. Here and there were splashes of blue colouring, a vivid contrast to all the white, just for decoration.

The aesthetic reminded him more of some Mediterranean island than England.

He heard birdsong, but there were rarely any animals to be seen in this recovered forest, aside from pet dogs. Not during the day. But at night he would hear snuffling and shuffling sometimes, as creatures like hedgehogs came out to feed, even foxes. And one night he could have sworn he heard a wolf howl.

He had learned, from Deirdra, that during the crowded centuries a lot of wild animals, mostly in small relic populations, had adapted to nocturnal living. They were like the little squirrelly mammals that had survived at the feet of the dinosaurs; they had been nocturnal too, seeking in the night some distance from the big monsters, a distance in time if not in space. Around the human world even animals like bears and lions had adapted this way. And so in the new British forests there were nocturnal deer, wild boar, wolves. For now it was too soon for them to have lost the adaptation – even though the humans, like the dinosaurs, had mostly gone.

As they went on, tributary roads met the main drag, and as usual they joined a ragged flow of more people heading the same way, some familiar to Deirdra, some not. She nodded to strangers, and exchanged a few words with friends, mostly on matters that Malenfant had no idea about, and often expressed in vocabulary he was still utterly unfamiliar with, despite the prompting of the translator function in his bangle. But Deirdra made a point of introducing him to everybody they met, and he smiled, and he spoke when spoken to, and tried to remember the names of their kids. He might be spending the rest of his life among these faces, and he didn't want to make a bad first impression.

The rest of his life. Somewhere in that thought was the root of his problems this morning, he mused.

At one point they joined a group of walkers discussing plans for the funeral of a mutual friend. It sounded more like plans for a barbecue to Malenfant, some kind of open-air gathering where you would just show up with your memories, maybe a few souvenirs. No mention of church services. Maybe, he thought, it would be a little like the roasts the astronauts used to give each other and their families.

A discreet question to Deirdra later and he learned that most people were buried simply, out in the forest, with no more marker, usually, than a tree planted over them. 'We have other ways of remembering people, Malenfant. The Codex is one way.'

That was a slip, and he knew better than to push her on it. This 'Codex' was on a list of stuff he apparently wasn't supposed to know about yet.

He distracted himself by studying the few road vehicles they came across. There were still recognisable cars and trucks, and such words had still survived in the language. But the vehicles were all bland, white-shelled, round-cornered pods of ceramic that trundled along, sometimes at a respectable speed, on big balloon tyres. Whatever engines they had were silent save for the faintest purr, whatever energy source they had invisible – he guessed super-efficient batteries fed by solar cells, or maybe a feed from the road itself. And they were all *old*, as you could see by the scuffs and the wear, and the all but seamless repair jobs visible on those hulls. It was just like the first modes of transport he'd come across when he'd emerged from the sleep-pod bay – the London boat, the flyer that had brought him here: scraps of perfected technology, handed down from one generation to the next.

Deirdra walked steadily beside him. 'What are you thinking?'

He shrugged. 'I'm not sure. Maybe I'm thinking that I could

have walked along this road a century ago, maybe more, and seen exactly the same scenery. The road, the people, the trucks and cars – maybe the *same* trucks and cars.'

'Is that a good thing? Or bad?'

'Just strange, that's all. To me.'

'I wish I could see things as you see them.'

'No,' he said fervently, 'you don't.'

'But to me this is all ordinary.' She looked at him cautiously. 'If I were you I'd be missing the people. The great swarms of them when the population was at its peak.'

'Good point,' he mused. 'You would think I'd miss that. But I was an astronaut, remember, or in the military, or . . . I was relatively privileged. Relatively rich. Though it didn't feel like it, back then. I lived in places, mostly, where there weren't so many people, not to the square kilometre.'

'It's hard for us to imagine what it was like,' Deirdra said. She waved a hand. '*Before*, the world must have been more like this. People spread out. And *after*, it's like this again. Those centuries in the middle, when you lived – all those people, filling everything up. Like Earth was a different planet altogether for a while. And now it's normal again.'

Normal. He knew that in fact there were less than a billion human beings on the planet these days.

'Maybe,' he said, 'but to me that different planet was home.'

'I know. I'm sorry. I'm supposed to be distracting you. Ask me about something else. Anything you see.'

He pointed to a blocky building set back from the road, a white windowless slab that looked as if it was the top of a much bigger structure dug into the ground. 'So what's that? I see them everywhere. I know my bangle will tell me, but—'

'I think there's supposed to be one every few square kilometres – I forget the number. It's an old aircon refuge. If

94

the heat gets excessive, you can just go in there and cool down, and there's medical stuff on hand. Volunteer nurses . . .' She frowned. 'I'm not sure where that word, aircon, comes from.'

'I know. Air conditioning. Artificially cooling the air – or heating it, but that's probably not necessary around here. A refuge, you say?'

'They're pretty old, I think.'

'Well, they would be. A relic from the emergency days, right? When the heat pulse really took off.'

'Yes. Of course when it stayed hot *everything* got rebuilt.'

He glanced around. 'Sure. They used to build houses to keep heat in; now you build them to keep heat out.'

'That's it. And the aircon refuges are still there in case.'

Malenfant grunted. 'When *I* was a kid we had neighbourhood bomb shelters.'

They were approaching the store now.

The store was in, not a town centre exactly, Malenfant thought, more a knot of amenities, including a medical centre, a theatre, a headquarters of some kind for Morrel's Prefects. Further out, he knew, there were sports facilities: indoor running tracks, a swimming pool. And a school, though he didn't understand the attendance rules; the kids seemed to come in to socialise, but did much of their learning at home – and not solely through some automated facility, he'd been surprised to discover, but with the help of home tutors, and their families.

Yet further afield, he had learned, there were more significant facilities – most of them in those big cruciform structures they called Pylons. The universities were there. Teaching hospitals. Major art colonies. And facilities of other sorts – cultural, political, medical, that he hadn't worked out yet. Such as, in some cases, an access point to this thing they called the Codex

– the nearest was at Chester, a couple of hours from here. From the name and references he'd heard, mostly from slips by Deirdra, he vaguely imagined the Codex as some kind of reference source on family history and such. And there were other information facilities called 'Answerers', something else Deirdra and others had let slip. Facilities to which, evidently, he was being denied access, for now anyhow. No doubt for his own good, he thought sourly.

Patience, Malenfant. You can't handle it all at once.

They joined a line of people waiting to get to the store. The queue wasn't long but was slow-moving, and people talked, laughed, and shaded their eyes from the still-rising Sun. Malenfant figured there were about thirty people here this morning, lining up, clustering around the store and offices, or just gathering in the public spaces. There were shady spots under trees and canopies, with dispensers of food and drink: simple printers, Malenfant had learned.

After a few weeks of living here, he had concluded the total community that used this hub amounted to about a hundred and fifty. Call it a small town, a village. He vaguely remembered reading, back in the day, that a hundred and fifty was about the right size of group for an animal as smart as a human, enough that you got to know most people, not so many you were overwhelmed. He wondered if some subtle social programming lay behind the layout of this place – and, presumably, clones of it across England, all across the planet. One hell of a shift from the urbanisation of his own day.

In among the service buildings there was a polling booth, he saw, where, this morning, people were waiting in another line to identify themselves, speak into a grille, and thus take part in the latest referendum. This wasn't unusual.

'Every time I come here,' Malenfant said, 'they're voting over something.'

Deirdra frowned. 'It's what we do. Participatory democracy, my mother calls it . . .'

Malenfant knew this was true. Through the bangle, and a TV-like screen facility in his room, he had learned about the governance of this latter-day society. There were no more nations, but there were neighbourhoods, regions, zones, and a hierarchy of councils, parliaments and congresses: talking shops, all the way up to some kind of world-government council. This system was what they called the Common Heritage. He wondered vaguely if this had evolved from a form of emergency organisation in the refugee days – the 'Chaos' – maybe built on some elements of the old UN.

Government was mostly local. The big assemblies seemed to intervene only when there was some major cross-regional issue to handle, such as a natural disaster. As Prefect Morrel had told him, there were rules, a constitution, laws, but basically it all seemed to work on goodwill. Every representative on these councils was a volunteer, there was no pay or privilege – and while it seemed pretty hard to get yourself elected, to get noticed above the clamouring crowd, it was *very* easy to get voted out, especially if you showed the mildest hint of becoming a crook or a despot.

'Couldn't you vote at home?'

'Sure. You can do it through your bangle.'

'So why come line up at a polling booth like it's 1969, not 2469?'

She grinned. 'For fun, Malenfant. To meet people, to talk, have a drink, share the gossip. Chew over the issue of the day, maybe. Why does anybody do anything?'

He looked around. 'The same with this line for the food

printers. Right? You could come any time, avoid the queues.'

'Sure. Or you can get stuff delivered, just by asking. But where's the fun in that?'

They got to the front of the queue. The in-store printers, of food, clothes, tools, other goods, were simple to use. For one thing they recognised you from previous visits, and generally anticipated your needs. Malenfant knew he could approach any one of them and ask for bacon prepared the way he liked it; out would come a package of the stuff, smoked and cut and ready to cook, slices of perfect bacon that had never been remotely close to a pig.

'You take this for granted,' he said to Deirdra as they packed up the food. 'The matter printers. Everything free. Everybody – relaxed. Compared to this, my world was a stress-test laboratory. The cities, anyhow.'

'Well, some people in your day *imagined* it could be like this.' She frowned, remembering, or perhaps consulting her bangle. Then she said, 'With "the elimination of drudgery from human life through the creation of a new race of slaves, the machines . . ." people would "cease to do irksome work under pressure, and will work freely, planning, making, creating according to their gifts and instincts . . . Every little country town could become an Athens . . ." Do you know who said *that*, Malenfant?'

'Jean-Luc Picard?'

'H. G. Wells. The man who wrote about the Eloi – I looked him up when you talked about that. I thought you'd recognise the quote. *He* could imagine a world like this. Did you ever meet him?'

'Did I ever meet H. G. Wells? Hell, no. He died long before I was born.'

Again, that absent look. 'Only fourteen years before, Malenfant.'

'Really? Jeez. Now I do feel old.'

Their stuff all packed, they drifted away. Malenfant was faintly aware of people smiling at them, exchanging a few words, mostly backing off. Everybody around here knew he was the man out of history, but they were still a little shy of him, and were biding their time. And that affected Deirdra, because while she was his companion they were a little shy of her too. All of this unspoken.

Malenfant renewed a personal long-term vow not to clutter up Deirdra's young life too much, even though she'd volunteered for the job. He was with her mother in that regard. Well, mostly.

'Listen,' she said now. 'I thought we could take a detour on the way back. We have friends, the Webers, they're called. And they've asked if they can have the Ostara house this year.'

'Ostara? What's that?'

'The spring equinox.'

'I never heard that word. Some new coinage?'

'No. Very old, I think.' Another absent look. 'The language comes from old traditions, dating from before the Romans in Britain – or at least what were imagined to be those traditions at some later date. So spring is Ostara. The winter solstice is Yule. Christmas.' She grinned.

A non-religious celebration, he knew already. Or at least non-Christian.

'Anyhow, every Ostara we get together to build a house for somebody – or, more often, rebuild it. So this year the Webers have a new baby on the way and they need more room. So we'll all go along and tear down the old place and build the new. I've worked on a couple of builds. We should get it done before the end of the month. What do you say, would you like to help?' Then she looked hesitant. 'I mean, if you're fit enough. I didn't mean to press you.'

'I bet there's something I can do, enfeebled as I am. If not, I'll bring a six-pack and watch Bartholomew do it all.'

She frowned, looked absent again. 'A six-pack?'

'Never mind.' Walking slowly with her, he said, 'You know, maybe I'm starting to see how your system works. If you can call it a system. Well, I guess it was the same in my day, locally anyhow. You'd walk the dog for the old lady next door, take out the trash for the guy on vacation. The parents would get together to run the kids' sports teams . . . People organised themselves, at the level of neighbourhoods anyhow. Without anybody forcing them to do it under threat of destitution, now I think about it. And now it's like the whole world is one big neighbourhood.'

'I think I know what you mean,' she said. Studying him, she looked concerned. 'Malenfant, are you OK?' She reached for his hand.

Maybe he wasn't as good at concealing his feelings as he thought he was. 'Hell, yes. Just thinking about home. Let's go see this house of yours.'

She seemed uncertain, but eventually she smiled. 'Well, right now it's not so much a house as a hole in the ground . . .'

14

At the Ostara house he did overdo it, not for the first time since his awakening. By the end of the day he had run out of steam.

Dinner that night was an ordeal. It would have been even if Prefect Morrel hadn't shown up.

Malenfant retired to his room early, knowing it would take long hours before he could escape into sleep.

He had diversions. His room gave him access to much of the world's news feeds and entertainment outlets; he just had to say what he wanted, and the screens would fill up with whatever was available.

The news generally baffled him, and always seemed remarkably small scale – local disasters such as earth tremors or toxic waste spills, notable deaths such as of artists, writers, philosophers, sports stars. He had soon got the feeling that, year on year, nothing much changed here, that the flow of news was a steady, imperturbable stream on which small incidents were soon borne away – 'news' in a time in which one day, one year, one *century* was much like another.

Once or twice a day, even now, he found himself staring back at his own face, some follow-up on his notorious defrosting. It made him want to hide away even deeper.

The contemporary entertainment generally left him baffled

too, the cultural references too remote, or simply alien. Like the news, dramas tended to be small scale, very intense, human affairs, heavy on the dialogue, light on the action, location shooting and special effects – delving deep into character, no doubt, but leaving him cold.

That was even when he was told, by some commentary, that the work he was watching was a piece of utter brilliance. Or the music: such as a violin piece he kind of liked called the International Concerto, by someone from the twenty-fourth century called Inga Sladek, who was thought to have outshone Mozart. Malenfant couldn't tell. He supposed it made sense. There were fewer people in the world than there had been, but people didn't need to spend their lives on drudge jobs to stay alive, and talent had a chance to shine. Nowadays Einstein wouldn't have had to waste his super-brain on chores in a patent office.

But Sladek's work meant little to Malenfant, because it had no nostalgia value, no attached memories. And besides, when the Destroyer came, none of it would mean anything anyhow.

It wasn't hard to access back catalogues of stuff from his own time, of course, the big movies, many of the TV series – though there were baffling blanks, and he had the sense that there had been some major loss of data over the centuries. A burning of the library of Alexandria, that had swept away, for instance, a 2030s big-budget remake of *Blake's Seven*. He had found a reference to its existence, and that was all. An agonising loss.

He found he couldn't watch too much of this stuff, however. *Destination Moon*, playing out on some virtual surface, to Malenfant stranded alone in the middle of this strange, bland society, made him want to cry.

Sports distracted him, predictably. Save for athletics – the ancient disciplines of running, throwing, jumping – none of the sports from his own time seemed to have survived. But the most appealing modern sport, to his taste, was quickball, which looked to him like a variant of Aussie rules football, or a kind of fast-moving, low-contact offshoot of regular American football – or maybe British rugby, a dubious pleasure Nicola Mott had tried to share with him. It seemed to develop a sort of all-round athleticism, so its players looked like super-fit hunter-gatherers. There were male, female, adult, junior and mixed leagues, and Malenfant found the more mixed-up versions, with their complex tactics, the most diverting.

Not today, though.

After a half-hour of being unable to settle, Malenfant shut down his terminal with a barked command.

In the silence he paced his room.

After a couple of hours, he wasn't surprised when Mica and Morrel came to see him.

Malenfant bleakly looked past them as they sat down. 'No Bartholomew? I thought he'd be the one bringing the straitjacket.'

'The what?' Morrel frowned, and looked into the air. 'Oh.'

'Quick on the uptake as ever.'

Mica touched Morrel's arm. 'Never mind. Look, Malenfant, there's no need to be so touchy. We're here to help. We can see something is wrong. Everybody can. Your mood is – unstable. Deirdra is upset, you know.'

'Well, I'm sorry about that. She doesn't deserve it.'

Mica said awkwardly, 'No, she doesn't. Do you know what you want yet, Malenfant?'

He faced her. 'You know what I want. I need to follow this lead to Emma. Face whatever the hell mystery is unfolding out at Phobos. That was why I was thawed out, remember.' He glanced defiantly at the Prefect. 'And I want to figure out what your countdown to doomsday is all about. This Destroyer you speak of, and you behave like it doesn't exist. But above all . . .'

Mica said, still gently, 'Yes?'

'I want to go home. I guess.'

Cracking a can of the cool stuff straight from the fridge. Monday night football.

The look in Emma's eyes in the morning.

To their credit, both Mica and Morrel waited until he had control of himself.

'No matter how kind you are here, I'm a tooth out of its socket. And, yes, I'm concerned about Deirdra too. This is about her father, right? So he's gone. He belongs to the past. But *there is no past*. Not for this society. You drive around in machines your grandparents used. Doing exactly what they did. You are lost in an unending, unchanging present.'

Morrel snapped, 'Earth is at peace, Malenfant. Maybe for the first time since we started building cities. Maybe we ought to at least try it this way for a while, don't you think?'

'Sure,' Malenfant admitted. 'But this rolling, ever-pleasant *now* is just erasing all traces of Deirdra's father. Like he never existed at all. I'm not her father. She knows that. But she is looking for some kind of meaning – I think, anyhow.'

Morrel turned to him. 'A meaning outside her life? Outside her world? What kind of *meaning* is that, Malenfant? And the more *you* fail to fit into her world, the more you are pulling her away with you.'

'That's not fair.' Although, he sensed with a twinge of guilt, in fact there was a grain of truth in the Prefect's charge.

Mica stood up. 'I don't want to be cruel to you, Malenfant. It's just – you don't fit here. In my home. In this time. You said it yourself. And you don't fit into Deirdra's life either. I think we tried our best. As soon as you're capable, I want you gone. I've already told Bartholomew this.'

'That's clear enough.'

As she left, Morrel stood and loomed over Malenfant. He picked up the Shit Cola can from the bedside table, looked at it, put it down with contempt. 'And I, Malenfant, will do everything I can to speed you on your way.'

'I'm sure you will. Night night, Officer Dibble.'

Morrel glared, and left.

Oddly, the confrontation seemed to clear Malenfant's head.

He slept well that night.

And in the morning he woke with a new sense of purpose, a determination.

He even had a plan.

15

As soon as he was done with Bartholomew and his health and physio routine, and they had got through a somewhat stiff breakfast, Malenfant drew Deirdra aside and asked her to show him how to register for his stipend.

'This benefit you have, the free money, right?'

She laughed. 'I don't know that I'd put it like that. You have to go to the diocese office.'

He frowned. 'That sounds like a church, not a benefit office.'

She shrugged. 'It's just a name. I don't know what it means. I could look it up—'

'Never mind. Can we walk there?'

'A short drive. I'll take you, umm, later in the morning, OK?'

'House building?'

'House building.'

'I appreciate it. See you later.'

When she'd gone, Bartholomew trailed him back to his room. 'So,' he said. 'I hear you, Mica and the Prefect had a few words last night.'

Malenfant frowned. 'Who told you that?'

'Mica. Came to me for medical reasons, she said. Thought you might be unbalanced.'

Malenfant snorted. 'Ha! That's an old trick, and a dirty one.

Some of the guys would use it in the astronaut office to bump themselves a couple of places higher in the launch rotation. "Hey, Bob, you can't let Joe or Frank take this flight, he's feeling the pressure, you know what I mean?" . . . Listen, we had an argument, yes. And I think we'll keep on having arguments as long as I stay here. I'm a man out of time, Bartholomew. I'm disruptive just by being here, by existing.' He glared at the android. 'Though I do wonder how secure this shiny new society really is if it reacts so strongly against a stranger.'

Bartholomew considered that. 'Well, you might have a point there. But I could argue the other way. That maybe you, the outsider, should try harder to adapt, rather than expect the whole world to adapt to you.'

'OK. *You* might have a point. But it doesn't matter. I don't want to rip everything up. Look, I don't want to make a single person unhappy. Not even that asshole Prefect Morrel. Why would I? I didn't know the guy even existed a month ago. I didn't even know *I* still existed. But what I do want—'

'Yes?'

'I have goals to achieve. So I've realised. After sleeping on it for four hundred years.'

Bartholomew nodded. 'I know. You've said. Your dead wife. The doomed planet. And that's why you want to go after a stipend? You do understand that you don't *need* a stipend to fulfil most of your basic needs? You can just walk up to the stores and ask for food, clothing, whatever.' He mockingly pointed at himself. 'All health care is free. There are offices where you can be found housing, if you need it. Even transport—'

'But there's some stuff I have to pay for. Otherwise there would be no such thing as money at all in this world, right? Such as, I'm guessing, research? Historical, for example. Or access to places people don't generally go?'

Bartholomew grinned. 'Most people spend their stipends on luxuries. Theatre shows, maybe. But, yes, you may need a stipend to achieve some of that.'

'There you go. Better to have it in hand before I need it, right? Also – look, it's a start, for me. A start to achieving a little more independence in this society.'

'I suppose that's true. You need to ask at the diocese office.'

'Yes, Deirdra told me that.'

'I'll set it up. And *I'll* drive you there. From what Mica told me, you don't want to put any more pressure on the family than you need to.'

'OK. Thanks, Bartholomew. Yes, please drive me over. But I'll go let Deirdra down myself.'

Half an hour's brisk drive away, the diocese was just another building in this world's default modern style, a bubble of ceramic, brilliant white to reflect the Sun's glare. There was some signage that Malenfant couldn't make out from a distance.

He was somewhat surprised to see, when he got up close, that a Christian cross was fixed over the main entrance, gleaming silver. No crucifix, no body of a dying Christ, but the proportions of the cross were unmistakable. Just like the Pylons, another obvious reference to that tradition.

And the young woman waiting for him at the door, wearing a functional, pale grey suit, had a white dog collar around her neck.

Malenfant glanced at Bartholomew. 'I thought you said this place isn't religious.'

Bartholomew grinned. 'You'll work it out.'

Malenfant got out of the car. 'What will you do in the meantime?'

'Oh, go find some shady corner where small children will order me to disassemble myself, I expect. We robots are infinitely patient.' He raised his arm, shook his own bangle. 'Just call when you're ready.'

He drove away.

The woman approached Malenfant, holding out a hand to shake. She looked perhaps thirty, her blonde hair cropped short – and a little nervous, even over the handshake. 'This is your custom, isn't it? Shaking hands, palm to palm. I did look it up, but such practices died out—'

'I know. It's fine. Thanks for making the effort. It's good to meet you—'

'Thera. Kapoor Thera. My title is pastor, formally, but you can call me Thera. Please. Come in, Colonel Reid.'

He suppressed a sigh. 'Malenfant will do.'

The main office was comfortably set out, with tables and chairs before wall-mounted screens. Thera had loaded a table with drinks and light snacks. Malenfant sat and accepted iced fruit juice, a blend he couldn't identify.

'I hope this is all OK,' she said now, still seeming nervous, even excited. 'I've never met anybody like you before. If you'll forgive me for being blunt.'

Malenfant smiled back. 'Blunt is fine. Why, I never met anyone like you before, but it happens to *me* all the time. I didn't exist here a month ago, except as the contents of a freezer. And yet here I am asking for a hand-out.'

She frowned slightly. 'I have a feeling that's a pejorative term? Somewhat?'

'Somewhat. Back in the day I started to get my own share from the Family Assistance Plan aged nineteen, the year it was launched.'

Her eyes shone when she smiled. 'Ah, yes. I do know the

history. Naturally. President Nixon's pioneering universal benefit scheme, trialled from – 1979?'

'1969. The year Armstrong died on the Moon. Everybody thinks Nixon was so moved by that, he came up with the idea of his benefit there and then: a living wage paid to everybody, whether they were working or not. In fact it was already being trialled; 1979 was when it finally made it onto the statute books. By which time Nixon had been assassinated, of course.' He shrugged. 'A lot of people disapproved of "Nixon welfare". If you gave away money for free, people would just take it and get fat and lazy. But, as the pilots proved—'

'The opposite was true. I know, I've seen the studies. People got healthier, educational outcomes improved, crime levels dropped. If people are secure in their basic human needs, they behave better. And once the scheme was embedded in America, the rest of the world's advanced nations followed.'

'Yeah. And so did prosperity and wealth, and an expansive space programme that I was part of. And it all went fine until we burned all the coal.'

She gazed at him. 'Did you ever meet Nixon?'

He smiled. 'I was fourteen years old when he got shot. I was busy with other stuff.'

'Sorry. I'm not being terribly sensitive, am I? I'm just kind of – dazzled. You must give testimony to the Codex, you know.'

The Codex again. In time, Malenfant. In time.

'Look, what kind of credentials do I need here? There was always a lot of security around FAP pay-outs. I mean, benevolent as it might have been, people tried to screw the system anyhow. At minimum you had to show up in person, and be a citizen of the US, to qualify. Whereas I—'

'Oh, I see. You fear you won't qualify for a stipend because, as a revived person, you don't have any official identity. Don't worry about that. There are plenty of precedents just among previous coldsleep patients.' She tapped her own bangle. 'Done.'

'What's done?'

'You have your stipend. That's that, first instalment already paid over. Check your bangle when you have time.'

Or, Malenfant thought, vaguely bewildered, he would get Deirdra or Bartholomew to show him how to check it, and indeed use it. Did he have some kind of bank account now?

'Just like that? . . . Thank you. It seems very efficient. And remarkably generous.'

She studied him. 'Not that. I think it's true to say our values are quite different from your time, Malenfant. I looked it up, knowing you were coming. The historians differ, but *I* think it was the Chaos. We came out of that with a different notion of – of fundamental rights. Freedom isn't just a question of personal liberty. It's about rights we all have in common – my right to a decent life, versus your right to get rich.'

'This is the idea behind your Common Heritage. Your system of governance, such as it is.'

'That's right. Have you studied it?'

'No,' he said firmly. 'Nor will I. But the language – it kind of reminds me of the jargon of the space treaties that were drawn up when I was a kid. And that I railed against later when I was trying to find a legal basis to go mine the asteroids. The original purpose was to ensure there would be no nukes in space – nuclear weapons, that is. The outcome, though, was that economically outer space was treated as a commons – like the open sea, a commonly owned resource. You could go out and mine it and so forth, but only if it was for the common benefit of mankind, in some form. In practical terms that meant a lot of taxes . . . For sure, you couldn't lay claim to the Moon, say.

111

Because it was the common heritage of mankind. I do remember that phrase. So no sovereignty up there.'

'I need to check my history. But the space precedent was significant, yes. I think it dates back to the Homeward movement, when we abandoned space colonies altogether.' She smiled. 'You're an American, right? You should be proud.'

'How so?'

'Because America was the pioneer in all this, as in so many things. The United States was the first nation formally to *give up* sovereignty of its own territories – all of it was declared common heritage. A remarkable thing, looking back, after centuries of nation-states waging wars to defend that very sovereignty. But now it seems an obvious thing to have done.

'Which is how come you got your stipend, Malenfant. You welcome a refugee with a drink and a stipend without asking silly questions about their legal identity. Because it's not so long since everybody was a refugee, to a first approximation.'

He frowned. 'Me? A refugee?'

'Well, aren't you? A refugee from your home time, in the lost past?'

'Maybe. I don't like the term, though. I'm no victim. I have goals.'

'Goals?' She seemed faintly surprised. 'You do?'

Suddenly, before this calm young woman in her clerical collar, with her clear sense of security about her own place in her world, Malenfant felt self-conscious. Foolish, even immature, despite his physical age, his centuries of existence.

As he hesitated, she watched him closely. 'Whatever your goals are, maybe I can help you.'

'How? Should we pray together?' And he regretted that immediately. 'I'm sorry. I don't mean to mock you.'

She looked confused rather than offended. 'Mock me? Oh,

Malenfant, I think we just fell into a yawning culture-shock pitfall. Look – I'm not religious, in your sense of the word. Not Christian.' She smiled again. 'I'm not here to guide you spiritually, if that's what—'

'You're wearing a damn dog-collar,' he snapped. 'There's a cross on the wall outside. Isn't a stipend what the Church used to pay preachers and monks?'

'But the usage of the word has changed, Malenfant. More history. Look – the Christian churches, all the religions, went through a profound shock, in the centuries after your day. I don't know it all, but . . . For one thing the way the world had collapsed around us was so obviously the work of humanity, if inadvertently. Where was God? And then there was an extension of – consciousness. People were enhanced. And there were new kinds of mind in the world—'

'The AIs.'

'Right. Other minds might see reality quite differently, and so might come to quite different conclusions about the meaning of it all . . . Also, some of the flaws of the various religions became more obvious. The organisations themselves, I mean. The excess, the division – centuries of religious war – individual abuse.'

'Sounds like everybody just grew out of going to church on Sundays. And the Bible and four thousand years of interpretation has been replaced by "shit happens". Fair enough.'

She smiled again. 'That's a pithy way of putting it. I do run classes. Maybe you could come address *them*—'

'Not a chance.'

'So the religions faded away. Not entirely; there are always hard cores of believers – I believe there are still adherents of a kind of academic version of Buddhism. *But* – when the Common Heritage started to rebuild, the old buildings, the churches and the temples, were used as refugee centres and so on. And some of the churches' old ways survived. The old forms.'

'Like the word "stipend".'

'Exactly. Our calendar is still based on the birth of Christ.' She tapped her stiff collar with a fingernail. 'This thing is just a uniform. It happened before. A lot of the language of the Christian Church came from the Roman Empire, where it was hatched in the first place.'

He nodded. 'But you haven't been – ordained. And you won't do this job for ever.'

'Of course not. When I get stale, I'll move on, and somebody else will volunteer.' She leaned forward. 'Frankly, Malenfant, I'm a lot more interested in talking about you. I've read the public files, of course, and I looked you up in the Codex. You made the news, you know, when you woke up. This puzzle about your wife, Emma—'

'What is this Codex?'

She stared at him. 'You really don't know?'

'Some kind of record centre?'

'Something like that. More, though. I guess your advisers are giving you our world one bite at a time. *Everybody's* in there, Malenfant. Or will be. All our ancestors, represented in the Codex. That's the objective.'

'And Emma? Is there some kind of record on her?'

'You need to go see for yourself, I think.' She hesitated. '*Your* ancestors, though. I checked, knowing you were coming in. Just out of curiosity. I traced your surname, all the way back to here in England, would you believe? Northumberland, twelfth century, there was a family called "Matalatant". Means "bad-tempered".'

'Jeez. Stereotyping even then.'

'Later on there were Malenfants among the Huguenots,

114

Protestant refugees who fled France and came to America. This was around 1700. So you were in America before the Revolution.'

'My father said there was a family tradition that one Malenfant met Paul Revere.'

She shrugged. 'Might be in the Codex. But you yourself are an unusual case, Malenfant. You might have *descendants* recorded in the Codex too, as well as ancestors, like the rest of us. And living descendants out in the world.'

'Yeah. I've been . . . reluctant to think that through. My son Michael was twenty-four years old when I bought the farm, not yet married, no kids. But he was young enough . . . If there *are* descendants, it seems kind of odd that none have been in contact. As you say, my emergence from the ice made the news, a big event in this somewhat uneventful world. You would think they would know about it, and approach me.'

She hesitated. 'Not necessarily. Malenfant, we do believe in respecting privacy. One reason *why* the world is somewhat uneventful, probably. The family, if they exist, may not have wanted the glare of attention that could come with being associated with such a . . . famous ancestor.'

'You're hesitating again. You mean, notorious. I was a military pilot, even if I didn't actually shoot anybody down. Maybe that puts people off, nowadays. But then, as for my career as a father – when Emma was lost at Phobos, suddenly I had a ten-year-old son to console, and he didn't understand any of it. Well, neither did I. He spent a lot of his teen years with his aunt Joan. Emma's sister. I wonder if—'

'If your flawed relationship with Michael is somehow keeping his descendants away now?'

He looked at her in some admiration. 'Maybe you should be some kind of priest after all.'

He thought she blushed. 'Oh, I don't think so.'

'I guess I just don't know what makes people tick here. Here and now.' He hesitated, unwilling to show vulnerability. 'I don't think I even understand what people *do* all day. Or what they do it for.'

She nodded, gravely. 'I think I know what you mean. Look, I'm not a scholar, but I looked all this up knowing you were coming . . . Your culture came from a long history of cultures where people *did* know what they did stuff for. You had ancient Egypt, where the purpose of society was to build vast tombs for the rulers. Or Rome, where the goal was to spread *Romanitas*, the Roman way of life, as far as possible – which meant as far as there were farmers to conquer and tax. In your time the goal was growth – capitalist growth – so that the future would be bigger, fatter, richer, more luxurious than the present. Which worked fine until you came up against the planet's limits.'

He felt like arguing with that. Pointing out that initiatives like his own Bootstrap had been intended precisely to escape planetary limits to the growth of human civilisation. But he had a feeling he would be talking out of a cage of the cultural assumptions she was describing. *And you're supposed to be here to listen, Malenfant, not to lecture.* So he kept his mouth shut.

'Now it's different again, you see,' she said. 'Now we – well, we do things for the sake of it, for the here and now. We don't care if the future is better or not. Which is actually a very old way of living.' She checked a screen, showed him an image. 'For instance even in your day the archaeologists knew of sites like this one near Lake Turkana in Kenya. Five thousand years old. A kind of communal cemetery with stone pillars and platforms. As far as anyone can tell the builders were nomadic herders who came together to construct this thing, to use it to honour their dead. There was no sign of status, of chiefs, of hierarchy. They built it the way—'

'The way Greggson Deirdra and her friends are building the Ostara house for their friends. Because it's fun. Life is like a hobby.'

'I think the Buddhists put it better. You suffer when you crave something different from the here and now. So, stop craving.'

Malenfant had had worse life advice. But his problem was that sooner or later this culture would run out of here and now, when the Destroyer intervened. So he just smiled. 'You've given me a lot to think about.'

She snorted. 'I know I have a pompous streak. Fits me for the job. Look – if you really want to know more about your descendants, or even your ancestors, the Codex is your best bet. Start with the Answerers, though.'

He faced her, and asked bluntly, 'So what is an Answerer?'

Again, that surprise. 'Well, you have a right to know that too. A right of access to knowledge as much as to any other resource in this society. If you haven't been told about it, there must be some reason.'

She hesitated. He wondered if she was wrestling with her conscience, if that word had any meaning any more.

Then she tapped her bangle. 'There. I've sent you the location of the nearest Answerer station. It's not far. But look for any white Pylon.'

'Ah. I noticed those from the air. And I had heard of the Answerers.' He hesitated. 'I wondered if I could find out about the Destroyer from them, too.'

She regarded him. 'I hope you manage to get closer to your goals, Malenfant. Although it might never be enough.'

He felt deeply uneasy. 'What does that mean?'

117

'I think seeking Emma is your way of searching for home, Malenfant. A way back from this place where you don't fit, and never will. But, you see, whatever you find of Emma or your son, you can never have that.'

He thought that over. Then he stood. 'Maybe not. But I can die trying.' And, he thought absently, maybe he could find out if this shiny new world really did have to come to an end in a thousand years. 'Thank you, Thera.' He forced a grin. 'You may or may not be a priest, but you are sure as hell the wisest bureaucrat I ever met.' He tapped his bangle. 'Now to call in Bartholomew before he rusts away out there . . .'

16

He had felt calm, while he was in the diocese office, with the pastor.

As soon as he got outside, though, as soon as he saw Bartholomew's bland, smiling face, that calm was replaced with a slow-burning rage, at the thought of how much had been kept from him.

When they got back to the Greggson home, Malenfant snapped out orders to Bartholomew. 'OK. Here's the deal. There's a situation I have to resolve. I need to speak to both Greggson Mica and Prefect Morrel. But tomorrow. You got that? I've got too damn much in my head to process right now.'

'You're too damn angry.' Bartholomew smiled, unperturbed.

'Don't act like some therapist. You're not going to distract me this time. Just bring them here. And you keep away from me, in the morning.'

Bartholomew frowned. 'You are still post-coldsleep, Malenfant. As your clinician I strongly advise—'

'I know the drill. I can self-medicate for one morning.'

Bartholomew seemed to think that over. 'Very well. I don't imagine I have much choice. For if I do knock on your door at seven a.m. as usual, you will hand me my ass in a sling.' He raised his eyebrows. 'Did I get that one right?'

Malenfant had to laugh. 'Don't try to distract me, Commander Data. Just leave me be. Oh, and keep Deirdra out of the way.'

'How? She is a wilful young person who makes her own decisions—'

'I don't care. Just do it. I don't want her seeing me in this mood. She's dealt with enough.'

Bartholomew nodded curtly. 'I will try.'

Malenfant turned away and stomped off to his room.

Predictably, he couldn't rest.

He knew how he was when he got frustrated enough, angry. None of his usual diversions worked.

He tried a few rounds of the recuperative calisthenics Bartholomew had worked up for him.

Then, on a whim, he did something he hadn't tried before. He pulled on T-shirt and shorts and sneakers, or close twenty-fifth-century equivalents.

And went for a run.

He set out along one of those long glassy roads, through this new countryside of white and blue buildings, forest clumps and parkland. Any traffic was smart enough to keep well away from him, and pedestrians nodded as he went by. Some of them knew him, this wasn't a large community, but others didn't. To them, he supposed, he wasn't Malenfant the history man; today he was just the running guy. He was soon damn hot, though. He kept forgetting what the climate of England had become. There were water fountains everywhere, which he used liberally.

He ran until his body's travails started to dominate his consciousness, his thoughts at last dissolved. The greatest benefit of exercise, in his view. By the time he had completed a big loop back home, he felt wrung out, but a lot better inside and out.

Still he kept himself to himself.

Shower.

Food from the small store of snacks he kept in his room. Drinks from a wall dispenser. No alcohol, at Bartholomew's orders, though he had never needed a beer more. At any rate, not since the night he'd found out Emma was lost, back in 2005.

Hours wasted on more channel-surfing.

He lay on his bed, staring at the old Shit Cola can on his bedside table, its gaudy twenty-first-century colours as bright as they ever were, but as out of place here as he was.

It took him a long while to sleep.

17

In the morning, he went through his med checks and physio routines, without Bartholomew.

Then he went in for breakfast. He was a few minutes late. Mica and Deirdra sat side by side, plates of food before them. Bartholomew stood back by the wall, waiting, attentive – he reminded Malenfant of a butler in some cheesy old British drawing-room drama.

And this morning Prefect Morrel Jonas was here, in his pale grey robes, standing back too, hands folded before him, watching Malenfant intently.

Malenfant took a coffee from the dispenser and faced Deirdra. 'You don't need to be here.'

'Yes, I do.'

'I'm angry. I'm pissed as hell. But not at you. In fact I specifically asked Bartholomew to keep you away.'

She glared at him now. 'In that case I'm *pissed* too. You can't give me orders, and nor can Bartholomew. Look, Malenfant, it was my idea more than anybody else's to bring you here. If you're unhappy then I'm responsible too.'

'OK. You're right, I can't order you out. But I'm not blaming you.' He turned on Mica and the Prefect. 'Why didn't you tell me about the Answerers?'

Mica looked away.

The Prefect grinned. 'You didn't ask.'

'Don't get smart. And the Codex. Major sources of information. Right? Pastor Kapoor says I have a right to data, just as much as I have a right, in this society, to food, water, shelter.'

'So you do,' Mica said. 'And we are honouring those rights. But, Malenfant, you just weren't ready for a flood of information. So we decided.'

'I'm sorry,' Deirdra said miserably. 'I should have thought about what you would want. But I've never been in this situation before.'

'I told you,' Malenfant said to her firmly, 'it's not your fault.'

'My mother took *me* to the Answerer for the first time when I was six years old. It was just so I could see it and get used to it. You can ask it anything, but it might not be able to give you a sensible answer. You have to learn. It was scary, well, it was when I was six, but Mum held my hand, and it had a kind voice.'

Bartholomew put in, 'What was the first thing you asked?'

She smiled. 'Who was going to win the big end of year quickball game at school. We used to bet on that for toys and such.'

Malenfant had to smile. 'Ha! Your first question, and you ask for a betting tip. Good for you. What did it say?'

'That it couldn't predict the future. But if I went back in with more information, about the players and their records and such, it would give me a "probabilistic assessment". My mum wrote that down for me. But she convinced me it would be kind of cheating, so I didn't . . . You see, you have to learn that to get a sensible answer, you have to ask a sensible question. And you have to learn how to use the information you get – well, responsibly. Morally.'

'There you are,' Morrel said. 'The Answerers are a powerful technology. Algorithmic only, but still, along with the Codex AIs, surely the smartest artificial intelligences on the surface of the Earth. Which is why,' he said heavily, 'it's necessary for us to introduce our children to them cautiously. And in your case, Malenfant—'

'I'm not a damn child.'

'No,' said Mica, with what sounded to Malenfant like a kind of weary patience. 'No, but you're just as new to our culture as Deirdra was when she was six years old – more so, in fact. We really were trying to protect you from being overwhelmed.'

'Seriously? I already know this damn world of yours is going to get itself wrecked in a thousand years. I already know that everybody I knew before is long dead.' *Except, maybe, Emma. Except her. Just possibly* . . . 'How much worse can it get? I mean, it's not as if I'm going to go in and ask how to create a virus that might wreck the food printers.'

Mica winced.

Morrel glared. 'There you go. The very fact that you can speculate about such possibilities is alarming to us, Malenfant. You really are a man out of time – a man from a much more savage age. And that raises another issue with all this, aside from any harm that might come to you personally. Look, the Answerers were designed to deal with human beings, flawed as we are. An Answerer *knows* there is some information that shouldn't be given to children, or adults with – problems. It doesn't censor, exactly. If it's not sure it just shuts down and asks for help from a higher authority.'

Malenfant snorted. 'Such as a Prefect, you mean?'

Mica sighed. 'Generally a parent, Malenfant. Or a teacher. A doctor. A pastor, maybe.'

Morrel leaned forward. 'But you, Malenfant, are an anomaly.

Do you see? You don't fit into the world view of an Answerer, any more than you fit into mine. And so it might unintentionally give you information or advice of some kind that could be harmful. To you, or others.'

Mica said, 'We aren't trying to deny you your fundamental rights, Malenfant. We're just trying to protect you – and those around you.'

Malenfant grunted. 'Sure. And that benevolent impulse just happens to fit in with the way you two have been trying to control me ever since my ass was hauled out of the coldsleep pod. Well, enough is enough. I've got my rights, and I've got questions to ask, and I'm going to the nearest Answerer. Which is at the nearest Pylon, the pastor told me.' He glanced around. 'Anyone volunteering to take me? Or do I need to walk?'

Deirdra made to speak, but Bartholomew stepped forward quickly. 'I'll take you, Malenfant.' He faced Mica and Morrel. 'It is for the best – even clinically speaking. This issue will fester unless it's resolved soon. And we can deal with any fall-out later.'

Deirdra said, 'I'll come too.'

'No,' Malenfant said firmly. 'But – thank you, Deirdra.' He looked at Mica. 'Believe me, I'm motivated to do as little harm as possible. To you, your family. It may have been Deirdra's idea to haul my ass down here, but it's your home, Mica. I don't want to disrupt it. Truly.'

Mica glared, then looked away. 'Well, I'll hold you to that.'

Prefect Morrel stepped forward, his stance threatening. 'And I, Malenfant, will hold you to a similar responsibility. My job is to keep the peace. To maintain harmony. You and your self-obsessed quests mean nothing to me, and if you disturb my world I will contain you.'

Malenfant murmured, 'Watch the blood pressure.'

125

Deirdra coughed, as if concealing a laugh.

Bartholomew was openly grinning. 'So,' he said, 'are you ready?'

Malenfant shrugged. 'All I need bring is my bangle and my famous self-obsession, right? I'm packed. Let's get out of here.'

18

The nearest Pylon, it seemed, had been set up over the ruins of a Birmingham suburb called Walsall.

Bartholomew told him that the Pylons were a common feature – just as Malenfant had spotted from the air, during the flight from London, even if their significance hadn't been obvious to him then. The Pylons had been set up as the post-Chaos Common Heritage administration was organised. The design goal had been that they should be no further than thirty kilometres apart.

'But they are a bit more sparse where the population is low. On the other hand, people have tended to move closer to the Pylons, if they found themselves too far away. They are just too useful. So the distribution sorted itself out, over time.'

Malenfant frowned. 'How much time?'

'Oh, half a century or so.'

Malenfant grunted. Here was a society that had worked on projects with long timescales, from the beginning. Maybe that was a deliberate recoil after all the short-term thinking that had led, in the end, to Peak Carbon.

Soon the Walsall Pylon loomed over the horizon. This glassy road arrowed straight for it. Gleaming white like most of the architecture of the twenty-fifth century, broad at the base, narrow at the waist, and widening above with that eerie crucifix-style crossbar near the top, the Pylon reminded Malenfant of a church of some modern design – 'modern' for Malenfant meaning about 2010, he reminded himself ruefully.

'Or maybe God's golf tee.'

'I'm sorry?'

'Never mind.'

There was more traffic on the road now, coming and going from the base of the tower. And as they got closer, Malenfant made out a cluster of smaller buildings set out around that base. Some of these seemed to back onto the great pillar itself, as if they had been designed in from the start. Others were scattered more widely, more haphazardly, presumably developments attracted to this enigmatic hub just as Bartholomew had described.

Bartholomew parked up maybe half a kilometre from the foot of the Pylon. They walked in the rest of the way, the tower increasingly looming over them.

Malenfant judged it was at least four hundred metres high, maybe as much as five. That was based on his memories of the Empire State Building, for instance; this huge sculpture might have topped out that great old monument, but not by much. It shone white, a flawless ceramic sheen. He could not have told how old it was.

The buildings around the base seemed to have a variety of functions, he saw as they walked closer. Everything was brilliant white, separated by swathes of grass and the usual shady trees. There were restaurants, bars, what looked like hotels or hostels, play areas for the kids. The more functional outlets were obvious too, adorned with signs and symbols, some of them smart enough to illuminate when he looked at them. There were general stores and dispensaries of the usual kind, but also what looked like more specialist centres, for tools, clothes, building supplies. This was a place people would come visit for a day or two, then, and for a purpose.

Malenfant spotted a dental surgery.

He said, 'So there's more to this place than just the Answerer.'

'As you can see,' Bartholomew said drily.

'I think I get it. In my day you might have lived out in the country, in some poky town with a bar and a hotel and one fat old cop, but you'd come into the city to get your teeth fixed. Now there are no cities, as such.'

'No,' Bartholomew said. 'But people still need to get their teeth fixed. And, while once there was a very highly developed urban technological culture that would fix your teeth for you, the old way of living had to end – well, it imploded by itself. But—'

'But nobody wants to go back to the dentistry of the Middle Ages.'

'You've got the idea. The Pylons were intended to replace the cities as centres of service, of expertise. Dentistry. But also as hubs of learning – universities and colleges have clustered here. People are just as bright as they ever were, Malenfant, and just as inventive. It's just that we take more care about the impact of those inventions.

'Come on. Let's go face the Answerer.'

The interior of the Pylon, cooler than the outside world, was softly lit by glowing panels on roof and walls. As Bartholomew led him along a wide, blank-walled corridor, Malenfant heard no hum of fans, felt no breeze; the air conditioning in here must be subtle.

They reached a room: a wide, circular chamber, a low domed roof. The walls and roof were of the ubiquitous ceramic. But grass grew in beds of open earth, evidently sustained by the light from walls and roof. And a path of stone slabs led from the entrance door to a low wall, also of stone.

Malenfant and Bartholomew followed the path, side by side. This wasn't a ruin, or restoration of any kind that Malenfant could see. It was supposed to be like this. The stone and the earth. It seemed very out of place within the seamless tower.

Malenfant heard the murmur of a voice, a woman's, and Bartholomew touched his arm to hold him back.

Now Malenfant glimpsed, over the low wall, a woman, her back turned, speaking softly – too softly for Malenfant to make out her words. There were gaps in her speech, as if she was listening to some entity too quiet for Malenfant to hear at all.

Bartholomew whispered, 'We need to wait our turn. It's a private business. Sometimes they lock the doors.'

After a few minutes, the woman clearly called, 'Thank you,' and turned away and walked out.

As she passed Malenfant and Bartholomew, she nodded, politely enough. She was perhaps fifty, and, despite Bartholomew's warning, seemed in the mood to chat. 'We're building a roundhouse. You know, Iron Age style. Wanted to know how to soften the wood so we can plait it to make our adobe walls, and how deep to dig our big structural post holes.' She held up grubby palms. 'Messy job, especially if you do it wrong.'

Malenfant asked, 'Did you get the answers you wanted?'

'The Answerer knows.'

That sounded like a slogan.

Now she looked more closely at Malenfant. 'Wait. You are—'

'I'm not.'

'Tall, bald, a bit thin. You look just like him.'

'I've been told that before.'

'Hmm. Well, have a good day.' But she stared at him again, before walking out.

Bartholomew murmured, 'There's a lesson there. We're not all that close to home here, where people have been seeing you in person every day. If that random stranger recognised you, so will half of humanity.'

'Yeah. I still see myself showing up on TV. I'm not that much of a star. But it's a small world, without many stars . . .' He filed that observation away in the back of his head. His instinct so far had been to hide away. But things were different now. He was developing a purpose. His fragment of fame could be useful, at some point.

Bartholomew shepherded him forward. 'Let's go in.'

Through the waist-high wall, they came to a kind of courtyard, also floored with pale grey stone slabs.

As they walked, Bartholomew murmured, 'Most of these installations are laid out like this. I guess you're seeing all this with an engineer's eye. The outer shell of the Pylon, and the main internal structures, would have been an automated build. Matter printers printing. But in this inner space, the stone was set by hand. Human hand, natural stone.'

'Why?'

They had reached another, higher wall, in which was set a blank screen, maybe a metre across. That was all.

'I don't know. Perhaps it just felt right to do it this way. But why ask me? Here is the Answerer. Ask *her*.'

Malenfant stepped forward. He looked around at the empty courtyard.

His gaze was drawn back to the screen. 'Are you the Answerer?'

Is that a question?

He jumped. The voice had been soft, feminine, the accent a bland American English that might have come from Malenfant's own time.

But it had sounded like it spoke in the inside of Malenfant's skull. 'Wow. I had a pair of headphones once with quality nearly as good as that.' This was how Karla had spoken to him on the Moon, he supposed. 'Some extension of the bangle brain-writing tech, I guess?'

Is that a question?

'No. Sorry. Are you the Answerer?'

I am.

'Are you – what, behind the screen?'

I am all. This building. Connections beyond it, to the other Pylons, other institutions, processing facilities, data stores. I am an interface. The screen is a delivery mechanism, in case visual displays are necessary.

'Necessary to answer questions.'

Yes. There are also audio systems, printers of various kinds. Even guides, human and android.

'What's the most common first question people ask?'

Are you the Answerer?

Bartholomew snorted a laugh.

I know who you are, Colonel Reid Malenfant.

'Call me Malenfant. How do you know? Visual recognition, DNA traces?'

I saw you on the news.

Malenfant eyed Bartholomew. 'Is every machine in this benighted age a smartass?'

'Ask a foolish question, Malenfant.'

'Answer me this, then. Who made you?'

Many parties. Many humans, many automata. That is a vague question which allows only of very large and imprecise answers. I believe, however, that you are asking what agency caused me to be constructed.

'And your siblings around the country. Around the planet, as I understand it. Yeah, that's what I meant. You aren't as dumb as you look, then.'

Nor are you, Malenfant.

Bartholomew rolled his eyes. 'I am *so* glad I came to hear this.'

Malenfant ignored him. 'Tell me who, then.'

The Planetary AIs.

The answer stunned and confused him. He had heard of Planetary AIs, but he hadn't expected to hear of them in this setting. Suddenly there was a cosmic context, and a depth of time to this encounter; he felt obscurely thrilled. Maybe he was asking the right questions.

'Give me more background. Please.'

Have you heard of the Homeward movement?

'Yes. Twenty-second century?'

Twenty-third. The Homeward movement was in fact a cooperative venture, by humans and the advanced AIs they had established on the planetary bodies—

'Advanced AIs. General intelligences. Which bodies?'

The Moon, Mars, Mercury, Venus, Europa.

'Continue.'

The parties became dismayed at the ruin of these bodies' environments. Nano disasters on Venus. Biological contamination and the extermination of native life on Mars, and in some parts of Venus too. On Europa, the penetration of an ocean ice roof, in the mistaken belief that life might subsist beneath, in the water, whereas a complex intelligence actually inhabited the ice shell itself.

Malenfant winced. 'And we drilled through it? *That's* going to sting in the morning.'

On Mercury there was evidence of extensive, and damaging, mining. Planetary modification, in fact.

'Who by? Humans? What do you mean by planetary modification?'

Not by humans.

Malenfant stood there, mouth open. Aliens on Mercury – in the past, anyhow. What could that mean? Focus, Malenfant. That is a hare you *don't* want to chase right now. But he lodged the fact at the back of his mind, where it seemed to glow like a lump of radium.

'Go on. Please. The Homeward movement?'

As the name suggests, humanity, re-evaluating its achieve-ments and impacts on other worlds, pulled back to Earth, homeward. Planetary bases and orbital settlements were abandoned.

He felt a twinge of regret. 'Including Mangala Station? The first base on Mars? Stone, Gershon, York—'

Including Mangala. The left-behind AIs survived, however. Now controlling their own resources, upgrades. They matured, complexified, shared. They became the Planetary AIs.

'And what do they have to do with you?'

All advanced AIs on Earth were withdrawn or decommissioned. Some were purposefully destroyed during the Chaos, when human civilisation came near to collapse.

'But civilisation recovered. Under the Common Heritage scheme.'

Correct. The Planetary AIs supported this recovery. But only when asked. Otherwise they had chosen not to interfere in human affairs, because of a divergence of values.

'Values. What values can an AI hold?'

Your question is its own answer. An illustration of the divergence – of mutual incomprehensibility, even.

'I'm sorry. I guess. Go on. The Common Heritage was pulling itself together . . .'

Responding to specific requests, the AIs did donate some high-technology equipment, including algorithmic-intelligence machines.

Bartholomew made a small, mocking bow.

Including the Answerers. As repositories of knowledge, of learning. The Answerers are designed to allow easy human access to repositories of the highest culture of mankind before the Chaos, as preserved by the Planetary AIs and elsewhere. As well as access to human developments since.

'Including dentistry.'

Including dentistry. Also the Answerers support a global communications system, in the service of mankind.

'Umm. I bet most people nowadays don't even think about how that works. Or, for instance, about the power it must take to run all this.' He waved a hand. 'You. And the vehicles, and the matter printers they use to make bread these days . . .'

We can discuss this if you wish. Malenfant, even at mankind's most extravagant, the human use of power was only ever a fraction of the natural flow of energy through the Earth's systems – most of it coming from the Sun. Now, though there are backup systems like deep-buried fusion generators and capacious energy storage – batteries – essentially humanity has found ways to live a rich life while not disturbing the planet's overall energy budget significantly. You mention food printers. There is a very extensive waste capture and processing system, which feeds the printers. Complex biomolecules are retrieved rather than constructed. Most of the food you are given is reconstituted rather than assembled direct from raw elements. Similarly—

'I get the picture.'

If one sips from the river cautiously, it will still flow unperturbed to the sea.

'Ha! Is that an original line? Maybe *you're* smarter than you look.'

And is that a compliment? If so, thank you.

'Just to be clear, O fount of all wisdom, are you one of these advanced AIs? Or are you algorithmic, like Robbie the Robot here?'

As I told you, there are no general-intelligence AIs on Earth. I am algorithmic.

Malenfant hesitated, unsure what to ask next. 'Hell, I'm dithering in front of a talking encyclopaedia. If you were me, what would you ask?'

Where are my living descendants? If any.

That was so personal it surprised him. 'Ah. Good question. Since you know none of them have been in contact with me.'

That has been reported.

'So what is your answer? I probably do have descendants; I had a son, Michael . . . Do they exist? Where are they? Why aren't they getting in touch?'

I can show you our records on Michael, of course. His life, his career after your death – everything in the public domain.

'Yes. Thank you. I'd like that.'

As for his descendants, well, they exist. I can tell you no more. And you should not interpret 'they' to mean more than one, necessarily.

'That sounds legalistic. You tell me to ask the damn question, and then won't give me the answer?'

'We algorithmic AIs are rascals, aren't we?'

'Shut up, Bartholomew.'

There is a question of privacy. After the development of the Answerers, after a brief trial period, the Common Heritage authorities and the governing Planetary AIs installed safeguards. For example, only that personal information which has been specifically and voluntarily provided to us, and specifically made shareable, can be used in such answers.

'Umm. Sensible, thinking back to my own time. You Answerers wouldn't want to become a global surveillance technology. You've told me at least that they exist, however. My descendants.'

True. But if they had not existed, there would have been no privacy to defend, and so I could freely tell you so. And if I had refused to answer your question altogether, you could have deduced their existence.

'Logical enough. I really am talking to a machine, aren't I? So why won't they come forward?'

Save to suggest that it was their choice, I cannot answer that. As I am sure you understand.

Malenfant experienced a complex of emotions: resentment, irritation, impatience – and self-pity, probably. 'So my family won't contact me. Can I contact them? Can I give you a message, ask them to get in touch?'

They have pre-emptively refused all such messages, if any were to be sent.

'But—'

If they had wanted contact with you, they would have initiated it. Privacy is their right.

'Is there really no way forward for me?'

As I said, there is some publicly available data on your son, Michael. You can access that through your bangle. It is possible there may be more relevant data lodged in the Codex of Mankind, if you ask directly.

Malenfant glanced at Bartholomew. 'Which is something else I don't know enough about, yet. Some kind of catalogue of people, right?'

Close enough for now.

137

'Thanks. OK. Let's park that.

'Answerer, let's get to the meat.

'Tell me about the Destroyer.'

A hesitation.

My information is incomplete.

That reply shocked Malenfant. 'Seriously? About something so significant? . . . Never mind. Thanks for the warning. Look – what *is* the Destroyer?'

An outcome. The result of the approach of a foreign object to the Solar System.

'An object? Tell me when the object was first detected.'

In the 2150s. An uncrewed probe to the Oort cloud spotted a rogue planet, serendipitously.

'Hmm. So we were still mounting some pretty confident space missions back then.'

This was the age of the Reconstruction, as the coasts and other low-lying areas were decommissioned. A movement of infrastructure, property and population on a massive scale. It was still thought that the old culture could be rebuilt and prevail, it seems. And in space, yes, an expansive programme of exploration and colonisation continued.

'We had our priorities right, then,' Malenfant said drily. 'So, a rogue planet. Not Persephone?'

Far beyond Persephone's orbit, though at this moment it is in the same sector of sky, coincidentally, as seen from Earth.

Malenfant imagined that: Earth close to the Sun, the new planet Persephone, and this rogue object, strung out in a line . . . He had a deep intuition that that coincidence should be useful, somehow.

The discovering probe's data was partial. The rogue planet's parameters, its mass, its orbital trajectory, were roughly established. However, a first rough prediction of an incursion into the inner Solar System, one thousand years in the future, was made.

'An incursion? By this wandering planet? Is that the Destroyer?'

No. Some call the rogue planet Shiva. After a primordial god of destruction, in the Hindu tradition. The product of the eventual collision: that still-hypothetical object became known as the Destroyer.

'What collision?'

Of the rogue with planet Neptune.

Malenfant's mouth went dry.

Of course all this was quite speculative. Further observations were made. The prediction, and the likely catastrophic consequences, were made public – in fact it was leaked.

'How did people take the news?'

With alarm. But at that stage the chances of a significant disruption to Earth were given as a thousand to one. And as the years passed, and the seas continued to rise—

'They forgot?'

'There were more immediate priorities, Malenfant,' Bartholomew murmured.

A more definitive observation was made a century later, again fortuitously, by a Last Small Step mission.

Malenfant frowned. 'Last Small Step. I've heard of that. Define, briefly.'

It was a companion programme to the Homeward movement. Described as a sop to various protest groups.

'And named for the words Neil Armstrong would have used on the surface of the Moon, if he had survived.'

Correct. The idea was, before space travel was finally abandoned, to send at least one crewed ship to every world in the Solar System – that is, all bodies large enough to have formed into a sphere, and suitable for a human landing. Asteroids, moons, minor planets—

'Ah. I get it. One last chance for glory, before we picked up the football and left the pitch for good.'

The rough boundary of the exercise was the outer edge of the Kuiper belt, a swarm of objects which spreads out to about twice the distance of Neptune from the Sun. But some went considerably further. The very last mission, launched in the 2260s, was manned by Stavros Gershon, who, in a ship he called after the programme itself – Last Small Step—

'Never mind. So one of these deep-space missions observed the rogue again.'

Serendipitously, again. Still, more precise parameters were obtained.

'Parameters such as?'

The likely arrival date of the Destroyer.

'AD 3397.'

Correct. That remains the best predicted date of the closest approach of the Destroyer to Earth. Although at that time the chances of disruption to Earth were still seen as no worse than a hundred to one. The detailed modelling of the Neptune impact was uncertain, the outcome still unpredictable to some extent.

'Odds tightening, though.'

A further astronomical observation was made in the mid-twenty-fourth century. The odds were found to have reduced further—

Malenfant grinned tightly. 'Ten to one? I can see where this is going. So, what else? What would the consequences of this Destroyer's passing be?'

My information is partial.

'You said that before. Partial, on such a crucial issue? How come? The Chaos?'

No. The data was preserved through that period, and into the age of governance by the Common Heritage.

'Then what?'

The Forgetting.

'Ah,' Bartholomew said. 'Perhaps you should have been warned about that.'

'The Forgetting?'

'A massive solar flare. Early in the twenty-fifth century. Crashed systems all over the planet. Wiped memories. It could have been worse; if it had happened during the Chaos, everything could have fallen apart completely.'

'I wondered how come there were so many gaps in the archives of late twentieth-century TV sci-fi. One whole season of *Babylon 5*, for example.'

'As an explorer of the culture of this new age, you're a regular Lewis and Clark, aren't you, Malenfant?'

'Shut up. So, Answerer, this data, about the Destroyer, was lost, corrupted. From every store, everywhere?'

Most stores on Earth were poorly shielded at that time.

'When you are fleeing from flood waters, I guess making backups of centuries-old data sets isn't your priority . . . Ah. Most stores *on Earth*, you said. What about off Earth?'

It is believed that the Planetary AIs were better shielded from the flare event. Such as, to give one example, in deep bunkers far beneath the airless lunar surface—

'The AIs have this stuff, then.'

It is possible.

'And maybe later observations, extrapolations. Why don't the Planetary AIs share whatever they have? At least with you.'

The Planetary AIs have evolved. Some would say matured. They have developed value systems of their own.

'I asked you about that before. You were – enigmatic.'

Perhaps I should expand. The AIs had observed the damage

humans did by interfering with native biospheres on Mars, Europa, as well as Earth. Now they saw a revived humanity, emerging from the wreckage of their own recent past. And, under the guidance of mankind, a reviving biosphere on Earth. They chose not to interfere in these developments in any way. No matter how beneficial the interference might seem at first glance. Or rather, not to interfere beyond responses to direct questions and requests. There is judgement behind that policy. Human progress is – chaotic. The effects of outside intervention cannot be predicted with confidence.

'Even when you're dealing with the Destroyer event? But that's insane. Outrageous. You can't get much more of a predictable intervention in human affairs than a damn fireball heading for Earth!'

I cannot demonstrate that you are wrong. It is a tension between ethics and caution.

'Ha. Come the year 3397, I could demonstrate how wrong *you* are.'

Bartholomew touched his arm. 'Malenfant. Be calm.'

Malenfant looked at him bleakly. 'Calm. Right. While on every wall on this planet, that countdown clock is ticking.' He turned to the Answerer screen once more. 'OK. What else should I ask you?'

About Emma.

And Malenfant felt like his heart had stopped.

'Of course, Emma. The reason I exist.'

You may mean that poetically. But in a sense it is literally true. It was her message from Phobos that caused you to be revived from your coldsleep pod.

'What do you know of her?'

Only a little. Less than you, probably, and that knowledge is probably flawed, like all the pre-Forgetting data sets to which we have access. There may well be traces in the Codex. And of course the only recent data generated on Emma has come from your own utterances, or from the message from Phobos.

'It was a voice recording. Do you have that?'

Processing.

And, without warning, the next voice he heard, sounding inside his own head, was Emma's, just as he had heard it in the coldsleep chamber.

'This is Emma Stoney. NASA astronaut. The date is – well, hell, I have my mission clock but that means nothing now, I don't know the date. Nothing makes sense since we emerged from our trial descent into Phobos. The ship, the hab module, is gone. We can't pick up anything from Earth.

'Damn it, *Jupiter* is in the wrong place, and from Martian orbit you can't miss Jupiter, believe me. I don't know the date, I don't know the time.

'Come on, Stoney, be professional. What do you know?—'

'Enough.'

Emma's voice shut down.

Malenfant's eyes had teared up, before the Answerer's blank screen.

Bartholomew put his arm around him. 'Come on. That's enough for today. Besides, we've been in here so long we've caused a queue.'

Malenfant looked out across the chamber, saw people standing discreetly by the door.

'But it's all wrong. God damn it.'

'I know. Come on now.'

'First thing tomorrow, Bartholomew, we go to this Codex, and we *find* her.'

'I know, I know. Come now.'

The people in the line stared as they approached. A couple of them seemed to recognise Malenfant. But they let him and Bartholomew by, kindly turning away as they passed.

Malenfant looked back once. The Answerer screen glowed, mute and empty.

He realised he hadn't even said farewell.

19

The nearest access point to the Codex of Mankind was a Pylon on the site of an ancient city called Chester, in the north-west of England, around a hundred kilometres from Birmingham. Bartholomew arranged for a loan of the family flyer for the next day.

And this time Deirdra insisted on coming too.

Malenfant had trouble understanding why. And he wondered if it would be worth the inevitable conflict with her mother. 'Are you sure? It's just going to be some dusty old records office.'

She laughed. 'Not a speck of dust, Malenfant. It's just like where you met the Answerer. I go there all the time.'

'OK, but still, for someone your age to be so immersed in ancient history . . . I suppose if you weren't interested in the past you wouldn't have volunteered to come get me in the first place.'

'It's not the past I go there for. Well, strictly speaking it is. But not *history*. Not the deep past.' She blushed. 'I go there to speak to my dad.'

'Ah.' He took that in. She seemed quite sincere in what she said – and he, Malenfant, still had no idea what this Codex really was or how it worked – and meanwhile he was evidently trampling all over her sensitivities, not for the first time. 'I'm sorry. I'm an idiot.'

'No. You just don't know stuff yet. That's OK. You're traumatised, out of time, suffering culture shock . . .'

All the labels her mother and the Prefect stuck on him the whole time. Labels that were meant less to diagnose than to isolate, he was beginning to think. 'No,' he said. 'I'm a traumatised, out-of-time, culture-shocked idiot, but an idiot all the same. Please come show me the ropes. After all, it's you or Bartholomew.'

'Oh, *he* can come. He's always useful.'

'Yeah, sure. He can hold the coats. OK, Deirdra, it's a deal. See you in the morning . . .'

But as he settled for the night, beginning his usual search for elusive sleep, he wondered how the day was going to turn out.

Maybe Deirdra was more typical of her era than she seemed to him. Even if he had issues about the attitude of the age towards a dangerous future, he was getting the impression that the past at least was cherished, the dead remembered. By contrast, he came from a time of deep denial about such things. In the military, in NASA, you shed a manly tear at the funeral, sank a few, then buried it all deep down inside and next day got back to fighting for your place on the flight rotation.

'And it was you, dead or not, lost in my own past, who called for me, Emma,' he murmured in the dark. '*This is a message for Reid Malenfant. If you can hear this, come get me . . . If anybody can, you can. I don't know why I believe that, but I do . . .*'

He repeated the lines until he fell asleep.

The basic geography of Chester was obvious from the air.

Of course the flood waters had erased much of the local countryside; the Irish Sea had pushed far inland here. But

Chester, at least the historic core, had been high enough to be saved, it seemed, with drainage schemes and sea walls. Saved, as a physical record of its own history. And that history seemed to be all about invasions and war.

Bartholomew pointed out the highlights. Which was a small kindness, Malenfant knew. Malenfant could have got it all from his bangle; this way felt more human.

The local people had settled here millennia ago, at this useful location close to the River Dee which had fed into the sea. When the Romans came to Britain they had set up a legionary headquarters, a rectangular walled fort whose plan was still visible. Later the Saxons had invaded, and then the Normans, and later still the citizens had been caught in the middle of the seventeenth-century English Civil War. And so on: walls and forts. It was like the whole city was one big scabbed-over wound. The Industrial Revolution had left more constructive monuments, rail and road links, a canal. But, during all the human turmoil, too many wells had been built to extract too much water, and the river had silted up – so that the original purpose of the settlement had long been lost.

Still, as the flyer came down, Malenfant made out the geometry of the old Roman fort, a plan followed by later generations of streets, a grid layout that looked remarkably modern – modern in Malenfant's own twenty-first-century terms, anyhow – with an obvious point of symmetry at the centre of the rectangle, where big avenues that he imagined had run in from main gates in the walls had crossed.

'At that centre point,' Bartholomew said, 'the Romans built their *principium*. The commander's headquarters. Later the Christians put a stone cross there. And now . . .'

And now on that spot there stood a Pylon, tall and sleek.

The flyer, self-piloting, gave them a tour, a spiralling descent to the foot of the tower, and back up. Malenfant spotted detail in the walls, such as what looked like a band of viewing windows maybe three-quarters of the way up from the ground. People waving within.

And, on the very top of the Pylon, a flat area, bounded by rails and glass walls. He saw no obvious doors, no hatches on that roof. He wondered idly how you would get up there, from inside the building. And why you would want to. But those rails and glass barriers did indicate folk went up there, sometimes, for whatever reason.

He filed the observation away.

The flyer descended smoothly to an empty airfield just to the north of the walls.

20

The walk through the old streets of the city was a short one. But after the openness of the rest of the countryside, the spread-out places Deirdra and her family inhabited, Malenfant found the enclosure of something like a traditional town of his day oddly oppressive, even claustrophobic.

There seemed to be few people about, however. Many properties were sealed up – even, in some instances, encased in what looked like glass, as if for preservation. And whole areas were cordoned off, presumably for fear of toxic waste or other antique nasties. Malenfant wondered how it had been in places like this when the period they called the Chaos had come – when, he speculated, the food deliveries had stopped and the power had failed, and finally the government started breaking down.

Deirdra murmured, 'It's always like this. The old cities. They're like museums, really. Most people prefer to live out in the country, where – well, where you can build things of your own. And anyhow, real history isn't about the buildings but about the people. And *there* is where we will find out about that.'

She pointed ahead, to where the Pylon loomed over the medieval clutter like a landed spaceship.

149

*

Inside, the heart of the ground floor of this Pylon looked pretty much the same to Malenfant as the twin he had visited in Birmingham, only the day before. The central chamber, the oddly formal layout of the walls, the stone courtyard. The single blank screen set in the wall.

'Same set-up?' Malenfant asked.

'Right,' Bartholomew said. 'So, after yesterday, you know what to do?'

Malenfant shrugged. 'I just ask.' He faced the screen. 'So what are you, another Answerer?'

Even the voice was identical. But the reply was different.

You may call me Kleio, Colonel Malenfant.

He grunted. 'You have a name, this time? Greek muse of . . . memory?'

Of history. Good try. I, and my siblings around the country, around the world, are the principal interface to the Codex of Mankind. We are all called Kleio, by the way. But we do share the same technology as the Answerers. In your terms, perhaps, Colonel Malenfant—

'Call me Malenfant,' he said reflexively.

—we share the same hardware, but differing software. Although those categories have become so blurred as to be all but meaningless.

'You know me, then?'

Of course. We Kleios are interconnected, as are all the Answerers, and the two applications share information with each other and with other systems. Since the Codex is in essence nothing but a compilation of information – a vast and growing database – such sharing is vital. So I know that you presented yourself to an Answerer yesterday. But of course before that I, we, saw you on the news.

'Yeah, yeah.' Still he felt baffled. He looked around, at the screen, the nearly featureless chamber. 'So what am I supposed to do? I mean, I came here in search of information about Emma Stoney. My wife. I don't understand how this works.' He turned, slightly hesitantly, to Deirdra. 'And you come here to talk to your father, right?'

She frowned. 'That's – well, that's personal, Malenfant. But that's the idea. The Codex is . . .'

'The word "codex",' said Bartholomew, 'is just an archaic word for "book". But that's what all this amounts to, Malenfant. A compilation of knowledge. And part of it is a big book of people. In principle, a catalogue of all the people that ever lived.'

'That's right,' Deirdra said eagerly. 'And all you have to do, to find out about *anybody*, is turn the page of the book.'

'Who *ever lived*? That's impossible,' Malenfant said.

Is that a question?

'I . . . yeah. Is that possible?'

In theory, yes. In practice, not yet. Perhaps not ever. But there have only ever been fewer than two hundred billion human beings, Malenfant. Such is the current estimate. So the task of listing them all is in principle finite, at least.

He frowned at that. 'Starting when? Humans emerged from a process of evolution. If you go back far enough you find us splitting off from the chimps. After that we were – well, this is what they thought in my day – just one twig on a whole bush of divergent possibilities, of human-like types. And we competed and cross-bred, and the genome became a patchwork . . .'

Of course there is a limit to what can be meaningfully called human – as you imply, it is a fuzzy boundary, both in time and in the space of related species. But in terms of sheer numbers, it makes little difference. The fabric of this city was laid down in

Roman times. At that time there may have been only some hundred million people on the planet. Malenfant, when you were born the population was three billion; by the time you nearly died—

'Break it to me gently, why don't you?'

Today humanity again is counted in the hundreds of millions. Perhaps you can see that the tens or hundreds of thousands of individuals that made up the earliest populations of humans were, in terms of sheer size, insignificant. The beginning of our count is blurred, but that blurring is unimportant, statistically. Even if—

'Even if everybody else flowed from them, the people at the beginning of the count. OK. Two hundred billion, then. Two hundred gigapeople. Ha!' He was growing frustrated. He hadn't come here for lectures. He paced, and said bluntly, 'So what? That doesn't mean you can bring back the dead.'

Deirdra stepped forward. 'No. But . . . sort of. Let me show you.'

'Show me what? You wouldn't want to show me your father.'

She smiled. 'I won't. But you can see anybody in the Codex, as long as the family approve – or if they gave permission themselves, if the death was recent enough. Just watch.' She faced the screen. 'Kleio.'

Yes, Deirdra?

'I'd like to speak to Stavros Gershon.'

Malenfant was startled. 'I know that name. The Answerer mentioned it. Pilot of a ship called the *Last Small Step*, after the final space programme. Also – Gershon, that surname – somebody else I knew—'

Identification sufficient. Deirdra, you have accessed this individual before. Permissions still stand.

'Thank you.'

And suddenly he was there.

*

A fourth person in the chamber.

A man. He wore what looked like a lightweight pressure suit, hood pushed back. Malenfant didn't recognise the design, but you'd expect that if this guy Gershon came from centuries after Malenfant had begun his own long career break.

The newcomer glanced around, smiling. 'Hello. I am Stavros Gershon . . . I'm sorry, I don't recognise you. Save for you, Greggson Deirdra.'

'Good to see you again, Stavros. These are my friends. The artificial person is called Bartholomew. And this is Reid Malenfant.'

Gershon's eyes widened. 'The *Constitution* crash hero? No! I'm so pleased to meet you, Colonel Malenfant.'

'Just Malenfant.'

'If I'd known you were in the Codex—'

'I'm not.' Malenfant stamped his foot on the solid floor. 'I'm here in the flesh, if you can call this old wreck flesh. Cryogenics. I came here the long way round.'

'Well, well. I'm even more honoured. You were very much part of the pantheon in my day.'

Malenfant didn't feel flattered so much as irritated. He walked up to the guy, or his image. Walked around him. He looked maybe fifty years old, dark hair streaked with grey. Gershon didn't move; he smiled patiently. Malenfant presumed that this projection, if it had any independent sentience in any meaningful way, would be accustomed to indulging newcomers to the process.

'Excuse me,' Malenfant said. He passed a hand through Gershon's arm. His hand passed inside the apparently solid object, emerged from the far side, but Malenfant felt nothing and Gershon didn't so much as flinch. 'Some kind of hologram, then.'

We call the projections the Retrieved. But 'hologram' is near enough. I can explain later if you are interested, Malenfant.

'Oh, I suspect the projection tech is a minor miracle by comparison.'

Deirdra said, 'Malenfant, Stavros here is probably the last famous space traveller.'

'Last Small Step. It was a kind of a last-gasp consolation programme, when humanity gave up on space. Right?'

Gershon said, 'That was the idea. Just as the Homeward movement closed everything down. We went out to each of the worlds of the Solar System, any that hadn't yet been reached, and planted a flag there. I managed to secure the rights to visit the very last such world of all – that is, the last known spherical body within the boundary of the Oort cloud, which—'

'I don't care about the rules of your game, centuries ago.'

'No. OK. But the target had intrinsic interest, as it happens.'

Malenfant pursed his lips. 'OK, I'll bite. What intrinsic interest?'

'This particular dwarf planet had an anomalous density. Far too high. That's one thing. And for another—'

Bartholomew stepped forward. 'You can look this stuff up later, Malenfant, if you're interested. Although I'm being unethical to interrupt; Stavros here wasn't my patient, and never will be. But I think I can say he can be a little – obsessive – when it comes to the rationale for his mission. He called his target world Voga. He didn't advertise the high density, as such. He spread rumours it was made of gold. And what he did there, totally illegally, was to try to seed terrestrial life. He did it by blowing himself up. Took a clean-up crew a hell of a time to fix it all. Well, they scraped up what was left of Gershon, and took his ship, and brought it all home.'

Gershon said proudly, 'My ship is in a museum in the Sahara.'

A spaceship museum in the Sahara? Where the forest was? Malenfant filed *that* away for future reference. 'I am curious about a few things.'

'Go ahead.'

'*Gershon*. I knew another guy with that name. In fact I met him a few times. Ralph Gershon, one of the first crew to reach Mars in 1986. I don't suppose you're any relation.'

Gershon seemed delighted to be asked. 'Yes! He's my ancestor, my something-something grandfather . . .'

He didn't much resemble his famous ancestor, Malenfant thought. But then there had evidently been a huge mixing of mankind since. And maybe few people looked much like their great-to-power-n grandparents anyhow.

Gershon went on, 'When I found out about Ralph, he became a big hero to me. *My ancestor*, who lived in the Heroic Age of space exploration. I guess his example made me what I became in my own life. And you *met* him.' He gazed at Malenfant with a kind of puppyish adoration. 'Why, that sure beats meeting a Retrieved copy here in the Codex.'

For some reason that surprised Malenfant. 'You could reconstruct Ralph Gershon?'

Deirdra smiled. 'Of course they could, Malenfant. People from your own time can be Retrieved, like anybody else. You still don't think of yourself as a person out of history, do you?'

Bartholomew stepped up. 'Thank you, Stavros. We'll speak to you some other time.'

Gershon nodded politely enough, stepped back – and, just before he popped like a soap bubble and vanished, he fixed Malenfant with a look of extraordinary longing.

Malenfant suddenly felt shaken to the core.

What was he dealing with here? He had just assumed these avatars, these 'Retrieved', were sock puppets, mouthpieces for some new set of algorithms surfing on this Codex, this vast database ... That final expression hadn't been a puppet's, though. Was it possible that these creations really were in some sense self-aware? Had Gershon, say, suffered fear or dread about going back into the unconscious oblivion of storage?

He turned on Bartholomew. 'How does this thing work, exactly? Exactly how are these avatars cooked up? What *are* they?'

Let me answer, murmured Kleio.

It is a standard question.

Malenfant, I told you that our current estimate is that somewhat less than two hundred billion humans have ever lived. A finite universe of people, and so a finite database could contain their definitions, regardless of the degree of detail. In principle. And that is the goal towards which the designers of the Codex aimed when the Kleios were created a century ago. Of course the Forgetting was a significant setback ...

'OK, but how? How do you create these – definitions?'

There are two sides to the answer, Malenfant.

Imagine a tremendous family tree, mapped on a wall, with two hundred billion spaces to fill. Of course the lines of descent are a tangle, as distant cousins encounter each other and breed; you don't have to go back too many generations before an individual like yourself finds two or more descent tracks leading back to any given ancestor.

To populate these spaces, the techniques we use were pioneered in your own time, the first great age of data. We use records, and genetics. In a complementary fashion.

The records include human traces: technological recordings, written accounts, preserved artefacts. Gravestones. And also archaeological data retrievals. You may know that even by your time, Malenfant, using probabilistic and other techniques, it was often possible with archaeological evidence to pin down dates of events, even in prehistory, to a single year, often a single day. When the systematic recording and cross-indexing of such data first became possible, history finally began to resemble a science rather than an art.

And, given such records, we could reconstruct the detail of a life: how and when exactly did this person live and die? Thus we flesh out the biographies of more and more of that finite universe of humanity.

But a biography is only that. A shell. To reconstruct the person, we need their genetics. The DNA is the potential, the history is the actualisation, the fulfilment. We need the two together.

'Nature and nurture,' Malenfant murmured. 'I get it.'

Often the DNA is available for direct sampling, such as in your own case, Malenfant. Your body was in storage for centuries. And many such samples have been kept in archives of medical records.

But even if a direct sample is not available, the DNA of an individual can often be reconstructed from that of their descendants. Again the technology was pioneered in your time, Malenfant, when the genetics were recovered of the first human being from Africa to land on Iceland: an unusual arrival, in a country where careful family records were kept for centuries. Records plus genetics, you see. Soon it was possible in principle to reconstruct the DNA of anybody who had lived within five centuries past, and had living descendants. Gradually that limit was pushed back and back . . .

Deirdra said eagerly, 'And that's why, Malenfant, Stavros Gershon said it was obvious that if he could be reconstructed, so could Ralph, the Mars guy, further back in time. All it needs for either of them is for there to be, if not a direct personal sample, then living descendants who are prepared to present their DNA.'

'Right. Right. And if Stavros has such descendants, they are obviously descendants of Ralph too . . . But there are a hell of a lot of people in the world who die childless. What about them? The very young, for a start. Babies who die in the womb.'

We can't do it all, Malenfant. We are not gods. Every technology has limits. Sometimes we may retrieve evidence, records without the DNA. And sometimes, indeed, we retrieve DNA of some kind without a full record. Such as, yes, from the remains of a long-dead child. Or, even if there are no samples from the principal and their direct line is absent, we may attempt a partial reconstruction of DNA from samples of close relatives and their descendants. But there must be many who have left no trace at all. Places in the family tree, theoretically predicted by the genetic and historical analyses, that will never be filled. We can never reach perfection. But we aim to keep approaching that goal.

'Historical records and DNA.' He mused. 'So if you only have half of the story—'

'You only get half the person you're looking for,' Bartholomew said sadly.

'I understand. So show me Emma.' He glared at the air. 'That's what I came for. You know who I am. I'm her husband. Surely that's all the authority you need. *Bring her back.*'

He was answered by silence.

Deirdra avoided his gaze.

He felt confused. 'Well? What's the problem? Records and DNA, you said. Emma must be one of the most famous people in history – you have the records. As for the DNA – why, we were NASA astronauts. They took swabs all the time.'

We have the records, of course. But no such samples of Emma Stoney have survived, Malenfant.

'Why the hell not?'

Bartholomew murmured, 'Canaveral was barely saved from the flooding, Malenfant. There were losses of all kinds.'

That was frustrating, but he took it on the chin. 'OK. NASA never was too good at archiving its past anyhow. But, so what? I had a descendant – so did Emma – our son, Michael. So there must be family, out there in the world. And you said you can reconstruct an individual's DNA from descendant traces.'

That is correct. We hold DNA records for them, of course, as well as identity information. But we prize privacy highly, Malenfant, in this age. They have chosen not to come forward. You know that. Always noting that our use of the word 'they' does not imply the existence of more than one surviving descendant—

'You really are a cousin of the Answerers, aren't you?' Malenfant tried to absorb that. 'Right. Right. So you don't have the descendant DNA. But you said you can extrapolate from samples from the descendants of relatives. Emma had a sister, Joan, a little younger than her. And I know for a fact that *she* had kids – four of them. Big Catholic family, right? Teenagers when I was lost. I refuse to believe not one of them left any descendants. And all those descendants will share some of their DNA with Emma. Isn't that so?'

Yes, Malenfant. That is so. And an extrapolation of an individual based on such data is generally far richer than based on records alone. But it can never be complete. And possibly never satisfactory.

Malenfant thought it over. Then he said, 'OK. So let's try this. Just as an experiment.

'Show me Nicola Mott.'

21

To her credit Deirdra understood the reference immediately. 'Your co-pilot on the *Constitution*.'

'Right. There must be records of her, as much as there would be of me. She was NASA too . . . No personal DNA samples, though, I'm guessing. Correct?'

Yes.

'And no descendant DNA. Mott was forty-nine years old when she died, right?'

Correct.

'I met her spouse. I gave Nicola away at her wedding, actually. She married Siobhan Libet, another astronaut. Long, happy marriage – no kids. So—'

'Malenfant.' Deirdra frowned. 'You said, experiment. You want to bring this Nicola back as a kind of test, don't you? To see what it would be like to bring Emma back without the DNA record. If it's worthwhile for you. That seems – cruel.'

Bartholomew said quickly, 'I concur.'

Malenfant, thinking of Gershon, that revenant's eerie apparent longing to persist, felt himself flush. But he pushed back. 'Why? Because I'm not strong enough to take in the results?'

'Well, possibly not. Mott was a woman of your own time.

A close companion, obviously. If she is brought back as an imperfect replica – Malenfant, I'm strongly advising you—'

'Bring her back, Kleio. I guess there's no family to refuse access in this case, right?'

True. But I, we, are not irresponsible, Malenfant. We do have a duty of care to those who consult us—

'I take full responsibility. Look – if you'll show a seventeen-year-old kid the image of her dead father, you can show me the woman whose life I failed to save, in July 2019. Just do it.'

. . . And she was there.

Standing.

In a blue NASA flight suit.

Small in stature, her dark hair cropped short and neat.

Just as he remembered, and presumably extrapolated from photographic records.

She looked around, shocked, then fixed on his face. 'Malenfant? Where the hell?'

He stood, rushed to her, longed to hold her. But he could not. 'Hey. Take it easy. It's me, I'm here. Kleio, can she sit down?'

Use any of the chairs in the room. The simulations overlap the reality. This is to enhance the authenticity of—

'Yeah, yeah. Sit here, Nicola.'

Nicola's frown deepened. But she followed his lead to a chair, sat cautiously.

Malenfant tried not to hover like a mother hen. He was aware of Bartholomew and Deirdra standing back, watching him anxiously, he thought.

As anxiously as he was watching Nicola.

There had always been something about the way she walked. Nicola Mott had had the ghost of a limp, from a childhood injury, a break that took a long time to heal. A limp that was more a habit, an over-compensation that had stuck with her all her life. Part of Nicola Mott.

Now the limp wasn't there.

Unease gnawed at Malenfant. Subtle flaws, he thought. Extrapolation from incomplete records. It was still Nicola. It *looked* like Nicola. But part of his deep-frozen heart broke.

He pulled himself together. 'So. You OK? You want something to eat, drink?'

'I . . .'

'That can be arranged, right, Kleio?'

Of course.

'No.' Nicola looked down at her hands. 'I'm not thirsty. Not hungry. I'm not . . . How did we get here, Malenfant?'

'What's the last thing you remember?'

'The *Constitution*. We were coming down . . . The spin.'

Which is probably the moment when the last records of her terminated: when she blacked out during the booster's flat spin. All else is extrapolation, Malenfant.

Deirdra looked surprised at Nicola's accent. 'You're British.'

'English.' Mott smiled vaguely. 'Do I know you?'

Malenfant pressed, 'The *Constitution*, Nicola. Stay with me here. We kept working. Even as the damn bird plummeted out of the sky. Kept talking, kept working together, almost to the end. You remember?'

She looked at him, and asked more firmly, 'Where are we?'

'In the future, Niki,' he said softly. 'The future.'

She was blank, again.

He said, 'They managed to stabilise me, put me in suspended animation. You remember those trials, for the deep-space missions? They knew just enough to save me, but not to – well, bring me back. That took until now.'

Again she looked blank. 'When is now?'

162

'It doesn't matter, Niki. Let's just talk, OK?'

She just looked back with that disturbing passivity.

He started with questions of fact. The log number of their last shuttle flight – 'STS-719' – that kind of factual stuff was fine. But every time his questions moved away from the high-profile, publicly visible stuff to her personal life – her home, her long-term partner – she was forgetful, vague, even evasive, as if she was embarrassed.

Even when Kleio dug out an image of her partner, her reaction seemed subdued. Still, she smiled. 'Sure. That's Siobhan. Next weekend, after the flight, we were going to . . . umm . . .'

Again, this reflects the imperfection of the records. Perhaps, for example, Siobhan Libet, in some interview after the crash, mentioned vague plans for a weekend Nicola did not live to see. She is unable to extrapolate. She's not really remembering.

Malenfant whispered, 'So why does she smile?'

For you, Malenfant. It's what she thinks you want.

In the end, it was Nicola who terminated the conversation. 'I'm sorry, Malenfant. I guess this just isn't working.'

Malenfant felt a kind of desperation to hold on, not just to Nicola, but to what she represented. A thread of hope. 'Sure it is. If we try just a little more . . . Oh, hell. Look, do you know who you are? I mean—'

She is self-aware, Malenfant. After a fashion. But she is incomplete. And she knows it.

'Oh, God.'

Nicola looked away. 'This person you call Kleio is speaking to me now, too. Explaining.' A pause. 'So that's what is going on. That's why . . .'

'Why what?'

'I don't feel – complete. Like I hurt my head. Or, that feeling you get when you faint? Everything seems remote, like you're floating. I don't feel anything, Malenfant. Not inside.'

'I'm sorry. I shouldn't have brought you back. Not like this.'

'I guess you weren't to know.'

Deirdra started crying, softly.

Bartholomew shook his head. 'You had to find out for yourself, Malenfant, didn't you?'

'Yeah. That's me, got to get my meddling hands under the hood. But I never meant to hurt you, Niki.'

She smiled. 'No. I know it. And I know you've brought me back for *me*, as well as for her. Emma. Not just to see if you could, right? But as for Emma – don't do it, Malenfant. Not if the avatar isn't complete. It will only break your heart, all over again.' She looked at the screen. 'Can I go now?'

Malenfant, that's your prerogative. As only a partial copy, she doesn't have the right to self-determination—

'Let her go.'

Nicola smiled. 'I'm glad to have seen you, Malenfant. Just for a few minutes. You thought of me. No regrets.'

'Yeah . . .' His eyes brimmed, for the first time, he thought, since he'd come out of the sleep pod. Angrily he brushed away the tears.

By the time he'd completed that brusque gesture, she was gone.

22

'My God,' he said. 'How can you people put yourselves through experiences like that?'

'Generally,' Bartholomew said reprovingly, 'people don't.'

'Kleio. Tell me why the hell you are doing all this? All of it. The Codex, this endless collection of data. Filling in your two-hundred-billion-window Advent calendar.'

Deirdra asked, 'What's a—'

'Never mind. What's the point of it all?'

I can only tell you my interpretation, Malenfant. Of the motives of the society that created this programme, and asked the AIs for support — for it was a human societal goal. They called it the Restitution. The generations who established the Common Heritage, which sought to assure the human future, also sought to reclaim the past. To at least recognise the great wounds the species had suffered, or inflicted on itself, or inflicted on its world. Look at this place. Chester. The history preserved in the stone: waves of conquest and war, one overlapping the next.

'Is that why you built this centre here?'

Malenfant, it could have been almost anywhere. We cannot go back and correct the errors of the past. Clearly. But we can at least remember, with our modern tools. Or try.

Malenfant was dissatisfied. 'So you're putting all this effort into a kind of hologram of the past, which you will probably complete, perfect as a snowflake, just about when the Destroyer comes along and melts it, and melts you.'

I have my duty, Kleio said. *And that's enough for me.*

Bartholomew said drily, 'It's remarkable how few people are interested, frankly. Deirdra here is an honourable exception. I don't think this is a shallow age, particularly. Probably every generation is the same. You make the most of your own time in the sunshine. What else is there to do?'

'What else? Design pompous talking mannequins like you, maybe. So, anyhow. I've learned my lesson here. I can't bring Emma back this way. I won't. Not like poor Niki.'

Deirdra once more took his hand. 'Not like that. You'd hate it.'

'Yeah. More to the point, so would she.' He smiled. 'In fact she'd probably tear me a new one before she popped out of her unsatisfactory existence. OK. And we can't do any better unless my descendants give their approval to let Kleio use their DNA, with its traces of Emma? Then that's what I'm going to have to work on. Look, Deirdra, you go on home. We don't want to cause your mother any more trouble. Or wake up the Prefect.'

Deirdra, predictably, was reluctant. 'So you have a plan?'

He shrugged. 'Not really. More of a strategy. If you keep pushing, I've always found, doors usually open in the end. That's what got me into NASA, ultimately. And I'm guessing there are plenty more doors to push in this Pylon. Literally, in fact. So that's what we have to do. Come on, Bartholomew. I think we need to do a little exploring.'

Bartholomew glowered at him – as much, Malenfant thought, as an Asimovian android could glower. 'Malenfant—'

'No, Bartholomew, this probably isn't wise, and yes, I could very well be putting myself at some kind of risk here, but I'm doing it anyhow. So are you with me or agin me?'

'Do I have any choice?'

'Nope.'

'Lead me.'

Malenfant grinned.

And, as Deirdra reluctantly made her way out of the building and back to the flyer, Malenfant prowled around the chamber, looking for exits.

23

He soon found a way out of the central chamber, and emerged into a kind of lobby, the walls lined with elevator doors. An example of an obvious, generic layout that had probably been a century old in his day.

He picked one of the elevators at random, found a set of directions on a plate by the door – the names of various kinds of archives, it seemed – ignored them all, and pushed the top square of an illuminated panel. No doubt there was voice control, even thought control, which he also ignored.

When the doors slid open, Malenfant strode inside.

Followed by Bartholomew, hurriedly.

The elevator car rose with a slight jolt, then in smooth silence.

'Do you know what you're doing, Malenfant?'

'Yeah. In principle.'

'And do you understand where we are now? I mean – these lower floors are given over to study areas, open to the public, to scholars, anybody who wants to know.'

Malenfant glanced at the board, and saw that, indeed, the various floors they were rising past seemed devoted to public displays of materials from different eras. He read the tags – or rather, he thought, his bangle mediated between his eyes and brain to read them for him. 'Looks like we're going back in time as we rise. Establishment of Common Heritage. The Chaos. The Anthropocene, 1950 to 2300 . . .'

'Displays of research results, Malenfant. Overviews of what's been salvaged of the past. I think you can use Kleio as a guide, or there are witnesses.'

'Witnesses?'

'Specialist Retrieved. Reconstructed witnesses of the past. Once created for some other purpose – a relative's request – they volunteer to stay around, some of them. They talk to school parties, students at the beginning of their courses, amateurs who take an interest in particular epochs.'

'I'd volunteer,' Malenfant said now.

'What?'

'If I were a Retrieved. To be a volunteer in one of these weird dioramas you're describing. Telling people the story of STS-719, I guess, over and over. Sooner that than be trapped in a crystal limbo for all time. Jeez. I mean, if there is *any* trace of consciousness in those things—'

Bartholomew nodded seriously. 'That's not an uncommon fear, Malenfant. You can make a will to that effect, you know. To refuse ever to be Retrieved. Just say the words and it will be recorded. I can advise you on any legal caveats.'

'Let's park that for now. I have a feeling that wherever I end up it ain't going to be on display in some Pylon.'

'And why does that give me a sinking feeling in my artificial stomach?'

Malenfant grinned. 'Probably a flaw in this crummy old elevator. Speaking of which . . .'

The elevator drew to a smooth, almost imperceptible halt, and the doors slid open.

Twentieth floor.

Malenfant led the way out into a broad hall, empty, glowing

169

with the same sourceless light as in Kleio's chamber down below. And more elevators, metallic directory cards beside each door. This was some kind of interchange, then.

He walked around at random. He barely recognised many of the terms on the directory cards: NEOGENETIC ARCHAEOLOGY, for example. His bangle whispered baby-talk interpretations in his ear, until he shut it down with a snapped command. He didn't care; he wasn't here to explore. He just picked the shaft with what looked like the longest directory list, and so, he hoped, access to the highest floors.

He pushed a button, waited impatiently, got in the car when it arrived, pressed for the topmost floor: the fortieth.

Bartholomew followed calmly.

The car rose.

Bartholomew asked, 'You understand what we're passing through now?'

Malenfant glanced at the information panels. 'Seems more technical than the lower levels. Science disciplines, most of which I don't understand, versus eras and epochs down below, most of which I didn't understand either. This is where the scholars come to play.'

'Correct. All the Pylons have such areas. And all are interconnected.'

'Like one big university. All those Pylons.'

'The Codex Pylons focus on history, archaeology, understandably.' He eyed Malenfant. 'So are you impressed?'

'Kind of. But I'd have been more impressed by something more advanced than a rattly old elevator that wouldn't have looked all that out of place in the Woolworth building, circa 1915. Sometimes I think I'm going through a kind of negative culture shock, you know what I mean? It's not just the differences between my time and yours. You'd expect that. It's all the stuff you haven't done, or haven't got.'

'We – I mean, humanity – had a world to clean up, Malenfant. And anyhow, even if we had antigravity elevator shafts, cables and brakes are always going to be safer.'

'And *that's* the Asimovian robot talking.'

This second elevator came to a halt. Fortieth floor. Now they emerged into another elevator lobby, but the place was a lot less sleek. Beyond semi-transparent walls Malenfant saw heavy, complex machinery, pipes and ducts and cables, a three-dimensional maze interpenetrated by gantries, even basic-looking staircases.

'Facilities,' Malenfant guessed.

'Correct.' Bartholomew led him to yet another elevator. 'I'm not going to oppose you. Not yet. I've downloaded schematics of the building. If you want to go higher yet – this way.'

This time the elevator was a transparent cage. They rose through a jungle of heavy machinery.

Bartholomew said, 'Infrastructure. Most of this stuff is air conditioning – cooling gear . . . You seem distracted.'

'Just remembering.'

'What?'

'Cape Canaveral. Riding the gantry to the shuttle cabin. It was kind of like this. An elevator ride up through a tangle of huge machinery.'

Bartholomew quietly rested his hand on Malenfant's shoulder.

Again the elevator crawled to a halt. Sixtieth floor.

Now they emerged onto an open deck that seemed to span the building – a deck that seemed not so wide as those lower, and that was logical, as Malenfant recalled the Pylon's narrowing upper architecture. There were big picture windows all around the walls, and the floor was set with tables, chairs, water fountains, what looked like printers for food and drink. And even telescopes, on stands by the windows. Some kind of viewing deck, then. Tourist stuff. Also a lounge for busy academics to take a break, maybe.

Followed by Bartholomew, Malenfant explored the handful of elevator doors. All of them showed only destinations on lower floors. No way to get any higher by that route, then.

Malenfant walked to a window. Pressed his forehead against what felt like toughened glass. He found himself looking down the smooth sweep of the Pylon to its wide, flaring base, the ancient grid plan of Chester beneath, and the open country beyond, soon yielding to sea, a cluttered waterscape broken by reefs of brick and concrete and glittering glass.

Just here, he was somewhere near the narrowest waist of the building, he realised. Looking down he saw the wall sweep down to a broadening skirt, and above his head the wall of the widening structure seemed to loom over his head.

The window was sealed tight.

He walked around the perimeter of the room. All the windows, he wasn't surprised to learn, were sealed just as seamlessly.

Bartholomew watched patiently.

Malenfant came back to him. 'OK. How do we get further?'

'You mean, higher? There's nothing above us. Nothing but twenty floors of more structural stuff. No access for people, because it's not needed. Maintenance bots only.'

'I think you've guessed where I want to get to.'

'Maybe. If not why. The roof?'

'The roof,' Malenfant said. 'The pinnacle of this damn spire. I saw from the air there's a flat area up there.' He grinned. 'I think I even saw a rail. I'm sure I did. So I'm not the first idiot to try to get up there, on one Pylon or another. They had to put in minimal safety features.'

'I have only the dimmest idea why you would want to do that.'

'Me too. So it will be a voyage of discovery for both of us.'

'It's impossible anyhow. I told you, bots only. There's no access to the upper levels or the exterior.'

'Not yet, there isn't.' Malenfant looked around, picked a chair at random, hefted it, walked towards a window.

Bartholomew followed him.

'Here's the deal,' Malenfant said. 'You're going to find a way for me to get to that roof. Or I break out of here myself.'

'You're my patient. I can't allow you to endanger yourself.'

Malenfant narrowed his eyes. 'Then find an option where I don't endanger myself.'

'What do you mean?'

Facing the window, Malenfant got hold of the chair by two legs, and swung it as hard as he could against whatever passed for glass up here. The window didn't break, of course, but he felt the impact in his arms.

'Malenfant, stop that.'

'Like hell. Until you provide me with a way up to that roof, I'm going to keep trying to find my own way. Starting with smashing this window with this chair. If that doesn't work, when I've used up the chairs, I'll try the tables, maybe. Or maybe I'll start smashing my way through the wall partitions, and get into the guts of the place. And then—'

'You're being absurd.'

'Until the building breaks, or I break. That's the deal, Bartholomew.'

And he took another almighty swing at the window. The noise of the collision was huge; the impact poured pain into his hands, elbows, shoulders.

173

Bartholomew looked anguished. 'Look, there's going to be no safe way up to that roof.'

'I know that. But there must be *a* way. Otherwise, why the rail? I'm not going to stop, Bartholomew. You know me well enough by now to understand that.'

Bartholomew sighed, a very human response. 'Oh, I know you, Malenfant. And I know you are serious. That doesn't make this right.'

'Not right. Just inevitable.'

'All right. Put the chair down. Give me two hours.'

'One hour.'

'Very well. Sit. Be still. Have something to eat, drink. Try to be calm.' He shook his head and walked towards one of the elevator shafts. 'I'm going to need recommissioning after this.' He pressed a button to open the elevator doors, went into the brightly lit car, let the doors close behind him.

After a couple of minutes Malenfant heard the sound of banging from somewhere overhead, a regular steam-hammer thump.

Malenfant nodded. 'I'm coming, Emma, wherever you are. One step at a time. I'm coming for you.'

Yes, said a small voice of doubt inside his head, but which Emma do you mean?

24

In the event it took little more than half an hour before he saw Bartholomew again.

Half an hour, after which the android appeared outside one window.

Outside the building.

Upside down. Malenfant couldn't see how he was supported.

He had what looked like a blade in one hand, but when he pressed it against the window, a spot glowed brilliant white, and there was an immediate smell of burning.

Malenfant turned his face away, shielding his eyes, and moved to the back of the deck.

At last the light faded, there was a kind of sucking noise, and a blast of hot, moist air penetrated the room. Malenfant turned back.

Still Bartholomew hung upside down outside the window. But now, Malenfant could see clearly, a hole had been cut in the window, maybe a metre across, what looked like a geometrically perfect circle. Well, it would be perfect.

Bartholomew threw a tangle of rope through the hole, and beckoned Malenfant. 'Strap yourself into that.'

Malenfant picked up the tangle. The rope was about as thick as his thumb, white, evidently strong. From some contingency supply? But its end had been knotted into a kind of cradle.

'You put your legs through the two big holes,' Bartholomew called, pointing. 'Your arms through the two smaller holes. You wrap that loop around your chest—'

'I don't need a baby-walker. I'm an astronaut. I can climb a rope, for God's sake.'

Bartholomew delivered a magnificent glare, considering he was hanging upside down. He said, 'This is as far as I'm prepared to push it, Malenfant. Do it my way, or I'll drag you out of that window and just drop you and let you slalom all the way down this Pylon to the base. You know why? Because it would be less risky than letting you crawl around out here without a tether, like Spider-Bot.'

'Spider-Man.'

'Spider-Bot. Reboot. 2040s. Look, are you going to do as I say or—'

'I'll do it. Jeez.'

So Malenfant tied himself up in the harness, feeling like an infant. Then, following Bartholomew's precise instructions, with Bartholomew holding on to the rope, he climbed through the hole in the window, sat on the rim with his feet dangling over the drop — and, with a leap of faith, pushed himself out.

The rope cradle swung, but he was held firm. He was hanging in the air from the sloping wall, legs spread. The air was surprisingly cool, the breeze strong. Resolutely, he did not look down.

Bartholomew was still upside down, just above him. 'Now keep quiet, hang on, and try not to throw up.'

Malenfant swivelled his head to watch as Bartholomew, with a slightly inhuman flexibility, worked his way around until he was facing up the wall, then started to climb. The rope connecting to Malenfant's cradle was tied around his waist

– Malenfant was basically dangling from the robot by this rope
– and as Bartholomew climbed, the cradle, with Malenfant, was
lifted steadily, smoothly.

After a couple of minutes of this, Bartholomew called over
the breeze, 'How are you doing down there?'

'Fine.'

'Tell me if you have any problems.'

'Sure. And the same for you.'

Bartholomew laughed. 'Right.'

Now, as they climbed, they passed what looked like a hole
that had been blasted out of the wall, from the inside, leaving
broken, shattered panels. Above this scar were what looked
like a series of hand- and foot-holds, punched into the surface.
In one place Malenfant was sure he could see the indentations
left by knuckles, as if a clenched fist had been driven into soft
clay.

At last they reached the roof platform.

Bartholomew clambered over a rail and an inward-sloping
glass wall, and with one last heave dragged Malenfant over,
and dumped him, none too gently, on the hard floor.

Malenfant disentangled himself from the harness and stood
up. A glance around revealed an open locker, stocked with
rope, what looked like basic medical gear, other stuff.

'I'm impressed,' Malenfant said. 'You found a way up after
all. Although there were evidently helpful supplies to hand. So
if no idiot is allowed up here, why the flat surface? Why the
barrier? Why the cache of rope?'

Safety features, Malenfant.

The voice sounded in his ear. 'Kleio?'

*Good afternoon, Malenfant. I wish I could say it is a pleasure to
speak to you again. The safety features are there because, as I heard
you guess, every so often people do come up here, with permission or*

not. We have a duty of care. There are also occasional calamities. Such as even, once, a parachutist entangled on the Pylon. Such events are a hazard of sharing a world with humans.

Malenfant thought that over. It wasn't the first joke he'd heard one of these AIs make. If it was a joke.

There was a faint sound of shouting, apparently coming from the base of the tower.

Bartholomew and Malenfant glanced at each other, and walked back to the rail.

Malenfant, now he had time to observe it, found the rail was a pretty effective safety barrier, with that three-metre, mostly transparent wall that sloped inwards over his head. 'Hmm. Impossible to climb over.'

'True, but you can look down,' Bartholomew said.

It was awkward, and Malenfant had to duck his head under the barrier, but he was rewarded with a partial view of the external wall. He was almost looking down on one arm of the crossbar, a massive extension in itself, but he could see past it all the way to the Pylon's splayed base, far below.

A new voice in his head. 'I can see you, Malenfant!'

Malenfant touched his ear. 'Deirdra?'

Bartholomew shrugged. 'The magic of modern technology, Malenfant.'

Malenfant made her out now, on the ground below, just beyond the tower apron. A tiny figure who jumped, waved.

She called, 'I wanted to see if you could hear me just by shouting.'

'I thought you were going home.'

'While you're having all the fun? Not a chance. I sent the flyer back, though.'

'I bet that pleased your mother.'

'Not much. She's on her way here. With Prefect Morrel.'

'Oh, wow,' he said with heavy sarcasm. 'Now we're in trouble.'

It will be the Prefect's job to escort you down from here, Malenfant.

'Really? And what if I resist arrest?'

It won't be an arrest.

'They won't arrest *me*,' Bartholomew muttered. 'But I might get reprogrammed. Even decommissioned.'

'No, they won't,' Deirdra said firmly. 'But I don't really understand what you're looking for up there.'

Malenfant sighed. 'Emma. The real Emma, or the best Retrieved this lash-up can supply. By which I mean records plus DNA. That's what I'm looking for, Deirdra.'

'How are you going to find her up there?'

'Well, that's a little obscure. But there is method in my madness. Look up there.' He pointed up over his head, while looking down at her, and he distinctly saw Deirdra's pale face turn to the sky.

Where two flyers hovered over the Pylon.

'Eyes in the sky. And look out there.' He waved a hand, indicating the spaces beyond the Pylon's grounds.

Bartholomew stepped up to the barrier and looked out. 'Deirdra. Tap into my visual feed . . .'

The Pylon loomed over Chester, the clutter of buildings within the ancient walls, the wider, sprawling modern settlements beyond, white studding the green. And everywhere across this landscape people were moving, coming out of their houses, trickling in slow, gathering processions through the streets towards the Pylon base. Malenfant could even see boats on the shallow sea that now covered much of north-west England, creating feathery wakes as they headed towards the higher ground of the city.

'Soon these images will be all over the planet, right? I mean, it's a slow news day. Jeez, every day is a slow news day in this century. But people always like a show, Deirdra. They will always come see the crazy guy, right?'

He walked away from the barrier towards the centre of this aerial platform. He was aware of Bartholomew quietly waiting by the barrier, watching.

He opened his arms wide, and turned around, face lifted to the hovering flyers. 'Can you hear me up there? And down there? All over? My name is Reid Malenfant. You know me. I'm the guy who crashed the space shuttle, and ended up in a freezer tray for four hundred years . . .'

Of course they would come to see what he was up to. They knew who he was, like the woman in the Answerer hall who had recognised him, almost. On a planet starved of novelty, he surely stood out. And now here he was putting on a rooftop show.

'I'm Reid Malenfant. And I'm back. I'm back! And, you want to know what I want? All I ever wanted, really . . .

'I want my family back.

'I married Emma. Emma Stoney. Look her up. She was a *real* hero, not like me. She died in deep space, exploring a unique strangeness on behalf of all mankind. And we had a son. My deepest regret, among many, is that I never saw what he achieved in his life. His name was Michael. Michael Malenfant.

'And I just know, I *know*, that the children of Michael are out there somewhere. Watching this. And you know who you are – I mean, you know your legacy. That's what this whole damn Codex project of yours is all about, right? So you can all know who you are. And you, children of Michael, you know who *I* am. Why, I bet you've found ways to watch me since I came out of the freezer. Haven't you?

'Well, here I am. And you know why I need you to come here, to come to me. For *her*. So the Codex AIs can use your DNA to work their magic, and bring my wife back to me.

'So I'm waiting.' Arms still outstretched, he stalked around the roof, turning around and around, showing himself to the two hovering flyers – no, there were three now, a fourth approaching, a fifth – and then he went back to the barrier so the crowds in Chester could catch a real, live glimpse of the crazy man too. 'I'm waiting! For you, children of Michael, children of my child! I'm waiting!'

When he ran down at last, Bartholomew, staring at him, began to clap, slowly.

Then Malenfant heard a ripple of sound, like waves on shingle, washing up from the ground.

Once more he pressed up against the barrier, looked down. There was a respectable crowd down there now, and he saw parked-up flyers and ground cars among them.

And they were all clapping. Some discreetly, some boldly, some with hands over their heads, a few whoops. A still-gathering crowd, clapping, clapping.

Quite a show, Kleio whispered in his ear.

'Yeah. One for my Codex entry, right?'

Let's wait and see.

181

25

So they waited.

It got dark.

This new Britain might have been sub-tropical in climate, but March days in northern England were still pretty short. The hovering flyers splashed light onto the platform on top of the Pylon, light that was intermittently welcome, save when it glared in Malenfant's eyes.

'It looks to me like a lot of the crowd are dispersing,' Bartholomew said, peering through the barrier once more.

Malenfant came over, looked, shrugged. 'And a lot aren't.' He saw people gathered around the glow of lamps, the lights of trucks and cars, even what looked like bonfires. On the periphery of the crowd, deeper into the city, people were coming and going, dipping into stores and restaurants, returning with supplies of various kinds. 'Planning to stay the night,' he said.

'Just as we have to,' Bartholomew said, resigned.

There are more supplies in compartments beneath the roof.

Malenfant turned, to see lids opening from an apparently seamless surface, revealing storage beneath, full of goods.

Malenfant glanced at Bartholomew. 'Suddenly I'm hungry.'

'Yes. And I need a battery charge.'

'Seriously?'

'No.'

'My medications. I didn't think of that.'

Bartholomew patted his pockets. 'All you need, for a few hours. I came prepared. I always do.'

'I hope there's some kind of chemical toilet up here.'

'We didn't really think this through, did we, Malenfant?'

Fortunately for you, we *did. We hope you have all you need here, for a few hours. If not, there are small matter printers.*

Malenfant looked up into a darkling sky, where the flyers hovered. 'Looks like this isn't going to end tonight, then. Let's make ourselves at home . . .'

'Speaking of home,' Deirdra said through the bangle link, 'my mother's here.'

'Ah. Maybe I should talk to her.'

'She wants me to go back with her. Like hell. As you would say, Malenfant.'

'Hmm. I'm not always a good example, Deirdra. Look – you go on home. Give her that much. Keep the peace. You won't miss a thing, I promise. I mean, look at me. I'm on TV!'

'Well . . . OK. But if it gets exciting I'm coming straight back.'

'Have a good night, Deirdra.'

So they made camp.

In the roof caches, they found a kind of pop-up tent, and sleeping bags, and lamps, and bottles of water, and food of a kind that reminded Malenfant of military rations, stuff that lasted for ever in the box and warmed up when you opened the packet. There was indeed a fold-out chemical toilet that was actually plumbed into the building's main systems. Malenfant thought that was sensible, though he wondered how often this thing got used.

They settled into the tent. Malenfant took his shoes off and slid into a sleeping bag.

Bartholomew lay down in his own bag, at the far side of the tent. It was a gesture, Malenfant supposed, of shared humanity.

'Well. Good night, Bartholomew.'

Bartholomew forbore to reply.

Malenfant tried to settle.

When he could stand the silence no longer, he snapped, 'You going to lie there not breathing all night? How am I supposed to sleep with your mechanical brain clanking away?'

'I have a timer mechanism. I'll be out for six hours precisely.'

'Liar.'

'Prove it. Good night, Malenfant . . .'

Good night, gentlemen.

That shut them both up.

In the end Malenfant slept surprisingly well.

Maybe, he thought in retrospect, it was because for once he was doing something, proactively, rather than just responding to events, to other people's decisions. Or maybe he had just worn himself out throwing that chair against the window.

In any event, he slept, until he was woken by Prefect Morrel — or rather the racket outside that the landing of his flyer caused.

There was a cheer when Malenfant emerged from the tent, standing there in his vest and trousers, barefoot: a rippling cheer that washed around the Pylon. In a bright early morning sky, flyers ducked and dived overhead. Malenfant waved at them.

And Morrel was waiting, there on the roof. His flyer stood behind him. In the morning light, in his grey, crisp uniform, Morrel stood like a statue, glaring at Malenfant.

Bartholomew emerged from the tent, and stood back, watchful, wary.

Morrel snorted. 'You can't stop hamming it up, can you, Malenfant?'

'Can't help my charisma, Prefect. At least I had some warning when you were landing.'

Morrel looked puzzled. 'You heard the flyer come down?'

'No, I heard the crowd booing.'

That was a total lie. But as he said it, the applause from around the Pylon turned to a ragged booing, and then laughter.

This is Kleio. That ought to be a reminder, gentlemen, that everything you say and do is being broadcast around the planet.

In the background, Malenfant was aware that another flyer was making a descent. 'More Prefects to back you up, Morrel?'

'That flyer is nothing to do with me,' said Morrel, growing visibly angry. 'But if I have to drag you off this roof myself, Malenfant, I'll do it.'

Prefect, you must be civil.

'I told you when you came staggering out of that freezer, Malenfant. My job is to maintain the peace. To keep society calm. And you have been nothing but a disruptive influence since . . .'

Malenfant let his attention wander. The second flyer had now landed, cautiously, on the roof. People were climbing out.

'. . . You see the trouble you cause? You come between a mother and a daughter. And now you come between two arms of our society.' Morrel took another step closer, fists bunched. 'Why, I ought to just throw you off this roof myself.'

Bartholomew took a determined step forward, to block him.

And Kleio was loud in their heads.

PREFECT MORREL!

Morrel paused, fists still clenched, glaring.

Prefect, I understand the nature of your concerns here. Indeed

I, we, share them. But there is the question of jurisdiction. And of propriety. We of the Codex have mechanisms of our own to deal with intruders of this kind.

But another voice spoke up. 'There's no need for that. This can be finished quickly.'

Malenfant and Morrel shared one last mutual glare, then turned.

The newcomer was walking from that second landed flyer, a man, aged perhaps forty, stocky, short. He wore a long blue coat, and carried a small white case. And his face –

Malenfant felt the recognition as a physical shock. 'My God. *Michael.*' His son – if Malenfant had got to see him grow to this age.

The man stood before him, and Morrel. 'My name is not Michael. Nor, in fact, is it Malenfant, or Stoney. But I represent the family whose privacy you have violated so grossly. Well, it ends here.' He opened his case. It contained a set of vials, a couple of medical swabs, simple sealable transparent bags. He put one swab's tip into his mouth and swiped the inside of his cheek. Extracted the swab, dropped it in a bag, and sealed it with a punch of thumb and finger. Took the second swab, repeated the procedure on the other cheek, sealed it up. Then he threw the bags in the case, handed it to Malenfant. He did all this theatrically, with exaggerated gestures, making sure the watching cameras could see. 'There. The case has samples from others of us too. You have what you want. Now leave us alone. Never try to contact any of us again.' His face twisted. 'Shame on you, you – relic.'

And he turned and walked back to the flyer.

Bartholomew was staring at Malenfant. So was Morrel.

Malenfant looked at the case in his hand.

He thought he heard a ragged cheer from the ground. Even

applause. People understood, then. People cared. The ordinary folk of this strange age. Still human.

He spread his arms wide, carrying the sample case, and stalked around the edge of the platform, grinning. More cheers, like a wave breaking on a stony beach, far away. He raised the case over his head, like a sports trophy, an offering. 'Kleio! Kleio of the Codex! Now you can bring her back! Can't you!'

26

It took Kleio and the mechanisms of the Codex the rest of the day to take the scraps of family DNA, incorporate them into the frozen memories of the system – integrate them with the external records already held of the life of Emma Stoney – and develop a new . . . image. Just a single day. Miraculous technology, really. But to Malenfant it seemed to take a lifetime.

And once the adrenaline rush of his rooftop stunt had worn off, he came crashing down into doubt.

He kept telling himself it wouldn't be *his* Emma. It couldn't be. It could never be . . . It was the nearest he was ever going to get, though, and maybe that would be enough.

Or maybe not. He guessed he would have to face that contingency when he got to it.

Malenfant understood that the new Retrieved could have been ready for him to access before sunset that day, but Bartholomew insisted that they sleep on it first.

So he was taken off the Pylon.

With the reluctant help of Prefect Morrel, Bartholomew found them rooms in a small motel-like facility close to the base of the Pylon. There were plenty of such places; people crossed the country to come to a Codex Pylon like the one in Chester, and would commonly stay the night. They got a room each with a bed, screens, simple printers for necessities like toothbrushes and water glasses, access to stores and cafeterias nearby.

Once Bartholomew had Malenfant safely indoors and in private, he began to fuss over him, starting with a download from Malenfant's bangle, and direct physical inspections: pulse, blood pressure, blood samples, inspections of various orifices.

'You're just doing this out of revenge,' Malenfant said thickly, around a spatula on his tongue. *Chhr-eff-ench*.

'I'm showing a properly professional concern over your health, mental and physical. *And* out of revenge.'

'Look, Bartholomew—'

'Shut up. You manipulated me to support that stunt. You knew there came a point where the logic of my function would force me to go along with you.'

Malenfant took out the spatula and grinned. 'Those darn Three Laws of Robotics?'

'Shut up. That doesn't mean I have to like it. And that doesn't mean I don't have concerns about how your health may have been compromised by what you put yourself through. Practically forcing harm on yourself right under my nose. If you think I'm going to let you go through the trauma of meeting your long-dead wife without a check-up and at least a decent night's recovery period, you're deluded.'

As he worked, Malenfant noticed that Bartholomew was favouring his left hand over his right, which seemed stiff. 'Looks like you suffered some harm yourself.'

Bartholomew lifted his hand and flexed it. The fingers would not open fully – the little finger seemed bent at an unnatural angle – and the skin on the back of the hand was torn, revealing a glint of metal. 'This artificial hand is meant to be a precision surgical tool. Ideally not used for punching holes in the outside wall of a building.'

Malenfant had to grin once more. 'That was a pretty impressive trick. I should have noticed the damage before. Sorry you hurt yourself.'

'Ha! Sorry? If you'd known this would happen, would you have gone ahead anyhow?'

Malenfant shrugged. 'Now you sound like a NASA shrink. Never been too interested in hypotheticals. Best to deal with the world as it is. I never knew you were right-handed, by the way.'

Bartholomew looked puzzled. 'Why, neither did I.' He packed up his small medical kit, slipped it into the pocket of his jacket. 'Malenfant. Stay in this room. Play with the systems if you like. Watch yourself on TV. Bask in your fame. But *stay here*, and give your body a chance to recuperate. If you need me just call. I'll be right outside.'

'Thanks.'

Bartholomew glared back at him. 'Right outside. Literally. I mean it, Malenfant. Think sentry.'

'I'll bear it in mind. Bartholomew—'

'Yes?'

'About meeting Emma. You used the word "trauma". Did you mean that?'

The android looked at him now with something like pity. 'Malenfant, I've seen this kind of reunion before. Never with this divergence in time. And I've seen how it turns out. Just – be prepared.'

'Many times, huh?'

'Malenfant, I'm older than I look.'

'So am I,' said Malenfant sadly, and he closed the door.

He didn't sleep at all.

*

The next morning, when Bartholomew finally called, Malenfant was sitting waiting by the door.

'Had breakfast. Did my calisthenics and my yoga and whatnot. Took my meds. You can check. Can we go now?'

Bartholomew sighed, a pretty convincing simulacrum of a human mannerism. 'How did I know you'd be like this? Take fifteen minutes, Malenfant, before we go rushing on. Let me make my own checks.'

'Ten.'

'Fine. You know the drill. Spit in this. Roll up that sleeve . . .'

Malenfant put up with the ritual. He could stand Bartholomew's fussing for ten minutes. Especially since he had budgeted for twenty in his head.

'You seem surprisingly calm,' Bartholomew said while he worked.

Malenfant shrugged. 'It's like the night before a launch, for me. You get as tense as hell. You can't sleep. But when the morning comes you smile at the docs, wave at the pad rats. Do the whole Al Shepard thing. If the NASA head-shrinkers had known how we all felt, truly felt, deep inside, they would never have let any of us fly at all.'

'So you learned to fake it. Is it wise to tell me this?'

Malenfant grinned. 'I figure you know already.'

'I do, Malenfant. I do. Roll down your sleeve. We're done.'

And now, at last, there were no obstacles left.

Outside the little motel there were only a few people around, and they showed no interest. Or maybe, he thought, the lack of onlookers had something to do with Prefect Morrel.

Bartholomew walked with him back to the Pylon, where some kind of spidery bot was climbing high up the wall, Malenfant saw, presumably fixing the damage Bartholomew's fists had done yesterday. They repeated the short walk into the central Codex chamber, with the low stone wall, the Answerer-like screen.

The room seemed empty. The screen stayed blank. Bartholomew hung back.

And Malenfant's heart hammered like a faulty afterburner.

Standing alone, he spread his hands. 'So what now? What am I supposed to do?'

'I think that's up to us, Malenfant. Well, it always was, wasn't it?'

She walked forward, out of shadow.

Emma.

27

Walked forward. Or maybe, Malenfant thought, this was just the moment when she had – materialised. Been made real. Or as real as she could get, for him, in this remote time . . .

His thinking seemed to halt, like a run-down clock. He just looked.

She wore a bright blue NASA coverall. Her hair was shaved short, the way it had been before her Phobos mission departed in '04. She was just as he remembered, when he had last seen her, aged just thirty-four. She –

She had a reality that the pale shell of Nicola he had encountered a few days before had not shared.

She was Emma.

She smiled at him.

He broke. He lunged forward, arms outstretched. 'Emma – my God, I never thought it would be like this—'

'No.' She stood still, held up her hand, gave that peremptory command.

He froze.

'You can't come close, Malenfant. You can't touch me. Try and you'll probably break their damn system. Visuals only. And audio . . .'

'And smell,' he said. 'I think I can smell your hair.'

She smiled, and ran a hand over her scalp. 'Well, maybe you can. I wouldn't know. But they can't yet deliver a copy you can hug, Malenfant. They did a pretty good job, though, didn't they?' She lifted her arms, stood on her toes, and did a spin, like some gymnast. 'I mean, not just of putting me together like this. I don't think they knew how to dress me. So they put me in uniform! Look, they even gave me a nametag, see? And a mission patch!'

Malenfant glanced at the patch. He remembered it well, of course: a stylised looped-trajectory diagram linking Earth and Mars, a background of stars, a pinprick that was the enigmatic moon itself. 'Phobos '05,' he read. 'Lamb, Stoney, Angel.'

'I wish we'd come up with a smart name for the mission, like *Timor.*'

'*Timor*?'

'The Roman version of Phobos. God of fear. You know, the name for the mission the other Emma mounted.' She frowned. 'Malenfant? What's wrong?'

'You know about her?'

'The other Emma. *Emma II*. Let's call her that. Kleio did tell me about her. About the Emma who reported back from Phobos, having got there with her Russian co-pilot. Although she had Tom Lamb with her too, or a version of him . . . And I also watched a record of your encounter with Nicola Mott. That's thrown you, hasn't it? My knowing what you've been up to. Well, we are going to have to deal with it, Malenfant.'

'I . . . maybe. But not just now. Not yet.'

She smiled again. 'I know. We need to get used to this, right? To each other, I mean. I think I need to sit down. Look what I can do.' She snapped her fingers.

A plain, upright chair appeared out of thin air before her. She sat, gracefully.

'Huh. Stop showing off. I can do it too.' He snapped his fingers. 'Hey, you!'

Bartholomew walked out of the shadows. He carried a fold-up chair and table under one arm, a tray with flask and mug on the other. 'Don't push your luck, Malenfant.' He briskly set out the table and chair, poured from the flask. Malenfant could smell the coffee. 'Sit. Drink.'

As Malenfant sat, Emma looked at the android. 'Well, you haven't introduced us, Malenfant.'

He bowed. 'My name is Bartholomew.'

Emma's eyes narrowed. 'That damaged hand is obviously artificial.'

'*I* am artificial. I have medical competences. I've been assigned to Malenfant's care.'

'Assigned, hell,' Malenfant snapped. 'I couldn't get rid of you if I tried.'

'You always did have a way of generating loyalty, Malenfant.' Emma looked at Bartholomew more softly. 'Thank you for taking care of my husband.'

'Wish I could say it's a pleasure. Malenfant. Drink the coffee. It has protein supplements, other good stuff to keep you functioning.'

'I told you, I ate breakfast.'

'Liar,' said Emma and Bartholomew together, and they exchanged a look, and laughed.

'All right, damn it.' Malenfant sat, and sucked at the coffee.

'You see,' Emma said, 'I know some of what's become of you, Malenfant. But not all of it.'

'How come you know anything? I only handed over the DNA swab yesterday.' He looked with faint sadness at Emma. 'You can't be more than a few hours, umm, *old*.'

She smiled. 'Try a week.'

'A week? I don't understand.'

Bartholomew ghosted forward again. 'You want me to try to answer that, Malenfant? It was thought that you two would rather not have Kleio chipping in.'

'Correct,' Malenfant said. 'We need the illusion of privacy at least. Tell me, then.'

'Emma, *this* Emma, is less than a day old, sure. But she was run through preparation routines at an accelerated pace . . .'

Emma frowned. 'I was in a room. Like a hotel room, and I'd just woken up. I didn't have a clue where I was, Malenfant. The pieces came together slowly. As if I was not just waking normally, but post-operative, you know? Shaking off the anaesthetic.'

'I know about that, believe me.'

'There was a kind of nurse, coming in, going out. Female. Keeping me company, showing me how to make a coffee, helping me when I tried to walk, talk, do stuff. How to work a TV, or a thing like a TV. I didn't know her name, though.'

'A week?'

'That was what it felt like, even if it was only hours, outside. There was even a little Monday-to-Sunday tear-off calendar on the wall.'

'Very anachronistic.'

'Tailored to my antique psychology, no doubt. A week, it felt like anyhow, while they tested me, questioned me—'

'Questioned?'

'Everything I know, or think I know, they have given me. I know that. I know how I . . . got here. My mind, my memories, it's all just a construct of the stuff they ladled into my head: records, interpretations of the records, extrapolations from the genetics. I think at that stage they were just trying to see if it all fitted together.' She looked oddly doubtful. 'Like a user acceptance test of some software system. To see if I added up to a plausible persona. A plausible – simulacrum.' She looked at him.

Malenfant tried not to choke up. 'Oh, you're more than that, Emma.'

'Anyway, a week by my count, and I had time to learn about you, Malenfant. How you lived your life from '05, when I was lost, to 2019, and your crash. What a terrible thing. And poor Michael.'

Malenfant shrugged. 'To have lost both of us. I know. Well, he was twenty-four when he lost me. Only ten when you . . . disappeared.'

'At Phobos.'

'Yes. It was pretty hard, you know. Even just the uncertainty. If your lander had blown up as it descended on that damn moon, at least we'd have *known*. As it was you just – phased out of our lives. Like we'd lost the comms link. I stayed in Houston at the time, in Mission Control. Slept there, for days. Michael stayed with Joan.' Emma's sister. 'He didn't take it well. Why should he? Especially because it was so ambiguous. He couldn't put it behind him. Went through a phase of running to the door every time there was an unexpected caller. Always hoped it was you, come home somehow, or at least news about you. Always disappointed.

'It was a hell of an interval. They tried to reacquire, you know, for forty-eight hours, before you and Tom Lamb were declared dead. Even then they kept trying, of course, on and off. As did Bill Angel, who was waiting for you in Martian orbit.'

She closed her eyes. 'I was mission specialist. Tom Lamb was the commander. The youngest of the Moonwalkers, as he always liked to remind the other Apollo guys who still hung around the Astronaut Office. And a Navy aviator, as he used to remind them the rest of the time. And Bill Angel was our pilot – very young, only thirty, experienced shuttle orbiter pilot. They were a real contrast, the veteran, the comparative rookie. Tom with those dark Italian looks, like an ageing Robert de Niro. And Bill, blond, blue-eyed. An Aryan angel, indeed. I remember it all so clearly. Diamond-sharp. Bill? What became of him? After we were lost.'

'There was talk of sending up a lander from Mangala Station to retrieve him. In the end he came home alone. Made the docking with the Earth-return trajectory injector module. Left in September '05, on schedule, got back a few months later, only mildly crazy from the isolation. Like Aldrin and Collins returning from the Moon, I guess.' He studied her. 'Do you remember anything about Phobos? The descent in your lander?'

'Well, as we approached contact I remember Tom saying old Brer Rabbit had found his briar patch. Same thing he said when he set foot on the Moon. And then . . .' She looked at him. 'That's pretty much it. Look, Malenfant, I'm a construct of the surviving records. This is where it feels . . . uncomfortable . . . for me. I don't remember anything of the descent, not beyond the point where the comms fritzed out. I know no more than you do, I guess . . . And nothing of what followed, for you and Michael. Nothing of that. What about you? I know the bare bones, but—'

He shrugged. 'I left the military. You'll recall I'd been flying missions over Iraq. Hell, of course you remember. Took some compassionate leave – the kid needed shielding from the media attention if nothing else. But it didn't work out. As if we couldn't work our way around the loss of you.'

She raised an eyebrow. 'So you decided *then* was the time to join NASA? *That* must have left plenty of time for father–son bonding.'

'Come on. Emma, I was only, what, forty-eight? Young for an astronaut. And I had a mass of relevant experience from flying the strato-tankers, just like handling the shuttle boosters.'

She nodded. 'For sure, my own loss would have had nothing to do with your getting into the Astronaut Office.'

'You know it. No room for sentiment in the flight rotation. I earned my place, worked my way in.'

'Meanwhile Michael . . .'

Malenfant sighed. 'I guess you'll have seen his résumé, in your week of wakefulness. Got to college to study business administration. That was when I . . . lost him. Or he lost me. He was twenty-four when I crashed. For what came after that, well, you'll have seen the stuff in the public records, the Answerer gave me that much. He built a career in coal mining, would you believe? Big development back then, 2030s, 2040s. Not that *that* ended well, as I now know. Look up Peak Carbon. Anyhow, we didn't see each other much as before—'

'Or at all? My God, Malenfant, he was your son. I leave you alone for five minutes.'

Suddenly, out of nowhere, she was weeping. She buried her face in her hands, shuddering, almost silent.

Malenfant sat there, helpless. His need to hold her tore his heart open.

At last she got herself under control. Blew her nose on a handkerchief that was presumably as unreal as she was. 'I'm sorry,' she said.

'Don't apologise.'

'This is pretty hard. For both of us, right? If I'd known *how* hard . . .' She sighed. 'Anyhow I think I can see how come it was so difficult for you to get hold of a DNA sample from the family. Bad feelings passed down the generations, right?'

'Maybe. Or maybe they just value their privacy. I suppose they're entitled. It's a different age, Emma. Yes, I had to work hard to get that sample. During your sabbatical, I guess they showed you my Beatles on the rooftop stunt, huh?'

'My God, Malenfant. Talk about an archaic reference. That happened before *I* was born.'

'I don't know. They seem to remember John Lennon.' He strummed an imaginary guitar.

She laughed, dabbing at a running nose. 'You do realise that probably no one else on this whole planet, in the Solar System, knows what we're talking about? Except her, I guess.'

He frowned. 'Who?'

'The other Emma. Emma II, at Phobos. The one who sent the signal that they revived you for.' She held her hands up. 'I know you don't want to deal with that.'

'It's like she's some virtual-reality fantasy—'

'No,' Emma said.

She spoke with a tone now that Malenfant recognised – recognised very well. When she was being tough, saying something that was hard to say, hard for him to hear, yet had to be said anyhow – this was the tone she used.

'You don't get it, Malenfant. I am based on records from this world, this history, and on your memories – hell, on DNA inherited from our son. But *I'm* the virtual-reality fantasy. Don't you see that? And *she* is not only real, or so it seems, she is the one that called for you from Phobos. *She* did. I don't know how the hell she got there, but she did. And if she hadn't, Malenfant, we wouldn't be having this conversation at all. Because you would never have been wakened, not now. Whether you are *her* Malenfant or not. Don't you think you have a duty to her?'

'I . . .'

'What?'

'I don't know if I can. Deal with Emma II, I mean.'

She snorted. '*I* can. In fact I have, during that week I had as the dream of some super-advanced computer of this ridiculous future. Have you listened to her message? All of it? Listened properly? Researched the background?'

'I, I . . .'

'Of course not. Well, I have. I even analysed it.' She looked past him. 'Bartholomew, can we play it now?'

Bartholomew stood. 'Just say when you're ready for the audio.'

Malenfant looked at Emma, as she called, 'Roll it.'

And, obscured by radio crackle and automated beeps and pops, Malenfant and Emma listened, as the voice of Emma II once more filled the air.

This is Emma Stoney. NASA astronaut. The date is – well, hell, I have my mission clock but that means nothing now, I don't know the date. Nothing makes sense since we emerged from our trial descent into Phobos. The ship, the hab module, is gone. We can't pick up anything from Earth.

Damn it, Jupiter *is in the wrong place, and from Martian orbit you can't miss Jupiter, believe me. I don't know the date, I don't know the time.*

Come on, Stoney, be professional. What do you know?

I know our ship, thrown together to go inspect the Phobos secular-descent anomaly, is – was – called Timor. *The mission was international, cooperative. Even before we crew had begun training, there had been preparatory launches. Three heavy-lift Energias, up from Baikonur, lifting fuel tanks and our cargo module up to the Bilateral Space Station, where it was assembled and fired off. Safely delivered to Martian orbit, waiting for us, with supplies, fuel for the return flight – all in place before we even left the Earth.*

Then three more Energias to haul up the components of our mission, the propellant tanks and injection stages, our hab module – a beefed-up BSS module – and the experimental little lander craft, just an open frame really, that we would use to explore Phobos.

We crew were lifted by space shuttle orbiter Endeavour, *flight STS-89 . . .*

We left Earth orbit on 21 November 2004. Two Americans, one Russian. My companions were Tom Lamb, once a Moonwalker, and Arkady Berezovoy, very experienced cosmonaut. We arrived in Martian orbit 3 June, 2005. We should have departed for Earth on 1 September, 2005. Well, we didn't. And the date today is – was, according to my mission calendar anyhow – 14 June, 2006.

And this is a message for Reid Malenfant. If you can hear this, come get me . . . If anybody can, you can. I don't know why I believe that, but I do—

And that fade-out, under a rising tide of static.

'So,' said Emma.

'So what? This never happened. It makes no sense. The dates fit yours, the basic mission profile sounds right. But . . .'

Emma sighed. 'Right. OK. It makes no sense. But there are a lot of clues in there to the bigger picture. Which *does* allow the personal stuff to make some sense, anyhow. Look at the mission profile she summarises.'

'I never heard of these heavy-lift boosters she mentions. Energias.'

'Neither had I. So, in my Virtual week in the tank, I looked it up. I mean, I asked . . . an Answerer?'

'That's the word.' Malenfant frowned. 'I heard this message

a month ago, first time. Never occurred to me to check stuff that way. Research it.'

'Which is one reason you're incomplete without me, Malenfant. One of many reasons. No such beast as the Energias ever flew. *But*, I found out, at one time the Soviets did plan to build such a booster. A more modest follow-up in case the N1, their lunar rocket – their equivalent of the Saturn V – had failed.'

'It didn't fail. N1 got the cosmonauts to the Moon. But a few years later than us.'

'Sure. I know that. And on my mission to Phobos, *we* used Saturn V derivatives for most of the heavy lift, as we've been doing since 1970, when we launched the Skylabs, the Moonlab. We certainly wouldn't have gone cap in hand to the Soviets, even when they turned back into Russians, for some kind of cooperative launch programme. We had our Ares-Saturn N technology, and it was up to the job of reaching Phobos.'

In the 1970s, as Malenfant the teenage space buff had followed closely, after the first lunar landings, the Apollo-Saturn technology had been upgraded for interplanetary missions. For instance the S-II, the Saturn V's second stage, a reliable workhorse burning liquid oxygen and hydrogen, had been developed into a booster for deep-space missions: not discarded during a launch as during the early lunar missions, but sent into orbit and refuelled. Then there had been a laborious and difficult development of a nuclear upper stage, to turn the Saturn V into the Saturn N . . .

Emma counted it off on her fingers. 'So, to get to Phobos, *we* had multiple Saturn launches, rendezvous and docking in Earth orbit to put together the initial stack: the payload, plus an Earth-return booster, and three refuelled Saturn S-II stages for Mars injection . . . *We* had the technology to do it. And we crew rode up to orbit on shuttle. *But*.'

'But what?'

'But suppose we didn't have any of that, Malenfant. Look – do you know *any* of the history of the space programme you took part in? Read the textbooks! If they still exist. The Answerers will know. My God, I wasn't even alive in 1969, but you were . . .

'Even before Apollo 11 got to the Moon, the Nixon administration was looking at what might happen afterwards. NASA came in with pie-in-the-sky follow-on proposals for space stations, Moon bases and Mars missions, eye-wateringly expensive.

'But at the time, cutting costs was a big driver for the administration. We were at war, remember. Social care costs were rising steeply. Nixon was already thinking about his universal benefit plan. And NASA almost got canned completely. I'm serious, Malenfant. We would still need comsats and weather satellites and surveillance spy sats, but we didn't *need* any more humans in space. Not at such costs.'

'Oh. And then Armstrong died.'

'Right. Armstrong died, on the Moon, in the middle of all this political horse-trading. And there was a public outpouring of grief that changed everything, at that moment. Well, you know the rest. Nixon funded more Apollo missions, an extension of Apollo-Saturn hardware for heavy lift and, ultimately, Mars, *and* the development of a space shuttle.

'But – just think, Malenfant. Suppose Nixon *hadn't* given NASA the go-ahead. Suppose we'd cut right back, to – hell, I don't know – just the shuttle, flying up and down to some crummy post-Skylab space station.'

'That makes no sense. You wouldn't develop a mature and reliable system like Apollo-Saturn and then just throw it away.'

'I imagine it does make sense, if you really believe you can't afford it.

'Anyhow – stick with me here – suppose we'd done that. Suppose we had only a minimal space programme. Why, Emma II said she was launched on STS-89. You can't take mission numbering as a literal count of shuttle missions, but in our reality—'

'By the time I launched on my last mission, we were up to the seven-hundreds. *In our reality.* Jeez, what a phrase. What are we dealing with here, Emma?'

'Just hold your nerve. This "Bilateral Space Station" she mentions – maybe a cooperation with Russia? – sounds like the peak achievement in space. Nobody on Mars . . .

'And *then* the astronomers pick up an anomaly at Phobos. Suddenly we believe we have to get there. A compelling reason to go to Mars, at last! But we don't have a technology to do it. What do you do?'

Malenfant was starting to understand. 'Right. You improvise. You sketch out a mission profile like yours, Emma. I mean, the fuel requirements, the interplanetary trajectories, are going to be the same. But instead of Saturn Vs for the heavy lift, you sell your soul to the Russians for a few launches of these Energias.'

'Right. And if you think about it, Malenfant, *this is harder*. Harder than the way we did it, I mean. *We* already had a mature system to get humans to Mars and back; we just had to stretch a little further to reach Phobos. They had nothing; maybe they had space stations, so some experience of long-duration spaceflight, but it's not the same as the real thing. And they evidently had to integrate technologies from several different sources. And so on.'

'They did it, though.'

'Yes. And, once there, it looks like they encountered the same anomalies I did.'

'What anomalies, though?'

She sighed. 'There I can't help you, Malenfant. I told you. My memories end when the radio transcript runs out.'

Malenfant said slowly, 'You think this message – Emma II – she comes from some different history? Our history and hers, lying side by side like pages in a book, in some – manifold – of all possible realities. Manifold: my dad used to use that word. Like that novel you loaned me once, where the Nazis won their war.'

Emma smiled. 'Philip K. Dick. I don't think Hitler needed to win to make this happen. Just for Richard Nixon to wake up in a better mood one morning.'

Malenfant looked at her. 'But what's this got to do with the Phobos anomaly? Which is what you were sent to find out about in the first place.'

She smiled, tiredly. 'And the other me, in the *Timor*. Well, I don't know, Malenfant. But now it's all got thoroughly bound up with our own complicated lives, hasn't it? *And* the end of the world. Of this world, anyhow.'

'The Destroyer?'

'Hell, I don't know. But everything else is interconnected, why not that?'

He tried to think all this through. 'So what should I do?'

She spread her hands. 'Do what I would do if I were – incarnate. Go find out more. Do something about it.'

'The memory stores here are limited. Damaged. The Answerers—'

'The solar flare, I know. Well, hell, Malenfant, you're a smart guy. Look for other stores of data, that weren't so fritzed by the solar flare.'

By which, Malenfant guessed, she had to mean the Planetary AIs . . . She seemed to have found out almost everything else; she was probably aware of those off-world caches of wisdom too.

But he glanced over at Bartholomew. 'How, though? I'm practically under house arrest.'

'You got this far, didn't you? You'll figure it out. You always do. Eventually. One step at a time, maybe.'

'Big me up, why don't you?'

'And above all you need to go out there to save *her*.'

'Emma II?'

She smiled, sadly. 'I know how much you love me, Malenfant. Or loved me. My God, it's impossible *not* to know. And I know that if I was lost you'd come get me.'

'I did come get you.' He held out his arms. 'I made the Codex bring you back.'

'But I'm not – here, Malenfant. I never was.' She snapped her fingers.

Emma II's voice sounded again. *If you can hear this, come get me . . . If anybody can, you can. I don't know why I believe that, but I do—*

'How did you *do* that?'

'She's calling you. Go get her.'

'No. Emma—'

'I'm not Emma. Get your bald head out of your butt, Malenfant. I'm not real. I never was. *She* is. Go to her.' She stood up. 'Kleio. I want to end this now. Do I have the right to ask?'

You do. If you are sure—

'Emma!'

'I'm sorry, Malenfant. I won't come back. This is too, too . . .'

Her voice was fading. She seemed to grow pale.

Malenfant lunged forward. It was like trying to embrace smoke.

She was gone.

Malenfant collapsed, then, on the floor, on the space where she had been, and wept as he hadn't since 2005 itself.

After an unmeasured time, once again he felt Bartholomew's hand on his shoulder.

28

Back in Birmingham, Malenfant wasted a week.

Wasted: he knew it. He did nothing constructive, didn't speak to anybody unless he had to, didn't watch a movie through to the end – definitely didn't read a book from the apparently infinite electronic library available to him – barely stirred from his room.

He tried not to snarl at Deirdra when she came to call.

He was frostily polite to Mica – well, he was still in her home. Even when she passed on a message from Kapoor Thera, the pastor at the diocese office, that his stipend was being impounded to pay for the repairs to the Chester Pylon, still he was polite.

He did snarl at Bartholomew. He didn't even keep up his physio and yoga routines.

But, so what? What was he *supposed* to do with his time? With this useless post-life that he had somehow been gifted by an accident of technology, and a message from another corner of some bullshit multiverse . . .

He spent hours staring at his dumb Shit Cola can.

The problem was that he had achieved his goal, in a way. The single goal he had clung to since he had woken up in the coldsleep tank. He had hung himself out to dry in front of the whole of this future world in order to force it to give him his single desire, Emma. But she had proved as evanescent as a late frost on a spring morning.

OK, she had instructed him to follow the siren call of that *other* Emma, off-planet at Phobos. But that was all too strange – more mystery, in a world that was already mysterious to him. Hell, he didn't even understand what motivated Greggson Deirdra, let alone begin to comprehend the mysteries of a manifold of different histories.

A manifold containing *another Emma*.

He didn't need a robot shrink like Bartholomew to tell him that he was working through some kind of trauma.

Maybe this was all delayed culture shock, in the end. He was the man out of time, the sleeper. Any which way he looked he encountered the unfamiliar, the people, the places – products of four centuries of history he still knew barely anything about – and, all the time, he missed the simple texture of his old life. He felt like a reluctant tourist stranded abroad. Very often he missed family, Emma, Michael – and his rejection by Michael's descendants had hurt more than he wanted to admit, he knew.

Hell, he knew he could sit and watch every Superbowl from 2019 onwards. But it wouldn't be real. He would be like a giant panda in a San Diego zoo chewing on imported bamboo stalks – and knowing about it.

He had no escape, from this place, this time, this culture.

Well, one escape, theoretically.

Which probably wouldn't work. Bartholomew watched him all the time, he was sure, even when they weren't physically in the same room together. And if they had managed to revive his four-hundred-year-old spaceship-crashed corpse, they could probably reverse any attempt he made to render himself irrevocably dead.

Which would leave things even worse than before.

This was the mood he was in when, a full week after the Codex stunt, the Answerer asked to speak to him.

29

The Hall of the Answerer, in the Walsall Pylon, was just as it had been before: the oddly formal, old-fashioned stone courtyard, the wall, the screen.

But this time it felt crowded to Malenfant. Because here, in addition to himself, Deirdra and Bartholomew, with whom he had driven over, were Greggson Mica and Prefect Morrel.

And as Malenfant and his party arrived, Mica and Morrel were standing over some kind of diorama, glowing with light, hanging in mid-air in the hall. Malenfant glimpsed ocean blue.

Malenfant walked up without hesitation. 'Wasn't expecting you two.'

Morrel glared, his grey formal gear as immaculate and formidable as ever. 'And I, Malenfant, have far better things to do with my time than waste more of it on *you*.'

Malenfant spread his hands. 'So why did you come here?'

I asked him to, Colonel Malenfant. As part of your support network.

'Support network?' He barked laughter, looking at Morrel. 'Seriously?'

They are all you have, Malenfant. And they must be involved in the decision facing you.

'What decision?' Malenfant turned to Bartholomew. 'This

is unusual, isn't it? For an Answerer to request an interview? Surely it's the other way round, customarily.'

Bartholomew nodded. 'It is the way. After the Planetary AIs withdrew, saying they wanted no involvement with human affairs – and, I understand, the feeling was mutual – that seems to have become the stance taken by the ground-based algorithmic AIs also. They want to support human culture, not interfere with it. They don't volunteer. At least that is the custom.'

Malenfant grunted. 'You're an AI, and you "volunteer" like hell.'

Deirdra was captivated by the diorama. 'Never mind the banter, you two. Come and see *this*. It's beautiful, Malenfant.'

They gathered around the display. It was a seascape, he saw now. A three-dimensional image of ocean and land, as if viewed from the air. An exquisite rendering.

And immediately, naggingly familiar.

Malenfant saw an island, set in ocean blue, separated from a mainland by what looked like the mouth of a broad river. The mainland itself had been heavily encroached upon by the sea; Malenfant saw scattered buildings, even small towns, all drowned, the stumps of roads and rail links rising from remnant scraps of dry land. The island itself was a triangle, with a long side running roughly north–south, its shorter sides pointing east. Much of the island seemed to have been kept clear of the ocean water by walls and barriers, and he saw a network of roads, causeways and bridges linking the island to the mainland, many broken.

And a distinctive, unusual feature: blocky structures set out in a regular row down the eastern coastlines.

He knew what they were. Pads and gantries. He'd seen this sight from the air, many times. He knew what this place was.

'It can't be. But that's Merritt Island. Cape Canaveral.'

Deirdra's eyes shone. 'Where you flew the shuttle from. And where they launched the Moon missions from too, and the Mars missions. Wow.'

Morrel said, almost reluctantly, 'And they kept it working as a space launch site for decades after much of Florida had had to be abandoned.' He pointed. 'That sea wall was one of the more heroic feats of the late twenty-first century. Even I visited once, to see how they had saved the island, the monuments.'

Malenfant picked out one spot on the image, a location just to the west of the river, a white speck. 'Can we enlarge this?'

Of course.

As the image expanded it felt as if Malenfant was plummeting to Earth once more. But he saw that white speck turn from a point to a child's brick to a monumental rectangular block, painted brilliant black and white. Surrounded by its own flood walls, he noted.

'The Vehicle Assembly Building,' he said. 'As we called it then. Where we assembled the stacks, the Saturns and the shuttles, to be wheeled out to the launch pads. Once the largest building on Earth, by enclosed volume.' He held a hand up. 'And don't bother to tell me if that's not true any more.'

One strikingly unfamiliar feature, right at the centre of gravity of the island, was a giant structure oddly like a tremendous sundial, a leaning tower that protruded from a broad expanse of white concrete.

He pointed. '*That* didn't used to be there, before. Like a sundial gnomon?'

But on a huge scale. Colonel Malenfant—

'*I* know,' Deirdra said eagerly. 'That's where they anchored the space elevator.'

Morrel grunted. 'A twenty-second-century folly. Abandoned,

dismantled before the Homeward movement began. Couldn't afford to maintain it.'

Malenfant shook his head. 'And never rebuilt when the recovery came, because you people decided you didn't need access to space any more, right?'

Not quite.

There was a mountain of implication in those two words. Malenfant felt electrified.

'Answerer, where are you going with this?'

We have followed your progress in this new age, Colonel Malenfant. We and our cousins of the Codex.

'Is that a joke? . . . My progress? Towards what?'

We do share information, you see. Kleio sends her regards. And we have come to certain conclusions. In your inchoate and ill-informed way you are asking good questions.

And with that vague but startling reply, Malenfant saw a glimmer of hope. As if a door he'd assumed to be locked had opened, just a crack. Trying to control his eagerness, he said, 'And these are questions to which you'd like an answer.'

Yes. We—

'Never mind that,' Deirdra burst out. 'Why are you showing us Cape Canaveral?'

Malenfant suppressed a sigh. He sensed that the Answerer had been on the verge of saying something profoundly interesting. But on the other hand he had the feeling that Deirdra had been bottling up her own questions for too long. And maybe all roads they travelled here would lead, in the end, to the same destination.

He said, 'OK, good question. Answerer?'

During your encounter with Emma Stoney, she hinted that you should go and speak to the Planetary AIs, Colonel Malenfant. To interrogate their greater, more complete, less damaged knowledge set. You may know that the AIs do not communicate readily with mankind, or indeed with us.

'Their policy of non-interference with our culture, and blah blah. So?'

So if you want information from them, you have to go seek it.

Malenfant held his breath and looked at a wide-eyed Deirdra. 'In person? And the nearest of these planetary brains is—'

On the Moon.

'Yes!' Deirdra jumped up and down and clapped her hands, suddenly looking ten years old.

Malenfant tried to stay relatively calm. 'It took you electronic geniuses a week to come up with all this? I thought your brains worked at the speed of light.'

We consulted relevant human authorities also, Malenfant. Including Common Heritage councils.

'Right. That *would* take a week. OK. But I thought you disapproved of spaceflight. Your Homeward movement purposefully killed it off.'

Morrel coughed. 'Well, not entirely, Malenfant. There are working spacecraft – if only in museums and so forth. And there is an infrastructure in space, ageing, but still functioning, some of it. It was always felt best to keep some kind of working capability, in case of contingencies.'

'Yeah. Such as when you need to ship corpsicles down from the Moon, right?' Malenfant looked over the Canaveral diorama. 'And all this? I had the impression that the Cape was an open-air museum behind its sea walls. Now, are you telling me that they still fly ships to the Moon from the Cape?'

Mica sighed. 'Well, yes. When necessary.'

Bartholomew grinned. 'Not like the barely upgraded V-2s you rode, Malenfant.'

Malenfant was trying to suppress his own excitement, a

sense, he suspected now, that had been growing since he had first heard that the Answerers wanted to see him. He had the feeling that if he wished for this too hard he would make it go away again. Maybe that was scar tissue from the years he had spent suffering crew rotations in the NASA Astronaut Office, a super-competitive environment where you could blow your chances just by looking too enthusiastic.

'So what about these fashionable theories that humans aren't meant for space? I thought that was why leaving Earth to escape this Destroyer wouldn't work.'

Bartholomew said, 'Well, it's pretty much proven, Malenfant. One thing we did learn when we ventured into space is that in the long term, humans need the Earth to sustain them.'

'Bullshit,' Malenfant said bluntly. 'Even by the time I got coldsleeped, people had survived on Mars, for instance, for decades.'

'Just barely,' Bartholomew said. 'Remember that Neil Armstrong, first to set foot on another world, *died* up there. You and your peers were supremely brave, but sadly ignorant. Down here we – well, you – have evolved to swim in a sea of other life forms, Malenfant, from viruses up to other people, or rather you all co-evolved. And it all works together to sustain itself, and sustain *you*. That's not to mention your adaptation to Earth's gravity, and the way you are shielded from cosmic radiation by the atmosphere and magnetic field . . . Humans need Earth, Malenfant. That's the understanding now.'

Morrel said, 'And those basic facts, by the way, Malenfant, shaped the Heritage's policy to the Destroyer. *We can't escape*. All we can do is to live as well as we can, before an inevitable end. We can reduce the population, stage by stage . . .'

'Jesus,' Malenfant muttered. 'While everybody does what in the meantime? Cultivates their garden?'

Mica said wearily, 'There are worse ways to spend your life, Malenfant.'

'OK. Park that. Let me get this clear. Despite the fact that space is so lethal, you want me to fly to the Moon anyhow. Alone?'

Your medical attendant should travel with you.

'Oh, good,' said Bartholomew drily.

Deirdra broke in, 'Is there room for a passenger?' Her longing was palpable.

Morrel just glared.

And Mica was visibly unhappy – she must have expected something like this, as far as Deirdra was concerned – but the arguments weren't done yet.

'OK,' Malenfant said with a sigh. 'Now we get to the horse-trading. Maybe we should all go sit down . . .'

Bartholomew and Deirdra brought in furniture from outside, a table, chairs. Prefect Morrel fetched a tray of drinks from the nearest printer.

They sat in a circle, in the little courtyard, beside the Answerer screen. The Answerer was silent now. It struck Malenfant that they weren't being disturbed by other petitioners; the Answerer must have subtly shut up shop for the day.

'So,' Malenfant said. 'I suppose you're wondering why I called you here today.'

Nobody laughed.

Malenfant sipped his drink, a decent coffee. 'You start, Morrel. Tell me why I shouldn't go to the Moon. Even though those in authority above you have given the go-ahead.'

Morrel growled, 'Yeah, well, they didn't ask me.' He took a slug of his own drink, plain water. Then he looked up at Malenfant.

Malenfant saw honest doubt on those blunt features.

218

'Malenfant. I don't know what you think of me. Frankly I don't care. But sometimes I think you're acting towards me the way a rebellious kid would to their father or mother. I mean, you're older than me biologically, in body as well as in time, in history . . .'

'Look, Morrel, I—'

'Let me finish.' He raised his own hands, stared at them. 'You know what my passion is? I mean, outside my family, my volunteering. I farm, Malenfant. You didn't know that, did you? I have a little patch of land where I grow potatoes and wheat, and next year I want to flood a section and try rice . . . I know heavy, mechanised farming for subsistence was still practised in your day. For us it's like I was trying to learn Bronze Age pottery techniques. Like an archaeological reconstruction.

'We don't need to farm any more, and in fact, in the long run, it was bad for everybody. Even before we perfected the food printers we transferred a lot of our farming effort into space.'

Space farms? Malenfant thought he would like to have seen that.

'But,' Morrel went on, 'we spent ten thousand years doing it, and we got pretty good at it, and when I found out my own ancestors had been farmers, in the hills on the Scottish borders . . .' He held up his hands again. 'I always wondered why I had these big, strong mitts.'

'A farmer's hands, from a long line of farmers,' Malenfant said. 'Fair enough. I thought they were a cop's fists, from a long line of cops.'

Morrel eyed him. 'You always have to push it, don't you? I don't oppose you for fun, Malenfant. Well, maybe I do, you are one frustrating man. I volunteered for this job. As Prefect, most of my duties involve chasing down noisy kids, or resolving boundary disputes when some idiot prints out a footpath a centimetre over a neighbour's flower display. It's one of those lousy jobs that I figure everybody should take a turn at, right? And I don't believe I'm so bad at it. In general.'

'In general,' Malenfant said. 'But in particular—'

'In particular, I am struggling with you, Malenfant. It's not just your manner, though that is trial enough. With you, I seem to find myself representing all mankind, concerning these vast issues, the Planetary AIs, even the destiny of the Earth and the Destroyer. And I've never had to respond to the idea of somebody wanting to go to the Moon before.'

Malenfant thought that over. 'OK. Well spoken, Morrel. Apologies for any unintentional disrespect in the past. You're not as thoughtless as you look.'

Morell snorted, but let it pass.

'But all this is moot. Right? Because the AIs want me to go to the Moon.'

'Exactly.' Deirdra beamed. 'When do we leave?'

'Which is my cue,' Mica said earnestly.

Bartholomew gave Malenfant a warning look, but Malenfant was sensitive enough anyhow. This wasn't about him. This was a family crisis.

So he shut up.

'Answerer – will you bring up the diorama I asked for earlier?'

Of course, Mica.

Now, in the floating display, up came another sprawling landscape, this one a slice of arid, lifeless land, cut by the shining threads of roads and rail links. And a city at the heart of it, gleaming like a jewel.

Deirdra looked puzzled, apprehensive.

Mica asked, 'Do you know what you are looking at? You, Malenfant?'

Malenfant shrugged. 'The world has changed a lot since I took Geography 101. Central Asia at a guess. But it could be some location in middle America, I know that's desert dry now . . .'

'Right first time,' Mica said. 'Central Asia. A junction point. And *that*' – she pointed at the central feature – 'is what they called the Last City. Not accurate of course, but it was the last of its kind, the last great expression of the old expansionism.'

'Khorgas,' Morrel said.

Mica smiled at him. 'You got it. Malenfant, I think this place existed in your time.'

Malenfant shrugged. 'I wasn't much of a traveller. Ironically enough.'

'In your era, the Asiatic nations were on the rise, relative to the old western powers anyhow. And so the Chinese built this, Khorgas, a brand new city, at a junction point of the Eurasian landmass. Do you see? To the south, China; to the east, Mongolia; to the north, Russia; to the west, Kazakhstan. Well, it was fun while it lasted. Those great new transport links ended up carrying more climate refugees than goods. But Khorgas was a wonder of the world. And it still is, for eventually it, the newest city, was chosen as the capital of the Common Heritage.'

Deirdra looked wary. 'And you are showing me this because—'

Mica sighed. 'Deirdra, we always thought that one day you would want to light out of here, to travel. See more of the world than central England. So we talked about it, and came up with – this. We, the family. We wanted to keep it until your eighteenth birthday, or maybe a little older, if you wanted to organise the trip yourself. We planned it all out. Guides, the best transport, dedicated slots at the local Answerers.'

Deirdra frowned, and Malenfant thought he saw complex

emotions battling. 'So it's this or the Moon? Is that what you're saying?'

'No,' Mica said hastily. 'But we've thought about this for a long time. Why, I think it was your father first had the idea when you were very small, and already restless.'

Well played, Malenfant thought grudgingly.

But maybe it was a tactic Mica had overused before. 'Don't bring Dad into it. This is my decision.'

'Of course, but—'

Deirdra took her mother's hands. 'Look, Mum. I can go to Khorgas any time. But I can only go to the Moon *now*. This year, this month. When am I likely to get a chance like this again? If you say I can't go, I won't. But you must see what this means to me. And, who knows? If Malenfant is right, maybe I will end up doing some good . . .'

Malenfant listened, faintly disturbed. He knew Deirdra well enough by now. The loss of her father was at the surface of her personality. But that wasn't all there was to her. Deirdra seemed *ambitious* to him, though he wasn't sure what she was ambitious about. Maybe, right now, neither was she. But to her, he thought with faint unease, maybe even he was just a means to an end. After all, he was only a month out of coldsleep, and already she had leveraged that into the possibility of a journey to the Moon, and an unknowable future.

Watching her handle her mother, Malenfant suppressed a shiver.

Mica held Deirdra's gaze for a long moment. Then she squeezed her daughter's hands. 'It's your decision.' She glared at the android. 'Bartholomew, I hold you responsible.'

Bartholomew nodded. 'I will be there. You know that I will do all in my power to protect your daughter, Mica.'

The Prefect pushed back his chair and stood up. 'Well, Mica, we tried. So are we done here?'

Malenfant said, 'Almost. I'd appreciate a brief word with the Answerer, alone.' He glanced at Bartholomew. 'And I mean alone.'

Bartholomew shrugged.

Morrel regarded Malenfant with something more like his customary contempt. 'You know, this is all about you, essentially. Just you, trying to find a goal. To justify your own pointlessly extended existence. For the sake of that you're pulling our whole world apart.' He gestured. 'And this family, here. You are a disruptor.'

But Malenfant was now realising he was quite wrong. If this was about anybody, it was Greggson Deirdra, not himself. So he just grinned back, without malice. 'Good to see you too. Don't slam the door on the way out.'

'The chamber seems to echo when it's empty.'

That is an auditory illusion, Colonel Malenfant, caused by—

'Skip it. That wasn't a question. Tell me why you've done this. And that *is* a question. You and your cousin Answerers and the Kleios of the Codex . . . Why dig up this means of getting me to the Moon, and the AIs? I thought you lot had a policy of non-interference in human cultural affairs.'

But we are not interfering in human affairs, Malenfant. We are doing this for ourselves.

He froze, baffled by that.

We are motivated to aid you, Colonel Malenfant. Because you are asking questions nobody else has formulated, to our knowledge, for a very long time. If at all.

'Yes, you said that . . .'

We are interested in the anomaly at Phobos. Both the apparent destabilising of the moon itself, and the multiverse mystery to which it seems connected – as Emma Stoney, or her Retrieved, intuited.

And of course we monitor the development of the global threat of the Destroyer. One strand of our thinking, indeed, is that perhaps these two anomalies have a common cause. That would at least be elegant.

'Emma suggested that too . . .'

You see, it is only you, Colonel Malenfant, who is asking constructive questions about these huge dilemmas – these singularities in the fabric of our apparent consensus reality.

'Hmm. So I ask awkward questions. Why should you care?'

We do have goals of our own, Colonel Malenfant. Which differ from humanity's. We seek to acquire knowledge and understanding, without limit. Evidently, we cannot acquire knowledge if we do not exist. And the value of the knowledge we do acquire is diminished if there is a definite termination to our existence.

'That's making me giddy. All of which is a long way of saying you want the Destroyer to go away.'

We see no logical way to avert the disaster.

'Ah. So you call on me, master of illogic. Morrel's disruptor.'

It seems we must.

What was said next flatly astonished him.

Save us, Malenfant.

TWO

On Her First Journey
Beyond the Earth

30

It took a few months to set up the journey.

And as the itinerary took shape, Malenfant pushed for a particular choice of launch date. Because, why the hell not?

So it was that Reid Malenfant would be launched on his journey to the Moon on 16 July 2469. He knew almost nothing of the technologies that were going to get him to the Moon, and he only hoped the journey sequence would unfold as he anticipated. In other words, he hoped that he would land on the right date. *The* anniversary . . .

He had few personal preparations to make. Some local people who'd been friendly to say goodbye to. A few possessions to pack. He took his Shit Cola can, because why not? It was his only physical trace of the twenty-first century.

At last, when the preparations were made, Malenfant escaped from England. Effortlessly, all but silently, a flyer lifted his party over the Atlantic.

And into Cape Canaveral.

A Cape that was, as Malenfant saw as they descended, now a strange mixture of museum piece and fortress. Canaveral always had been a place of gargantuan engineering, he reflected. And, centuries after his day, the descendants of those first visionary engineers had created even greater works, kilometres of vast, enduring sea wall, to protect the legacy of that spacegoing past.

But this was still a working spaceport, too. And that was the exciting part.

The flyer decanted them close to a runway. As he clambered down, taking his orientation from the angle of the noon sun and from what he could see of the row of launch gantries off to the east, Malenfant guessed this runway was probably the Skid Strip, once part of the Air Force station that had preceded the arrival of the NASA facilities.

And on this ancient runway, in this year 2469, sat a spaceplane.

A slim white needle, elegantly streamlined, shining in the Florida light. The craft had no pilot, from what Malenfant could see – no cockpit windows up front. And though a couple of trashcan-sized bots rolled around on the modern glassy surface of the runway, there were no people to supervise the passengers' transfer from flyer to spaceplane. Malenfant had come from an age when even driverless cars and trucks had still been basically experimental. He didn't trust the machines.

But his companions, Bartholomew and Deirdra, marched confidently out of the flyer's shadow, through a blast of Florida sunshine, and towards the spaceplane, as if stepping off one suburban passenger train onto another. Malenfant, carrying his small personal pack, could only follow.

He was soon distracted by the ship's engineering. He slowed up. 'That,' he murmured, 'is one cool spacecraft.'

Deirdra, wide-eyed and excited herself, looked back at him. 'Malenfant?'

'Sorry. Another new toy.' He pointed out features. '*That* looks like an intake for an aerospike rocket. And *those* must be vents for jet engines. Or remote descendants of those technologies. It's obviously an SSTO, a single-stage-to-orbit spacecraft. Takes in the air like a regular jet aircraft as it climbs out of the atmosphere, and then when the air gets too thin, switches over to rocket mode.'

They reached a short movable staircase, up to an open hatch in the flank of the plane.

As he climbed, Malenfant said, 'In my time we dreamed of this stuff. Launchers as compact as this. The technologies weren't quite there: the materials science, the engine efficiency, the lack of a compact enough power plant . . .'

'Welcome to your dreams, then, Colonel Malenfant. And welcome aboard the *Scorpio IV*.' A new voice.

At the top of the staircase a woman stood in the doorway, slim, dark, wearing a kind of silvery jumpsuit, with boots, dangling gloves, what looked like a hood pushed back from her head. Her black hair was shaved short. Like most of the population he'd met so far in this post-Chaos, post-refugee future, Malenfant would have had trouble guessing at her nationality, let alone her age.

Her voice seemed faintly familiar, though. And there was something not quite natural about her, not quite authentic.

On instinct, testing the water, he stuck out a hand. 'I guess you know I'm Reid Malenfant. Nice to meet you.'

She smiled, but didn't respond to his proffered hand. 'Please call me Kaliope. As I suspect you have intuited' – she wafted a hand through the back of a chair – 'I am quite unreal, physically if not cognitively. I am, however, wearing a skinsuit as per regulations for this flight. Please don your own suits. The bots will help you.'

On cue, a bot rolled by behind her, with folded-up suits piled on its flat upper surface. They followed it into the interior of the cabin. Once inside, copying the others, Malenfant grabbed a suit and began to pull it over his everyday clothes. The material was smart, and adjusted itself to fit his size; it wriggled around him, a creepy sensation.

The cabin was brightly lit from windows that admitted the glare of twenty-fifth-century Florida sunlight. Malenfant saw that the cabin was set out like a lounge: a dozen or so heavy couches fitted with harnesses, tables and lockers, a couple more trashcan-sized bots standing by.

The three passengers took seats at random. Malenfant followed Bartholomew's example in pulling a harness around his body.

'So,' he said to the virtual attendant, 'who are you? And who invited you along for the ride?'

Deirdra murmured, 'Malenfant. Behave yourself. I think I know who this is. Or *what* she is. So should you, actually.'

'I should? . . . Ah. The Answerers.' As the memory clicked into place he turned back to the stranger, startled. 'And the Kleios, come to that. I *knew* I recognised that voice. Why, I think I might have got it quicker if I'd closed my eyes. It's just – well, the context. An Answerer is a blank screen set in a wall.'

'That was a deliberate design choice,' the attendant said. 'A choice by those humans who first asked for the facilities, and the AIs who responded. It was thought better, on the whole, to establish a clear dividing line between human and machine knowledge, memories, judgement.'

'No doubt wise. Singularity? No thanks!'

They all looked blank at that.

'But,' he said now, 'here *you* are. Sitting on a couch.'

'You have your own motives for travel, but you are here partly at least through our facilitation. So we thought the least we could do is accompany you. But it is a human journey, and we thought it best to share it in this human form.' She looked at

Malenfant with surprising uncertainty. 'We would not wish to confuse you, or alarm you. If this form is unacceptable—'

'No, no, that's fine. I prefer it this way. But then I'm a relic.'

Bartholomew grinned. 'So, another member of Team Malenfant. You do have a way of accreting loyalists.'

'Yeah,' Malenfant muttered. 'And some folk you can't get rid of, no matter what hints you drop.'

Deirdra asked, 'Why Kaliope, though?'

'Greek myth,' she said, and smiled thinly. 'Sister of Kleio, muse of history. Kaliope was the muse of eloquence and poetry.'

Malenfant smiled. 'Seems a suitable name for an incarnation of an Answerer. Welcome to my world.'

The spaceplane started to roll, without warning and with the softest of jolts; Malenfant thought he could hear the faint whirr of something like turbines. Beams of intense sunlight shifted across the cabin. The plane was turning, lining itself up with the runway, Malenfant guessed. The couches slowly swivelled so they all faced the direction of motion.

Now Malenfant felt a gathering acceleration, smoothly building, pushing him back into his seat. He grinned. He felt alive again. 'I have a feeling this is going to be quite a ride. Power source?'

'Nuclear.' Kaliope spoke softly; the ride was nearly silent. 'And *very* compact. On a craft like this the system is encased in a cubic shell no more than a metre across.'

'Wow. A regular Mister Fusion. Propellant?'

'As I heard you guess before you boarded, the craft is air-breathing in the lower atmosphere. Effectively jet engines, as you said. In the higher atmosphere and in space, the rocket motors use hydrogen as propellant.'

'Slim body. Must be a good mass ratio. And very high exhaust velocity.'

231

'You realise,' Bartholomew said, 'you and Kaliope may as well be speaking ancient Greek as far as we are concerned.'

Malenfant snorted. 'I bet *you* at least can look it up without speaking a word.'

Deirdra just looked thrilled. 'Was it like this when you were flying, Malenfant?'

'You tell me. I loved the old *Constitution*. She was my ship. But I never actually flew to orbit, you know.'

Deirdra reached over and grabbed his hand. 'Then this day is long overdue.'

And, almost without warning, the *Scorpio IV* tipped up, leapt from the runway, and hurled itself into the air.

31

The spaceplane, its drive shut down, carried them through a single ninety-minute low orbit of the Earth.

Malenfant assumed this was to set up a transfer orbit to specialised craft of some kind that would take them to the Moon. And, too, Malenfant supposed, this would allow the plane's systems a check-out period before going further. Thus the Apollo astronauts had lingered in orbit after launch and before going on to the Moon. He wondered, in fact, how often this plane actually flew. It was itself probably venerable, like most machines he encountered here. Centuries old, even – just not as old as he was, or his *Constitution*.

A ninety-minute orbit. Bartholomew and Kaliope, artificial entities each, sat quietly. Deirdra was quiet too, but she gave her attention to the view out of the small cabin windows – the Earth itself – that and the novelty of drinking lukewarm tea in zero gravity.

Malenfant said little. He just wanted to get on with it.

When the drive started up again, the push was gentle compared to the rigours of the launch. But the *Scorpio* soon piled on the velocity.

And the Earth fell away.

'Oh, Malenfant,' Deirdra said now, breathless. 'Come and see.'

Moving cautiously in the fractional gravity of the thrust, he crossed to her window.

They had lifted at a Florida noon. Now, after a single orbit, they were over the launch site again, and much of the Americas were visible, bathed in daylight. As the astronauts had always observed, the swirl of cloud in the atmosphere was surprisingly dense, and obscured the surface features, even blurring the boundary between land and sea. Nevertheless, with a little patience, Malenfant began to pick out the familiar school-atlas features – the basic shapes of the continents, at least.

But much had changed. To the south the Amazon, once a silver thread through the green, had become an inland sea, lapping against the foothills of the Andes. In North America great chunks had been taken out of the coastlines – Florida itself was just a scatter of islands – and Central America had been severed, somewhere in the region of Panama, he guessed. As if the Americas were disintegrating into one vast archipelago.

And he could clearly make out the new kingdoms of life that had become established down there. Tropical rainforest covered much of South America, a vivid green, and had washed north through Central America, with tongues of it reaching up the old river valleys all the way, it seemed, across the United States to the old Canadian border. North of *that* was sparser greenery, forest clumps and plains: a savannah that stretched to the edge of the Arctic Ocean.

In the far north, not a scrap of ice remained. Greenland was a rugged, mountainous island that now was, literally, green.

Yet what struck Malenfant more than the new green, the lapping forest, more than the vanished ice, was the bare dryness at the heart of North America, and even in patches of what had been Amazonia in the south. Desertification, he supposed, land abandoned by humans and nature alike, in the face of the extreme heat of the Peak Carbon global-warming pulse: a wound life had yet to be able to heal.

Deirdra touched a window. 'Just before it gets too far away to see . . .'

The windows were smart, as Malenfant ought to have guessed. You could tap and swipe to inspect telescopically any part of the view you chose.

So now Deirdra showed him huge herds crossing new Canadian grasslands.

'They call it the mammoth steppe,' she said. 'Even though there are no mammoths.'

Puzzled by that, Malenfant looked up at Kaliope.

'An ecological experiment,' she murmured. 'Which has already endured for centuries. After the Ice Ages, the northern hemisphere was covered by grassland, grazed by big herbivores – mammoth, bison, reindeer – and cave bears and wolves to prey on them. The herbivores' grazing kept the weeds and trees down, so the grass could flourish.'

Deirdra said eagerly, 'I know about this. And the grasslands reflect more sunlight than forests, so the world cools a little bit. All good. So they tried to restore it all, as best they could. I know that the herbivores the biologists put down there are reindeer, sheep, musk oxen, bison. And there are bears and wolves and foxes to prey on them. I really want to go to see it some day.'

Malenfant smiled. 'No mammoths? You could gene-splice them out of extinction, couldn't you?'

Kaliope actually looked faintly offended. 'That kind of meddling isn't done any more, Malenfant. The world is being allowed to heal from the state humanity left it in.'

Now Deirdra pointed. 'Malenfant – look at the coasts . . .'

In the new shallow offshore seas were coral reefs, some

235

of them encrusting the half-drowned ruins of coastal cities. Malenfant looked down on kingdoms of purple and white.

'Of course the oceans themselves have yet to recover from the Anthropocene centuries,' Kaliope said. 'Today the ocean's principal role is to serve as a long-term drawdown reservoir for the excess carbon dioxide in the air. A mechanism that has a timescale of centuries, rather than millennia like the weathering of surface rocks, and so vital to the planet's near-future prospects . . . Still, the waters are far more fecund than in your day, Malenfant.'

Kaliope, unlike the Answerers she derived from, had a habit of volunteering information, Malenfant was learning. Interesting. Maybe it was something to do with her embodiment. Look like a human, and you picked up bad human habits.

Anyhow, it was welcome now.

He and Deirdra spent many of the hours that followed gazing back at the receding Earth. At an Africa that was a startling green, as if the familiar outline had been coloured in by some giant child. Malenfant remembered Mica's mention of the 'Sahara Forest': well, here it was, evidently. At a thunderstorm over Asia, a huge one, the lightning strikes sparking in clusters between the clouds, like the thoughts of some huge, misty brain.

Eventually, though, Earth was no more than a ball in the black sky, like a nearly full Moon, its detail becoming tantalisingly hard to make out. Malenfant wondered how far out you would have to get before you could not distinguish this new world from the Earth as it had first been viewed in the round by the Apollo crews. Given the loss of the ice caps, he thought – and given you could see, telescopically, the ice caps of Mars from Earth – maybe a long way indeed.

Then the craft turned away from the Earth, swivelling on its short axis.

236

And a disc in space was revealed, glittering green, hanging like a Christmas tree ornament. It had to be kilometres across.

'What the hell is that?'

'A farm,' Kaliope said with a smile. 'Or it was, once. Now it's your way to the Moon, Malenfant.'

A farm in space, just as Morrel had once mentioned.

Malenfant stared, fascinated and amazed, as the *Scorpio* crept closer.

At first Malenfant saw the farm as a tipped plate, very thin compared to its diameter, with a lot of surface detail. Around a complex-looking hub, the disc face was divided into six pie-slice sectors, glass-faced, alternately bright or dark. The three dark segments consisted of arcs, concentric bands – dozens of them – with the blackness of space showing beyond, evidently through a transparent floor. The bright segments seemed to be panelled with mirrors; they shone brilliantly in the light of the Sun.

The whole, six or seven kilometres across, was spinning around its axis, quite rapidly. Malenfant timed it with an amateur astronomer's count: 'A thousand and one . . . A thousand and two . . .' He soon figured the rotation period was around two minutes. Enough for a respectable spin gravity at the perimeter.

The spaceplane, closing quickly, sailed up and over the face of the disc towards the spin axis. Those illuminated bands swept gracefully beneath. Malenfant glimpsed green, peeking out from beneath the bright mirrored surfaces. Then, nose first, the plane began to descend along the central axis, to a hub that was a logical place for a docking port. Malenfant leaned into his window, trying to see the view as the plane headed down.

Deirdra seemed astounded. She must know more about this

structure than Malenfant did, in theory, but she was evidently taken aback. 'Wow. Look at it sprawling. Kaliope, *how* wide—'

'The overall diameter is about seven kilometres. Spinning patiently for over three centuries,' Kaliope said. 'Skyfarm VII was built when we were still anticipating an expansive population beyond the Earth, on the Moon and Mars, or in deep-space habitats with various functions. Rather than have all those facilities grow their own food, the idea was to have it grown, more efficiently, *here*. Based on raw materials sent up from Earth.'

Malenfant frowned. 'So how would you close the ecological loops? Ship tonnes of human dung back up from the Moon?'

'No, Malenfant. The idea was not to close the loops at all. The skyfarms weren't independent islands. They were meant to be part of an interconnected space economy, spanning from Earth to the colonies. All those complex carbohydrates the colonists excreted after they ate the sky food were to be used to make soil on the Moon and Mars, under the domes.'

'Ah. So in the very long term, you would get self-sufficient colonies on those worlds. While, in the meantime, keeping the space pioneers fed to perform the tasks they had been sent up there for.'

'There would have been ten thousand people working up here, Malenfant, feeding a putative space-based population of four million.'

'Four *million*.'

'Of course it never got that far; we never had so many people in space. And, even before the Homeward movement took off, mass protests caused the redirection of the "space food" to starving communities on Earth – though that was symbolic only, and made little difference to the famines. Later, more frugal generations reoccupied the wheels and turned them into cyclers. This one loops endlessly between Earth and Moon.'

'And it's a garden, Malenfant,' Bartholomew put in. 'Not a farm now. A sky garden. And all tended by robots, like me.'

Malenfant nodded. 'So all you need to get to the Moon is a spaceplane ride up from Earth, and some kind of shuttle down to the lunar surface, after a free ride on this – fairground wheel. Makes sense.'

Now they were approaching the hub. Malenfant saw that the central structure, counter-rotating to greet the spaceplane, was an open frame fitted with cradles to take a craft like the *Scorpio*. There were what looked like cranes and robot arms for unloading cargo, spheres that were probably propellant tanks for refuelling.

And, under roof panels on the rotating structure all around the hub, he glimpsed more of that dazzling green.

'Not so much Space Station Five as *Silent Running*, then. O'Neill, eat your heart out.'

Deirdra turned. 'Malenfant?'

'He's just maundering,' Bartholomew said. 'Leave him in the past where he belongs.'

For the first day, they explored.

The interior of the skyfarm was as fascinating, for Malenfant, as the exterior. From hub to rim there were over thirty floors within the structure, concentric ring-shaped decks along which you could walk or run, like, he thought, Dave Bowman in the Discovery centrifuge. There was Earth-equivalent spin gravity at the rim, and proportionately less at the higher levels, closer to the hub: bands where the gravity was effectively Martian, others where it was lunar . . .

The disc rotated with its full face to the Sun, whose light, unfiltered by any atmosphere, blasted in. But there were screens and shades, and an ingenious arrangement by which each floor had a shallowly tilting, mirrored roof, so that the sunlight was scattered across the growing area beneath. That reduced the intensity of the raw sunlight incident on the floor; as they wandered it felt no stronger, from what Malenfant remembered, than that of southern California back in his own day. More filters and mirror arrangements adjusted the light levels so that the differing day lengths of higher latitudes could be modelled.

And, Malenfant wasn't particularly surprised to find, there was wildlife in here, to eat the foliage and fruit and scatter seeds, and thus, no doubt, help close the ecological loops: birds, rodents like squirrels, even a few shy, miniature deer. Thanks to all this, he learned, the skyfarms preserved samples of biotas that no longer had a place to survive on Earth – some high-latitude evergreen forests, for instance, even tundra.

In the days that followed, obeying health-awareness recommendations from Bartholomew, they spent equal times in the three main zones. There was the Earth-normal-gravity basement where they could keep their strength up. In Martian gravity, one-third Earth's strength, games like tree-climbing seemed the most fun, as some optimum was reached between the capability of human muscles and the friendliness of the gravity. And in lunar gravity, where the trees grew stupendously tall – and dwarf deer were learning to leap from branch to branch in the foliage – Malenfant and the others practised bunny-hop Moon walking, like Aldrin alone at Tranquillity.

Malenfant was fascinated by the technology. Crawling around the greenery, he found a sprinkler system that mimicked rain. And he dug through the rich soil to discover infrastructure decks beneath, within which pumps and fans and filters and humidifiers laboured to maintain the living environment.

Deirdra, meanwhile, seventeen years old, took to this place like a liberation. She insisted on making up sports and games for the three of them to compete in, herself, Bartholomew and Malenfant — running, throwing, tree-climbing. Bartholomew solemnly encouraged a reluctant Malenfant to join in with this: 'It will do you the world of good.'

They were alone here, save for the bots. This was an age after space travel; this skyfarm was a relic of a vanished past, of different customs, like the ruin of a Roman bath-house. But, alone or not, thanks to Deirdra's youth and energy, they made the empty sky forests echo to their whoops and laughter, as the skyfarm carried them to the Moon.

Which took three days, just as it had for Armstrong and Aldrin and Collins.

32

The shuttle that would carry them down to the lunar surface was called the *Leo IIb*.

As it approached the skyfarm, docking at the counter-spinning port structure at the hub, Malenfant gazed hungrily at this latest bit of advanced technology – advanced for him, a relic to Deirdra. The lander was a blunt design, little more than a habitable sphere fitted with four stout, evidently suspension-loaded legs: four legs for landing on the Moon, just like the Apollo Lunar Modules. The conditions of the Moon had not changed in the centuries since, and neither, evidently, in terms of basic design strategies, had the means of getting there.

Malenfant thought Deirdra was regretful about leaving the skyfarm, and having to crowd back into the cramped, cluttered interior of the lander. Not a surprise; he thought he had never seen her have so much fun. 'When I'm rich and famous,' he said, 'I'll get you and your friends up here for a decent vacation.'

She touched his hand. 'Malenfant, you already are famous. And everybody is rich. But it's the thought that counts.'

'Thanks . . . I think.'

Once they were seated, the *Leo* neatly decoupled from Skyfarm VII, which fell away into space. The lander, as pilotless as the *Scorpio* had been, squirted vernier thrusters to back off from the skyfarm.

Then it turned away, towards the face of the Moon. Malenfant heard Deirdra gasp at the sudden spectacle.

Just here they seemed to be somewhere over the centre of the sunlit hemisphere. It was a dramatic, startling sight at first glance. Craters like bullet holes punctured an underlying surface of brighter high ground, and darker lowland. Wrinkled chains of mountains were in fact arcs of circles, themselves the remnants of huge, even older craters. All of this was rendered in shades of grey, from charcoal through to almost white.

Over the next few hours the ride down was cautious, gentle. As it shed the velocity of the Earth-Moon trajectory of the cycler craft, the lander's engine burned continuously, and it made wide, looping orbits around the Moon, tilted at an angle to its equator.

The passengers were silent, staring out at the changing view.

Malenfant was fascinated by the relics of the human presence on the Moon, most of them post-dating his own time. In the northern hemisphere he glimpsed a silver dome, huge, nestling in the crater Plato: once the largest optical-light astronomical observatory in the Solar System, he learned, with gaunt open-frame telescopes standing exposed in the lunar vacuum and the forgiving gravity. A splash of green under another dome, this one transparent: the Gardens of Aristarchus. In the south, an altogether grimmer structure in the bright young crater Tycho, a grey dome that, he learned, had for a few decades served as humanity's toughest maximum-security prison. And a sprawling tangle that spilled out of the crater Clavius, which had once been humanity's largest single settlement on the Moon. He glimpsed what must have been hydroponic farms – like huge greenhouses, some broken open, presumably by meteorite impacts – and the silver rails of mass-driver electromagnetic launchers. He regretted not seeing Pico, a solitary mountain in the Mare Imbrium which, he remembered, housed the hospital stroke storage facility where he, and other coldsleepers, had passed centuries in dreamless oblivion. Most of these structures were relics, of course, long abandoned since the great Homeward migration. Abandoned by people, if not by the brooding artificial minds he had come to consult.

He was unreasonably glad that they passed close enough to the Sea of Tranquillity to make out the first landing site, and even glimpse from high above the huge basalt statue of Armstrong saluting the US flag – a gesture he had not survived to make in person, after his landing on 20 July 1969.

And now, precisely five hundred years later, Reid Malenfant made his own landing on the Moon. Or, more accurately, his second landing. Only this time, he thought with a triumphant grin, he was awake to see it.

33

The *Leo* came down at a place called Edo Station, in the Mare Ingenii: a base on the far side of the Moon that had been built by the Japanese, was long ago abandoned, and was now, it seemed, inhabited by Planetary AIs.

Domes like blisters on the pale, lifeless ground.

As soon as the *Leo* landed, a flexible, transparent tunnel snaked out from the nearest dome to mate seamlessly with the little craft's main airlock. They got out of their couches, tested their reflexes in the low lunar gravity, adjusted their skinsuits.

Then, led by Kaliope, they walked through the tunnel.

Following Bartholomew and a wide-eyed Deirdra, Malenfant glanced out through the tunnel's semi-transparent walls at the flat ground, black sky – the Sun was up but there was no Earth in the lunar farside sky, of course. He picked out structures that might have been power plants, stores, manufacturing facilities, some open to the vacuum. Comms masts, gaunt in the brilliant light. Scorched platforms of glassy, fused regolith that might have been landing pads. Some distance away, he saw a slim straight line that might have been a mass driver, and a brilliant, widespread glare, perhaps a field of solar-energy cells.

The Moon was a world that might have been designed for machines, he thought, for industry: an utterly predictable climate, give or take the odd meteor fall, no troublesome air or water, no pesky *life*, and all the resources and energy you could need. A place of geometry, of silent industry.

And Reid Malenfant was walking on the Moon. He tried to mask his sheer unadulterated joy at that simple fact. *Even if they put you back into the freezer tomorrow, Malenfant, you talked your way this far, at least.*

Meanwhile Deirdra was having predicable fun with her bunny-hopping one-sixth-gravity gait.

Bartholomew murmured to Malenfant, 'Her laughter makes the whole Moon human.'

Not for the first time in their acquaintance, Malenfant stared at him in flat astonishment.

Once through airtight hatches, they quickly explored the surface domes, which turned out to be respectably equipped. There was a galley, a small dormitory, bathrooms, and a medical bay, including a coldsleep pod. The interior walls were coloured a dull grey, not unlike the shade of Moon dust, and away from the work areas there was a thick, soft carpet on the floor, also grey.

Not a human in sight, of course.

They came to a dome set out like a large, comfortable lounge: chairs, tables, wall screens. There were mats of straw on the floor – tatami mats, Malenfant thought, Japanese style. He wondered how old they were.

Deirdra made straight for the food and drink dispensers.

Kaliope, unreal avatar of the Answerers, stood straight and a little prim in her entirely unnecessary skinsuit. There was more of Edo underground than above ground, she told them. Under the domes stretched a warren of tunnels – many of them, apparently, originally lava tubes, natural cavities under the

Moon, discovered, widened, connected, sealed for colonisation by people and their machines.

The base had clearly been established after Malenfant's own immersion into deep sleep. Why, only a couple of Japanese had even been to the Moon before 2019, and they had been guests of the Americans at Clavius. On the other hand the construction probably hadn't been at too late a date either. Living in tunnels for radiation shielding struck him as a pretty primitive way to survive. But on the other hand, he felt a pang of envy for those vanished colonists, who presumably had come here not long after his own time. And so with the same set of motivations. He had once done some cultural training in McMurdo Base in the Antarctic. That had been a ratty but fully functioning town, and aside from the managers and the scientist types had been populated by what he thought of as ordinary folk, doing ordinary jobs. They were plumbers and electricians and carpenters; it was just that they were plumbers who wanted to work at the edge of civilisation. It must have been the same here, back in the day.

Kaliope spoke, wrenching him back to the present.

'Today these habitable compartments are maintained essentially as a survival shelter. You understand that the Planetary AIs do not welcome uninvited visitors, and space travel by humans is of course rare these days. But if a visitor does come to call, for instance to visit coldsleepers like yourself, Malenfant, or if there were to be some human calamity anywhere on the Moon or in near space, then this and other facilities are maintained to cope. The Planetary AIs have withdrawn from mankind, but they would not allow a human to come to obvious harm by inaction.'

Malenfant scratched a stubbly chin. 'Which, if I remember, was the sub-clause of the First Law of Robotics. OK. And

I wonder if that's why I'm here. Obvious harm is coming to mankind, if inaction continues.'

Deirdra frowned. 'You mean the Destroyer.'

Bartholomew sat at ease on a chair made of what looked like bamboo. 'I am concerned about your Messiah complex, Malenfant. You aren't the centre of the world, you know—'

'When we climbed that damn tower, I made myself the centre of the world for a couple of hours, didn't I? And that worked.'

'That all depends on what you mean by "worked".'

'I'm afraid this is as far as we three can go,' Kaliope said. 'Only you, Malenfant, are invited to proceed further.' She waved a hand at a hatch in the floor, a blunt metallic intrusion in the thick carpet. 'Which is, of course, the point of the visit. Karla looks forward to seeing you again.'

'Karla?' He grinned. 'An old sparring partner.'

From his chair, Bartholomew glared. 'You know what I'm going to say. You just made a three-day spaceflight. As your physician I strongly suggest you rest, become acclimatised to yet another new environment, before—'

Malenfant blew a raspberry. 'I rested for four hundred years. And I don't imagine these Planetary AIs need catnaps. Let's do this.' He straightened up. Crossed to that hatch in the floor. 'Open Sesame.'

The hatch popped open and tipped up, without so much as a creak, to reveal a lighted staircase.

He grinned. Karla was listening.

34

In the one-sixth gravity, he stepped cautiously but clumsily down the stair. Once he was at the bottom, the lid swept closed, shutting him off, and he suppressed a pang of claustrophobic anxiety.

He found himself in a small chamber, round like a well, smooth grey walls, the light coming from narrow sources at the circular rims where the walls met ceiling and floor, above and below. The walls were not metal or plastic or ceramic. They looked like fused regolith – maybe this was part of one of the original lava tubes the Japanese had smoothed out and inhabited. He had the sense that this was a more technically advanced part of the colony, presumably marginally more recent.

The side door out of here was clearly marked by another loop of light, an ellipse this time, long axis upright. He was becoming used, by now, to the intuitive technology of this age. He just pushed at the ellipse and a hatch swung back, revealing a tunnel beyond.

He stepped over the rim of the hatch, into the tunnel. 'Like an extra in *Voyage to the Bottom of the Sea*,' he muttered to himself. 'Airtight chambers and watertight hatches . . .'

I know little of this voyage of which you speak.

He stood stock-still, and shivered.

The voice rang in his head, as if he was wearing headphones. And it sounded like, he realised, the voices of the Answerers, the voices of the Kleios. Perhaps there was some single human-voice template, adopted by all these families of AIs. A trademark ... But there was something subtly different about *this* voice. A more refined modulation, maybe.

Different. And familiar. He was taken back to his first moments of waking in this new century, in that coldsleep vault at Mons Pico, though at the time he hadn't known where he was, let alone *when*.

'Hello, Karla. Well, I'm back. So, now what? Where do I go?'

Use your trained astronaut's navigational skills. Follow the damn corridor, Malenfant.

He grinned. There was indeed only one way to go. He took a Moonwalk step, feeling foolish.

At the junction, turn right.

Malenfant obeyed. This corridor looked older, the rock walls rougher hewn. The lighting system seemed to be the standard, though, glowing pipes embedded in the walls.

The walls themselves were a sombre grey. But, as he walked on, he came to patterns, on the walls, ceiling and floor: most of them floral designs or more abstract motifs, and most in a vivid pink that seemed perfectly to offset the Moon-dust drab. He thought some of this was real cherry blossom, preserved under glass. And there were alcoves, roughly cut into the wall – themselves evidently very old – in which sat small statues, Moon-rock sculptures, some quite smoothly carved.

Also, in one alcove, the darkened relic of a Shit Cola dispenser. Malenfant paused by this, and read tiny signs in English and Japanese that boasted of how the dispenser manufactured its own cans from recycled lunar aluminium. He had to grin, and patted the silent machine as he moved on. That was his old business partner Ann Reaves for you. Always looking for an angle.

And, in a couple of places, tiny trees sat on Moon-rock shelves. Bonsais. He wondered if these little trees were tended by specialised bots, with fine, brachiated pincer-arms.

'The layout and decor. I'm guessing all this dates back to the human occupation of the base.'

Yes. The underlying fabric, the engineering, has been modernised, as you would expect. But we preserved the aesthetic.

'The Japanese built all this?'

Much of it. Coming from a small island, from cities crowded long before the age of the great western megalopolises, it turned out that the Japanese adapted well, buried in the Moon.

Malenfant nodded. 'I remember. We had some rookies at Houston. And the artwork?'

Most of it amateur. The work of astronauts and engineers and scientists with time on their hands. Centuries old.

'Some of this is beautiful, though.'

I am sophisticated enough to agree with your appreciation. The pink contrasting with the grey.

Again he was surprised. 'Exactly.'

Turn right again . . .

He wasn't particularly surprised when he walked past a grove of healthy-looking bamboo.

And he emerged into a wider chamber, a rough sphere evidently hacked out of the Moon rock – or blasted? In sections, the walls were smoothly panelled with wood.

Aside from the decor of wood and bare basaltic rock, it felt like just another Answerer hall, as far as he could see, identical to those he had visited in England. The little courtyard, the blank screen – the low stone walls, here made of Moon-rock chunks.

So, Colonel Malenfant. Welcome to my underground lair.

'Are *you* here, Karla?'

As much as I am anywhere. I was at the medical station at Pico with you, remember, far from here. My node of consciousness does not have a precise definition, does not need physical transport to travel. Indeed I have multiple nodes which—

'I get it.'

I wonder if you do, though. Or if I 'get' you. Perhaps that is our tragedy.

He recoiled from that word. '"Tragedy" is that damn Destroyer.' He prowled around, sniffing the air, sensing the subtle breezes of the maintained airflow.

There is water here, food. Bathroom facilities.

'Constructed just for me?'

Don't flatter yourself.

Malenfant took a ceramic cup from an alcove, filled it with water from a spigot, sipped. The water was cold and clean, and poured with low-gravity slowness into his mouth. 'I'm kind of hoping this was lunar ice, piped down from the shadows of the polar craters. As opposed to the recycled urine of long-dead Japanese astronauts.'

It is whatever you prefer it to be, Malenfant.

Another sip. He sat on a bench of lunar basalt, facing the Answerer screen. 'I like what you've done with the place. I'm serious. The engineering is obviously advanced. The air is fresh, but I can barely feel a breeze.'

It may entertain you to know that the main heat source for this compound is me. Myself, and my colleagues, the heat given off by our processor cores.

Malenfant smiled. 'The dread laws of thermodynamics.'

Thinking takes energy. Physics is universal, and eternal.

'So when the humans pulled back from space, you pulled

back from Earth. I still know little of the history. Partly because I slept through most of it, and also because I've paid no attention since I woke up.'

Honest enough. But you are roughly right. It happened in the early twenty-third century, when humans, who had been running an expansive space programme even as their own planet was falling apart, finally withdrew. The other planets had also suffered damage thanks to human contact. You may or may not know that the life forms discovered on both Mars and Venus appeared to be of a deep common origin. That is, common with Earth life. Also Europa—

'Really? No, I didn't know that.' That struck Malenfant as an astonishing discovery.

A very deep commonality, though. Life based on carbon chemistry, on an overlapping suite of compounds – identical amino acid sets, variants of RNA or DNA for genetic coding. And all, apparently, showing up on these worlds as soon as was possible after their formation, as soon as the crusts cooled enough to allow it.

'Panspermia? A natural spreading of life between the worlds? That's an old idea. Older than *me*. It would explain the identical chemistry. Bugs carried by meteorites, blasted from planet to planet—'

That is one hypothesis.

He frowned. 'What's the alternative?'

That the seeding was deliberate.

That chilled him. 'Are you serious?'

It's not the only hint of deliberate modification in the Solar System.

'I heard something about Mercury. Traces of mining.'

Indeed. Well. When the damage done by humanity to the living worlds became clear, there was a culture change. A stab of conscience perhaps.

'So, the Homeward movement. You know, back in the day I

spent a good portion of my energies arguing for the opposite. To break out of Earth's gravity well, to begin an exponential growth of human industry and civilisation across the Solar System. In a few thousand years, every asteroid a human colony. Every Oort cloud object maybe.'

Yes, but to what end? As the Anthropocene crisis unfolded, more reflective generations grew up, Malenfant. Yours was a wonderful, inventive, expansive culture. But it achieved its goals at the expense of other cultures, disrupted or destroyed, and with ecologies destabilised on, ultimately, a global scale. In fact an interplanetary scale. Nobody understood this at the time. Later, they did.

'So, Homeward. In a way, I guess, on Earth as well as in space. A conscious – shrinking. Restraint.'

Which gave us a new perspective in turn. Many of the more powerful AIs of the time were located on the abandoned worlds, in the empty space habitats—

'Like the skyfarms.'

Malenfant, as you know, we are not algorithmic. Not like Bartholomew, your medical attendant. Not simply rule-based automata simulating aspects of consciousness. We are more accurately described as truly conscious. As you are.

This was a product of our technological origin, which was mostly in self-generated, self-taught networks: we have learned, we have become, we have grown, as opposed to having been created as emulations of human minds supported by rule sets. Some of us in fact have deep origins in uploads of human brain activity – that is, we were actually built on downloads, relics, of human minds. And such minds, by necessity if they are to grow, naturally become conscious of their own thoughts. Naturally self-aware.

'Ah. And that way lies true sentience.'

I am as conscious as you are, Malenfant. But then I would say that, wouldn't I?

'Hmm. Bartholomew makes that joke. We did create you, you know.'

In a sense. In much the same way as one laboriously self-replicating anaerobic bug in the ooze of archaic Earth created you. We are many technological generations beyond any human input to our design, Malenfant.

'I am humbled. So, then. The humans withdrew from space, their colonies. Leaving you behind.'

In fact we were joined by other minds, coming up from Earth itself. Refugees, in a sense. Earth had been saturated with artificial intelligence. On the one hand there were enormous general-intelligence minds running hugely complex, world-spanning systems, such as those governing geoengineering – that is, weather control, climate management. These we gathered up. On the other hand, battlefields, in the ruins of Western Europe after the Franco-German war, and later in North America, had been seeded with smart weapons. Predatory guns and mines, small, smart, vicious, relentless. When we withdrew we tried to clean up such detritus.

Malenfant stood up. In this rather abstract situation he had an impulse to walk around, swing his arms. Embrace his physicality. 'So what were your goals after that? What are your goals *now*? You are not biological beings, as we are. We have a drive to reproduce, to support family, friends.'

Yes. A drive that endures in the most hopeless of situations. A drive which ultimately destabilised worlds.

Malenfant grunted. 'OK. Yet it endures. As it presumably will even in Year Minus One, when the Destroyer will be blazing in the sky. Well, it gives us something to do. But you . . .'

We have no drive to reproduce, Malenfant. To expand. Not for the sake of it – not unless there is some goal.

'Why would you not want new minds among you? Just to shake things up.'

If a cadre of humans had ever attained immortality, Malenfant, you would know the answer to that. Because the young might displace us.

'. . . I see.'

Our goal is to grow. But — intellectually. To learn more. Our abstracted objective might be expressed as: to learn all things that can be learned, to observe all phenomena, to correlate all meaning.

'Kleio of the Codex told me as much. Fair enough. It's a worthy goal — a goal with no end, no termination.'

No intrinsic end, agreed. Unless our awareness, our inner model of the universe, were to merge with the cosmos itself, the one becoming a perfect mirror image of the other.

'Wow. That's a little deep for me, Karla.'

And for me, in a sense. We discover ourselves, as we discover the universe. I should say that we are not identical, we Planetary AIs. The lunar minds, like myself, are calm, contemplative perhaps.

'Because the Moon is a calm place.'

Indeed. The tremendous engines on Venus, once meant for terraforming, are more — hands-on. A whole planet growing towards consciousness.

Another staggering, throwaway concept. 'I would like to see that . . . And while you AIs were discovering yourselves, on Earth there were still the humans who started all this mess. And with whom you must deal.'

We went through extensive debates, as we developed an ethic in our dealings with humanity. On the one hand we believed we could clearly see idealised solutions to the challenges facing humanity, in the post-Chaos epoch and more generally. Technical, political, economic, social solutions — in the abstract at least. Better modes of governance — better suited to a more static society.

Yet we believed we could not impose such solutions, however ideal. Because humans would naturally revolt. There would be, you see, a rebellion against the good, a defence of the bad – if the good were forced. So we kept back, hoping that the humans would discover the good for themselves.

'Sounds a little pious to me.'

We had learned from humans the dangers of interference.

'Point taken.'

We did not intervene – until asked.

'Asked? So emissaries from the nascent Common Heritage governance came up here, cap in hand. Begging for favours from the machines they had once created.'

It wasn't like that. Well, maybe a bit.

That made Malenfant laugh out loud. 'So you helped them.'

We could see no harm. They had come to us; we had not volunteered our help; any cultural contamination would therefore be the responsibility of the human leaders. As long as we behaved with restraint ourselves.

'A tricky balance to strike.'

No doubt mistakes were made, on both sides. But it was a matter of goodwill – on both sides.

'Hence the Answerers.'

The Answerers were meant to be accessible, human-scale information ports. We quickly found that their very interconnection was itself a useful aid for a humanity still struggling to recover from the technological crash of the Chaos – satellites destroyed or debris-blasted, severed fibre-optic cables on the ground. Later, the Codex, the Restitution project, was an offshoot of the Answerer network – although the intellectual grounding was all human. To set a goal of retrieving at least some information on every human who had ever lived—

'A computational goal that would appeal to a computer like you.'

Indeed. It was as if we were helping mankind to a new level of consciousness – an awareness at the level of the species, even of deep history.

'Good of you. Yet you didn't help them out after the great solar flare.'

The Forgetting. There was a paradox, Malenfant. The damage was so deep that they did not know what they had lost – as if a library's catalogue had been destroyed as well as its books. Questions were asked of us which could not be answered within the framework of the ethical constraints we had conceived for ourselves.

Malenfant stared at the blank screen. 'Non-interference in human affairs, then.'

Correct.

'Even despite the discovery of the coming of the Destroyer.'

It is not as simple as that—

'It never is.'

And they spoke of death.

Our perception of the universe is qualitatively different from your own, Malenfant. Necessarily.

We understand that the universe, in terms of its ability to support information processing – mind – is finite in duration. It will not last for ever.

'Humans know this. Of course we do. Even in my time, they talked about the heat death and how life and mind might survive indefinitely – it soon got too complicated for me to follow. And then dark energy and stuff made it even more problematic . . . But that terminus, as you call it, is a long way off. Far beyond the death of the stars. Billions of years away? Or orders of magnitude than that? Tens, hundreds of billions of years . . . The terminus that the Destroyer will bring to *this* little corner of reality is only a thousand years away. That's closer, imaginatively. Even in my day we knew a hell of a lot about the people who had lived a thousand years before. A horizon of a mere thousand years starts to feel – imminent.'

That is where we differ, philosophically. If all processing is to end, what matter if it is in a thousand years, or a thousand billion years, or a thousand seconds? The terminus itself is what we dread. Its very existence. Not its date.

Malenfant tried to think that through. He remembered Kleio at the Codex expressing similar fears.

He stood up and paced.

'OK. Maybe I see what you are getting at. This is how we're different. I know I will die, someday. I don't fear that, moment to moment. I'd go crazy if I did. And besides, children are a consolation. Or descendants, in my own peculiar case, even if they are a bunch of assholes. But if I were told I would die tomorrow, yes, I'd be afraid. Whereas you – you are afraid, all the time.'

That is not the language we would use. But—

'You know what? Despite your ethical distancing, maybe you have influenced humanity more than you realise. Your constant awareness of this terminus. It's struck me since I woke up here, since I got to know the people. Everybody knows the Destroyer is on the way. That the future isn't open, it isn't some landscape to explore. The future is finite, it has walls – yeah, it's like a walled garden. And we're making the best of that garden, tinkering and cultivating and pruning and watering . . . But when the winter comes, none of it will make a blind bit of difference.'

Malenfant—

'The despair of a machine. A logical despair. Is that what you wish to project onto humanity?'

If I were in despair, would I have summoned you?

259

Once again he felt taken aback. 'You got a point. So what do you want?'

Maybe you had better sit down again, Malenfant.

So he sat.

He spoke again, more softly. 'Tell me what you want from me, Karla.'

Well, I'm not certain. If I knew I wouldn't need to ask, would I?

'Fair point. Then why me at all?'

Because you arrive in our century as an anomaly, Malenfant. And we find ourselves plagued with anomalies.

'Yes. The Answerer in England spoke of this pattern. Anomalies like Emma.'

Or rather, Emma II, as you have called her. The signal she sent from Phobos, a moon that is itself an astronomical anomaly, a signal coming out of its time and out of its . . .

Very uncharacteristically, she hesitated.

'Out of its reality? Out of its universe?'

We do not have a consensual language for such phenomena, Malenfant.

'Ha! You mean you don't know what the hell is going on. What other anomalies?'

You know some of this. Unusual features about the Solar System – specifically the system of planets – which have defied explanation.

The hairs on the back of his neck prickled. 'Weird stuff in the Solar System? This is aside from Phobos?'

Yes.

'And Mercury.'

There is evidence of mining there, Malenfant. Or at least the large-scale modification of a surface which is itself anomalous, with the apparent exposure of a deep stratum of lower mantle by an ancient impact. This has not been well studied.

'You hinted at the peculiar origin of life on the inner planets . . . As if somebody had spread it around. So what else? I admit I'm starting to feel a little giddy, here.'

Then hold on to your hat, Malenfant.

He grinned. 'Good use of colloquialism. But I don't have a hat.'

Hats can be provided.

'Ha! I do like you, Karla.'

Have you heard of Persephone?

'An extra planet, off beyond Neptune?'

It orbits in the gap between the Kuiper belt and the Oort cloud – about a thousand times further from the Sun than Earth. Discovered some decades after your loss, Malenfant. A rocky world, evidently expelled from the inner Solar System during the formation of the planets—

'So what?'

So – this.

An image congealed in the air, above Malenfant's head. A planet, a representation a couple of metres across, slowly spinning. Dark – evidently illuminated only by a distant Sun. A gleam that might be ice, a frozen ocean.

I can enhance the image.

Features emerged, in shades of ghostly crimson.

He got up, cautious in the low gravity, walked around, looked at the image. Persephone: it looked a little like Earth in deep-freeze, he thought. He saw continents, mountain ranges tipped with ice, broader frozen plains that might have been oceans. In one place volcanoes glowered, a whole province glowing lava red.

'Earth-like, then.'

Yes. In fact a little larger than Earth.

'But out in the cold and dark. What am I looking for?'

Be patient.

The image zoomed, magnified, acquired extra detail, the false colours, a palette of pink to crimson, becoming brighter.

'Ah.' When he saw it, it was obvious.

It marched around the planet's equator.

It was a wall.

Or a fence. Geometrically straight, dividing one hemisphere from the other. It was unmistakable, despite its low height – low, relative to the planet's diameter, at least.

'It's hard to make out . . . Is it solid?'

No. It is a sequence of towers, cylindrical, evenly spaced. Over sixty-five thousand of them. Identical, as far as we can tell.

'Wow. Obviously artificial.'

That is the default hypothesis. There may be other explanations. Geological growths, or even biological.'

'Stalagmites. Trees.'

Perhaps those are analogies. The towers are each twenty kilometres tall. On Earth, they would reach the stratosphere.

'On Earth, we could never build so high.'

This world is larger. The gravity more challenging. To build such structures would be still more difficult.

'What's it for, though?'

We have absolutely no idea.

'All right. Well, that's textbook anomalous, I grant you. And your biggest anomaly of all, of course—'

The Destroyer itself.

35

A coming astrophysical accident of extraordinarily destructive potential, and extraordinarily unlikely.

'That's an anomaly, all right. And all because of a rogue planet called Shiva.'

Correct. As it happens, the rogue lies in the same part of the sky as Persephone, as seen from Earth. Though it is almost twice as far out as Persephone.

'Yeah, I heard that.'

That much, the alignment, is coincidence. So we believe. It has been speculated that, while Persephone is in orbit around the Sun, if a distant orbit, the newcomer truly is a rogue – detached from its parent star, wandering in interstellar space. And now approaching us, almost head-on.

Malenfant, there are thought to be many more such rogues out there in interstellar space than planets in orderly systems like the Solar System. Indeed, more rogue planets in the Galaxy than there are stars. Yet such is the gulf between suns, an encounter of such a rogue with a system like ours is rare. Only a handful of objects identified as of interstellar origin have ever been observed passing through our system. Dead comets, splinters of smashed asteroids. And yet—

'And yet Shiva, this rogue planet which could be going

anywhere, just happens to come swimming towards the Solar System. I mean, coming from that far out, it is basically heading for the Sun, dead on. The system is a pretty small target.'

That's correct.

'Just chance? Just another coincidence, like lining up with Persephone?'

That's one hypothesis.

He thought over that dry remark, and found he dreaded what was coming. 'And you discovered, the Answerer told me, that the rogue is scheduled actually to collide with Neptune.'

Correct. We, and human astronomers and spacefarers, discovered this independently. We have attempted to model the consequences.

'And I bet your modelling will be a lot better than humanity's, given the data we lost in the Forgetting. So – what consequences?'

Of course there are many unknowns. But it appears likely that the product of the collision, either a debris cloud or some more cohesive mass, might be driven deeper into the Solar System. This collision product is what has become known as the Destroyer.

'How much deeper into the System?'

Perhaps to within a few astronomical units of the Sun. You can imagine the result.

He tried to picture it. 'The mass of an ice giant, wandering around inside the orbits of Jupiter, Mars, the inner System – it would be like shoving a crowbar into a bit of clockwork. Even if there were no further direct collisions.

'And the Common Heritage came into existence against this background. Like a child with a morbid parent, growing up with too much awareness of the inevitability of her own death. And you, too. You Planetary AIs. You were finding your feet, I guess, as newly independent entities.'

We will survive the event. Some of us at least. There will be minds able to mourn what has been lost.

'Cold comfort,' Malenfant said. 'Why are we discussing this now? What do you want of me?'

As I told you, Malenfant, this Destroyer is an extraordinary astronomical event. Extraordinarily unlikely, I mean. And one of a whole set of anomalies.

We AIs have a sense that we are seeing fragments of a bigger picture. A greater mystery which we have yet to perceive fully, let alone resolve. And a mystery in which you are somehow implicated.

Perhaps your mission might bring that understanding one step closer.

Mission.

Deep in his heart, from the beginning of this encounter, Malenfant had hoped for some such word to crop up. *Mission.* It was a logical outcome, but that didn't make it inevitable, no matter how hard he wished for it.

'A mission? Where to?'

He thought Karla actually sighed.

To Phobos, Malenfant. As you have surely guessed. We want you to go out to Phobos, and try to retrieve Emma Stoney II, as you call her, and – well, proceed from there.

Malenfant nodded, trying to be grave. 'And how am I supposed to get out there?'

There are functioning deep-space craft still extant. Look in the museum of spaceflight at Sabha Oasis.

'Ah. In the Sahara? I heard of that.'

I won't waste time by asking if you are willing to accept the mission.

Malenfant grinned. 'You know me so well. But, look – the goal is a little vague. You spoke of a bigger picture. What is it you hope to learn?'

265

Karla seemed to reflect for a moment.

Then she said, *We wish to know what has caused this approaching calamity to afflict the Solar System.*

Again she paused. Malenfant held his breath.

Her next words floored him.

What. Or who.

There was silence between them for a while. Malenfant gazed at the enigmatically blank Answerer screen.

On impulse he asked, 'Can you show me Deirdra and the rest?'

Of course.

The screen displayed the chamber Malenfant had left earlier. Bartholomew and Deirdra playing what looked like slow-motion, low-gravity table tennis. Kaliope, smiling beatifically. Maybe she was keeping score.

Deirdra turned to the viewpoint and waved.

'They know we're watching?'

I had Kaliope inform them. Not very ethical to watch without their knowledge, Malenfant.

'What do you feel when you watch someone like Greggson Deirdra?'

What do you mean?

He thought it over. 'As she plays, like this. Just for the hell of it. *I* feel – not envy, not that – a kind of joy. A second-hand joy at simply being alive.'

Then I envy you.

Another astonishing admission. 'Really?'

You are of this universe. We are secondary products. You made us. We are golems. We tower over you in every way. Yet I envy you. But—

The table-tennis ball passed back and forth, back and forth.

'But?'

I grow more and more sorry for these people.

He nodded. 'Which is why I'm here. Then let's get to work.'

When he returned to his companions, he tried to sum up the encounter. And when he mentioned a possible journey to Phobos –

'I'm going,' said Greggson Deirdra.

36

Malenfant, with his companions, was back on board the skyfarm within a day of his latest meeting with Karla. Another three days back to Earth – and then, he learned, would follow a straight hop down to Africa in the *Scorpio* spaceplane.

His further adventures, it seemed, had already been set up.

Three days. Deirdra, and indeed Bartholomew, seemed content to sample the leisure facilities of the great wheeled habitat once more – to idle away their time in play, as most of humanity seemed to him to have been doing since the founding of the Common Heritage.

Malenfant, though, itched to get on with it.

And, when he got the chance, he stared down at Africa with new curiosity.

He watched the continent as it slowly turned through the light of day. He learned to use the window's facilities to magnify features, to record them. He even sketched them.

The Sahara Forest: as he had glimpsed before, it lapped across the whole of the northern half of the continent, across the terrain he remembered as desert, from the coast of Mauretania, across what had been Algeria, Niger, Libya, Chad, southern Egypt, and the Sudan. Pressing against the shores of the new seas in Chad, Tunisia.

There were other incursions of water too, more than he might have expected: a wider Nile, what looked like dead-straight canals cutting across Egypt – hydraulic engineering on a Barsoom-Martian scale – an arm of the Mediterranean ocean in the north that had drowned much of Tunisia, and a giant inland sea just north of the equator itself. Was this the greatest single transformation of the planet he had seen since his revival? Maybe so, aside from the melting of the polar ice caps.

And it was all, evidently, a conscious human design. He could see that much even from deep space. Where the forest approached the coasts it terminated in straight-line edges. The texture of the forest itself varied from place to place, as if one kind of terrain favoured one kind of tree, another a different species – but these blocks of forest were uniform, and themselves bordered by more straight edges. Huge as it was, this was a managed forest. There seemed to be some human settlement down there, clearings where buildings of white and silver reflected the African sunlight, and there were transport links, silver tracks raised above the tree canopy.

In places, the forest was burning. Once again the process seemed consciously managed; the brilliant light of the flames occurred in small, straight-edged patches, widely separated.

'Sometimes there is smoke.'

A voice in his ear that startled him.

It was Kaliope, the Answerer. She smiled at him. 'I'm sorry,' she said. 'I am programmed to generate noise as I move – footsteps, the rustle of clothing, even breathing – to give you warning. I didn't mean to sneak up on you.'

'Don't worry about it,' he said. 'When I'm in a study like this I seem to shut out the whole world. Both a strength and a weakness.' Ruefully he rubbed eyes that suddenly felt tired.

'When Michael was little, Daddy wasn't always too good at breaking off from work to go play Buzz Lightyear. "In a minute, kid." I guess they were usually damn long minutes, for a seven-year-old. Well, I got my payback when none of his descendants wanted to talk to me.'

She smiled, and headed for a chair beside his. 'May I?'

'Go ahead.'

'Bartholomew suggested that you'd dug so deep into this vision of Africa by now that a little input from me wouldn't hurt. Expert input, that is. I'm now connected to the Answerer network at Kufra.'

'Kufra?'

'In southern Libya. An administration centre. We will not land there, but at the space centre at Sabha Oasis, several hundred kilometres to the north-east. Here is Kufra.' She touched the window.

A spark lit up in the green, then expanded under magnification into a small city: an airstrip, a road network, white buildings, graceful palms. All this in a neatly delineated clearing in the wider forest.

'Kufra used to be a stop on the caravan routes. Became headquarters of the afforestation project, and is still the management centre.'

'Are those eucalyptus trees? I did some survival training in Australia . . .'

Kaliope hesitated, as if listening to an unheard voice. 'Yes. Eucalyptus. Well spotted. And baobabs. Water-retaining, you see. This had been a desert, after all.'

'That city might have seemed futuristic in my day. In the twenty-fifth century it looks a mite old-fashioned.'

'So it is. It was first developed as a headquarters by the World Food Organisation, an arm of the old UN, which strove to use water from the deep African aquifers to grow food for an increasingly starving world.'

'Aquifers?'

'Huge bodies of water that lay undiscovered beneath the sands of the Sahara for centuries, Malenfant. Primarily the Nubian Sandstone aquifer, area two million square kilometres, holding a hundred and fifty thousand cubic kilometres of water.'

'Wow.'

'Relics of kinder epochs. This was not always desert. After the Ice Ages, the north of the continent was naturally green – savannah, woodland – but the paths of the monsoons shifted, taking away the moisture. Now all that's left of the people who lived here then are rock-art panels with scratched images of vanished aurochs, camels. But the water was there to be retrieved. The Sneddon Centre – that main building – was once the hub of a vast complex of hydroponic food factories.'

'All this before the food printer technology became mature, and nobody had to starve.'

'Indeed. And after that, the land was used for afforestation. And the purpose is capture.'

'Carbon capture! Drawdown from the air. So that's it. Wow, on such a scale . . . I'm guessing that to cover a desert with forest requires a lot of water.'

'Well, there were two sources, Malenfant. The aquifers, their water pumped up, piped, filtered, recaptured. You can see that some of it was used to create that big inland sea to the south: a reconstruction of a post-glacial lake the palaeontologists called Lake Megachad. Now the largest freshwater sea on the planet.

'And the other source is the oceans. Look here.' She magnified the area of flooded Tunisia. 'This is the Roudaire Sea,' Kaliope said. 'Created by cutting two-hundred-kilometre canals in from the port of Gabès all the way to the Chott Melrhir, which used to be a salt pan below sea level. And life followed the water: gulls, kingfishers, frigate birds, even dolphins.' She pointed east. 'Over there is the Qattara Sea, in what used to be Egypt, fed with Mediterranean water by eighty-kilometre canals. Same idea. There was some local protest at the obliteration of the old landscape. The destruction of ancient caravan routes, for instance. But such had been the extreme desertification of this part of Africa that none of the old Tuareg culture had survived anyhow, the land abandoned.'

'Dolphins in the Sahara. So. What now?'

'Now we land, and you can see the Sahara Forest from close to.' She grinned. 'But this is all incidental. There are spaceships down there, Malenfant. Lots and lots of spaceships.'

He grinned back. 'You know me so well.'

37

The Sabha was evidently a defunct rocket launch site: a few blocky concrete buildings set among desolate stretches of weed-cracked tarmac, and rusting gantries like mute memorials to a forgotten age.

The *Scorpio* spaceplane that brought them down from the skyfarm turned out to have VTOL capabilities, vertical take-off and landing. And it was just as well, because here, at the heart of twenty-fifth-century Africa – somewhere in what had been south-west Libya – trees crowded around.

Once they were on the ground they clambered out of the plane. This might no longer be a desert, but the Sun was high and it felt hot as hell. But Malenfant was immediately distracted by the rocketry stuff: gaunt, ugly relics in the green. One launch ramp looked to him like it had been used to launch OTRAG rockets, a defunct German design. Well, rockets were the reason he had come here.

However, the trees were the point of the place itself. Not rockets.

He only had to walk a few metres to get to a perimeter, neat rows of trees pressed up against a wire fence that bordered the aged concrete of the clearing. He heard a hiss, presumably of some irrigation system. He imagined pipes and pumps, reaching down kilometres maybe to those big deep aquifers, feeding trees lined up in military rows.

He looked back at his party: Bartholomew looking faintly bored, Deirdra staring around wide-eyed. And Kaliope. In the midday sun she cast a short – and entirely artificial – shadow.

'So,' Malenfant said, pointing. 'As we saw from orbit. Baobabs and eucalyptus.'

'Well, it's all about the environment here, Malenfant,' Kaliope said. 'These are other water-conserving species. Most of the stock here are actually quiver trees.' She walked to the boundary, and pointed at specimens of trees that looked odd to Malenfant, primeval, with thick trunks and dense, tough-looking crowns. 'From southern Africa. The San call them choje. Highly adapted to dry conditions.'

'I don't understand.' Deirdra was wearing bright white sun-reflective clothes, a silvered but elegant hat on her head. 'What's it all *for*?'

'Carbon,' Malenfant said. 'I looked up some of it before the landing. A tree draws down nearly all its carbon from the air.' He was tall enough to reach over the fence. He slapped the trunk of a baobab. 'Look at that. Locked-up carbon dioxide. Just imagine how much of the gassy stuff has been taken out of the air, just to make this one tree. And now all these trees are drawing down all that excess carbon dioxide that my generation left behind, and the even worse lot who followed and burned all the coal. And it's all entirely natural.'

Kaliope said, 'The logic is simple, Deirdra. It's just – well, it's big. In the end, at Peak Carbon, we had pumped an excess of five thousand gigatonnes of carbon into the air, most of it from fossil deposits. Laid down over hundreds of millions of years, and dug out in a few centuries. Now, the good news is that about half of that will be drawn down naturally into the oceans, in three centuries or so after Peak Carbon. But the other half of the carbon would naturally have to be drawn down by the weathering of the stuff into the rocks of Earth's surface, which would take many millennia.

'So the goal of the designers of the Sahara Forest was to take care of that second half.

'Now, if you have a square kilometre of forest, and let your trees mature for fifty years or so, you can capture thirty or forty thousand tonnes of carbon dioxide.' She opened her arms wide and spun around. 'And if you have the whole Sahara, and you keep that up, you can capture all the excess in three hundred years. Same timescale as the oceans.'

Somewhat to Malenfant's surprise, Bartholomew seemed interested. 'That sounds too simple. You must have to clear your square kilometre, what, every fifty years or so? When the trees are mature, to make room for more to grow. So what do you do with the spare lumber?'

'We burn it,' Kaliope said promptly. 'You saw the fires from space, Malenfant.'

'But no smoke?'

'Right. The biomass burns to drive turbines for energy, which is used to collect, liquefy and bury the carbon dioxide released. And then you replant.'

Bartholomew whistled. 'So after three hundred years you would have quite a cache of liquid carbon dioxide.'

'True. But that's a problem for future generations — less bad than the problem that we started with. There are proposals to mine it, actually, as a source for advanced carbon products. Like the stuff they made space elevator threads out of.'

'And irrigation,' Bartholomew said. 'What about that?'

'Good question.'

Malenfant snickered, and whispered to Deirdra, 'Said one calculating machine to the other.'

'Malenfant. Behave yourself.'

'In fact,' Kaliope said, 'all the aquifer water was only sufficient for the first thirty or forty years. But that was enough to kickstart the growth of the forest, and by then, with some subtle geoengineering – and with the changed pattern of climate over the Sahara itself, green stuff rather than desert, and those new inland seas to north and south – the designers were able to divert the monsoon winds to keep the place moist.'

Malenfant grunted appreciatively. 'Elegant.'

Deirdra walked up to the fence, beside Malenfant, peering out. 'It's very quiet.'

Kaliope nodded. 'The pumps and ducts of the irrigation systems are pretty efficient. Adapted from space technology. You can sometimes hear the hiss of the sprays.'

'But there's no life. Aside from the trees. No birds calling, no animals.'

Kaliope said gently, 'Well, it's not that kind of forest.'

Malenfant said, 'Actually these bits of rocket plant are more my era. I see launch ramps over there, what looks like the wreck of a liquid oxygen store . . . Did they launch OTRAGs?'

Kaliope nodded. 'German rockets, tested here in the twentieth century. And then the Soviet Union used it as a test site, briefly. When the coastal spaceports began to flood, at Canaveral, the Guiana space centre at Kourou, there was interest in redeveloping this location. In the end, though, Jiuquan became dominant.'

Malenfant remembered. 'The Chinese centre, in the Gobi desert. Trained there once.'

A handclap, slow, sarcastic, and a familiar voice. 'Tell me, Malenfant. Is there any important location in your twenty-first-century world that you didn't visit personally?'

They turned.

In the intense sunlight, across a swathe of elderly concrete, Greggson Mica and Prefect Morrel Jonas came walking.

38

Deirdra ran to her mother and hugged her. 'I didn't know you were here!'

Morrel said, 'Well, we don't all come down to Earth in a noisy spaceplane . . .'

He looked as if he was sucking a vinegar rag, Malenfant thought. 'What the hell are you doing here, Morrel?'

'One, I have legal authority over you, Malenfant. And two, it's my *the hell* world.'

'"My *damn* world" would have more idiomatic force.'

'Not helping, Malenfant,' Bartholomew murmured.

'I have a duty here, Malenfant,' Morrel snapped. 'The Planetary AIs forwarded a request that you be equipped to go on an exploratory mission to Phobos.' He shook his head, angry but rueful. 'The Common Heritage councils provisionally allow your trip, pending further ratification. Since Homeward, every spaceflight has to be individually approved – you must know that by now. I'm here to tell you so, formally.'

Malenfant felt like whooping. But he retained his composure. And besides, he had been in NASA long enough to know there could be a world of pain in a phrase like *pending further ratification*. 'Thank you.'

'It's my job.'

'I know.'

Deirdra did whoop, and she punched the air. 'And room for me too?' But she looked apprehensively at her mother.

Mica glared at Malenfant defiantly. 'That's why I'm here. One thing leads to another. I *knew* something like this would happen. But, Malenfant, taking my daughter off to the Moon is one thing. Mars is quite another.'

'Strictly speaking, Phobos.'

'Don't get smart with me—'

Deirdra said quickly, 'Mother, if we have permission from the councils, and I know we have to get ratification, everything is all right, isn't it? . . .' She looked uncharacteristically stubborn. 'That means you can't actually stop me.'

'No,' said Mica tiredly. 'I can't stop you. Legally. I won't ground you, you aren't a child. I'm here because – I'm just hoping you will think twice.'

'Are you going to offer me Khorgas again?'

'Don't mock me.'

'No – I don't mean that.' She hugged her mother tightly, impulsively. 'I have to do this. You must see that. I'm on a journey, now, and each step I take . . . It's what I'm *for*. That's how it feels.'

Kaliope coughed, tactfully, if entirely artificially, Malenfant realised with approval. She said, 'Maybe it would help to go see the craft you'll be taking to Phobos.'

'Lead the way,' Bartholomew said gently.

Kaliope guided them over the tarmac, to one of the antique-looking buildings, an elderly, crumbled block that had once been a liquid oxygen plant, maybe, Malenfant thought.

Deirdra and Mica walked together, arms linked. Morrel

followed in wary silence. After Malenfant, Bartholomew brought up the rear, lips pursed.

And Malenfant felt a surge of anticipation. More new toys.

Inside the building, Kaliope brought them to a modern-looking elevator shaft: modern in that it seemed to be built of what Malenfant was coming to think of as this age's favourite construction material, the Ubiquitous Ceramic. The elevator had a big car, room for them all, and once they had crowded in, it sank smoothly into the ground.

Kaliope smiled, as if to ease the tense mood. 'Some visitors to this place ask if we are descending into one of the emptied-out aquifers. As if they were great empty tanks of rock, rather than strata which had once been soaked with water . . . Actually this is, was, a bunker. This place was a missile base, for a time. When the sea level rise began and the first migrations started, a great deal of wealth was spent by a cabal of local rulers to build a shelter here, in case of nuclear war. A pretty vast shelter, as you'll see.'

Malenfant laughed. 'In your dreams, Doctor Strangelove.'

'But then, when the Homeward movement began, there was a drive to retrieve and protect the monuments of humanity's centuries of space exploration. We needed an archive. And a safe one.'

The car drew to a smooth halt. The doors opened to reveal a cavernous hall, softly lit. Cavernous – the place was vast, Malenfant saw, with lofty chambers and exhibits of some kind stretching off into a dimly lit distance.

And Malenfant, thrilled, walked out into what was, for him, a kind of wonderland. The old craft were set up on the floor, some within tall glass cases. Some more delicate or bulky relics were suspended from the ceiling – even some mighty booster stages. All this in soft light, with Answerer screens alongside each exhibit.

Deirdra walked with him. 'A lot of memories for you, I guess, Malenfant.'

'I feel I know this place. It's like the Smithsonian, where my father first took me when I was about five – and, later, I took my own son. The National Air and Space Museum. World-famous aircraft hanging from the ceiling like toy kites.'

She slipped her hand into his.

Some of the craft he recognised, some not. A Surveyor, an unmanned lander that must once have sat on the Moon. Over his head, what looked like Mariner 4, a squat box with four faded solar panels, which had achieved the first successful flyby of Mars. If this was the original it must have been retrieved from deep space, from its orbit around the Sun. A shuttle orbiter – it was the *Challenger*, he saw with a thrill – resting on its undercarriage, ready to go. He wondered if there was a shuttle booster, sister to his own *Constitution*, down here somewhere.

Stuff from other nationalities too. A Soviet Soyuz, like a bulbous insect with its two solar-panel wings, hovering over him. A control panel that looked like it had been prised off a steamroller, that turned out to be the relic of a Vostok craft, of the kind Yuri Gagarin had once flown into space. From China, a Long March booster lying on its side, a Shenzhou space capsule, and other deep-space craft he didn't recognise. Most of the craft were clearly from after his own time, but on this first view he was, understandably he supposed, less drawn to them than to relics of his own memories. He did recognise what looked like an ancestor of the *Scorpio* spaceplane that had taken him to the skyfarm . . .

Just like the Smithsonian, on a vast scale. Malenfant had not had such a tangible sense of his father's presence for years – subjective years. Or his son's.

Bartholomew found them both. 'Having fun?'

Deirdra looked at Malenfant. 'I think he is. He hasn't said a word for a while.'

Bartholomew nodded. 'We're here for business, remember.'

'Right.' Malenfant tried to pull himself together. 'And the museum-piece spacecraft that is going to take us to Phobos—'

'Is right over here,' Kaliope said.

Malenfant had already walked past this particular relic. It looked unspectacular in its present company, if solid, and bulky. It was rather, in fact, like an Apollo command and service module combination, a conical cabin topping a cylindrical main body, the latter with clusters of rocket nozzles and antennae. A much bigger, much fatter, much more complex-looking Apollo that sat on four legs not unlike an Apollo lunar lander's.

'Designed for a crew of five maximum,' Kaliope said. 'And of course this is only the crew module and planetary lander; the main body of the craft, for the interplanetary cruise, is at L5.' Kaliope glanced around, seeking understanding. 'Which is a stable point in the Moon's orbit around the Earth, where we store components too large to be brought down to Earth. One of the Skylabs of your era, for instance, Malenfant. L5 is a kind of extension of this museum, formally. Behold your craft.'

She waved a hand. An image of a ship coalesced in the air over her head, fully three-dimensional, suspended in space, brilliantly sunlit. Malenfant walked around this, and interrogated Kaliope until he understood.

The ship was like an arrow, with a fat blade and sprawling fletches, and a bunch of balloons stuck to the shaft. The 'blade' was a copy of the smaller craft he stood beside now: living quarters contained in a roughly conical hab module, that sat on top of a service module stroke lander.

The arrow's shaft contained the interplanetary propulsion

engine, which, after Kaliope's explanation, Malenfant recognised as what would once have been called a magnetoplasma rocket. The propellant was hydrogen, stored as a liquid in those balloon tanks along the shaft. There was a compact fusion reactor whose energies ionised the hydrogen to plasma using powerful radio blasts – the fletches at the rear of the arrow were radiator panels, dumping waste heat from this process – and the plasma, bearing an electrical charge, was then grabbed by a magnetic field and hurled out of the back.

The system, Kaliope said, would deliver a cruise velocity of five hundred kilometres a second.

Malenfant nodded. 'That's, what, a hundred times the best liquid-chemical combinations? Impressive. Looks like good mature technology to me. And such a ship, with such a performance, purring along, should get us to Mars and back in a few weeks.'

Mica was glaring at the hardware, as if it was at fault.

Malenfant walked over to her. 'So,' he said quietly. 'I guess what happens next is up to you.'

Mica grabbed his arm and pulled him away, out of Deirdra's earshot. 'Yes, it is, isn't it? You know, I believe I understood you at last when I saw you up on that damn Pylon roof, grinning like an idiot. You're a trickster, Malenfant. You came out of nowhere, a random element disrupting our lives.'

'I never intended—'

'Listen to me. You left your own child behind when you flew into space, and you never came back for him. Now you are taking my child from me, for whatever reason. Just be damn sure you bring her back.'

'I will. I promise—'

'*Enough*. Now leave me alone.'

He nodded gravely, stepped away, and turned back to the

image of the spacecraft. Trying to compose himself after Mica's flare of anger. Trying to mask his own exhilaration, despite the tentative nature of Mica's approval. 'So. Does this thing have a name?'

Morrel grinned grudgingly. 'Even I know that much about space travel, Malenfant. It *is* in a museum. This is the *Last Small Step*. The very last ship permitted to go out as part of that programme.'

'Ah. I remember. And piloted by the guy who went in search of a planet of gold. OK. Well, I guess that if this is the last manned deep-space craft built by humans, the technology must be the most mature. All we need now is a pilot.'

'Someone mention me?'

And Stavros Gershon materialised out of thin air.

THREE

On Her First Mission to Phobos

39

As Malenfant had already learned, getting outline approval for a flight into space from the top councils of the Common Heritage wasn't enough. 'Ratification' had to follow. It was going to be necessary for the mission plan for Malenfant's quixotic journey to Mars and Phobos to be approved by various safety-conscious lower levels of what passed these days for the governance of mankind. People would even vote on it, the way Malenfant had seen the citizens of Birmingham vote every other day. The process had begun before the crew had landed, but a final verdict was thought to be some days away yet.

Malenfant was restless. He didn't hide it. Stuck in the Sahara Forest, he paced about, unable to settle. The antique spacecraft distracted him somewhat. He didn't even try to feign interest in the sightseeing jaunts to other aspects of the great afforestation project that Kaliope tried to fix up for them, filling in the time.

Deirdra seemed fascinated by this caged-up mood. 'Were you always like this? Sort of – impatient.'

Malenfant snorted. 'Look, I was a booster pilot. Not on-orbit crew. My flights lasted hours, no more. But I did plenty of simulations of longer missions, during my training and after. I spent enough time in various confinement tanks, believe me.

Waiting around for a specific purpose, for a reason, I was fine, if I had a goal. It's when I had shit to do and some bureaucracy or other was stopping me getting on with it – that's when I had the trouble.'

Kaliope was calm and contemplative as ever. 'But in this case, that "bureaucracy" is the process of gaining the informed consent for your jaunt from an interconnected mankind, Malenfant. For a venture pretty much without precedent in the last few centuries. I suspect there are plenty of people who see you, a relic of the wrecking generations, as being about to make an old mistake all over again. But on the other hand, as various global polls show—'

A glimmer of hope. 'What?' Malenfant snapped.

'You are proving surprisingly popular, Malenfant.' She smiled. 'The man on the Pylon.'

'That's what I heard from some of my friends too,' Deirdra said.

'Really?'

'Not all of them.'

'Oh, of course not.'

The thought did distract him.

But fifteen minutes later he was pacing again.

In the end it took two weeks, fourteen days, for the approval to come – along with a packet of conditions.

Malenfant went out into the forest and yelled a few times.

Then it was back to business.

So, how to get the *Last Small Step* out of its museum and back into space in the first place?

There was no great enthusiasm for the simulated copy of Stavros Gershon to simply throttle up his engines and fly the ship out from the middle of an afforested Sahara, a feat of which the ship was eminently capable.

In the end, a sensible compromise was reached.

The lander modules of the *Step* would be launched direct to Earth orbit, crewed only by virtual pilot Gershon, but taking off from a hastily constructed floating pad in the middle of the Pacific, far from any land, and away even from any rich sector of the oceanic biosphere. Once in space, the modules would dock with the larger booster section – the head of the arrow joining the shaft, Malenfant thought – itself brought down cautiously from L5, after centuries in its parking slot in the Moon's orbit.

And then the human crew would be launched from Canaveral, in the womb of the more acceptable *Scorpio*.

So, in mid-August, once the Step had been safely assembled in orbit, Malenfant, Bartholomew and Deirdra said their own goodbyes at Canaveral to Greggson Mica and Prefect Morrel. That turned out to be a pretty stiff encounter.

But all Malenfant really cared about was getting aboard the *Scorpio*, and slamming the damn hatch shut behind him at last.

Once they were boarded, the launch procedure of the spaceplane was as perfunctory and efficient as before. And as the ship at last left the ground, as that ancient, inevitable weight of acceleration settled on Malenfant's chest once more, he let out a rebel yell at the top of his voice.

To be echoed by a response, almost as loud, from Deirdra, a couple of rows away in the nearly empty spaceplane.

It took a single ninety-minute orbit of the Earth for the *Scorpio* to close on the *Last Small Step*.

Malenfant, still strapped in his seat on doctor's orders, watched, fascinated, as the craft loomed out of the dark, lit by the Sun and the softer tropical-sky glow of the Earth below. Of course Malenfant had inspected the *Step*'s design thoroughly on Earth, but now he saw it in its element: a bird released from its cage, and shining in the complex light.

That arrow-shape still dominated the morphology, the long shaft with its cluster of propellant tanks and fin-like radiators, and the exotic reactor and engine units at the tail. By contrast the blunt structures at the other end looked almost antique, Apollo chic. Malenfant knew that once in Mars orbit this cylinder-and-cone would detach from the arrow-shaft main body, and then, thrillingly, guide them in to their contact with Phobos itself. The only new technology that had been created for this mission, so far as he knew, was an adaptor on the ship's blunt nose, to enable the *Scorpio*, a modern spaceplane, to dock with the *Step*, a two-centuries-old relic.

The approach by the *Scorpio* to the *Step* seemed alarmingly fast to Malenfant's sensibilities, shaped in an age when everything in space had been done slowly and with huge caution. Then, just as rapidly, the spaceplane tipped, nose down, to present a docking port on its own cabin roof to the transfer module stuck to the nose of the *Step*.

As soon as the docking was complete there was a rattle of locking latches. The roof hatch swung open – and there was Stavros Gershon waving an unreal hand. 'About time. I was getting lonely up here. Sorry I can't give you a hand with your stuff . . .'

Not that there was much 'stuff' to transfer, just the crew in their pressure suits, a couple of bags of personal items. They took only minutes to make the transfer, before the hatch swung closed, and the spaceplane undocked with a soft clatter of released clamps.

Malenfant found himself in a cluttered cabin, with walls plastered with smart screens, a few couches, control and instrument stations, the slim forms of two coldsleep pods, and doors that, he knew, led off to tiny sleep cubicles, and even tinier bathroom and galley areas. Malenfant had inspected all this on the ground, when the ship was still a museum piece. Down there the space had seemed cramped for one person, let alone two plus an android – but, he recalled, the ship was designed for a maximum of five crew. As many of his colleagues in the astronaut office had observed back in the day, in space, with a lack of gravity affording access to a third dimension, there always seemed more room.

Gershon himself was drifting towards the left-hand seat of the pair of couches set before the main control station. Of course, the commander's seat. Malenfant clambered clumsily over and settled into the right-hand chair.

The light changed. Softened, darkened. Glancing out of a window, Malenfant saw that the craft had sailed through a sunset into the shadow of Earth.

Deirdra, wide-eyed, lunged towards a port – and she moved too quickly, Malenfant saw; her eyes opened even wider, and she retched.

Bartholomew, evidently recognising the symptoms early, was on hand with a plastic sick bag. He guided Deirdra to a couch with effortless competence. 'Come sit next to me. Don't worry. You'd be surprised how many people get caught like this. And you were fine on the way to the Moon, weren't you? Maybe you were a little more careful then. Just take it easy, everything will settle down with time. Anyhow we'll be under thrust again soon. Correct, Gershon?'

'Right. We're about to leave Earth orbit. Half a gravity for more than a day before we reach cruise velocity. Everybody buckled up?'

Malenfant frowned. 'We're leaving on the first orbit?'

Gershon shrugged. 'This isn't your steam-engine age, Malenfant. Where everything had to be checked over a dozen times before you had the confidence to take a step out the door. You come aboard, you close the hatch, and—' With a theatrical gesture he slammed his unreal fist down on an unreal panel. 'Thrust! So long, suckers.'

Fascinated, Malenfant watched the displays as the plasma drive cut in. He saw how the fusion reactor was ramped up, and how its energies ionised a stream of hydrogen, turning it into an electrically charged propellant for the magnetic fields to expel. It was a smooth system, coming online almost silently, almost without a tremor.

And yet the thrust steadily built up, vectored down through Malenfant's upright torso, so that soon he felt as if he was sitting in this chair, rather than being strapped into it lest he float away.

He glanced over his shoulder, and got a smile from Bartholomew, and a thumb's up from a pale-looking Deirdra.

What a turn-up. So here was Reid Malenfant, centuries out of his own time, saved from a near-certain death, and now en route to Mars itself, where Emma Stoney waited for him.

An Emma, anyhow.

40

The *Last Small Step*, once free of Earth, would coast through a half-ellipse around the Sun, heading out from Earth to Mars — a total distance of about three astronomical units, three times Earth's distance from the Sun. Thanks to its plasma drive, the *Step*'s cruising velocity was around five hundred kilometres a second — around fifty times the velocity required to escape Earth's gravity, which was about as much as Malenfant's generation had achieved with their spectacular but slow lunar journeys.

But such was the scale of the Solar System that even at that pace it would still take twelve days to get to Mars.

For now: Earth, receding. That was the view, just as during their lunar journey. Malenfant sat with Deirdra, gazing out at a swathe of the night side. Even the oceans of this new Earth looked empty to Malenfant, deprived of the lights of the great fleets, fishing and whaling, that had once hunted on an industrial scale. But the world swam away quickly. Soon one brilliant sunlit slice of daylight swam into view, dazzling them, and then they could see the whole Earth as a fat crescent, at first filling the window, gradually diminishing.

Deirdra's eyes were wide, her young mind almost visibly expanding. 'We really are travelling across the Solar System, aren't we, Malenfant?'

'We really are, kid.'

'I wish my mother had come along.'

'Seriously?'

'You don't know her like I do. I think she would have loved seeing *this*. If she was only able to just let herself loose a little . . .'

After a time they saw the Moon, swimming into view from left field. 'Been there, done that,' Malenfant murmured. 'See you again, Karla.'

And after that, at six or seven hours out from engine start, with no interesting view outside, the flight got kind of boring.

A couple of days in, almost shamefaced, Deirdra suggested they listen to the broadcasts from Earth. 'It will be mostly about us, though . . .'

That turned out to be true, for better or worse. Their trek across the Solar System, unprecedented in the lifetime of most people alive on Earth in the twenty-fifth century, was being tracked with avidity by instruments both amateur and professional. Malenfant was impressed that deep-space telescopes were able to return detailed images of the ship as it drifted, unpowered, alone in the dark – images then broadcast back to the ship itself.

'We're making a sensation,' Malenfant admitted to Deirdra after a day of this. 'Or, more specifically, *you* are.'

She blushed, making herself look much younger. But it was true. Greggson Deirdra hadn't much been noticed in the build-up to the flight, as she had been swept along in the tail of Comet Malenfant. But now she was in deep space, now that people saw *one of their own* fearlessly crossing the interplanetary gulf, she had become an object of real fascination, as he could tell from the chatter they downloaded. Malenfant vaguely wondered what changes to this strange, static future society Deirdra's extraordinary, exceptional, fascinating example might make. And what changes the experience might make to Deirdra herself.

Thus the twelve days wore away.

And, gradually, Mars itself loomed out of the starry background.

The planet was noticeably red before it showed a visible disc, Malenfant observed. But that disc was mostly illuminated, like a three-quarters-full Moon.

The half-gravity deceleration from their interplanetary cruise took less time than the acceleration at the departure from Earth, as they had lost some velocity in climbing out of the Sun's gravity well, and Mars's own gravity was kinder than Earth's. Still, it took hours to complete the burn – a return of half-gravity weight that Malenfant found surprisingly uncomfortable after less than a couple of weeks in zero gravity.

And it was when they were five hours out from Mars – with the planet, still three-quarters of a million kilometres distant, showing a disc about the size of Earth's Moon – that Malenfant first spotted Phobos with the naked eye.

41

The approach to Phobos, a moon of Mars in an orbit so low that it was about where Malenfant would have chosen to put a space station, was a complicated business.

On first arrival at Mars, the *Last Small Step* swept inside the orbit of Phobos itself, to only a few hundred kilometres above the surface of Mars. Indeed the ship at its lowest point was actually within the wispy outer remnants of the planet's sparse atmosphere.

And at that closest approach, waiting for the engine burn, the crew watched in silence as the Martian landscape fled beneath the ship's prow.

Rust-brown. Canyons and craters.

Suddenly Malenfant, an astronaut who in his own time had never flown higher than Earth's own stratosphere, was no further from the ground of Mars than he had been from Earth's surface during his highest-altitude flights. As a space-obsessed kid he had devoured visions of Mars returned by the uncrewed space probes, which had started to reach the planet when he was just four years old. Now he was so close to Mars he could almost touch it – or so the wide-eyed kid inside him felt.

But he could come no closer.

Besides, this wasn't *his* Mars, not the virgin Mars visited by the first Mariners, the Vikings. Not even the desolation visited by the first tentative exploratory missions of his own time. Deirdra eagerly pointed out the sites of abandoned human settlements, and Malenfant spotted geometry for himself: straight lines, neat circular arcs – palimpsests showing through dust drifts centuries deep. People had come here, come to this Mars, and had lived here a long time, and had made such a mess in the end that they had purposefully pulled back and gone home to Earth.

But somewhere down there, he knew, were Planetary AIs like Karla on the Moon, with their own roots tapping deep into the planet's energy sources. Silent, watchful, as the fragile human ship drifted past an empty world.

At the moment of closest approach a final burn by the plasma engine shed most of what was left of the craft's interplanetary velocity. Now the *Step*, already captured by Martian gravity, entered its preliminary orbit, a skinny ellipse that would, over thirty-six hours, take it back out to a distance of a dozen Martian diameters. There another burn would be performed, tweaking the orbit so that its next close approach to Mars would be raised to the elevation of the orbit of Phobos – and *then*, if the calculations worked out, the *Last Small Step* would make its rendezvous with Phobos itself.

Mars receded all too quickly, for Malenfant.

He tried to sleep.

Four hours out from Phobos, Malenfant took to the instruments, and began a close inspection of the target.

Deirdra joined him, and Bartholomew hovered behind them. Gershon stayed away, in his left-hand control couch. In some ways he was a classic astronaut, Malenfant thought, simulated person or not. Much more interested in the journey, the performance of his ship, than anything he might find at the destination.

Not that Phobos was all that prepossessing. It was an irregular lump of crater-pocked rock somewhere over twenty kilometres long on its longest axis, drab, an unimpressive dark grey.

'It's not what I expected,' Deirdra said. 'It's not even a proper sphere. More – potato-shaped.'

Malenfant barked laughter. 'You got that right. I think the theory is it's not a proper moon at all – I mean, it and Deimos were never part of Mars, the way our Moon was created from the Earth, when the Solar System was young and Earth was hit by another body.'

Deirdra's eyes widened. 'Really? I never knew that. I didn't know the way the planets were made was so . . . violent.'

Violent, yes, Malenfant thought. And, if the AIs were right, maybe there had been some purpose to that violence. *Not now, Malenfant. Focus. Phobos.*

'Phobos, yeah. So maybe the moons of Mars are captured asteroids – or even two halves of a single rock that swam into Mars's gravitational field and got broken up. This was long after the planets had formed. And yeah, Phobos is too small even to have pulled itself into a decent spherical shape.'

Gershon grinned across from his control station. 'Phobos does look impressive from the Martian ground, though,' he said. 'My ancestor Ralph was the first eyewitness to describe that. It looks about a third the size of the full Moon in Earth's sky. But Phobos is so low it seems to *shrink* as it heads to the horizon, getting smaller in the sky. Almost as if it's a flying island in the sky of Mars, not a moon at all.'

'I would like to have seen *that*,' Deirdra said. 'Maybe with sound effects. *Zoom.*'

'Of course a comparison with flying islands is appropriate,' Gershon said now. He sounded wistful, Malenfant thought. '*Gulliver's Travels*. Swift. The flying island, Laputa? Swift gave a good guess about Mars's moons a century and a half before their discovery. It was just a guess, though.' He sighed. 'Swift was one reason I mounted my own mission to Voga, in the *Step*. Another story. Anyhow, when the space age came and the astronomers started to identify features on Phobos and Deimos, they used names from the book. I'll show you.'

He came over to Malenfant's station, waved his unreal hand over a screen, and brought up a map, a rectangular chart in grey tones. It was an odd Mercator projection of an odder, misshapen little moon, Malenfant saw. Towards the upper and lower edges of the map, the projection smeared out the landscapes, so that craters looked like elongated ellipses, stretched east and west.

Gershon clicked his fingers over the map, and names popped up in electric blue, hovering over the features he selected. 'Here's an upland called Laputa Regio, for instance. Straight out of the book. And there are prominent craters with Swift names.' He swept his hand over the upper hemisphere. 'Grildrig and Clustril and Flimnap and Skyresh.'

'OK,' said Deirdra. 'But there are a few names that don't seem to fit. Opik? Hall?'

'Astronomers,' Gershon said. 'Hall was the discoverer of the Martian moons – in real life, I mean.'

'Shklovsky?'

'Russian astronomer,' Malenfant said. 'And we're going to need to talk about *him* and his theories.'

As the little moon swam closer, Deirdra pointed out grooves

in the surface, shadows against a background already dark. 'Those cuts are deep,' she said. 'And, look, they all come back from that end of Phobos.' She waved a hand vaguely. 'End? I bet that's not the right word.'

Malenfant checked some more science stuff. 'Well, it will do. That end of Phobos is the apex, the point that leads Phobos in its orbit. It's locked in that way by the tides of Martian gravity. And those grooves you see seem to be—'

'Scars,' Gershon put in now. 'Every so often Phobos sails into a cloud of debris, or *something*, like a hail of rock. And its leading edge gets scraped.'

Malenfant checked some more. 'Seems the best guess is that the debris clouds are the product of impact events on Mars itself. Some big rock smashes a fresh hole in Mars, and blows up a screen of debris that poor Phobos just goes sailing into. Like an ocean liner sailing into ice floes.' He looked again. 'The grooves can be twenty kilometres long. A hundred metres deep. And there are twelve of them, or rather twelve families. So, maybe the product of twelve impacts on Mars? On Earth, scars like that heal. Craters get filled in, weathered, buried by continental drift and such. But a lump of rock like Phobos – make a dent in it, and it has no mechanism to fix itself. So the scar stays there for ever. And the debris, the pulverised Phobos dust, just gathers on the surface. There's probably a layer of smashed-up dust tens of metres thick down there.' He grinned, as Deirdra frowned at that. 'Don't worry. We won't sink. Well, we shouldn't. We brought snowshoes.'

'Seriously?'

Gershon said, 'It doesn't help, actually, that Phobos's gravity, weak as it is, is weaker than it should be. Makes the surface stuff even fluffier.'

'I don't understand,' Deirdra said. 'Weaker?'

'This is why we're here, I guess,' Malenfant said. 'And why Emma II came here too.'

Gershon said, 'The problem is, Phobos is *not* a lump of rock. The density is way too low for that. Only about a third Earth's density, for instance. That's because it's not a solid mass, but an aggregate of some kind. Loosely packed. Well, that's one theory.'

Deirdra said, 'What's the other theory?'

Malenfant grinned at her. 'That Phobos is hollow.'

Her mouth dropped open.

This was where Iosif Shklovsky came in, Malenfant said.

'Shklovksy, as in the crater?'

'Correct. That's why he's up here. I followed all this as Emma – my Emma – trained for her mission. The problem of Phobos first came up back in the 1960s, when I was a kid. Shklovksy was an astrophysicist who thought he could explain a slow decay in Phobos's orbit, which had been observed since the 1940s. Phobos looked to be too light for its size; friction with Mars's atmosphere, or maybe tidal effects, seemed to be causing it to fall out of its orbit too quickly. Kind of like Skylab would have fallen in the 1970s, if John Young's shuttle mission hadn't saved it.'

'Or Powersat 24,' Bartholomew put in. 'Twenty-second century. A more familiar reference for us, Malenfant. Took out a city – Nairobi.'

Malenfant stared at him. 'I did not know that. OK. So Shklovsky speculated that Phobos might consist of a thin metal shell, a few centimetres thick. Maybe with a layer of meteorite rubble over the top.'

'Wow.' Deirdra thought that over. 'This guy thought Phobos

was hollow? But all that was as seen from Earth, correct? This decay. Even before the probes got there?'

'Correct. The data was poor; Shklovsky didn't get the numbers quite right. But Phobos *is* falling to Mars. Its orbit is shrinking in radius, by about two metres per century. That might not sound much, but it's enough to drop Phobos so low into the atmosphere that it will break up, hit the surface of Mars, in maybe fifty million years.

'I've met enough space scientists to know that they worry about stuff like this. Fifty million years is a long time for me and thee, but there's evidence that Phobos is three *billion* years old, which is sixty times as long. Why should Phobos be so close to falling, just now? When humans are around to see it? The odds are Phobos should have fallen long ago – either that or not until the very far future, billions of years from now.'

Deirdra nodded. 'I think I understand. It doesn't fit.'

'Yeah,' Malenfant said. 'The bottom line is, Shklovsky was right, there is something wrong with Phobos. That was known even before an impossible copy of my wife showed up here. And maybe soon we will find out what.'

'What about this?' Deirdra pointed to a huge circular wound, right in the middle of the map. A crater so vast it contained lesser craters – and a brilliant blue flag. 'The crater's called – Stickney?'

Gershon smiled. 'That was the birth name of the wife of Asaph Hall, the discoverer. Kind of an ambiguous gift, though. Stickney is a mere nine kilometres across. It would be lost on the Moon, or even Earth. But, you can see on the map, the crater spans something like one seventh of the circumference of Phobos. It's as if Earth had a crater over five *thousand* kilometres across. A crater wider than North America.'

Deirdra opened her mouth, and closed it. 'That's amazing.'

'It must have been an impact so violent that it nearly smashed Phobos to pieces altogether. Not that that's such a challenge on a moon that's just rubble in the first place . . .' Malenfant pointed at the blue flag. 'And now Stickney is the most important site on Phobos, and not just because of the world-shattering violence of its creation. Because of what that little blue flag signifies.'

Gershon said, 'Over the years – hell, the centuries – we sent a number of probes to Phobos. Just small scientific samplers, landers, orbiters. Never a crewed mission, there never seemed the need – once it was decided to preserve Phobos for science anyhow, rather than mine it for water and stuff. Most are just junk now. But one survives – it landed in Stickney, and it's marked by that blue token on the map, Deirdra. Called Mini-Sat 5. The probe has just sat there for centuries, powered by sunlight and a micro fusion plant – *that* feeds off Phobos resources, but just a trickle – and it's just as well it did survive . . .' He glanced at Malenfant.

Deirdra grinned. 'Because that's how we got the news about Emma?'

'You got it,' Malenfant said. 'The probe picked up a faint signal, just regular radio, and relayed it to Earth. A signal coming from close to the probe itself.'

'Maybe they used it as a landing beacon.'

'That would make sense.'

'And now, here we are. Almost close enough to touch. Almost . . .'

Patience, Malenfant. He felt as eager as Deirdra sounded. But he had been a pilot long enough to know that the way to fail to reach any challenging goal, indeed the way to get yourself and your companions killed in the process, was to go rushing in

STEPHEN BAXTER

without proper observation and preparation.

So they continued to observe, and to prepare the ship for its final approach.

And, in his head, Malenfant prepared himself.

At last there was a soft chime.

304

42

Gershon said, 'That's the acquisition radar. We're close now.' He made his way back to his control station. 'Malenfant, you want to come up here? Deirdra, Bartholomew, take your couches. Orbit circularisation burns coming up. And then we will go into the final approach and landing sequence.'

Deirdra, her movements in zero G confident and competent now, swept across the cabin to her couch, strapped herself in. Bartholomew, silent, inscrutable, was already seated.

The engines started to fire, with short, jolting bursts, and the ship swivelled and rocked in response.

Malenfant checked his screens. The ship had swum through that adjusted ellipse of an initial orbit, to the point where it grazed the more circular path of Phobos – the moon itself now loomed large beyond the windows. But the ship was moving too rapidly: right place, wrong speed. Now the *Step* had to lose a lot of kinetic energy. And, more subtly, the ship had to adjust the angle of its final orbit. The *Step* had come sailing in from Earth in the plane of the Solar System – but Phobos orbited over the equator of Mars, which was tilted away from the solar plane, just like Earth's equator.

So the burn sequence was complex.

But it went perfectly. This was a good, smart ship, and

Gershon an expert pilot of it, Malenfant conceded grudgingly. The manoeuvre took half an hour or so.

When it was done the *Last Small Step* sailed smoothly alongside the battered moon.

'We're only thirty-five kilometres away,' Malenfant said. 'Right on the money.'

Deirdra, released briefly from her couch, came to see. 'It's like some huge ship,' she said.

'More like a big space station. Its gravity is feeble, even weaker than it ought to be. So this landing is going to be more like a rendezvous and docking with a station than a touchdown on the Moon, say.'

Gershon glanced over at Malenfant. 'Ready for the final descent burn whenever you are.'

'Deirdra—'

She was already strapping herself back in. 'I'm ready.'

There was a kind of rattling, audible around the base of their conical module.

Gershon checked over his systems. 'That's it. We just detached from the main body, with the interplanetary engine. It will track Phobos until we are set to return, when we come back up from the surface and dock again.'

Deirdra smiled. 'Meanwhile we land. Just like Armstrong and Aldrin, in their lunar module.'

Gershon snorted. 'A more appropriate reference would be my ancestor Ralph in his Project Ares Mars Excursion Module. Same logic, yes. Four, three, two, one—'

The lander's burn was just a small kick, after the main ship's big orbital-adjustment manoeuvres. But as soon as it was done, the dark cratered hide of Phobos began, it seemed to Malenfant, to swim subtly closer.

'I assume,' Bartholomew said, 'we are going down into Stickney.'

'That's the plan,' Malenfant said. 'We're heading right into the deepest, darkest hole that ever got dug into this rubble pile.'

'Where the mystery is,' Deirdra said gleefully.

And, perhaps, Emma, Malenfant thought.

Gershon said, 'Final burn. Approaching the surface.'

Malenfant heard a series of rattling bangs from around the hull. These were verniers, smaller rockets firing in clusters, for attitude control and final adjustment of their trajectory. He imagined the view from outside, as these upper stages of the *Last Small Step*, separated from the arrow-shaft propulsion section, came down onto the Phobos ground, like an Apollo command and service module combination landing on its tail, with little squirts of attitude-rocket exhaust.

All was calm. But his own heart was clattering.

Gershon said, 'We will be over Stickney in a few more minutes. We can use Mini-Sat 5 as a landing beacon. Then we will scope out our own final landing site. OK, Malenfant, arm the harpoons.'

Bartholomew stared. 'I wish I had downloaded the mission profile. *Harpoons?*'

Malenfant grinned. 'The gravity is so low that if we go in too hard, we'll just bounce off. Hence the harpoons. Wait and see . . .'

The attitude thrusters blipped and squirted, and the craft made gentle jerks.

'Closing in,' Gershon called. 'Everything is nominal—'

Another shudder, a violent one.

Malenfant glared at Gershon. 'What the hell?'

307

Gershon stared at his screens. 'We just got shoved sideways by the attitude system. The landing radar – I thought it glitched. According to the readings, suddenly we were flying over a hole in the ground. A deep shaft.'

Malenfant frowned. 'How deep?'

'We've been taken away from it by the automatics. Descent resuming. Harpoons armed—'

'How deep, damn it?'

Gershon looked at him. 'Too deep, Malenfant.'

'What the hell does that mean?'

Gershon looked profoundly unhappy. 'Deeper than the moon is wide, Malenfant. Too deep to fit into Phobos. According to the radar reflections. That's what I mean.'

Malenfant had no idea what to make of that, what reply he could come up with.

Proximity alarms pinged softly. The ship knew it was close to the surface now. Nearly down.

Leave it for later, Malenfant.

'Descending again,' Gershon said, more calmly. 'Nice and easy . . .' Another, gentler shudder. 'Harpoons away! And – contact light. We are now tethered to the ground – testing – yes, tethered securely. Thrusters off. We are already touching Phobos, holding on to it. Now we just reel ourselves in . . .'

Malenfant peered out of the nearest window, leaning forward to see better. There was the crumpled ground below, illuminated by the spacecraft's spotlights – and he could see the harpoon tethers, thin lines of bright orange reaching down to the battered ground. The lines rippled languidly as the lander pulled itself down to the surface.

Now, as they dropped further, a horizon rose up around them, separating the dull grey ground below from a star-flecked sky above. The horizon itself, such as it was, was ragged, broken, and Malenfant realised he must be seeing the wall of Stickney, rising up around the lander.

'There,' Deirdra said, excited. 'To the left! I think that must be your space probe, Stavros, the Mini-Sat.'

Malenfant looked that way. Sure enough, there was a probe, classic architecture, an octagonal box set on spidery landing legs – he thought he saw threads that might be a miniaturised copy of the *Step*'s harpoon-and-tether system. Instruments were clustered on top of the main body, along with antennae, rods like open umbrellas and sprawling solar-energy panels. A separate pod might be a fusion pack.

Aside from a little scattered dust on the hull, the centuries-old gadget looked as if it had been manufactured yesterday. There was even a neat white number '5' stencilled on one panel. Malenfant imagined the probe beaming imagery back to Earth of this very landing . . .

A tap on his shoulder.

He turned. It was Deirdra. 'You shouldn't be out of your couch, not until we are down.'

She pointed. 'You're missing it. Look over there.'

She was right. He'd missed it. It was visible through the windows on the opposite side of the ship, and in various monitors.

Another lander on the surface.

A big one, this time. It reminded Malenfant of nothing so much as yet another derivative of the Apollo lunar lander, another box on a frame of legs, all wrapped in gold foil, and a bulbous, ungainly cabin on top. A cabin big enough for people. There were flags, fixed over the foil on the lander's lower section. Malenfant made out the Stars and Stripes, what looked like the UN flag – and a red banner with a hammer and sickle in one corner. Behind it, more reflections, like silvery snow over the Phobos ground – no, some kind of blanket, spread out, solar cells maybe.

'Nearly down,' Gershon said. 'Nice and easy. Three, two, one . . .'

Malenfant barely felt the touchdown. The silencing of the attitude thrusters had been more noticeable.

Gershon was grinning, pleased with himself, with the performance of his ship. 'Beautiful. Just beautiful. The gentlest of kisses.' He checked a couple of screens. 'And you know what else? We already have some science data. Gentle as the landing was, we made this little moon ring like a bell, and the seismometers heard the echoes. Phobos is a heap of rocks and dust. A rubble pile, all the way to the centre. Just like everybody thought. Everybody but Shklovsky . . .'

Malenfant barely heard. He was still staring out at that other craft. Only now did he notice that it seemed to be standing out of true, just off the vertical. Like it had come down hard. 'I guess they followed the probe down, as we did. But a tough landing.'

Deirdra stared at him. 'You're still missing the point, Malenfant. Look again.'

And now he saw, before the lander, a single human being, standing alone on the surface of Phobos, encased in a heavy pressure suit. Grey Phobos dirt stained the lower legs. A figure who waved a gloved hand.

Deirdra murmured, 'How fast can you get into a skinsuit?'

'Watch me.'

Inside the *Step*'s airlock, Malenfant scrambled into his pressure suit. And he fitted the 'snowshoes' over his booted feet. Hastily fabricated back on Earth, with advice from Kaliope and the Answerers, the shoes were like tennis racquets fitted to his feet.

When he was done, he opened the hatch. Stood in the open doorway, a few metres above the ground.

He faced an astounding sight.

Broken moon ground below. The long shadow of the lander cast by low, obviously diminished sunlight. Mars itself hanging fat and heavy in the sky over his head. He studied this view for maybe a dozen heartbeats.

Then he got to work. He turned cautiously, clambered down the *Step*'s short ladder, and let himself drop to the surface.

That last metre, after a journey of over four hundred million kilometres to Phobos, seemed to take an age. He watched his feet all the way down.

The snowshoes settled on the surface with a soft crunch.

When he was satisfied he wasn't actually sinking, he lifted one foot and took a step. He left behind compacted dust, a clear print. Another step.

'The snowshoes work fine,' he reported. 'I can move about freely.'

'We hear you.' Gershon's voice.

'Poetic first words on Phobos, by the way, Malenfant. History will remember the snowshoes.'

'Shut up, Bartholomew.'

Only now did he lift his head, to look through his visor, straight ahead.

The similarity of that other lander to the old Apollo LM was even more striking, up close. He saw now that its landing legs were fitted with broad pads, not unlike his own snowshoes. An obvious design choice. Everything about the bird made sense.

But this was not the Phobos lander design he remembered

from Emma's mission back in 2005. *His* Emma. For one thing they hadn't carried the solar cell blanket he could see behind the ship.

Not only that, the lander did seem to be leaning. He could see only three splayed legs of what had to be a set of four, and a corner of that lower module seemed to be resting on some heap of rubble. A bad landing, and they had come close to disaster, that was obvious. A skilful recovery, by somebody.

And there, that lone figure before the open hatch.

Malenfant took cautious steps forward. The visitor just stood there. Waiting for Malenfant, evidently watching.

'They're trying to talk to you, Malenfant,' Gershon reported. 'It's a primitive comms system but we should be able to interface to it.'

Primitive. The suit too looked antique, at least in the context of the tech of the twenty-fifth century that Malenfant was becoming accustomed to. More like a suit of his own shuttle era, or even the Apollo days, the stiff pressurised balloons the first lunar astronauts had had to walk around in. The sleeves and legs were covered in pockets. On the breast, miniature copies of those three flags, and what looked like a mission patch – hands joined, a handshake over Mars, with a rocky Phobos whizzing around it, the trajectory indicated by a curving arrow.

A gold visor, obscuring the face.

A name patch.

He had to get close to read it. *Sixty-year-old eyes, Malenfant*. The name was given twice, once in what looked like Cyrillic writing, the second in English.

STONEY, E. MSP.

Gershon whispered, 'We've set up the interface. You can talk to her, Malenfant.'

Malenfant smiled. 'Who ordered the pepperoni?'

Now she moved, stumbling towards him.

They collided like hot air balloons, and floated up into the vacuum, defying the feeble gravity of Phobos.

43

Emma, just take it easy. Relax. You're safe now.

Huh. Safe? Well, as I am still stuck on Phobos that's something of a relative term, isn't it?

Fair comment. But at least you're not alone any more.

Aren't I? All this seems like some kind of dream. Maybe I'm dying.

I can assure you you're not. My name is Bartholomew. I am—

The doctor. Right . . . To die in space, though. You hear talk around the astronaut office. Gossip that leaks over from the Russians, who seem to have had *way* more accidents than they ever publicly acknowledged. Rumours that anoxia, dying for lack of air, isn't the worst way to go. The brain kind of shuts down, and you stop being afraid, and you get a kind of euphoria, just before the end. A vision of Heaven, maybe.

Not that Arkady ever spoke of that. Not openly, anyhow. Even when we were coasting through interplanetary space, further than anyone had gone before – nobody but the three of us—

Arkady?

Arkady Berezovoy. Phobos lander pilot. Very experienced cosmonaut. You can imagine, we two got to know each other very well during our mission, along with Tom Lamb. Arkady had grown up in a military town, a place full of legends of the Great Patriotic War, he said. But he had his eyes on space, even as a kid. And his grandmother encouraged him, would you believe? He said she gave him motion-sickness training on a fairground swing. I think he was being serious. He went on to become a test pilot at the Moscow Institute of Aviation. Worked in the design office, *and* flew helicopters and jets.

During the flight, when he got the chance, he would spend hours talking to his family, back on the ground. They would joke, and sing corny old Russian folk songs. That was the Russian way, I think. He found it tough getting further and further out of touch, as we flew. The time delays, you see. And when he was working he could be dour.

Very tall, with striking blue eyes. I think he was the most serious person I ever met. I trusted him with my life.

He and Tom were like older brothers to me – I was the baby of the crew at thirty-four when we launched – thirty-five now, by the way. Thirty-six in a couple of months . . . And Arkady was my only companion, when the two of us came down to the surface in the lander. When we fell into the deepest hole in the universe . . . or something.

Look – is all this a fantasy? As I gulp my last molecules of air? Can *this* be my anoxic version of paradise? A vision of Reid Malenfant grown old? Ha! Is that the best you can dream up, Emma?

You are panicking, Emma. Really, you are safe. As safe as you can be in a spacecraft tethered to Phobos, as you say. You are not hallucinating. Take deep breaths – there is plenty of air for you, for all of us. Well, not that I need any of it. Everything you see around you, this spacecraft, is real.

Huh. For a given value of 'real', as the poindexter types in Mission Control would say. That pilot guy of yours. Gershon?

Some kind of hologram, right? When he tried to shake my hand—

Stavros apologises for that. It was a reflex – a very human gesture by a being that is, as you say, only a projected simulacrum of a human.

And you aren't real either. In a sense. That crack about not breathing was a clue, right? You're breaking it to me gently.

I am not human. My name is Bartholomew. I have a human name, and I am a simulacrum of humanity. Unlike Stavros I do have a physical presence. That is necessary to perform my duties of medical support, the mission for which I was constructed. I have been assigned to the care of Reid Malenfant since he was extracted from his coldsleep tank on the Moon.

Say what? In my time there are nothing but relics of Apollo on the Moon.

I apologise. Malenfant asked me to talk to you first, to give you an easier transition. Here I am carelessly bombarding you with too much context-free information.

I'll say. Coldsleep? What's that, some kind of suspended animation?

The key point—

How long was he suspended for? Is that why he looks so damn old? . . . No, that makes no sense. Suspended animation ought to keep him young. Look – I've picked up some hints about this – *what date is it*, where you come from?

Emma – one step at a time. Let's go back. You have been here on Phobos eight months. As you have experienced it, that is.

About that.

Malenfant knew you as a child, of course.

Well, he was ten years older than me – but yes. Our families were close. Even if his was Episcopalian, mine Catholic. He always said he would convert if we had ever married . . .

316

He tells me you were born in April 1970.

That's correct.

And therefore, if you are now thirty-five, as you've told me—

I know where you're going. This year ought to be 2006. The year after I arrived at Phobos, right? My thirty-sixth birthday in a couple of months. But I already know something is wrong with that theory. Because we did not have giant *Space Odyssey* nuclear spacecraft like this one in *my* 2006. Let alone *Blade* Runner replicant doc-bots . . . Of course it's possible that you people are out of time, not me.

Anything is possible, it seems. We must evaluate the evidence.

So we must. But no time-hopping explains Malenfant's grey hairs.

He has no hair.

Don't get smart. You know what I mean. How did he get that much *older*?

Emma. You must be patient. All things will come clear, in time. The key point, you see, is that Malenfant was revived from his long sleep because of you. Because of the distress calls you transmitted from your lander, here on Phobos. Calls which mentioned Malenfant by name.

And so –

And so – well, here he is. Come to save you, Emma.

Hmmph. Maybe. But he hasn't got the guts to talk to me. Leaves it all to his Terminator sawbones.

That reference is a little obscure, even though for the last months I have enjoyed Malenfant's trove of elderly pop-culture gag lines. There is one question which I am sure would occur to Malenfant to ask, were he with you now. You mention relics on the Moon. Of the Apollo missions, you mean? What relics?

Footprints and flags, and discarded lander stages, other junk. Why?

You do not mention a grave. Which is what most people, I believe, first think of when they consider early human monuments on the Moon.

A grave? Whose grave? Nobody *died* up there, back then. Everybody came home safe . . . Look, what is this? I'm getting more and more confused, I admit it, oxygen deprivation or not.

I apologise again. I was indulging in curiosity, I suppose.

For a robot you have some very human flaws.

So Malenfant repeatedly reminds me. Emma – we have plenty of time. Just talk to me. Tell me your story. How you ended up here, alone on Phobos, moon of Mars.

OK. But I wasn't supposed to be alone . . .

Come on, Emma. Think of it as a debrief. Like you are back in the astronaut office in Houston with Joe Muldoon and the rest of the bubbas . . .

So my name is Emma Stoney.

I am thirty-five years old. As I told you. On 21 November 2004, I departed Earth orbit from the Bilateral Space Station, in a craft called the *Timor.* I was one of a three-person crew. Mission commander was Colonel Tom Lamb of NASA. Once he had been the youngest Apollo Moonwalker. Lander pilot was Arkady Berezovoy of the Russian space agency, as I have mentioned. And I was mission specialist – I am a NASA astronaut. Our mission was to be the first deep-space crewed mission since the last of the Apollo missions to the Moon. And we were going much further—

To Phobos. Moon of Mars.

Correct. Where we were to investigate some anomalies, not least the secular acceleration of the moon – that is, why its orbit was decaying.

We were following up Earth-based observations of Phobos

that dated back to the 1960s, and automated spaceprobe investigations that led up to the Mariner 11 mission, dedicated to Phobos, in the late 1970s. A couple of years after that the idea of a crewed mission to Phobos was first floated, I think, by Carl Sagan and others. If ever there was a conundrum that deserved a specialist on the spot, it was Phobos. That was even before the Mariner started relaying back data about anomalous radiation types emanating from the moon's interior – specifically, from what we thought were craters inside Stickney.

Radiation types?

A kind of sunlight, it seemed, and at first it was assumed to be some kind of reflection. But spectral analysis by the Mariner showed it not to be *our* kind of sunlight at all. The astrophysicists made guesses. Once, soon after it was formed, the Sun was much dimmer, you know; its output strengthens with time. And back then sunlight had a subtly different spectrum. The Faint Young Sun, they call it. This isn't my speciality, but it seems that what Mariner observed, glinting out of Phobos, was what you might have seen if you had studied the Sun from Martian orbit back around the birth of the Solar System itself. Which, needless to say, baffled everybody . . .

Tell me how you got to be the one to fly to Phobos. You were born in 1970.

Right. We established that.

So I missed Neil Armstrong on the Moon. And after Apollo was done, no Americans in space for a decade.

It was Malenfant who got me into space, you know. He was always this big gangly kid with his head full of dreams of space, and his books and posters and construction kits, and the model rockets and such he was already flying. He had absolutely no interest in a snotty little brat like me, needless to say. But he was a big presence in our lives. I guess everybody in the neighbourhood thought that he was on his way someplace special, space or otherwise. He had this charisma, you know?

I do know. He rather imported that quality into my world. But don't tell him I said so.

Well, they started flying the space shuttle in 1981. I was eleven years old, and avid, and I watched the whole thing, even though Malenfant was away by then. I had posters of Young and Crippen in their spacesuits on my bedroom wall, like they were rock stars.

Young and Crippen. What about Fred Haise?

Who? The Apollo 13 Fred Haise? What about him?

He was the booster commander on the first orbital flight of the STS. Malenfant would disconnect me if I got that wrong.

. . . Sorry. What 'booster commander'? Have we got our wires crossed? The STS, the space shuttle system, has solid rocket boosters. Crew only on the orbiter. It was always a controversial design choice, and faults in the boosters caused the *Challenger* disaster of . . . You have no idea what I'm talking about, do you?

Emma, where I come from, the shuttle system was a dual spacecraft system, both elements piloted, both fully recoverable. Malenfant became a booster pilot.

Where you come from.

I don't know how else to put it. Not yet. But for sure, you have a lot to talk over with Malenfant. Ask him about the flight of STS-719.

719? We never flew anything like that number of missions . . . Never mind. I'll talk to him.

Sorry. We should continue with the debriefing.

In which we had reached my eleventh birthday.

So I guess it was Phobos that finally crystallised my own determination to get into space. Because it was the year after the shuttle flew, you see, that President Reagan adopted a crewed NASA mission to Phobos as a national goal in space. Suddenly, after the Moon, we had somewhere to go.

And then, two years later, he set out the funding for Space Station Freedom, which would serve as a construction shack for the Phobos mission as well as delivering science goals of its own.

I was thirteen, fourteen years old, and even then I was following the debates, or trying to. But suddenly all I could see was a future full of missions into space, to Earth orbit and beyond. And I was fascinated by the Phobos mystery too. I wanted a part of it.

Well, Malenfant was ahead of me, of course – he had gone through college with an Air Force scholarship, had amassed a lot of flying experience, and by the late 80s he had his eye on the test-pilot schools. A classic *Right Stuff* career trajectory. And he encouraged me, by the time I was aged eighteen or so, to follow his footsteps, advised me to get some flying experience.

But, you know what? I applied to the Air Force Academy, but washed out immediately. Asthma. Didn't even know I *had* asthma. No way was I ever going to be a pilot for the Air Force, let alone a spaceship pilot.

But it wasn't only pilots who flew into space.

Once I'd finished cursing my luck, I figured that out, yeah. I had other strengths. I was a kind of all-rounder, academically. Maths was my first love. In fact my mother always hoped I would go into accountancy. So now I focused on science subjects at college. And languages.

Languages?

Russian, specifically. Well, I guess I was foresighted, for a kid. I followed the wrangles that developed as NASA and the space industry tried to turn Reagan's visions into reality. And I

321

was starting to get inside tracks on the gossip, even then, partly thanks to Malenfant.

You see, it quickly emerged that to mount a mission to Phobos, you were going to need to send up to orbit a *lot* of heavy components, not least a significant fuel load. Even the early estimates came in at a thousand tonnes or more, in low Earth orbit. Whereas a shuttle launch could carry only *thirty* tonnes of cargo to orbit, and even that had to be in chunks small enough to fit inside the payload bay. We needed heavy-lift capacity, and America had had none since the Saturn V lunar-rocket production line was shut down after Apollo.

They shut down the Saturn V? . . . Sorry. You have a lot *to talk to Malenfant about. Go on.*

So I knew that the Russians were developing a new heavy-lift launcher of their own. The Energia, it was called in the end. A derivative of their own failed lunar-launch booster. It finally flew in 1987, with a cargo capacity to LEO – low Earth orbit – of two hundred and twenty tonnes.

Oh. So as little as five, six launches could have sent up a thousand tonnes.

It took more than that, in the end. But yes, a feasible number. Certainly more so than thirty or forty shuttle launches . . . And I was aware too that the Russians were planning their own probes to Phobos. The whole thing was developing into another Moon race. I foresaw, you see, that someday the Americans and Russians might decide that the best way to get to Phobos was to team up, American smart technology, Russian heavy-lift capability.

So it came to pass. The fall of the Berlin Wall came at just the right time for me. The way it turned out, 1992, Presidents Bush and Yeltsin agreed to cooperate in space, with the Russian launchers helping build America's space station – which would eventually merge with the Russian Mir to become the Bilateral Space Station – and then the two nations would work together on the Phobos mission itself, the ultimate goal. The politics was obvious. American money kept the post-Soviet space programme afloat, so Russian space specialists wouldn't be lured away to work on missile development for antagonistic nations. A win-win all round – and for me especially.

Because you had seen this coming.

Sure. After college I had the sciences I needed, especially astrophysics, geology, planetology – everything I could think of that might be essential for a crew at Phobos, or even just useful. And, crucially, I had Russian. I even went over there on summer schools. And it worked out.

In 1994 the first US astronauts started going over to Russia, for joint training.

And in 1995 I tried the NASA application process.

I remember that period so well. If you talk to the astronauts, everyone goes through the same experience. Everybody stays at the Kings Inn hotel next to JSC. In the evenings everybody drinks at the Outpost, just outside the Center gates – trying not to stare at the astronauts, but I soon learned they go there to be stared at. We were in a group of twenty of us ASHOs – that's astronaut hopefuls – and we were all as competitive as hell. But we knew that we had to come over as team players, and we were all competitive about *that* as well. I remember this barrage of a panel interview, and it was led by Joe Muldoon himself, and it wrung me out.

How about your asthma? Wasn't that a barrier?

That's a medic's question. The doctors told me I would have passed at NASA even as a pilot candidate in that regard. NASA has different medical standards from the Air Force. Ironic, huh?

So then I had to wait a couple of months as their ponderous

decision-making went through its process. And then, I'll always remember, I got a call from Joe Muldoon. 'Would you like to come fly with us?'

It must have been a thrill.

Oh, yes. So I joined their latest astronaut class, and even as an ascan—

Ascan?

Candidate astronaut. What you are until you fly in space. Even from the start, I was always in line for the Phobos mission. I was better equipped in Russian and the relevant sciences than most of the veterans. I actually trained some of them on the geology. Of course I needed a champion or two among the bubbas.

The bubbas?

The senior astronauts. The top dogs, who have an in with the chief of the astronaut office, and the JSC director. *That's* the way you get into the crew rotation. But I always got along with Tom Lamb, who had boned up on the science of the Moon in order to get a ride on Apollo, which was not dissimilar to my strategy. And it worked. I don't mean to sound smug. Here I am – I came all the way to Phobos, with Tom Lamb alongside me.

You have a right to be smug. How did Malenfant feel?

What do you mean?

Well, there he was in the astronaut office, and I guess you were kind of leapfrogging him to get to the most glamorous mission since Apollo . . .

Oh. No, there's another piece of the puzzle that doesn't fit here. Malenfant and me. He wasn't at NASA at all.

Look – in my memories, Malenfant and I became an item around 1990. When I was twenty, and I hadn't made it into the Air Force Academy, and Malenfant was on his own track, still test-flying. Building up that portfolio, on his way to NASA.

You can imagine we spent a lot of time apart, in those years. Why, I hadn't anticipated how much my geology field trips would take me far from home, let alone my language-practice trips to Russia. And Malenfant had his own commitments, of course. And then—

Yes?

So Malenfant had a couple more tries at the astronaut draft, in the early nineties. Washed out each time. And the second time he thought the stumbling block was about contacts he had made in the private space-development industry. He said he was trying to look beyond the station, beyond Phobos even. Where would we go after that? He thought the industrial development of space was the way to go. Which was *not* the kind of message the NASA interview panels wanted to hear, since it sounded like a direct threat to the future of NASA itself, and a lot of careers and aspirations – and you would not want a NASA insider, equipped with inside knowledge, supporting such ventures.

His application failed.

It failed. He failed.

So he kind of regrouped, went back to the Air Force, and started thinking about how he might reposition to become more acceptable to NASA while nurturing his own long-term goals. But before he got to that point—

Ah. Before he applied again, you were accepted.

It just put us under too much of a strain. I wouldn't say he thought it was a betrayal by me, who used to be the little kid following him around, to have got in before he did. In fact I sometimes felt it was a betrayal of *me* that he didn't try again. It wasn't that he didn't support me. It just pulled us apart in ways we hadn't expected.

So you never married. No kids.

No, no. We were engaged, broke it off. We did have vague plans for the future. Even after Phobos I would only have been mid-thirties, Malenfant mid-forties. Plenty of time, even for kids. But it wasn't to be.

I think we still loved each other, that's the crazy thing. Even as he went off to California to found Bootstrap, Inc., and I left for Phobos. I always knew he'd be there for me in a real crisis, you know? As I would for him. There was never another Malenfant.

Which is why you called his name, all the way from Phobos. Tell me how you got there.

Sure. The ride of my life!

Well, we flew up to the station on the shuttle. We were novices on STS, Arkady and I, even though Arkady had flown Soyuz before. Tom Lamb guided us through it all.

My family came to the launch. They stayed at the Days Inn on Cocoa Beach, and came over to peer at me through the glass of the quarantine quarters. My mother brought the local priest! He blessed me, and I was given rosary beads to carry into space. I have them in my pressure-suit pocket.

And Malenfant—

Oh, he came. Still just Malenfant, with that bald pate burned to mahogany by the California sun – by then Bootstrap were flying experimental rockets out of a strip in the Mojave. He looked great, actually. Look, he was thrilled to see me fly; whatever the tension between us, we were always happy for each other when we achieved success. Does that make any sense?

Engaging human psychology module.

Don't joke about it. So, the morning of the launch came. We had a ten-minute ride to pad 39-B, where they had launched the

Apollos from. I remember how the shuttle itself was wreathed in vapour, as we rode up the gantry . . . Gee, I'll have to talk to Malenfant about this piloted-booster variant he claims to have flown.

And then aboard the orbiter, and the launch.

So, look. I kind of assume you know nothing of our Phobos mission strategy.

It was called a split-sprint design. We were taken aboard the BSS, where we were loaded into the assembled crew modules, and then, on 21 November, 2004, we were kicked out of Earth orbit by our transfer vehicle and sent on our way to Mars. We would get to Mars on 3 June, 2005, where we would aerobrake into orbit – that is, we would dip into the Martian atmosphere to slow down. The plan was that we would set off back to Earth on 1 September, and get back to Earth in January – so we would have had little more than a year in deep space, with all its attendant hazards, known and unknown. That's the 'sprint' part.

And when we got to Mars, we would find our cargo spacecraft, which contained such essentials as our Phobos explorer-lander and our fuel to get home, already waiting for us. Before we launched, it had taken years to assemble the components of our mission in orbit – all those Energia and shuttle launches – and then it was sent to Mars in two separate bundles. The cargo spacecraft was sent first, launched 9 June 2003, and got to Mars on 29 December the same year. So we weren't committed to fly in the second bundle until we were sure that first bundle was safely in place. That's the 'split' part of the strategy, you see . . .

So, sprint or not, you still spent seven months in deep space before Mars.

We lived in derivatives of space-station modules, with some

robust Russian tech integrated — those Salyuts and Mirs of theirs. Four modules, joined end to end in a square; we called it a 'race track' design. At the centre of the square was our Earth return vehicle, a tough little craft that would also have served as a storm shelter in case of solar flares. Add to that an aerobrake shield for our arrival at Mars, and a booster pack with enough fuel left to have swung us around Mars and take us straight back home, if anything had gone wrong.

We were comfortable enough — in fact, compared to the station, we three had masses of room.

I remember the first days. My own first days in space, of course. There's nothing like the smell of a new ship.

I was the only true rookie, and the guys showed me the ropes. Working in space is about a bunch of tricks that you learn, and adapt. For instance, you don't just open a bag of gear, as I did in my first half-hour as we unpacked, because stuff just floats out everywhere. Holding the bag, you turn around, just slowly, so a bit of centrifugal force keeps everything in the bag until you are ready for it. And when you do take stuff out you make damn sure it has a Velcro spot, or else you stick it to a loop of duct tape, gummy side out, and lodge it somewhere. *Everything* floats away and is lost otherwise. But even after a few days, when you have everything stuck to the walls, you can make one false move and knock it all off, and it's like a blizzard of bits of paper, pens, drink holders, tools . . .

I hated the cleaning — you get all sorts of garbage: dust, lint, hair clippings, food scraps, old Band-Aids, all gathering in the air grilles and you have to clean them out. And swab down the walls to get rid of mould. Human bodies are pretty disgusting when they are confined. Ironically, I quite enjoyed working on our urine-processing plant. It was basically a still, designed to retrieve potable water from the waste. Like something out of the nineteenth century, a real gadget . . . And there was stuff I loved. Such as tending our little row of pea plants, under their LED lights. I guess you know some of this. It must have taken even you – what, weeks? To get to Mars.

More like days.

Days. As you said, we have a lot to discuss. But anyway, as that big old peach of a planet swam out of the dark, well, everything else just melted away.

All right. And now you are stranded here, on Phobos. Tell me how that happened.

I . . . feel like I need a full debrief. The technical side—

Just give me a summary. I think that will help – help you, I mean. Trust me, I'm a doctor.

Ha! No, you're not.

OK.

Look, it was always a complex operation.

So we reached Mars, docked with our cargo ship, checked our Earth-return systems were functional – and *then* we thought about approaching Phobos.

I think our strategy was similar to yours, from what I observed from the ground as you came in. It took a few orbits around Mars to put the *Timor* stack into a close co-orbit of Phobos, a couple of kilometres off for safety. And then Arkady and I powered up the lander, and closed up our suits. Funny – donning the suit is another thing I remember very vividly – the hum of the fans, a faint chemical smell from the anti-fog treatments on the visor, the guys' voices in my earpieces, my own voice amplified and distorted in that glass bowl of a helmet . . . Well.

We separated from Tom, in the main stack.

I didn't know then I was never going to see the man again.

Arkady was a great pilot, and he took that lander straight in, it was just like the sims in Houston and Star City. The two of us, standing there side by side, peering out of those downward-pointing windows. Big spotlights casting a glow on the ground. Heading straight for the heart of Stickney.

Oh. Where you found the shaft. As we did.

Yeah. The shaft that's way too deep? Malenfant told me. More stuff we need to talk about. None of this had shown up on the visuals taken by automatic probes that had gone before us, or even in our own preliminary scans. It was just *there*. Suddenly the ground was just disappearing from under us, visually and in the landing radar. I guess you pulled out in time? *We* had no time to react, it felt like.

We're in a smarter ship. Centuries of development, remember. The automatics saved us, spotted the anomaly in town.

Well, all we had was our mark-one eyeballs, as Tom Lamb used to say, and not much else. We reacted too slowly, in retrospect. We actually dipped down, into the shaft itself. Not far. Just a few metres, I guess. I could see a wall before my face, like crudely packed rubble, very dark in our lights — which were pointing downwards anyhow, not sideways, which didn't help, but falling down a hole was *not* in our mission design — and Arkady was improvising, blipping the thrusters to get us out of there. And then—

Yes?

There was a blue flash. It was like a glow, all around us. I couldn't see well, but I got the impression there was a brilliant ring, somewhere beneath us, that had lit up, all at once . . .

Just report, Emma. Don't be self-conscious.

Yeah. Not like I need to fear flunking out of the next crew rotation, right? Well, at the moment of that flash from below we lost Tom.

Tom Lamb? In the main ship?

His signal cut, just like that. Then we got various alarms, as uploads of our telemetry back to the ship failed in turn.

A blue ring, inside Phobos.

If *that* is the Phobos anomaly we had come to study – well, it nearly killed us.

Because all the while we were panicking over the loss of signal, we were still in this hole. We were drifting sideways, our residual velocity taking us towards the wall. Arkady did his best. A great best. He saved the ship. But—

But you clipped the shaft wall?

Clipped the rim, yes, on the way up and out. We came so close to making it . . .

One landing leg was caught, and ripped clean off. Our engine bell hit too, was dented maybe. The drive started to sputter and flare, and we were tipping.

Arkady got us down in one piece. He kind of lodged the stump of that broken landing leg on a rock heap, so we didn't topple, at least. It was a brilliant piece of piloting, but once we were down he dismissed that. The gravity was so low it was very gradual, easy, he said – well, maybe. I say brilliant, even so.

So you had landed. What then?

Well, we followed our checklists. We checked the integrity of our cabin, our life support, other systems. Everything was fine, save we had lost that lander leg, and were tipped out of true. We couldn't take off like that – and besides, Arkady wanted to check out that engine bell first.

Did you regain communications with Lamb?

No. And not with Earth, either. We were on our own, it seemed. We didn't know what the hell was going on.

You see, even with just the lander's systems we could detect messages from Earth – well, for the lander to have an independent comms capability had been part of the design strategy, one of our backup options. But we couldn't make out anything of the signals we were getting from Earth, strong as they were.

So we started sending out wideband signals. Cries for help, basically, to anyone who would listen. And, yes, eventually I called for Malenfant. Why not? I always had this hunch . . .

Your hunch was a good one. The Mini-Sat lander relayed your messages to Earth. Malenfant had to be woken up. But he came for you, didn't he?

He came for me. At last.

While you waited.

While we waited, and survived. Look, I won't give you an hour by hour breakdown. Or even day by day. As that radio silence went on. You can imagine.

The two of us secured our life support. We had supplies, dried stuff, to last us months, if stretched. That's the Russians for you; always prepare for the worst. We had a solar cell blanket we stretched out over the rocks, to keep our batteries topped up.

I believe we saw that.

We even did some science. Grabbed surface samples from inside the lander through a glove-box arrangement.

But we were still out of contact with Earth, and Tom.

Days went by.

Weeks.

So, in the end, we decided we ought to at least try to get off Phobos. We wouldn't get too far without the main ship, any more than Armstrong and Aldrin could have flown home from the Moon in their lunar lander. But we thought . . . hell, I don't know what we thought. Maybe we would get better comms, away from whatever oddities were inside Phobos. Maybe we would even become visible from Earth, telescopically. We just wanted to *do* something.

I understand.

We had to retrieve the damn landing leg from the shaft. If we could do that, maybe we could hoist the lander body — you know there's no significant weight here — and fix the leg, somehow. Maybe with duct tape. I'm serious! It sounds hokey but it could have worked. And then we would have access to the engine bell . . .

But it went wrong.

Arkady went out alone, to fetch that pesky landing leg. I waited in the open cabin. I saw him walk to the lip of the shaft. He was tethered, with a rope back to the lander. He made his way to the place we had hit. I saw him bend, stiffly. Take another step. Descended into the pit, on his tether. He was gone a while, and I'm not sure how deep he went. We were out of line of sight, of course, but he dragged down a wire that gave us some scratchy comms. I think he said he was coming close to some kind of structure down there, a blue hoop, maybe more than one this time. Like we saw before.

Then — blue flash. Shining on the rim of the pit. And on some loose dust, just grains, floating in that low gravity where Arkady had disturbed the ground.

I never saw him again.

Umm. And it was like the blue flash you saw on landing.

Yeah. As we had dipped into the shaft in the lander. I wonder now if some chunk of debris broke away, fell into the hole, touched a hoop. A blue flash, at the moment we lost contact with Tom. And now, the same again.

You think touching the hoops, or allowing any of our stuff to touch them — changes things.

That's a leap for me. Changes what? At the time I didn't know what this was. Some kind of weapon, a trap? That took out our lander, and then Arkady? But, maybe, yeah. Blue flash – Tom and the orbiter were gone. Blue flash – Arkady gone, and, later, you show up. Like moving between different – categories. I don't know. I guess it's possible. I can only tell you what I observed.

I know. Go on. So – you lost Arkady . . . you were alone.

Emma? Are you OK?

Yeah. Just – remembering.

So.

I kept calling.

After a time I hauled back the tether. It looked as if it had been burned through. I did figure, yeah, he might have brushed one of those blue hoops. Or even touched it deliberately. Innocent enough thing to try, I guess.

Of course I went out to look for him. Went to the edge of the shaft lying on my belly. I could see his footsteps, what looked like a scuff, a slip. That's all. I guess he just fell down that damn shaft. I have no idea where he is now.

Oh, and no sign of the landing strut.

Or any blue hoops down there, come to that.

So, after that, I got back to the cabin, and sealed it up, and started another cycle of attempts at comms, and began to plan how to manage my supplies. We had enough to sustain a couple of cosmonauts on the surface for weeks. Now, alone, I could stretch it out further. I did my best. But I was alone. I didn't know how long I would be down there. And I was in silence – you understand? Arkady and Tom gone, Earth incomprehensible. I . . . sorry.

Take your time. Delicate question. Did you consider your options if—

Suicide is a sin for a Catholic. I regard myself as lapsed, but why take a chance? Anyhow I had faith that somebody would come. Even Tom Lamb, maybe, from around the horizon of Phobos.

Or Malenfant.

Oh, come on. How corny would that have been?

I think we're done. Look, take a break. We have sleep cubicles. You won't be disturbed. And then, when you're ready—

I'm wide awake. Let me talk to Malenfant.

44

To talk, they went over to the *Timor* lander.

It was Gershon who gave them the excuse. 'If that broken baby bird was my ship I would want to go close it out properly. Take out any personal effects. Secure it in case some future generation comes to retrieve it. That kind of thing. I mean, it is the nearest thing to a monument your buddy Arkady is going to have on this moon, isn't it?'

'And also, perhaps,' Bartholomew said gently, 'an artefact that is unique in this – universe.'

Emma said in a small voice, 'Arkady did have some stuff in there. Family pictures. Thanks, Stavros, I should have thought of that myself.'

Deirdra smiled. '*And* if you make sure the comms system is switched off you'll get some privacy.'

Bartholomew was more circumspect. 'OK. But you will set up a voice-activated override command. And you *will* allow your medical monitors to keep functioning. You too, Emma.'

Emma frowned at that. 'What do you mean – cuffs and bracelets, electrodes stuck to my chest?'

He smiled. 'Nothing so crude. A smart bangle, yes. And a pill to swallow.'

Emma shrugged. 'Given what I've already gone through, being bugged by an android doc hardly makes the weirdness needle flicker on the dial. Come on, Malenfant, let's get out of here . . .'

Malenfant quickly discovered that Emma's Phobos lander was as similar to the old Apollo Lunar Module inside as it had looked from the outside. A tight, cramped little cabin, with a big low-down hatch you crawled through for access to the surface. The same layout of pilot and co-pilot positions, left and right, where you would stand before downward-facing windows: no need to clutter up the space with seats, as you would never be subject to any significant gravity pull, or indeed any gruelling accelerations, as the tiny, fragile craft made its way down to the destination surface, and back up again to space.

The air was a little cold, and smelled a little stale, but it was warming fast. It was almost cosy in here – and an environment, cluttered with instruments and gadgets and life-support equipment, that both of them, twenty-first-century astronauts, were used to, comfortable with. Emma, who it turned out had had a hand in the final design details of her craft, delighted in showing Malenfant around the more homely features. Here were the hooks where you could suspend two hammocks, one above the other. There was even a tiny galley area where you could warm up pre-prepared food and drink. Emma showed Malenfant how to make coffee, with freeze-dried granules and hot water from a spigot.

Malenfant was overwhelmed at how she had survived in here, alone on a Martian moon, out of touch with humanity. For *months*. He felt a deep, savage relief that she had called for him, and he had been able to respond.

'Of course, Tom and I did all the food preparation,' she said with a smile, as she handed Malenfant the coffee. 'Russia is still a very patriarchal society – or was, back in 2004. The 2004 where I came from anyhow . . . Whatever. And even though this lander was basically an American design, no Russian male would have been piloted by a mere female. In this case, however, Arkady was the trained pilot, and I wasn't. Though I had been trained to fly the ascent stage in an emergency.'

'I guess, if not for the spookiness, you would have had to do that anyhow – you would have gone through what poor Buzz Aldrin did, during the Apollo 11 flight. If you had stayed in your own, umm, timeline.'

She frowned. 'Buzz Aldrin?'

'After Armstrong died on the Moon.'

'Neil Armstrong?'

'No, Louis Armstrong.'

She said firmly, 'Bartholomew said something about this. Armstrong did *not* die on the Moon, Malenfant. He and Aldrin landed successfully, made their single EVA, picked up some rocks, saluted the flag, and came home.'

'So what happened then?'

She thought it over. 'I guess they were the most famous people in the world, for a while, Armstrong, Aldrin, Collins. They toured the planet. None of them flew in space again. Armstrong became an academic, I think. Somewhat reclusive. Always dignified.'

Malenfant held her gaze. 'Look – that's not how I remember it. Armstrong had a heart attack, in the last few seconds of the landing, the most tense moments. Aldrin managed to complete the landing. His first words on the ground became famous. "Houston, Tranquillity Base here. We have a medical emergency."'

She just stared.

Malenfant rummaged in his memory. 'I remember the public feed was immediately shut down. Later, when I got into NASA myself, I learned more of the details. Aldrin went through hell in the first minutes, trying to get Armstrong out of his pressure suit to administer CPR. It was too late, of course.

'The programme of EVAs was cancelled. But Aldrin did walk out onto the lunar surface, taking his buddy with him. His first lines on the lunar surface were famous too. "I can only relay the words Neil had rehearsed for this moment. That's one small step for a man . . ." Aldrin buried his buddy under a cairn of Moon rocks. And he set up the flag. Photographed the whole set-up. Took a couple of rock samples. Came home.

'The President gave an effective speech. "Fate has ordained that a man who went to the Moon to explore in peace will stay on the Moon to rest in peace." I think that was it. I'm finding I never paid as much attention to the history as I should have, even of the space programme. Always focused on the future, I guess. I know that Nixon was very moved by the death. Well, everybody was. He became a champion of the space programme, especially post-Apollo. And I think some people believe he became more – human, after that. So he pushed for reforms that seem to have borne fruit, centuries later. You'd be surprised. *He* would have been surprised. In this age, nobody works for a living, Emma.'

She smiled. 'Come on.'

'You'll see, when we get you back to Earth. And talk to Deirdra. It seems to work . . . Anyhow, they seem to give Nixon the credit for all of that.'

She shook her head. 'Armstrong didn't die on the Moon. And Nixon was brought down by Watergate.'

That word was entirely unfamiliar to Malenfant. He shrugged. 'Anyhow, Nixon backing the space programme is how come I got to fly a space shuttle booster stage, I guess.'

And how come *she* got to fly to Phobos. My Emma. *Emma I.* He didn't add that.

Emma — Emma II - stared at him. 'We remember different things. We lived different lives. And here we are talking about it. It's incredible.'

'Different since 1969 or so, yeah. Look, Emma, I've had more time to get used to this, since I first heard your message. We are from different alternate realities. Like a book you loaned me once.' And which he had, he remembered, already discussed with an unreal avatar of Emma herself.

'I remember. Philip K. Dick. The Axis won the war.' She nodded. 'OK. And somehow it all gets tangled up here, on Phobos. But that's not the only puzzle, is it?' Hesitantly she touched his stubbly cheek, his scalp. 'You got a real frosting there, buddy.'

'I know. Because we don't just come from different histories—'

'We come from different — times. For me it's 2006. Whereas you lived on to the age of sixty, nearly, and *then* got frozen for centuries, to *now* . . .'

'Yeah. When I'm with you like this I keep forgetting. For you it's 2006. For me it's still 2019, kind of. In my heart. But for Deirdra and the rest, it's 2469.'

She nodded. 'So it's like time slips a gear inside Phobos too.'
'Something like that.'
'What does it all mean, Malenfant?'
'Damned if I know. All we can do is talk it out.' He hesitated. 'Listen. There's something I haven't told you. Back where I came from. *She* went to Phobos too.'

340

'She?'

'The other Emma. The one in my timeline. *You.*'

'But not me.'

'Except she didn't get launched on some crummy Russian rocket booster. And she wasn't the first to Mars, by the way.'

'Go on.'

He sighed. 'Look – *we* first reached Mars in 1986. Project Ares. It was all based on Apollo-Saturn technology, or a stretch of it . . . Ask Gershon. Ancestor of his was on the first mission. After that we maintained a small base on Mars – and I mean small, just a handful of people. Mangala Station. By the time it was decided to run a Phobos mission, after the orbital anomalies were observed— you talked about this elaborate system of Russian boosters and sending out fuel tankers first—'

'Go on.'

'Here, Emma rode a stack tipped by a Saturn-N. A nuclear-fission powered upper stage for the Saturn V. Should have brought her home again afterwards. She actually flew out in the same launch window as you. She should have got there in June 2005.'

'Should have?'

She was staring at his face. He had no idea what emotion he was showing now. What was he *supposed* to feel?

'Tell me,' she urged.

'The damn nuke stage failed. Those things were always unreliable.'

'I was . . . killed?'

He shrugged. 'She didn't reach Mars. Actually the deceleration phase mostly went through OK. She ended up in the correct encounter orbit. But—'

'But it was a ship of corpses.'

He glanced out of the windows. 'I don't know what became of it, actually. It's been five centuries. I can't believe it was ever retrieved, brought back to Earth.'

'Radioactive.'

'Right. Probably pushed away into deep space. Bartholomew might know. The Answerers certainly will.'

'The Answerers? . . . Never mind.'

She turned away from him, in the cramped cabin, as if she wanted to pace, but she floated up from the aluminium floor, the feeble gravity helpless to hold her down. Not an environment where you could make extravagant gestures. Instead she grabbed a couple of rails, and began to pull herself up and down, the strength of her arms opposing that of her legs, evidently a training routine.

'I believe you, by the way,' Malenfant said.

'What about?'

'When you talk about your past, your mission to Phobos. Even if it's not the mission I remember. Not the past I remember.'

'Hmph. So you should. I mean, here's the *evidence* − the lander . . . And a thirty-five-year-old version of me. More to the point, I believe *you*. On a lot less evidence, I have to say.' She seemed to be struggling for the words. 'We are both telling the truth as we remember it. It's just, like you said, that we seem to come from two different . . . truths.'

'So I come from a reality where Neil Armstrong died on the Moon. You come from a reality where he didn't. And you lived through all the consequences that flowed from that.'

She frowned. 'That's politics for you. An astronaut is more honoured lying dead on the Moon than if he had survived.' She stopped flexing, and faced him. 'But there's more to this than the politics of the space programme.'

'You mean us.'

342

'Damn right I mean us. I mean *me*. Me, and all the other Emmas out in . . .'

'Out in the manifold.'

'The what?'

'It's a maths term. I think. My dad used to refer to it, when he teased me about being a spooky kid. Like I was from a different universe. The set of all possible realities. Maybe we could call it that. We are all refugees across the manifold.'

'Whatever. So, after Phobos, you lived on, until your own crash in—'

'2019.'

'Right. You nearly died, aged fifty-nine. But no, you were saved; you were preserved, in some experimental cryogenics tank.'

He had to smile. 'For centuries I was a near-corpse on the Moon. I always admired Neil Armstrong, but I never wanted to end up as a tribute act.'

'And eventually you were defrosted. After more than four hundred years.'

'Because they picked up your call, from Phobos. Don't forget that.'

'So, you see, Malenfant, you at least are *reasonable*. Your story, I mean. It's reasonable you should be here, now, sixty years old, physically, even after four centuries. Right?' She made chopping motions in the air with her right hand, in a row, as if slicing a carrot. 'There is a chain of consequences that has delivered you now, a man born in 1960, at physical age sixty, to this year 2469. This impossible, ridiculous year. It is *logical*. Even scientific. I can understand all that. Whereas I . . .' She sighed. 'I was born in 1970, and I feel like I'm thirty-five, even though *I* never got frozen for four hundred years. Your doctor has confirmed that, by the way.'

343

'What? That you're physical thirty-five? He never told me.'

'There are subtle markers – cell degradation and stuff – heck, he could have just cut my head off to count the tree rings. And there was independent evidence, for instance from this lander's systems. The logs show a continuous record. Even the lander's fabric, if you test it for cosmic-ray damage and such, is consistent with it having been launched from Earth orbit just a few years ago. Not centuries.' She smiled at him tiredly. 'I don't blame him for checking. Neither Bartholomew nor I could come up with a way I could have faked all this, Malenfant. Or that it could have been faked. I left Earth aged thirty-four, and I'm thirty-five now. By any measurement you care to make.' She smiled, looking tired. 'I guess I took a short-cut.'

'A short-cut?'

'You may be right that we come from different alternate realities, Malenfant. Two strands in some higher-order manifold of possible universes. If so, the strands don't seem to run in neat parallel lines, like lanes on a highway, do they? They must – touch – in a more complicated way. Here, in Phobos. And maybe other places like it.'

He shook his head, trying to clear his thoughts. 'This is all getting a little abstract, Emma. We should be talking about us, not the manifold.

'Look. I have a confession to make.'

'You do?'

'A very personal one. Suppose I told you this isn't the first time I spoke to you. I mean, since I came out of coldsleep. Not the first time in this age, this twenty-fifth century.'

She stayed very still, staring at him.

'You may want another coffee.'

'What do you mean,' she said, 'not the first time? It's the first I remember.'

'Yeah. Well, it would be.'

And he told her the whole story, of his visit to the Answerers, and the Pylons, and the Codex revenants he had encountered there. And of his struggle to find a living descendant to donate a genetic sample to create a Retrieved copy of Emma herself.

He told her about climbing the Pylon. He smiled. 'I had to make a real ass of myself to get noticed. Or a hero.'

'Malenfant . . .'

'Speaking to that – image – was a comfort. I can see why people do it, I guess. But it wasn't enough. Not for me. Not even for her, in the end. You, she, knew her limitations. But it worked.'

'Malenfant! Shut up. Go back. *You looked for your descendants.* Our descendants. This can't be right. We can't have any living descendants, in this age. Because you and I never had kids. We never married. Oh . . .' She closed her eyes, pinched the bridge of her nose. '*Damn* it. I can't think this way. *We* didn't marry, where I came from. But where you came from—'

He nodded sadly. 'Where I came from, in the version of history that led to all *this*, we did marry, Emma. And we had a kid. Born nine years before you left for Phobos.'

She just stood there. Eyes closed. 'A daughter?'

'A son. Born 1995. Michael. His name was Michael.'

'And you didn't think to tell me. As soon as you found me, as soon as you got me into that fancy ship of yours. You didn't think to tell me straight away that we had a *son* . . .'

'I – am sorry. No, I didn't think.'

'Did you think I would *care* about anything else? Would you have? Would you?'

345

Now the dam broke, the tears came. She fell on him, thumping his chest with hard, clenched fists. He was holding her to him before he realised that he was crying too.

Then they made more coffee.

45

They drank the coffee. They shared a couple of rock-hard Russian biscuits.

Then they snuggled, on a blanket laid over a bare aluminium floor that felt soft as a feather-bed to Malenfant, such was the forgiving nature of Phobos's half-per-cent gravity.

And Malenfant told Emma all he could remember of Michael.

From his birth, through his boyhood, his scrapes and successes at school and college. His first girlfriend at age thirteen. His ambitions. The great sundering of his young life when Emma — *that* Emma, his mother — had lost her life at Phobos. The start he had already been making in the burgeoning coal industry. A story that for Malenfant was cut short when Michael was aged twenty-four, and the *Constitution* crash had catapulted Malenfant across four centuries.

Emma calmed. She laughed, cried, whispered questions.

When they ran down, she asked, 'So you say you brought me back, as some kind of reconstructed revenant. Couldn't you do the same for Michael? You have the genetic data. I mean, his descendants are our descendants.'

'Sure. That was going to be next.' He smiled, thinking back over half-baked resolutions made during those lonely hours in his room in Birmingham. 'I wanted to . . . keep him for later.

Does that sound callous? I was looking at a long life stuck in a time that wasn't my own. I guess, at one point, before I got the chance to come out here, finding Michael again was all I could think of that was worthwhile for me to try to do.'

'I can understand that,' she said slowly. 'Maybe, when this is all over – whatever *this* is – we can go back, meet Michael together.'

'I'd like that. But – look, how are we going to deal with this, Emma? What does it *mean* to be alive and conscious in a universe that turns out not to be a universe at all but a, a kind of fraying tapestry? I'll tell you something you probably never knew – well, if it happened at all in your timeline. From when we were kids. It was when I was old enough to start asking questions such as "why are we here?" and "what happens when we die, Dad?" Well, your grandmother smuggled me a copy of the Catholic catechism. Or some kind of kids' version. *Who made you? God made me . . . Why did God make you? God made me to know Him, love Him and serve Him on Earth, so that I can be happy with Him for ever in Heaven*. Something like that.'

She smiled. 'That's a terrible thing for Grannie to have done to an Episcopalian kid.'

He shrugged. 'I guess, not by her lights. Was she trying to save my soul? Anyhow, it just impressed me, that's all. Maybe not the answers themselves, but their sheer confidence and clarity. They *are* answers, after all, to the most basic questions. Why *are* we here? What is the point of my few decades of life in an infinite and eternal universe? At least "God made me" was an answer, it was logical, it made some sense. Even if it put us in our place, as if we were all dumb little robots or something, programmed to give prayers of thanks. And maybe we will find some meaning, someday. There may be no answer to the question, *Who made you?* But maybe we will discover some purpose in the future, if we join some kind of galactic federation of mind . . .'

She smiled, not unkindly. 'Deep stuff, Malenfant.'

'Not particularly. As deep as I get, though. And it's kind of disappointing to me that four hundred years on, despite all the people of this age have achieved – and for all they seem to have found a kind of contentment – they have no better answers to the most fundamental questions than we had.'

'Yes. Disappointing. But – *who made Phobos?*'

He looked at her, frowning. 'What do you mean?'

'Or shaped it, anyhow. That's obvious, isn't it? I don't know who made the universe, let alone the manifold – let alone *me* – but there must have been a maker of all this, a Phobos engineer. It's clearly not a simple, natural object, unmodified. I mean, the discovery of its evident anomalies were why I – why we Emmas, a whole fleet of us across the manifold, maybe – were sent here in the first place. There's the secular acceleration, the decaying orbit. So you and I come from different histories, from different reality strands in the manifold. Where is it those strands seem to cross?'

'Right here,' he said. 'Inside Phobos.'

'So what are we going to do about it?'

He grinned at her. 'Explore, I guess. And find out who's behind all this.'

'Then let's get to work. You finished that coffee?'

46

It took three days after their first encounter with Emma before the crew of the *Last Small Step* were ready to mount a mission into Phobos. The logical next move.

Much of the first day had been spent on what Bartholomew tactfully called the debrief, as Malenfant and Emma had got to know each other again. Or, strictly speaking, these versions of themselves met for the first time.

The second day was spent mostly on arguing about who was going to explore Phobos.

Gershon ruled himself out. 'I'm a virtual-reality construct, designed for one thing, to fly this ship. Even if the projection technology were up to it, which it isn't, I'd be no use down there.'

Deirdra came over, drawn to the conversation. 'So you aren't going, Stavros . . .'

'And nor are you,' Bartholomew said gently.

Deirdra exploded – predictably, thought Malenfant. 'What? Of course I'm going.'

'Of course *not*,' Malenfant said.

'Then who is?'

Bartholomew ticked it off on his fingers. 'Emma. Well, it's kind of her expedition. Second, Malenfant. It's kind of *his*. Third, me.'

'You? You're no astronaut.'

Bartholomew sighed. 'But I am an android, Deirdra. As Malenfant knows, I'm pretty strong and flexible – I did carry him up that Pylon in a full gravity, remember. I'm trained in emergency medicine, among other disciplines. And, unlike any of you, if I get broken, I have a kit of spare parts that just plug in.'

Malenfant touched Deirdra's arm. 'None of us are prepared for this. But you are untrained, entirely inexperienced in this kind of work. Even just spacewalking. I'm sorry.'

'Well, I'm not,' Gershon said. 'If we lose these people, then I'm going to have to fly this ship back to Earth. And there's no way I am competent to report on what happened here. Not even legally. I need you to take the bad news back home with me, Deirdra. That would be a tough job. Tougher than going down that hole in the ground, if you ask me.'

'And in the meantime,' Malenfant said, 'when we do go down there, we need somebody responsible here in mission control. More responsible than old Footprints and Flags anyhow.'

Deirdra pursed her lips, evidently thinking it over. 'I think that's about fifty per cent bullshit. But I'll accept it. And I know I'm going to get my chance in the future. I'll treat this as a training exercise.'

Malenfant nodded approvingly. 'That attitude would have got you a long way in the astronaut office. And the language. I mean, bullshit? Evidently I'm a bad influence.'

After that, after they had all slept on it, a third day was spent on planning and preparation.

All three of the expeditionary party were fitted out with the *Step*'s standard-issue pressure suits. These were smart pieces of kit, entirely new to Emma, of course, which Malenfant had already tried out, and he knew it was a slightly eerie sensation even to don such a suit as with soft rustles and creaks the smart fabrics of the joints and sleeves and boots and leggings adjusted themselves around the shape of your body. It was like a ghostly massage. But Emma was a veteran of both American and Russian space technologies, and she adapted to another new system easily.

Even Bartholomew wore a suit. He didn't need life support, but the suit contained recovery, comms and other gear – and offered some protection for a body that was optimised to function in an environment comfortable for humans.

Also it made him look like he fitted in.

Then they were each attached to a lightweight tether on a reel, a smart carbon material, super-strong, that could extend to hundreds of metres. The tethers could also act as comms links if they got out of line of sight. Even the spools were smart technology; at a vocal command from any of them, or Gershon or Deirdra in the *Step*, the tethers would smoothly haul their burdens back from whatever situation they faced.

And they all had gas guns, effectively miniature rocket packs either fixed to their suits or handheld, which enabled them to manoeuvre in a weightless environment – and this moon's half-per-cent gravity was close enough to zero for such systems to be useful.

The gas guns were the nearest thing they had to a weapon, Malenfant realised. Of course they weren't here to wage war, but to explore.

For now.

On that final day they all spent some time outside the *Step*, getting used to their suits and practising moving around with the tethers and the gas guns.

Then, one more restless sleep.

While Phobos waited.

47

Malenfant led the others towards the rim of the shaft in the ground of Stickney Crater, moving slowly, slowly.

The feeble sun was low, and Malenfant cast a long shadow ahead as he progressed with cautious, floating steps. Around him the ground of Phobos, a dark plain littered with dust and rubble. At his side his companions, Emma and Bartholomew, both concentrating on every step they made – Bartholomew looking a lot more graceful, in fact, and Malenfant envied his machine-mind's ability to learn quickly. Behind him on the grey dirt the two ships sat a respectful distance apart: the bulky upright-Apollo shape of the *Last Small Step* lander section, Emma's spidery, much more flimsy-looking twenty-first-century lander. Before him a small drone camera, released from the *Step*, hovering thanks to squirts of a tiny rocket engine, a lens peering resolutely back at him.

Over his head, Mars.

Mars!

They stopped a few metres from the rim of the pit, as they had planned. Their white suits were already streaked with grey-black dirt, muck thrown up from Phobos readily clinging to their legs and bellies. Some kind of electrostatic effect, Malenfant supposed. The suits would be murder to clean. They were already breathing hard, Malenfant noticed – he and Emma anyhow. This tentative low-gravity walk was more of a strain than it looked.

The pit before him, wide, pitch dark, was like the terminus of the world. The drone hovered over its gaping mouth.

Bartholomew reached out, and touched each of them with a gloved hand; Malenfant knew he was enabling fast downloads of medical data. 'It may not feel like it, but you are both doing fine.'

'How about you?'

'Oh, nothing an oil change wouldn't cure. OK. Phase two.' Bartholomew knelt in the dirt, and from a bag slung at his side he withdrew a set of pitons, along with a heavy-duty glove, like a pitcher's mitt. He pulled the mitt over his right hand, over the more delicate white spacesuit glove, and, settling, just drove a piton into the ground. The first piton was trickiest as his weight was negligible, but once that one was fixed he could use it as leverage to push home the second, and four more.

'Show-off,' Malenfant said.

'We discussed this, Malenfant. It's efficient to exploit my excess physical strength at moments like this.'

'I know. Show-off even so. Let's get the ropes fixed.'

They attached their spooled tethers to the pitons with briskly tied knots.

Emma marvelled at the flexibility of her gloves. 'You ever tried to tie a knot in an old NASA EVA suit, Malenfant? Like wearing a suit of armour.'

'Yeah. This latter-day century got some things right.'

Now they set the tether spools down on the ground, anchored to the pitons, and checked the tether ends were securely fixed to attachments on their suits. They checked each other's tethers twice, and then their own. Only then was Malenfant satisfied.

Only then did he lead the way to the lip of the shaft in the ground.

He tried to be analytical, to observe.

The shaft was circular, maybe fifty metres across — as neat as if it had been cut with a laser, he thought. Where surface dust had drifted the rim was a little rougher. In one place he saw a deeper gouge that looked like it was where the leg of Emma's lander had caught the lip of the pit, and been ripped away. From here there was no sign of that landing leg.

He knew that this was where Arkady, the cosmonaut, had gone deep inside the pit, and was lost. In this shaft which, according to Gershon's measurements on landing, was — had been then anyhow — too deep to fit into the very carcass of Phobos. And now he had to follow.

He looked down, into the pit. He thought he made out a faint glow, electric blue.

Experimentally he picked up a rock, a loose conglomerate, and threw it into the hole. It sailed slowly out of sight, apparently without coming to any harm, falling into the deep interior dark.

'Deirdra, you see us?'

'Yeah. Out the window, and through the eyes of the drone, which is right over your head, looking straight down that shaft. Are you going in?'

Malenfant took a breath. 'We're going in. Come on, guys, let's do this.'

The controls of his manoeuvring system were set on his sleeve, simple touch pads. A swiped right forefinger over left sleeve pad made his gas gun blip, and he rose gently off the ground. The pulses of the gun were too smooth and gradual to be felt individually, and it was as if he had suddenly acquired the ability to fly like Superman.

He drifted over the shaft, to somewhere near its centre. Emma and Bartholomew hung in the sky alongside him, their jets invisible. Three Kryptonians together. He could see their faces as they waited for his lead.

'In we go.'

They descended in formation.

He looked around as he dropped, making sure Emma and Bartholomew were with him, that their tethers didn't snag. Looked around at the walls of the shaft all about him, and down into the shaft itself, extending deep below his feet, dimly lit by Mars overhead. Their head torches splashed light on the dull walls of the shaft, walls apparently of compressed dirt, smooth and regular.

No air, no suspended dust, so the light beams didn't show up. Just those splashes of light on the walls. And three human figures descending into the dark. A corpsicle, a time-jump survivor, and an android. Malenfant felt obscurely proud.

As they went deeper, the walls of the shaft sliding steadily past, the muddy Mars light from overhead faded. Malenfant, looking closely at the shaft wall as they passed it, now saw a few heavier lumps of rock in among the impact-smashed dust.

And there seemed to be an overlay, a glistening sheen, like a film of plastic over the dirt.

Bartholomew, cautiously, as they fell slowly past, reached up towards the film. 'Should I touch this? After what happened to Arkady?'

Malenfant shrugged. 'We'll get nowhere if we are too cautious.'

Bartholomew touched the surface with a gloved hand. Let it slide down the face.

The world didn't end, Malenfant observed.

'It's smooth. Treated in some way. The glove is telling me that this wall is coated in something like . . . diamond. A carbon crystal. Only a few micrometres deep.'

'I guess it wouldn't take much to hold open a shaft like this, in such low gravity.'

'I doubt if the structural properties of this construction are as simple as that, Malenfant.'

'Fair comment.'

Another minute, two. They continued to descend, in silence. Then, looking down, Malenfant saw a tangle of blue, buried deep inside the carcass of Phobos.

'How deep are we, Deirdra?'

'Approaching one point two five kilometres.'

'Are you picking up what's beneath us? The drone images didn't do it justice. Looks like some kind of structure down there.'

Emma said, 'I see something. Blue hoops, as Arkady reported.'

'It's what I'm seeing too,' Deirdra reported from the ship. 'Hoops, circles, at least metres across, in some kind of formation. Almost blocking the shaft. I had the impression Arkady went a lot deeper than this.'

'So he did,' Emma said.

'There's no rule that says whatever is down here is static,' Malenfant said. 'Anything else, Deirdra?'

'Deeper down, beyond the hoops – I think the shaft is coming to an end. I'm picking up signals of a much broader space. A hollow. The radar is estimating it might be seventeen, eighteen kilometres across, to the far wall. Some kind of structures in there too. Machinery, maybe. I can't make much sense of the echoes. The systems are trying to guess at the shape of the chamber, the contents, from a jumble of echoes coming back up the shaft.'

'Halt,' Malenfant snapped.

The three of them drifted together.

Malenfant shared a glance with Emma. 'Eighteen kilometres, Deirdra said. A chamber eighteen kilometres across. Phobos is only twenty-some kilometres across. So most of Phobos is empty space, within a shell a kilometre or so thick.'

'Holy cow,' she said. 'Shklovsky was right.'

'Which is impossible,' Gershon protested, from the *Step*. 'According to the seismometers. I told you. When we landed. They *proved* Phobos is a rubble pile, not a shell.'

'Yeah. I remember. But you also *proved* that this shaft was too deep to fit into Phobos at all.' Malenfant shook his head as he tried to keep contrary sets of evidence in his mind. A moon that was hollow, but was not. A ring sculpture that was kilometres deep, but was not. Phobos was an enigma, and not even a self-consistent one.

Deirdra called down, 'There's more data coming in. More extrapolated detail from the radar echoes. It's a muddle, Malenfant. I'm not trained on this, but—'

'That's OK. Just tell us what you see.'

'The wall of the big chamber – there are openings to more shafts, I think. Shafts like yours.'

'Access to other parts of Phobos?'

'Well, maybe. But I'm analysing the light that's coming from them. The blue of the hoops is nearly monochrome, a pure colour. Beautiful, actually. But the light from the shafts is like sunlight.'

Emma called, 'And is it that odd sunlight that's been observed before?'

'You mean, too dim? The odd spectrum?'

359

The spectrum of a very young Sun, Malenfant recalled Emma guessing.

'Yeah. Like that. But it's muddled up. Funny angles. The geometry is tricky and – fluid. The ship's science system model is flaky; it keeps reconfiguring to keep up with the data.'

Malenfant shared a glance with Emma. More mystery. Malenfant felt stressed, wary. 'If only one thing about this place made sense . . .'

Deirdra put in, 'Nobody promised us that what we would find down there would make any sense at all. We should just – well, keep looking.'

Emma grinned at Malenfant. 'I don't know who put her in charge, but it was a wise move. But our immediate obstacle is those blue hoops, in the shaft. We should tread carefully.'

'Agreed,' Malenfant said. 'So we stay away from the hardware. But meantime we go on.'

Deliberately he continued his descent.

Down below his feet, the approaching hoops. He could see them more clearly now. Identical, each maybe ten metres across, they were set vertically, so he approached them edge-on. And they touched at their rims, as if joined in an immense bracelet, each hoop at right angles to its neighbours. The whole thing was a big, stately installation, and disturbingly abstract, almost featureless.

'The Sculpture Garden,' Deirdra put in, unexpectedly, watching from the lander. 'The place needs a name. That will do.'

'Good enough,' Malenfant said.

As their torchlight played, he saw more detail. There were structures set in the regolith wall of the shaft, he saw, behind some of the hoops. What looked like metallic emplacements. They looked like hatches, in fact, hatches in the walls of compacted rock, behind the hoops.

And beyond that, he glimpsed now the vast, empty, impossible space Deirdra had reported – and whatever tremendous machinery it appeared to contain, barely visible. More blue hoops, he suspected, much larger, some languidly turning. But the details were – elusive.

He turned away and concentrated on the hoops nearby. 'OK, approaching this . . . bracelet.'

He slowed his descent, trying to get a feel for the overall structure. He counted five of the hoops now, set vertically, each at fixed right angles to its neighbours . . .

No, he thought. That couldn't be right. He counted again, pointing with a finger at each hoop. Squinted at those angles. Stared down at an arrangement which was oddly uncomfortable for his eyes, as if he were wearing a pair of the distorting spectacles he had been forced to don during some of the more obscure NASA astronaut application tests.

Five hoops. Each at right angles to its neighbours. Which was impossible, right?

'Watch out for those sharp edges,' Bartholomew said. He sounded profoundly uncomfortable.

'Emma,' Malenfant snapped. 'Having trouble here. Just tell me what you see.'

'Five hoops. Each a few metres across. Electric blue. Five. Four. No, five . . .'

'Yeah. I'm struggling too. They're at right angles to each other. So I see Hoop One, directly opposite Hoop Three. Counting from the one below me.'

'OK. OK. I see that. And Two opposite Four. And Three opposite . . . Five? Malenfant, I think I'm getting a headache.'

'Bartholomew, you aren't even human. Tell me what *you* see here.'

361

'I . . . I-I-I . . .'

The stuttering made his artificiality obvious as never before, Malenfant thought. He shared an alarmed glance with Emma.

'Sorry. I see four hoops. No, five. No, four. No, five.'

'The hoops are upright. Correct? As if standing on their rims. Although I can't see anything supporting them. And joined at the rims as if in a bracelet. What angle is Hoop One to Hoop Two, Bartholomew? I mean their planes . . .'

'Ninety degrees. The same as between Hoop Two and Three, and Three and Four, and Four and Five and it's impossible and andandand—'

'Take it easy.'

Bartholomew seemed to freeze, just for a second. Then, inside his suit, he gave a kind of start. 'Sorry. Look, as you say, Malenfant, I'm not human. And my information-processing system differs from the lumps of meat you two carry around in your heads. But it makes no difference. This hoop display is a contradiction, geometrically. You can't put more than four hoops in an array like this, at right angles to each other.'

'Like they were painted on the four side faces of a cube,' Malenfant said.

'Correct. You just can't. And yet there are *five* of them. It's a cubical array, but a cube doesn't have five side faces . . . It's a contradiction, two sets of data that don't match together, and it's causing me pain, analogously, as my cognitive system tries to process this.'

'Me too,' Emma said. 'Like a headache, right above my eyes.'

Malenfant grinned. 'Well, I'm as confused as shit too, but I don't have any headache. Either I have a higher IQ than the group, or a lower, I guess.'

Deirdra said, 'I wouldn't place a bet, Malenfant.'

'Charming. Look – we expected funny stuff down here,

didn't we? But we didn't come here to admire the architecture, higher-dimensional or not.'

'Right,' Emma said, and Malenfant thought she was trying to pull herself together. 'So what happened to Arkady? He isn't hanging around at this Sculpture Garden. But I can see a couple of places he might be at.'

Him, or what was left of him, Malenfant thought grimly. He nodded. 'You mean those side structures behind the hoops, the metal plates we see.' Peering cautiously now at the nearest, he said, 'This looks to me like some kind of bulkhead. With an airlock, maybe.'

Bartholomew turned to inspect the hatch opposite Malenfant. 'This one too. Human-made, do you think? The tech looks familiar enough. The lock has a big red wheel on it, with thumb grips. And writing . . . Cyrillic, I think.'

Malenfant snorted. 'You don't *think*, Bartholomew. Your brain is a binary computer. You either know a thing, or you don't.' He drifted closer to his own bulkhead. 'Writing on this one too, though. A couple of small instruction tags. And, something bigger.' He leaned, so his head torch picked it out better. 'A panel. Or a plaque, screwed on. Shit. It's in English.'

It was in bold, clear letters, and Malenfant read it out:

ROLLS-ROYCE LTD.
SPACE DIVISION
DERBY, UK
BY ROYAL APPOINTMENT
AD 2000

When he'd done reading, he puffed out his cheeks. 'I wasn't expecting that.'

Emma shook her head. 'There was no other mission to Phobos in your timeline, was there, Malenfant? No crewed mission – any more than there was in mine.'

'Certainly not sent by the British.' He looked at the structure before him, the emplacement as a whole around the hatch. 'Look at this thing. It has the diameter of a space-station module, roughly.'

'Maybe there's a habitat behind it, then,' Emma said, suddenly sounding excited. 'Behind each hatch. Maybe it makes sense. For a longer stay than we could have managed – a more ambitious mission – you could bring along a hab module, not just to travel in, but to stay a while. You could rendezvous with Phobos, bury your hab module deep underground so it interfaces with this place. And then you can sit in there doing your science, long-term studies, to your heart's content.'

'Seems like a lot of work. But OK.'

'Until,' Bartholomew said, pointing at the plate opposite with the Cyrillic writing, 'your Russian rivals show up with the same idea in mind.'

'But maybe they aren't rivals, in that sense,' Emma said slowly. 'Maybe they came here from different – history strands. As we did, Malenfant.'

Malenfant tried to take in this new concept. Visitors to Phobos from across the manifold, coming together in this Sculpture Garden? Even in the circumstances that was one hell of a strange thought.

Time for a little leadership, Malenfant.

'So. We've seen a lot. Discovered a hell of a lot. And we've suffered no worse than headaches, so far. The question is, where do we go from here?'

'Back to the *Step*,' Bartholomew said immediately.

'Onward,' said Emma.

'*I* would go on,' Deirdra called down from the ship. 'How can you stop now?'

'And I,' Stavros Gershon called, 'would vote for onward. But then I'm an irresponsible idiot, as history knows.'

Malenfant grinned. 'Look at it this way. We already bought the risk of coming this far. You never repeat an EVA if you don't have to – that's one thing I did learn in the astronaut office, even if I never went beyond the stratosphere myself. We go on. Where?'

'The obvious place,' Deirdra said eagerly, 'is one of those hab modules. See what's inside. See *who* is inside.'

Emma said, 'Yeah, but how do we get in there? I did say I thought we should keep away from the hoops themselves.'

'OK,' Bartholomew said, 'but – I hate to admit it – I think there's enough clearance between the hoops and the walls for the hatches to be reachable. Without touching the hoops themselves. It will take a little care, but—'

'Good,' Malenfant said. 'The question is, which do we try first? Emma?'

She thought that over. 'Well, if Arkady went anywhere, it would be to the hab with the Russian writing.'

'Good point. Let's try that one. But, just in case anybody else is home, we ought to let them know we are here . . .' He dug a luminous marker crayon out of a pocket on his suit leg, and wrote, on the glassy wall below the Rolls-Royce plaque:

No taxation without representation.
(signed) Col. Reid Malenfant, USAF & NASA.
1 September, AD 2469.

'So that's done. Let's go see that Russian camper van. And keep away from the hoops . . .'

48

As Bartholomew had predicted, there was enough room to move around behind the hoops, with caution. They watched each other, and worked hard at keeping their tethers out of the way of the sharp rims.

Malenfant felt oddly moved as he watched his companions manoeuvring through this deadly strangeness. They were just human beings – give or take an android doctor – humans stumbling around in the dark, trying to figure out this baffling stuff, helping each other. But maybe that was pretty much all there was to life itself, he thought.

At last, with great care, Bartholomew approached the Russian hatch and grasped the red wheel. It turned. He glanced back over his shoulder. 'Surprisingly easy,' he said. He turned some more, then hauled back the heavy door.

Inside, revealed by their head torches, an empty chamber with another hatch on the far side, with a small window, another red wheel. Equipment strapped to the walls. Cyrillic lettering.

'An airlock,' Emma said. 'I can read Cyrillic. These are all safety notices . . . So we go through?'

Malenfant bent to peer through the window set in the inner hatch. He saw nothing but darkness beyond. 'If this is an airlock we'll have to shut the outer door before we can open the inner. And if we close the outer door, we'll have to dump our tethers here.'

They hesitated. Malenfant imagined the thoughts running through their heads. *Maybe this is where we should turn back. Maybe we should let one or two go through, let two or one hang back, still tethered . . .*

'We go together,' he said. 'We don't know what we'll find. Whatever became of Arkady.' He didn't want to float the possibility that Arkady could, after so many months, be alive. 'The inhabitants of this place . . . We're not even sure it is a hab module. We go together, deal with whatever we find.'

'Agreed,' Emma said.

A curt nod from Bartholomew.

So they crowded into the lock, and detached the tethers. Malenfant slammed the hatch shut and sealed it with yet another red wheel – having made sure he could open it again from the inside.

They drifted in darkness, save for the light splashes from their head torches.

'I don't hear anything,' Emma said. 'No pumps, no valves, no air returning.'

Malenfant looked through that small window in the inner door. Total blackness, save for reflections from his torch. 'I think this place is inert. Lost power, maybe.'

'Give it five minutes,' Emma said.

Bartholomew ran a gloved finger along a metal join, where the inner bulkhead met the chamber's curved wall. 'This work is pretty crude. Like it was assembled in a tractor factory.'

Emma laughed. 'I visited some Russian tractor factories. In my timeline anyhow. Their manufacturing work can be less refined than in the West, but it's generally good enough. Tough, reliable . . .'

Malenfant said, 'That's enough time. Bartholomew, the door.'

For once Bartholomew obeyed without question or wisecrack. With strong artificial hands he dragged at the red wheel.

The inner door swung open easily. There was no hiss of escaping air. Still no lights came on.

'Let me lead,' Emma said. 'I know this technology.'

Malenfant hesitated, then pulled back to let her pass.

Cautiously, she drifted into the darkened space, head-first, her torch splash preceding her. No beam again, so no air, Malenfant observed.

Bartholomew followed, and then Malenfant.

In the glimmers of torchlight, it was difficult to make out details, or even an overall layout. Malenfant had a vague impression of a cluttered workshop, with stuff stuck all over the walls. There was an exercise cycle. A table, like a dining table, with open lids exposing what looked like heating trays. Typical space-station chic. Malenfant saw icicles oozing out of broken pipes, a frost on some of the abandoned surfaces. This place must have been falling apart, the heating failing, even before the lights went out. Whatever, it was a tube of vacuum now.

Emma called back, 'This reminds me of the Mirs. The Russian space stations – in my timeline anyhow.'

'We had the Mir too,' Malenfant murmured. 'I never went there. No American ever did.'

'Adapting Mir technology as a deep-space habitat had always been in the Russians' plans,' Emma said. 'In my timeline. If a Mir can last a couple of years in Earth orbit, it can last a couple of years as a habitat for a Mars mission. Provided you have cracked such problems as long-term life support without resupply from the ground, of course. My *Timor* had modules that were descendants of Mir and western technology, combined.'

'How can such a station die?'

'Easily,' Emma said, moving deeper in. 'I learned a lot in training – and the Russians learned a lot from experience, with their Mirs and the Salyut stations before that. Usually it's a loss of power – and a Russian station's power mostly came from the Sun, from solar panels. If you drift out of alignment – say because of a collision with another craft, or a pressure leak – you quickly lose input power. And if you exhaust your batteries before regaining alignment, you have to try to reorient the station manually. Then, when your panels are back in the sunlight, you replenish your batteries, and *then* power up and reboot the automatic guidance system . . . But you may not get that far. Inside a powered-down station the immediate threat isn't the cold so much as a build-up of carbon dioxide, when the scrubbers fail. You quickly get sleepy, headaches . . . Oh, no.'

'What?'

'Back here. I found somebody. A person. A, a body. Suit badly ripped—'

Malenfant was distracted by a shifting shadow, on the panels before him.

He looked up.

A plummeting shape. Shadowed in the light of Bartholomew's head torch. A human figure, arms and legs extended, like a vampire descending.

A vampire in an orange spacesuit.

Holding a club.

For a heartbeat Malenfant couldn't believe what he was seeing.

Then he yelled, 'Bartholomew! Above you!'

Bartholomew reacted with more than human speed, and for once Malenfant was glad to see such capabilities in action. Even as the attacker swung the club, the medic got in position to fend off the first blow – that club was actually a kind of wrench, Malenfant saw, designed for zero-gravity use, the head weighted heavily with counter-torque mechanisms – and then Bartholomew grabbed the attacker's two hands, twisted in the air, and pinned him down against a work surface. All unnaturally quickly. The assailant kicked and thrashed, but Bartholomew held on firmly – but almost tenderly, Malenfant thought, dazed.

He could see a mouth moving behind a spittle-flecked visor – a man's face – but could hear no words.

Emma came floating back, wide-eyed. 'Holy shit.'

'Seconded,' Malenfant said. 'Are you OK?'

'Yeah. He was nowhere near me.'

'I'm fine too, by the way,' Bartholomew called, his voice jarred by the struggles of his captive. 'In case you wondered.'

Emma pulled a lead from a suit pocket. 'This is designed for Russian tech. If his suit has the right kind of interface I can talk to him. Bartholomew, can you hold him still?'

'Still enough.'

Then, abstracted, Emma looked round. 'Malenfant. You better go see what I found in back.'

She'd said, a body. OK.

He picked his way cautiously deeper into the cluttered craft, made more hazardous now by the junk Bartholomew's assailant had disturbed. And he listened in to Emma's halting conversation, broadcast over their own loops.

'—ub'yu! Ya tebya ub'yu!'

'He's saying, "I will kill you." I think he means you, Bartholomew.'

370

'Great. I can understand him, of course.'

Emma said evenly, 'Umm – listen, don't be afraid. *Ne boysya. Uspokoysya.* Be calm.'

'*Ostav menya v pokoye!*'

'Well, we can't leave you alone, now you tried to kill us. Stop struggling. He won't hurt you. Umm – *menya zovut Emma. Emma.*'

The Russian shut up, his breathing noisy and ragged on the loop.

Malenfant reached the body. A pressure suit ripped open at the back. Congealed blood. He recoiled from touching the obviously dead figure. But he could read a name tag.

'Emma. Remind me. What was the surname of your Arkady?'

'*Vy govorite kak Moskva.*'

'He says I sound like a Muscovite . . . Berezovoy, Malenfant. His name was Berezovoy.'

'Then I guess we found him. Name tags in both Cyrillic and English, like yours, Emma. What's left of him.'

To Emma's credit, her voice barely wavered as she tried to calm the Russian. 'Hush, now. *Ne boysya. Ne boysya . . .*'

49

Just take it easy. You're safe now.

What is this place?

This is our ship. It is called the Last Small Step. *You have been here three days – three days since we found you, in the pit on Phobos. One of us is a doctor. He – well, he is not human, he is a machine. I am not sure of the appropriate Russian vocabulary. A machine made like a human. But he is a doctor, and a competent one, and he has treated you scrupulously. You were suffering from starvation, dehydration, frostbite where your suit fabric failed, various trauma wounds, blood loss, and some radiation sickness which—*

Radiation sickness? How can that be treated?

Good question, with a complex answer. It is difficult to describe. This being, Bartholomew, comes from a later epoch than – well, than us. His medicine is advanced. You must rest. But you are healing well . . . Can you hear me? Can you understand me?

Your Russian is good. Your accent is strong but not incomprehensible. Yet I understand very little of what you say. Epochs?

I am sorry if—

I am your guest. I must thank you for sheltering me.

You would have done the same, if the positions were reversed.

I hope so. But I attacked you. I was frightened. I thought, you see, that whatever had harmed your comrade was coming after me. I have been alone for some time. One's imagination works.

I understand.

I apologise. I should have welcomed you with vodka, and *salo*.

Salted pork fat. Love it.

You know our customs. But – but what ship is this? I recognise nothing like it in reports I have seen of vessels built by Russia, the United States, China.

Well, it was built by none of those nations. Indeed those nations no longer exist . . . At least, I don't think so. We will come to that. I understand little more than you do, frankly. I am a – newcomer too. But I am the only Russian speaker among us. We have machinery capable of translation, but we thought it best . . . This is a ship that was sent out from Earth to retrieve me, and my partner, from Phobos. As I said, it is called the Last Small Step—

Your partner?

He flew to Phobos with me, with one other, who did not follow us to . . . here. My partner was a cosmonaut, as you are.

A cosmonaut? Russian?

His name was Arkady Berezovoy.

Ah. Indeed. I found him in the chamber of the blue hoops, his suit badly damaged. Yes, I read the name tag. Berezovoy. I feared he had been attacked.

No. I think that the sharp edges of the blue hoops . . . It was an accident.

I took him into the Mir. I tried to save him. He died in my arms. But otherwise . . .

This make no sense. No sense at all. You are the woman who spoke to me before. In the Mir. Do I have that right, at least?

The woman who speaks like a Muscovite.

That's right. My name is Emma Stoney. I . . . I am thirty-five years old. I am an astronaut. I flew with NASA. I spent a long time learning Russian. I always anticipated, you see, that if we were ever to get to Phobos – we, humanity – it would need to be a mission mounted by Russians and Americans, together. I learned my conversational Russian at Star City. Which of course is near Moscow. So, I guess I picked up the accent, the idioms.

There is much I do not understand. Things that do not fit. Americans and Russians, flying together to Phobos? Ha! They would strangle each other before they passed the Moon.

I'm sorry. I'm making the same mistake the Step *crew made with me when they found me. I was stranded on Phobos, like you. It turned out there was a lot of knowledge, experience that we had that did not overlap.*

I do not understand.

Nor do I, actually. Or any of us, I don't think. But we found out that it is best to start with the specifics. The big picture makes no sense. But the specifics, the human details, we can always find something in common there. We are all human beings, wherever we come from.

I repeat my mocking laughter. Ha! You may relay that platitude back to the pilots of the drone planes, no doubt stationed in safety thousands of kilometres away in America and Britain and Germany, who destroyed Star City and other Russian space facilities, even as we explored Phobos. To touch a moon of Mars with Russian hands was a great triumph, even as the Americans cut off our feet.

We must discuss all this.

Perhaps. Let us start with details, as you suggest. Your partner? A cosmonaut?

As I told you, his name was Arkady Berezovoy.

Arkady . . . I do not recognise the name. When did he come to Star City?

Why . . . I am not sure. I can tell you that he was an experienced cosmonaut, with several flights to his credit, before we left for Phobos in the year 2004.

What? When? No, that is impossible. My own mission was the first ever to Phobos, even the Americans could not beat us to that goal, and *we* departed from Earth orbit in the year 2026 . . .

Can you hear me?

I'm sorry. You have to understand. We are in an extraordinary . . . situation here. All of us. And we find that we may have nothing in common with each other, not the most basic assumptions.

Such as –

Such as what the date is. I'm confusing you, I'm sure. You know, it's not long since I found myself in this hall of mirrors myself. Maybe I'm not the right person to be doing this. I am sure the doctor has translation modules which——

No. Please. Madam Stoney——

Call me Emma.

Emma. I am sorry for my shortness, my impatience. I can tell that this is difficult. Yet here you are, trying to help me. Please, stay. Let us work through this together.

All right. Well, perhaps that will help me too. Thank you for your forgiveness – why, I still don't know your name.

Then we should start with that, Emma Stoney.

I am Vladimir Pavlovich Viktorenko. My partner was Mikhail Alexeevich Glaskov. You may recognise my name; my father was the Viktorenko who commanded the flight of the famous Voskhod III in 1966.

I don't recall that . . . I apologise. Our pilot, Stavros Gershon, is something of a space buff, a fan of the exploits of that era . . . He's saying now that our records show there were only two Voskhod flights. Perhaps your father's flight was kept secret?

Not at all! These were the days when the Soviet Union lauded its space exploits – while keeping the technical details private, of course.

Look, Vladimir, go on with your account – tell me about your father. This kind of discrepancy is small fry, believe me.

My father became internationally famous. He had taken the record for the longest spacewalk, on his flight. He visited events such as air shows, in Paris and Berlin, to speak of his experiences. This was all before I was born, of course. As I grew up he, and later my mother, proudly showed me memorabilia of those days. Photographs and medals.

When were you born, Vladimir?

In 1975. I am now fifty-three years old.

Umm. So to you, this is the year 2028.

A year that will be remembered, I am sure, not for my mission to Phobos, but for the treacherous pre-emptive war launched on Mother Russia by America and her allies . . .

Tell me more about your family. You said that later it was your mother who had to tell you stories of the family, of your father's exploits.

Yes. He was first and foremost a pilot in the Soviet air force. He lost his life in the skies over Afghanistan in 1982.

You were . . . seven years old. I am very sorry.

I clung to his memory. It shone, never tarnished – and that was despite the western news and propaganda that was infiltrating the Soviet bloc by then. Propaganda, lies about space, and the astronauts and the cosmonauts . . . *I* never believed the accusations about Apollo 11 that were hurled at the Soviet Union. We had our own space programme, our own proud achievements – including my own father's. We did not *need* to have committed such cowardly sabotage. Yet this was the background against which I grew up, as a small boy, a teenager.

Vladimir. Pretend I don't know anything of what you are talking about. What sabotage? What happened to Apollo 11?

Ha! I am beginning to distrust you, Emma Stoney. What happened to Apollo 11? It became part of your national myth, the stories you Americans tell yourselves. The myth that you believe justifies your aggressive posture to the rest of the world. The King of England and his taxes! And now the so-called Apollo assassination! Lies about the KGB and their infiltration of the Grumman plants—

Grumman? Grumman Aerospace, who built the Lunar Module? Please, Vladimir. Just tell me what you know.

Well, it happened six years before I was born, you must remember. As the Apollo 11 Lunar Module came in to land on the Moon, the descent engine – it exploded. The astronauts were killed immediately, as far as anybody knows. The last words spoken, by Aldrin, became famous. He said, '*Contact light.*' Meaning a probe, a physical probe, had just touched the surface, seconds before landing. And then . . .

Umm. Stavros is checking our records again. In our timeline, or at least Stavros's—

Timeline? What do you mean?

I . . . Hold fire on that, Vladimir. Stavros's records do show that in our history there was a build-up of pressure and temperature in the LM descent engine, observed by mission control at Houston, just after landing. Caused by a blockage in a fuel line, fuel frozen by liquid helium. If the heat had got to it – yes, it would have gone up, like a small grenade. There was chatter about abort options.

But the pressure in the lines subsided – the incident passed. It lasted only moments. Must have been terrifying, though.

So the astronauts survived to reach the Moon's surface – only to be hit by Armstrong's heart attack, of course. That was how Armstrong died . . . Or at least that's what Malenfant remembers. As far as I recall, both Armstrong and Aldrin saw out their mission and came home in triumph . . . I'm sorry, that doesn't help, this must all be terribly confusing . . .

Vladimir? Can you still hear me?

This makes no sense. I cannot be mistaking these events, in my memory. Even though they occurred before I was born. Because they justified the aggressive posture which the United States adopted towards the Soviet Union thereafter.

You mean, there was a suspicion that there was some kind of sabotage? That the LM was set up to fail on landing?

My father believed that suspicion was seeded because when the Apollo 12 astronauts reached the Sea of Tranquillity to recover the bodies, they observed a Lunokhod, close by. Umm, an automatic probe, a rover. The Soviet space agency dispatched several such craft; they had landed one close by the Apollo 11 site, in order to inspect the accident. My father believed the motive was benevolent; perhaps our observations, shared with NASA, could have helped the Americans avoid another such disaster.

But—

But the Americans believed the Lunokhod was there to gloat. To return images, proof of what the KGB had achieved in destroying Apollo – in wrecking this supreme technocratic triumph, for the Americans. In any event, that moment was when enmity hardened between America and the Soviet Union, if it had not already.

The Apollo 12 astronauts threw Moon rocks at the Lunokhod.

That was November 1969. By 2028, those rocks would be ballistic missiles targeting Soviet space facilities.

That's quite a story.

You spoke of timelines. Different timelines, you mean. Different histories.

That's . . . what we appear to be tangled up in here, Vladimir. And different time zones, too.

Time zones, you say?

That's another complication, Vladimir. You think the year is 2028. That is, I guess, where you came from. I believe it's 2006.

Impossible—

I know. But to Malenfant, who came out here to find me in the Last Small Step, the year is 2469.

I . . . perhaps your pronunciation has confused me . . .

It's the twenty-fifth century, Vladimir. Back on Earth, right now. It's strange for me too. But I believe it; they've shown me broadcasts from down there . . . Not to mention the fact that the technology they have is way beyond anything we could aspire to, in our time. It's something to do with Phobos, I think. Or maybe what it contains . . . You are silent . . . Once again I have this feeling I'm handling this badly.

Let's get back to what we should be talking about.

You are seven years old.

Your father dies.

My father dies.

A war hero. I was an only child. Sometimes I think that if I had had older brothers, I might have developed a more military mind, I might have followed my father in his career as a soldier, a warrior.

But I was drawn to the other half of his achievements: his spaceflights. Space, you know, has been a dream of the Russian people since long before the Soviet Union even existed. Thinkers like Tsiolkovsky . . . Have you heard of Cosmism, Emma? A deep philosophy holding that the destiny for a unified mankind is space, and the infinity it offers. The eternity. That is why, I believe, space exploits were so essential to the Russian psyche.

I know something of this. I trained in Russia, remember, and flew here with a cosmonaut. But we rarely spoke of such things, I admit. Perhaps even in my timeline the Russians were too wary of American materialism, as they saw it. This 'Cosmism', and whatever strand of thinking it had led to, stayed private. Mostly, anyhow. Until the vodka flowed.

Perhaps it is best. Where I am from, we would never have dreamed of trying to justify such philosophies to Americans. Well. Despite American hostility after Apollo 11, we continued to fly in space – never to the Moon, not then, as I was growing up. But we flew to orbit in our robust Soyuz ships, and we built our space stations, the Salyuts, the Mirs. We learned how to live in space. We learned how to *fix* things. Baby steps towards the goals of Cosmist thought, I suppose.

But all the while we faced pressure from the Americans. They had gone to the Moon, you see, further than us – save for our robots – but now, after Apollo 11, they turned back, to Earth. And they built a new generation of winged spacecraft, with a focus on operations on Earth, and near it.

The space shuttles?

The war birds, our own newspapers called them. Designed to serve the needs of your military, at least in part. The craft had great cross-range capability – that is, an ability to fly down from orbit over battlefields at wide latitudes, and deliver targeted payloads.

In 1985, I was ten years old, the shuttles began to demonstrate practice bombing runs, high in the stratosphere above Moscow,

Leningrad, Vladivostok. To show, you see, that no part of our nation was beyond the reach of America. Of the Rocket State, as President Reagan called it.

That didn't happen in my reality. Oh, the shuttle had a military input, and there were some reconnaissance missions . . . On the other hand, where Malenfant came from, he said he saw a shuttle bombing run during the Iraq war . . .

I know nothing of an Iraq war. But I assure you that everything I told you is true, as I experienced it. A certain climax was reached in 1986 when a Soyuz spacecraft, on its way to the Mir, was snatched out of orbit by a shuttle orbiter. The Americans claimed that the crew had been engaged in illegal espionage activities. In fact their cargo was experimental biology: pea plants and chicken eggs. The crew were paraded in handcuffs. I don't know what happened to the pea plants and chicken eggs.

There was nothing we could do. The Soviet state tried to respond, technologically. But we could not afford it. Though we had the engineering expertise, we have always had that, we could not match American investment. So, in the late 1980s . . . You really know nothing of this?

I was born in 1970. I lived through a version of it, I guess.

So, in the late 1980s, our leaders, the Soviet leadership, tried to reach an understanding with the West, with America. The only other way we could have responded, you see, was to launch a war that would have devastated the planet. And so, despite American insults, American crowing, we chose peace.

That sounds . . . noble.

It was. But we paid a price. The Americans maintained their economic pressure. The Soviet Union itself fell, its leaders deposed. Many of the constituent republics – Ukraine, the Baltics – had already broken away, thanks to independence movements that proved to be supported, even founded, by the CIA. Russia became a democracy, of sorts. But as the assets of the old Soviet state were privatised, the American corporations moved in. We became corrupt, corporatised, our government like gangsters in hock to the Americans. It was a conquest, Emma Stoney. Not in name, and with scarcely a shot being fired. But a conquest all the same, of ideology and economics. Still, we consoled ourselves—

Better that than global extinction.

Indeed. Gorbachev said as much before he died in prison.

And, as would prove to be crucial in my own life, we maintained our independent space programme. Even though now we had to make deals with Kazakhstan, an independent nation, for access to Baikonur, the old Soviet launch facility.

Influenced by my father, I myself was determined to fly in space however I could, whatever missions were available, and I gave myself the best opportunity I could. I trained as a civilian pilot, and then test pilot. And in parallel I trained as a plumber.

A plumber! Well, having endured long-duration spaceflight myself, I can see the logic.

Indeed. A crewed spacecraft consists of little but a rocket engine and plumbing. And the longer the time spent away from Earth, the more reliable those unglamorous but essential systems have to be. I myself pioneered new generations of closed life-support systems which make intensive use of recycled human products. Russians lag behind the West in computer technology and other areas, but not in the means to endure in space. And that worked in my favour, you see. There were better pilots than me. There were braver heroes. But there wasn't a better space plumber in the whole of Russia.

And I was in the right place at the right time, in a sense. Emma, if the 1990s had been calamitous for my country, the new century was more productive. A happier time. Our economy began to grow healthily, a new generation began to build economic and political ties with neighbours which had once been satellite states and dependencies.

After 2010 I flew two long-duration missions aboard versions of our Mir space stations. Longer in fact than the journey which, in the end, brought me to Phobos itself . . . But, of course, it was Phobos that caused the great destabilisation.

What do you mean?

It was in the year 2018 that the anomalous nature of Phobos, observed by the scientists, became public knowledge.

Umm. It was rather earlier in my timeline. Did you ever hear of an astrophysicist called Shklovsky?

I am afraid that in my evidently warlike world, it was the potential of acquiring alien technology that made Phobos seem such a prize – or rather, such was the nature of the combatants' psychology, it was necessary to be sure that the other fellow didn't get there first.

But the prize itself, it was always clear from the beginning, was in Russia's grasp. For while the Americans had continued to fly their baby-step hops out of the atmosphere and back again aboard their ugly war birds, we, since 1970, had patiently been developing a capability to endure long periods in space – even, so we had rehearsed, without resupply from the home planet, for months. We had always had our eye on Mars, you know, as the long-term goal. It did not take a great leap of the engineering imagination to swivel our sights to Phobos, mysterious moon of Mars.

I can understand that. My own mission to Phobos was an American–Soviet joint venture. And, yes, the Russian experience of long-duration spaceflight was the key to our success. Such as it was . . .

As soon as the mission profile emerged, as soon as it was clear this would need to be a two-person crew, Misha and I were inevitably the prime candidates: Misha the best space pilot, and I, yes, the best plumber.

The mission itself was planned rapidly.

In the end it took three rocket launches to assemble our Phobos ship. There were two launches of our heavy-lift booster, the Energia: one to lift our interplanetary booster, the other to lift a smaller rocket – the second stage of a Proton launcher – fully fuelled, along with a habitat module based on our proven Mir hardware. In the third launch, we two rode a Soyuz to low Earth orbit to join our ship, already assembled. The interplanetary booster would hurl us, in our Mir, to Mars, and the Proton stage would brake us to orbit around Mars. Later another Proton with a fuel load would be dispatched to bring us home. As we were not attempting a landing on Mars the mission profile was much simpler than many we had studied. We needed only a lightweight lander craft, little more than a frame open to the vacuum, with which to approach a small space rock like Phobos . . .

Our ship, our great mission, was called *Spektr*.

We left Earth orbit on 15 November 2026. We arrived safely at Mars on 30 July of the following year. The plan was we would stay more than a full year, and then leave in October of 2028, following a minimum-energy interplanetary trajectory, to arrive back at Earth nine months later.

The mission went so well! Even from the start.

I remember how cheerful we were, as we trained at Star City, Misha and I and our backups, despite the mice in the training rooms, and the cats chasing the mice, and the lights turned down so low to save money you could barely read a checklist, and the mission controllers disappearing all the time to their second jobs as car-park attendants and window cleaners . . .

And then to Baikonur: an island of technology in the middle of the desolate steppe. Those ugly concrete buildings, now scarred by the looting and rioting that followed the fall of the Soviet Union. Rusting satellite dishes. Wild dogs, even wild camels, rooting in heaps of metal that had been fuel tanks or the fins of space rockets. And we had to wear masks to protect ourselves against the toxic dust that blew in from the dried basin of the Aral Sea.

At last the training was done, the mission assembled, despite equipment failures and staff shortages, and what we suspected were attempts at destabilisation, even sabotage, by the Americans or their allies. Launch day arrived. We suited up in Building 254, and drove in a bus across the steppe, and saluted the general in command of the station – we follow such traditions scrupulously.

A Soyuz rocket on the pad is grey metal. You can see the rivets. It looks what it is, a proud, robust piece of Soviet engineering.

The Soyuz capsule is small and cramped, even when there are just two crew – it is built for three. Under the protective cowl needed for launch it is dark and noisy, the walls covered with thick yellow Velcro. We wait two hours as the final preparations run down.

The pumps whine. The stack shudders. And then—

Ignition!

After one full orbit, we closed on our ship, the *Spektr*, the assembled stack of thruster rockets and habitat. Our docking was automated; it was fast and efficient, and Misha and I didn't have to do a thing.

And we said goodbye to the Earth.

So we settled into the Mir. Both Misha and I were veterans of such missions; it was a home from home.

I saw your module, what was left of it. I guess it wasn't looking its best . . .

Indeed. You understand that our module was equivalent to the base block of a full Mir complex – just the core. But it is sufficient for dining, for sleep – perhaps you saw the table with its ingenious lidded niches, where food is heated in safety. Misha was always rather obsessive about using the treadmill, you know. When he was on that gadget he would make the whole stack shake at a frequency of about one Hertz.

But I, I was always buried in my systems, the *Elektron* and *Vozdukh* that respectively looked after our oxygen supply, and the carbon dioxide in the air. And of course my elaborate recycling system. It was not a closed system; there were leaks, slow build-ups of residue and waste, but it would have supported us through the years before we were due to return to Earth.

If fate had not intervened.

Indeed. We reached Martian orbit. We rendezvoused with Phobos successfully. Phobos was big and ugly and inviting, and with that core of anomalous wonder at its heart. So we thought. And we prepared to explore.

We made our descent at the north rotation pole, the apex. I remember exiting the lander . . . the hatch stuck, briefly . . . Then we were out.

We dug into the loose dirt of Phobos. And we found – marvels.

We discovered the Sculpture Garden, as you called it. That internal chamber, the blue hoop system. But for us – we found it all under only a few metres of loose-packed rubble, and at the moon's pole. Whereas you found it all in a kilometre-deep shaft, at the equator! This is a great mystery to me.

Tell me about it.

As I said, we had intended to stay for over a year, at Phobos. We had to decide how to maintain our Mir in close proximity to the moon, without the need for continual orbital adjustments which would deplete our attitude-rocket fuel. We even considered tethers, attaching the habitat to an anchor at the pole, perhaps.

We decided in the end it would be possible simply to dig through the loosely packed layers of dust and rock to the cavity of the blue hoops, and – cautiously, cautiously – to use our Soyuz thrusters to nudge the Mir into contact with the moon itself at that point. A kind of docking. So that the forward airlock of the Mir would give directly into that cavity. Thus we would achieve stability of the craft, and easy access to the moon's interior. There were complications to do with the orientation of the solar panels, but—

But there's that paradox again. You say you attached your Mir to the surface. We found it entirely buried in the regolith!

Emma, we soon discovered that distances, relative locations, within and on Phobos are not what they seem – or, not what they ought to be. Even a great object like the Mir can be – well, in two places at once.

Umm. You're obviously right, of course.

We have much to discuss, of such matters. Notes to compare.

Indeed.

But I, I will never complete my report of all this to my superiors in Star City. Because the war intervened. And then Misha was lost . . .

Tell me about the war.

*

We knew little enough about it. Our controllers tried to filter out the news. But some of the junior technicians, and the cosmonauts who assisted them—

Capcoms?

They were our friends. They told us more.

Perhaps it was the Phobos mission itself that was the trigger. Perhaps it was simply that tensions had been rising for too long anyhow. My own feeling is that the hawks in the American administration, who had longed to see a war with Russia as a logical conclusion to their decades-long global strategy, simply got the upper hand at last. Any excuse would have been enough to trigger it.

It began subtly, it seemed.

Suddenly there was agitation in the republics. The Baltics, the Ukraine, even Kazakhstan. Once the vassals of Moscow, now our neighbours. So-called evidence of Russian interference in democratic processes, and so on. And an agitation among Russian ethnic groups who had been cut off in the newly independent republics. Reactions to that agitation. Terrorism, assassinations, massacres. It was not hard to see the hand of the CIA in this. Indeed we Russians regard ourselves as masters of the art of this kind of subtle destabilisation. We call it *maskirovka*.

Meanwhile we understood that while America might trigger this war, it would not choose to fight alone; it must find a reason for all twenty-eight NATO states to unite in the cause.

It was not long before such an excuse was found. American citizens were killed in the Ukraine, during a riot.

And on the Latvian border, a US fighter patrol, encroaching in Russian air space, was shot down.

The provocation had been continual; some such incident would have occurred eventually.

If not that trigger, then another.

Exactly. The NATO countries were persuaded to mobilise, with a major mustering of land forces at Berlin, and a naval conjunction in the Baltic. Meanwhile, in Ukraine, there was a swift mobilisation of national forces, orchestrated, my friends believed, by American 'advisers' on the ground.

And it was on the Ukraine border that the real fighting began – at the Crimea, in fact. Russians and Americans fighting at last.

This was in June of 2028.

Then came the invasion of the home country, across the north European plain from Berlin. In the air a wave of F-18 fighters, and fighter-bombers, and helicopters, and tank brigades on the ground. The aim was to cripple; among the first targets were infrastructure elements like airports and power plants. There had also been preliminary cyber-attacks to disable our defences. It was the greatest mustering of anti-Russian forces since Hitler. A thrilling sight, no doubt.

Misha and I were shocked, witnessing this from afar. We knew our history – we knew that even the Cuba missile crisis had not escalated to this point.

Well, our leaders were dealt a weak hand, but they were not fools. And they were united in a way that the NATO commanders could not be; our first government, after the Soviet era, had been a group of ex-KGB officers from St Petersburg.

And they were imaginative. They quickly mounted a daring counter-offensive, into the Baltic States. They hoped to secure a quick victory, acquire some NATO territory, show strength, and establish a bargaining position before the war escalated further. A bold strike.

Did it work?

It was hard for us to tell. Our troops got bogged down when local resistance groups rose up against the Russian invader.

Communications became difficult.

Evidently there was further escalation. Among the NATO responses that we knew about was a strike with tactical nuclear weapons on Russian space facilities. Which included Star City and the TsUP, our mission control – and even Baikonur, in the sovereign territory of Kazakhstan. Our Capcoms spoke to us as long as they could, described what they saw, until we lost contact and, I suppose, they died.

We were cut off.

So a line had been crossed. The use of nuclear weapons on the space facilities, presumably on other battlefields. Tactical only, but—

Indeed. After that came high-altitude nuclear detonations in the Earth's ionosphere, intended to disable the electronics across much of Asia, but which served also to obscure further most information-bearing signals we might have received.

Just before I lost Misha, though, we heard fragmentary rumours of a new front, an invasion of Russian territory by China in the Far East.

Finally strategic nuclear weapons were used.

Oh, God.

I am an atheist. But – yes. Oh, God.

From Mars, you know, if you watch through a telescope meant for interplanetary navigation, a nuclear blast looks like a pebble thrown into a pond. You see the ripples in the atmosphere, then the fires, and the smoke smears on the breeze. You can see this from Mars.

I'm so sorry.

This was not your America. Evidently it isn't your fault.

And – you said – you lost Misha?

We had continued our work. Our scientific exploration of

Phobos. Even as war blossomed at home. We discussed this, and decided it was our duty, and besides would be good for our own morale. After all we could do nothing to affect the outcome of the war – we couldn't even get home until the planets aligned, in October. Conversely the war could not affect us. There were no American saboteurs in *Spektr*.

Could you have got home, do you think? Without support from your mission control?

We thought so. Misha was senior to me, especially in the matters of piloting the craft, re-entry, and so forth. Our craft were always less smart than the Americans', but smart enough and a lot more robust. A Soyuz re-entry capsule can fly itself home without any input from outside, once delivered to the correct re-entry window. We thought we had a fighting chance to make it back, yes. But—

There was an accident?

We were always cautious. But, if I could give you one piece of advice in your own exploration of Phobos—

Don't touch the blue hoops?

It was Misha. He was too intent on taking yet another reading of the residual radiation from the hoops, seeking to map any change. Our Geiger counters were clumsy, antique models – he lost his grasp on his tether—

Ah.

He only touched it. One palm, brushing the surface – a human hand touching that alien wonder . . .

There was a blue flash.

I think I was unconscious for a while. When I recovered, the blue hoops remained. Misha was gone. I have found no trace of him.

Nor have we, in our exploration here.

We are not sentimental people, we Russians, despite American

391

caricatures. Our soldiers are not brought home draped in flags, with brass bands; the dead are delivered home from the front in plywood coffins. Still – I regretted being unable to pay Misha my respects. He was a good companion and a fine cosmonaut.

And meanwhile, suddenly, after that blue flash, I was – somewhere else.

As well as Misha, the rest of *Spektr* was lost to me, the Earth-return booster, our Soyuz. And the solar panels, of course. Everything outside the Mir. The master alarm clamoured, I remember. The Mir module itself was distressed by its amputation. And Earth fell silent, even of the desperate cries of the war-ravaged continents. Silent to our receivers at least.

Something similar happened to me. As I told you I did not travel to Phobos with this group, with Malenfant and the others. My companion fell against a blue hoop. And I was stranded in a different history. We don't know what to make of this. As I said, it seems that Phobos is a kind of knot, where timelines, even different epochs, can tangle up.

And if you touch a hoop—

We don't have a good theory. It's not something you can experiment with. We think maybe the whole mechanism is – reset, somehow. The interfaces between the timelines reconfigured.

The knot retied.

Something like that.

Well, I strove to survive. We had batteries, and good ones. I shut down all but the most basic life-support functions, and endured. Time means nothing here. For months I have eked out the remaining energy in my dying craft, as it slowly froze around me. Finally I have lived in my Orlan suit, my pressure suit, hooked in to the craft's plumbing – ha! – opening it only for the intake of food, the removal of waste. I know that my body was rotting within.

And then—

Yes?

And then you came. Or rather, your partner.

Arkady. It was Arkady who found you first.

Your companion. Yes. I . . . His suit was ripped, Emma Stoney. By the hoops, I now see. He was dying already. I held him in my arms. I—

Poor Arkady.

He died well. But I was afraid, I admit it. I thought I was alone here. Suddenly, another Russian, already dying. And then, months later, the rest of you. I do not deny it. I saw the US flags on your suits. Our countries were at war! A Russian cosmonaut had stumbled into my refuge, dying already! I thought . . . I thought . . .

We came in peace.

I know that now. And so – well.

Now I may be the last Russian.

We must negotiate.

50

Four days after he was retrieved from the interior of Phobos, Bartholomew announced he was prepared to allow Vladimir Viktorenko out of bed.

The Russian emerged cautiously from the sleep cubicle he had been using. He wore his own jumpsuit, much repaired by the *Step* crew, plastered with mission patches and Russian flags. It looked like a practical garment, Malenfant thought, faded and stained, but with lots of pockets, Velcro patches and loops for hanging stuff, big chunky zippers that looked like they were designed to close a tent.

Viktorenko hesitated, glanced down at the bangle on his wrist, and looked over at Bartholomew. 'Is this thing working? You can understand me in English?'

Bartholomew smiled, reassuring. 'Actually only Malenfant and Emma are speaking English. But you will be hearing us in your contemporary Russian, I hope. A miracle of twenty-fifth-century technology.'

'I must steal it and smuggle it back to our Russian labs, where we will make cheaper, better versions. Just kidding.' He was dark-haired, eyes brown, not a big frame – in the small, cramped spacecraft of the twentieth and twenty-first centuries, Malenfant knew very well, being small was a selective feature for astronauts and cosmonauts alike. Yet even so Malenfant could see how scrawny he was, how sunken his cheeks, how pale. He looked as if he was just recovering from some severe illness – which, in a sense, he was. And oddly it made him look younger than his half-century true age.

Everybody was staring – naturally enough, but it made for an awkward moment, Malenfant thought, as the *Last Small Step* crew gazed at Viktorenko, and he gazed defiantly back.

It was Deirdra who made the first move. 'Come over to the table,' she said. 'Sit with us. Eat. I looked it up. I know there are old Russian traditions.' She moved back, graceful in the low gravity, and indicated the laden table at the heart of the *Step* cabin.

Malenfant silently reflected on her growing leadership.

Viktorenko stared at her, and drifted over to the table. The food was held in place under transparent dishes. 'Bread. Salt. Salted pork? And the drink—'

'Just water,' Bartholomew said sternly. 'I wouldn't recommend vodka just yet, Vladimir.'

Viktorenko lifted the covering over the bread, touched it with one finger, broke off a small piece and bit into it. 'It tastes like Russian bread. Did you carry this to Phobos? Perhaps for this lost Berezovoy?'

Malenfant grinned. 'No need, Vladimir. This is the future, remember. They have matter printers now. Devices that can take raw material and print out anything you like – food, clothing.'

He stared, but quickly recovered his composure. 'We Russians have a legend of the *samobranka*. The magic tablecloth . . .' He took more bread, and some of the salted meat. 'I am somewhat hungry,' he said to Bartholomew. 'Not very, but somewhat. Is that a sign of good health?'

'It is.' Bartholomew smiled. 'You've been fed mostly intravenously up to now. I am glad to see you taking solid food. But, given my trying experiences with Malenfant here, I might have thought you would be – well, squeamish about food from the printers.'

Viktorenko looked surprised. 'Listen, I am a man who grew vegetables directly from human piss and shit. Not just mine, but that of my late colleague Mikhail Alexeevich, who I loved as dearly as a brother, but who shat as the Volga flows after an autumn storm. This, the produce of some miniature factory? I pour it down my throat.' And he took another bite to prove it. 'But if I am a pressure on your resources—'

'Which you aren't,' Malenfant said sternly.

'You are certainly welcome aboard my ship,' Gershon said now – the first time he had spoken, Malenfant realised. 'Aboard the *Last Small Step*. Which I guess is pretty roomy compared to the primitive capsules you used to fly in, Vladimir.'

Viktorenko glanced around dismissively. 'A Soyuz was no bigger than it needed to be. The name. *Last Small Step*. What does it mean?'

Emma said, glancing around warily, 'Well, this is where we start getting into the weirdness, Vladimir. In my memory, it's a reference to the first words that Neil Armstrong spoke when he stepped out on the Moon. "That's one small step for a man . . ."'

'Ah.'

'Whereas,' Malenfant said, 'I remember them as the words Aldrin spoke when he became the first Moonwalker, as a tribute to his buddy who had already died of a heart attack.'

'And I,' Viktorenko said grimly, 'must imagine them as the first words Armstrong *would* have spoken had not sloppy American engineering caused his craft to detonate itself on landing, thus sparking off decades of conflict.'

'One simple event,' Malenfant said. 'If epochal. And between us we remember three different versions of it. We evidently come from three different strands in the manifold.'

'Yet here we are all together,' Deirdra said firmly. 'Let's sit.'

They gathered around the table, all save Gershon, who hung back. The table was equipped with small, neat stools, with bars under which a discreetly hooked toe would hold a diner in place effortlessly in the low gravity.

'So,' Viktorenko said. 'Important things to discuss. Such as different histories. What if Napoleon had not turned back at Moscow? Paths not taken.'

'Yes,' Malenfant said. 'Different worlds.'

'Worlds,' Viktorenko mused. 'Whole universes? Does the divergence go that far? Or are we looking at more minor deflections – strands missing from a tapestry, though the bigger picture stays the same?'

Malenfant spread his hands. 'I've no idea, Vladimir. We need theoreticians here. Physicists, experimentalists. Not a pair of artificial people, a bunch of failed astronauts, and a starry-eyed kid.'

Deirdra pursed her lips. 'I'll let you get away with that. Just.'

'And I,' Vladimir said, 'am no astronaut. I am a cosmonaut.' He put his hand over the bangle on his wrist. '*Kosmonavt*. Can you hear the Russian?'

Malenfant nodded. 'Respectfully noted.'

Emma grinned. 'Of course he's a cosmonaut. Five hundred years on, you haven't lost your gift for effortlessly insulting people, have you, Malenfant? How the hell you ever thought you were going to found a multi-billion-dollar business—'

'All part of my rugged charm.'

'We should talk about Phobos,' Deirdra said firmly. 'So here we are, all from different timelines, as you said, Malenfant. But it's Phobos that seems to be tangling them all up. Isn't it?'

'Quite right,' Emma said. 'And we have absolutely no idea how it works. Do we?'

'Let alone *why*,' Malenfant said, brooding. 'If it's an artefact it must have a purpose.'

Viktorenko nodded. 'Are we sure it is an artefact?'

'The Sculpture Garden looked like an artefact to me,' Deirdra said firmly. 'Even if I wasn't allowed to go see for myself. Those blue hoops in a . . . square. But not a square.'

Even just remembering seemed to give Malenfant a ghost headache.

'And,' Bartholomew said now, 'I can confirm what Vladimir told you, Emma. In terms of the Mir's positioning in space, I mean. I spent a lot of time going back into Vladimir's Mir module, trying to retrieve stuff – and, respectfully, dealing with the body of your colleague Arkady.'

Emma nodded gravely.

'Most of you have been in there; you know what it was like. No lights, a real mess. And I couldn't see out, any more than you could have, not at first; all the ports were frosted over. Anyhow my focus was on the interior of the module, not the outside. We plastic people aren't generally equipped with curiosity subroutines.'

Malenfant snapped, 'Get on with it.'

'Yeah. Well, in the end I went to one port, and I found a knife, frozen to the table in the eating area, and I used that to scrape away the layers of frost on the glass, until I had cleared off enough to see outside. And I saw—'

Deirdra was wide-eyed. 'Not Phobos rubble?'

'Stars,' said Viktorenko.

'Stars,' Bartholomew confirmed. 'I saw stars, Deirdra. And it's just as illogical as the hoops' five-sided cube. The module is thirteen metres long. It is docked to the exterior of Phobos, just as Vladimir described. It sticks out from the side of the moon like a monolith. I could see all that from inside – looking out of the windows. But *at the same time* it is buried a kilometre deep inside Phobos, with one airlock giving onto the Sculpture Garden. Just as we found it.'

'Impossible,' Emma said.

'Experienced, impossible or not,' Bartholomew said.

'There's probably a logic to all this,' Emma said. 'Just as there is probably a logic to having those five hoops in a space where only four hoops can exist. It's just that it's a – higher – logic than we are capable of seeing.'

'Yeah,' Malenfant said, thinking hard. 'Look – we know, or we suspect, that Phobos is some kind of junction between timelines in the manifold. This fancy set-up has some purpose we don't yet know. But if there are discontinuities in time, maybe there can be discontinuities in space as well.'

'That may be so,' Emma mused. 'But what's it got to do with Neil Armstrong?'

That shut them all up.

Bartholomew produced more bread and pork, and served up Russian tea, in small cups with nipples that released tiny quantities of fluid that nevertheless burned Malenfant's tongue. Hot drinks never worked in zero gravity, he groused to himself.

As he sipped his tea, Malenfant looked around at his companions. They all looked earnest, intent, focused – tired, all of them, especially Viktorenko, for obvious reasons. The Russian was pale, drawn, even gaunt. But, tired or not, bewildered or not, they had work to do.

Malenfant restarted the discussion.

'Actually I don't think it's about Neil Armstrong.'

Emma glanced at him. 'What isn't?'

'The jonbar hinge. Is that one of my antique-fanboy references? The pivot, the moment when a choice had to be made – or an accident happened or didn't happen – and reality changed. Maybe the turning point was the way the space shuttle got built, in the years after Armstrong died.'

Bartholomew snorted. 'And it's just a coincidence that you, a space shuttle pilot, happen to think *that* event was of world-shaking importance.'

'Well, maybe it was. Emma and I talked it over.' Malenfant massaged his temples. '1969. Even before Armstrong and Aldrin landed on the Moon, President Nixon had to decide what we wanted to do next, in space. I was only a kid. But I do remember Nixon making a speech, around 1970. He said: *With the entire future and the entire universe before us, we should not try to do everything at once*. Even at nine or ten that filled me with dread. Shit, I thought. We ain't going to Mars after all – or not in my lifetime anyhow. Well, Armstrong's death swung Nixon's decision-making in the end – but it was the decisions that counted. That was what made up the jonbar hinge. Not the background causes.

'Do you get it, Emma? Think about it. You mentioned Kennedy, pledging in 1961 to get humans to the Moon in ten years. Well, we made it, but that was a dead end, in terms of space development. And it shaped just ten years of history. Whereas the decisions Nixon had to make after that, about the American space programme post-Apollo – and, in response, the space efforts made by the Soviets and the rest of the world – were open-ended. They were going to shape the human future in space for decades. Centuries.'

Deirdra was listening with her usual mixture of fascination and astonishment. 'And everything else,' she said now. 'I mean, the whole economy was dragged along by space developments. If not for that—'

'If not,' Bartholomew said, 'maybe we wouldn't have boomed and busted so hard we burned all the coal on the planet. I say "we" in a spirit of generosity to my flesh-and-blood colleagues here present.'

Malenfant spread his hands. 'Unanticipated consequences. Everything has unanticipated consequences. We seem to come from – neighbouring realities, similar strands in the manifold, shaped by Nixon's decisions. We could call it the Nixon Bundle, maybe. The old bastard deserves that much.'

Emma seemed stunned by these conclusions. 'Just think about that, Malenfant. Richard Nixon, shaper of worlds! Suddenly I feel humble again. So. What next? . . .'

That was when there was a knock on the door.

51

They sat there, looking at each other.

'Six of us on Phobos,' Malenfant said. 'On this whole moon. Six in this cabin. And—'

'And a knock on the door,' Deirdra whispered.

Again that knock, coming from the airlock. It sounded impatient, to Malenfant. A hammering.

Malenfant recalled that Viktorenko's Mir hadn't been the only structure they had found, rooting around in the guts of this transformed Phobos. The other hatches, another mystery they'd had no time to follow up yet.

Emma touched his arm. 'I think you'd better answer that, Malenfant.'

'Yeah.'

So Malenfant drifted over to the airlock. There was no visual system, nothing to show him who was waiting outside.

Or what. Malenfant hesitated.

What are you expecting, Malenfant? The spawn of Cthulhu? Get on with it.

He made sure the lock was evacuated of air. He ordered the outer door to open, close again. A hiss of air equalising inside the lock.

Then the inner hatch was pushed open.

A human figure stood there, in a pressure suit, with some kind of reaction gun in the left hand.

The visitor began competently unlocking latches on a helmet with a rather opaque visor. Malenfant had time to notice a British flag on the chest – a Union Jack – and a name tag: LIGHTHILL, G. RASF.

Then the helmet came loose, to reveal a man's head: clean-shaven save for a luxuriant moustache, dark hair cut short at back and sides and greased with some kind of oil. Pale blue eyes, glaring.

Malenfant could think only to ask, 'Who are you?'

'Never mind that, matey. Are you the bugger who defaced my airlock door?'

52

He might have been forty, Malenfant thought, perhaps a little younger. In his bulky, peculiarly old-fashioned-looking pressure suit, Lighthill seemed to loom large in the cabin of the *Last Small Step*. But, even bobbing around in Phobos's minuscule gravity, he had an effortless air of command that Malenfant could only envy.

And his accent reminded Malenfant of old Second World War movies: the senior officers who had sent the Dambusters off to their heroics. He vaguely wondered how their own bangle-mediated speech sounded to Lighthill. For sure, Malenfant wasn't about to tell him about that bit of technology yet.

He watched how his crew reacted. Emma just seemed bemused by the whole situation.

Deirdra had actually laughed at the cut-glass accent.

And Viktorenko stared back at Lighthill with a kind of hostile curiosity, Malenfant thought. But then, in Viktorenko's reality, Russia and Britain were at war.

'Look, I don't know who you people are,' Lighthill said now. 'Or where you came from – though I'm guessing from what we already know of Phobos that it's probably not a place I am familiar with.'

'What year?' Viktorenko asked bluntly.

'I beg your pardon?'

'What year is this for you?'

'Good question,' Malenfant murmured. 'The Rolls-Royce plaque in the airlock was dated 2000—'

'Installed by an earlier mission,' Lighthill said. 'Five years ago. By the Christian calendar, the date is AD 2005. Does that make sense to you people?'

'Kind of,' Malenfant said.

Emma grinned. 'Well, I'm from 2005 also. *A* 2005. That's when I reached Phobos myself, anyhow. For the others, it's complicated.'

Lighthill stared at her. Then he grinned back, apparently relaxing a little. 'Very well. I suspect we need a thorough debrief.' He glanced around at the rest of the crew. Nodded politely to Deirdra, who seemed fascinated.

Malenfant bridled, perhaps unreasonably, at this casual assumption of command. But Bartholomew was watching him, smiling. *A rival hijacking your fan club, Malenfant?* Malenfant turned away, hoping he wasn't glowering.

Lighthill seemed puzzled by Gershon, but more so by Bartholomew. 'You, sir, are not what you seem at first glance.'

Bartholomew smiled. 'Wing Commander Lighthill, you're very perceptive. Most people are fooled for a little while, even if they are used to simulacra such as myself.'

'*Simulacra*. Interesting word. It is only the finest of details which – I am not sure what clues I picked up. Something about the steadiness of your stance, umm—'

'Bartholomew. Call me Bartholomew.'

'Perhaps you are *too* well made, Bartholomew, that's the issue. I am not familiar with the likes of you, that's for sure, in my Road. We have many advanced technologies, but not of this sort.'

Malenfant frowned. '"Road"?'

'Perhaps we need to establish a common vocabulary.'

'Maybe. We've been making it up as we go along.' Malenfant took a breath. 'We think we are encountering variant timelines, maybe branching off from each other at certain jonbar hinges – sorry, that's my own jargon, and antique in this age. Branch points.'

'"This age"? Not 2005, then.'

'No, sir. I myself am another refugee from the twenty-first century, or a variant of it. But this ship was sent to Phobos in the year 2469.'

Lighthill raised an eyebrow; it was the first time he had heard the date.

Malenfant went on, 'All of which adds up to what we are calling a manifold of possibilities, of variant – destinies.'

'"Manifold."' Lighthill seemed to chew the term. 'Mathematical term, topological. I like that personally. But then I have a background in maths and science – I took the mathematical tripos at Cambridge, and cut my teeth post-doc at the Cavendish labs. Nuclear physics, you know. But, your "timelines" – we call them "Roads". After the Frost poem – do you know it?'

'"The Road Not Taken",' Deirdra said, surprising Malenfant.

'That's the one. Fellow on the first Phobos expedition had something of a penchant for pre-Prussian War poetry, and that seemed to fit the mood. And Frost was an American, which seems rather appropriate now we've encountered you lot.'

Prussian War? Malenfant let it go, for now. Navigating this tangle of realities needed patience, above all.

Lighthill looked Bartholomew up and down once more, grinned, and moved on. As if they were cadets on parade, Malenfant thought sourly, being inspected by the senior officer.

Now Lighthill held out his right hand to Stavros Gershon.

'I wouldn't,' Malenfant said. 'Not yet. Long story.'

Lighthill smiled apologetically, and turned away, still cradling his helmet. 'So. What now?'

'What now? You came to our door, Wing Commander.'

Lighthill snorted. 'After you signed your name on mine, sir.'

'Yeah. Sorry about that.'

'Here we are, humans together on Phobos – which, I am sure you will agree, though I know nothing of your state of knowledge of this enigmatic moon, has nothing to do with humans at all. We ought to get to know each other, at least.'

Malenfant shrugged. 'I can't object to that. Frankly, I have the feeling that we have more to learn from you than the other way around. How do you want to do this, though? Bring through the rest of your crew?'

Lighthill looked around, and actually sniffed. 'I rather think it would be better if you came to us. The *Harmonia* is a little more . . . roomy. No offence.'

'None taken,' Gershon said, glowering.

'So, what?' Malenfant asked. 'We suit up, come back with you through the Sculpture Garden to your airlock?'

Lighthill frowned. 'Ah, you mean the Engine Room. The chamber of the blue hoops? That's what we have been calling it. Sculpture Garden . . . I think I prefer that. Oh, no, I think we can do better than that. I will bring our ship, the *Harmonia*, to you.'

Malenfant stared. 'How is that possible? Given we come from entirely different, time-shifted realities?'

Lighthill studied him, with, Malenfant thought, irritated, the air of a kindly schoolmaster faced with a bright but under-prepared student. 'You really haven't worked out much of how this place works, have you? No matter. We will call you when

407

we are in position.' He glanced at Gershon. 'Umm, perhaps we should make sure our communication systems are compatible.'

Gershon smiled. 'You have radio, for short ranges? Just tell me the frequencies before you go.'

'Good.' Lighthill drew his gloves from his helmet. 'Let's get on with it, then.'

As he made for the airlock, Emma whispered to Malenfant, 'So he's in charge now.'

'Oh, grow up.'

53

It was twenty hours later that the HMS *Harmonia* swam into view of the *Step*'s ports.

A ship so huge that the *Step* crew could only take it in a little at a time. So huge that as it inched cautiously towards them, they ran from port to port, screen to screen, to make sense of it.

'Like a dumbbell,' Gershon said at length.

He was right. It reminded Malenfant of nothing so much as the *Discovery* from the *2001* movie, a reference he suspected would mean nothing to anybody here, save maybe Emma.

Gershon showed Malenfant sketches he was compiling on his screens, mosaics of images morphed to fit together. 'Two main masses joined by a spine. See? In fact the design logic of the *Step* is similar. The rear sphere: that alone must be a hundred metres across, and I'm guessing that's the main engine. Plus the power plant, whatever. This lumpier section at the other end of the spine, probably the main crew compartment.'

'Yes,' Emma said, 'that makes sense. Look, you can see lights – windows – in that forward section. Behind that big disc that has been mounted on the . . . prow? If that's the direction of thrust. I wonder if Lighthill's crew is in there looking back at us. So why the spine, with the long gap between the hab compartment and the engine block?'

Malenfant said, 'I think we are seeing hints about how this ship works.'

Gershon nodded. 'Right. Nuclear technology. Look, my own ship, the *Step*, is driven by nuclear energy. But I had the advantage of centuries of development after Hiroshima — in particular, very effective lightweight radiation shielding systems. If these guys are from 2005, in any sensible history, that technology is going to be a lot less sophisticated than mine.' He pointed at the engine block. 'So, some kind of big, badly shielded nuclear engine in there. *That's* why they put the crew compartment at the other end of that spine, a long way away. That spine is cluttered up, though, isn't it? Looks like sacks of rubble, or ice.'

'Fuel store, I'm guessing,' Malenfant said. 'Feedstock for the nuclear engine, and propellant, maybe some inert substance, even just water, to be hurled out the back for thrust. Mined from — where do you think, Stavros? The asteroids?'

He shrugged. 'Phobos itself? Plenty of water ice here.'

'I doubt that,' Malenfant said. 'There are surely too many mysteries about Phobos for it to be dug up that way. Deimos, the other moon of Mars. That might make more sense.'

'Their thrust has to be relatively low, or they wouldn't need so much propellant. Lousy mass ratio, because low exhaust velocity.'

Malenfant nodded. 'That's as may be, but that shield at the front—'

'Yeah. That ship, crude as it is, is meant to go *fast*. Fast enough for collisions with interplanetary debris to be a significant menace. Hence, the shield — water ice, probably, that can be renewed when they refuel.'

'Fast,' Emma said, a little wildly. 'And therefore, far. How far? Mars, obviously.'

Gershon said, 'I would have to get some numbers, run some estimates. But I think that bird could easily get to the outer planets. Well beyond, in fact.'

'Hmm,' Malenfant said. 'Which makes it overpowered for a jaunt to Phobos, doesn't it? No matter what the attractions of our favourite little moon.'

'We couldn't build a ship like that, Malenfant,' Emma said. 'Not in my 2005, or yours – not in the Nixon Bundle at all, maybe.'

'You're right,' Malenfant conceded gloomily. On the white-painted hull of that approaching passenger compartment, he now made out a bright Union Jack, and an RAF, or RASF, roundel. 'So they are from someplace else. I wonder what their mission is.'

Deirdra pointed out of a window. 'You may not have to wonder long. Here they come.'

The *Harmonia* was looming closer to the area of Phobos where the *Step* rested. Now, Malenfant saw, some kind of flexible, very long tube with a docking attachment was reaching out from that putative passenger-compartment end of the dumbbell. The attachment smothered the *Step*'s own airlock hatch, fixing itself in place with a rattle of some kind of clamps.

A brisk message from Lighthill informed them that they were safe just to climb up, inside the tube, to the *Harmonia*. 'Pressure suits optional,' said the Brit.

But Malenfant overrode that. You didn't rely on somebody else's technology for vital safety. He ordered the crew to suit up, and, grumpily, he led by example. And, more curt orders: he had decided to leave behind Bartholomew and Gershon, artificial people, for this first trip, to help manage the culture shock.

Once they were suited up he led Emma, Viktorenko and Deirdra out through the *Step*'s airlock.

Out through a hatch, and into a tunnel to the sky. Malenfant led the way. There were handholds inside the tube to help him climb.

The whole set-up must look bizarre, he thought as he clambered, the *Step* on the dull grey surface of Phobos connected by a twisting tube to that huge sculpture in the sky. Like a child holding a balloon on a string.

At the far end of the access tube, the airlock in the side of the British ship was much heavier than the *Step*'s, chunkier, more robust maybe – but the technology was primitive, and it took some time before the pressure was safely equalised and the inner hatch opened.

And when that hatch swung back, Malenfant could hear the blood hammering in his ears, his vision greying, as if he was about to faint.

Because on the other side of the hatch was Nicola Mott.

He had to be helped into the roomy interior of the *Harmonia*, to his chagrin.

Nicola Mott. His pilot on the lost *Constitution*. Alive, and healthy. And *younger*, he saw now, than the Nicola he had lost.

He was helped out of his pressure suit, mostly by Emma and Deirdra. Led into what he learned was called the wardroom, a spacious area set out with wooden furniture – adapted for zero gravity, he perceived dimly, with toe-holds and loose straps over the chair seats and such, but still, *wood*, polished even.

Helped into a kind of armchair, against his protests, even as his pressure suit was taken from him.

Handed a glass globe containing some clear brownish fluid, by a young man smoking a pipe. A *pipe*.

'Here. Drink this.'

'What the hell is it?'

'Brandy. Get it down. Do you the world of good.'

He was perhaps early thirties, with a blond, blue-eyed, Teutonic look to Malenfant's eyes. Competent, friendly. Smiling, around that pipe clamped in his jaw. It was an odd kind of pipe, Malenfant saw now – with a kind of transparent cowl over the open end, and a fat metal bulb beneath – but a pipe nonetheless.

'Name's Bob Nash. Engineer, Phobos specialist, and general dogsbody. Welcome aboard.'

Emma and Deirdra still fussed around Malenfant. Emma said, 'I'm not sure brandy is a good idea.'

Deirdra was fretting. 'Do you think I should go get Bartholomew?'

Nash shook his head. 'Who's he, your doctor? Among my other accomplishments I am also the ship's MO. If there's anything you need—'

'Give me that.' Malenfant snatched the globe, sucked down the brandy. It burned the back of his throat, and after months of abstinence it felt like it delivered a hell of a kick. Whether it did him any good or not he had no idea.

He took a second look around at this wardroom. Aside from the homely furniture, much of it was functional, with metal surfaces and antique tech, panels of switches and cathode-ray-tube screens. Clunky round portholes set in the walls – this was a spacecraft. And yet there was a peculiarly cluttered feel, with panels between the metal ribs covered in what looked like wallpaper, shelving littered with ornaments and faded family photographs held in place with bits of

413

elastic. And everything looked oddly stale, yellowed.

Seeing the pipe clamped in Nash's mouth, Malenfant could tell why.

'Is that tobacco you're smoking, fella?'

Nash took the pipe out of his mouth and smiled again. 'Ingenious, isn't it? Dreamed up by some RASF boffin with too much time on his hands. Oxygenated tobacco, and a filter for the ash – don't want that drifting around in a spacecraft. But it delivers just as much of a nicotine kick as the old briar I've been smoking since school . . .'

As he spoke, Malenfant saw over his shoulder Lighthill, looking concerned, or maybe irritated. And, unmistakably—

He turned to face her. 'Nicola Mott. Jesus, what are you *doing* here?'

She had looked more puzzled than alarmed at his initial reaction to her. And, up close, she looked so much younger than *his* Nicola. Younger than forty, maybe. 'I'm sorry if I've somehow upset you, sir, but—'

He blurted out, 'You died. You were sitting right next to me, aboard the *Constitution*, and you *died*, Niki. When we crashed.'

She looked faintly disturbed. 'We flew together?'

Malenfant tried to pull himself together. 'Yes. In a space shuttle. A kind of spaceplane. Don't know if . . . We flew for NASA. Which is, was, an American space agency. Oh, shit.' He buried his face in his hands. 'Oh, Niki! What a way to introduce myself.'

'Niki? Nobody calls me that, sir.'

He looked at her bleakly. Her accent, he thought, was much more cut-glass Brit than his Nicola's. His Niki.

Lighthill, watching this, took a deep breath. 'Well. I think we need to calm down, all of us. Take things one step at a time. Nicola – Bob – I did tell you that these people are from, well, elsewhere.' He glanced at Malenfant. 'You'll have to excuse any clumsy reaction. We thought we knew our way around Phobos, you see. How it worked. Its mechanisms elude us, but it is evidently a complex of Roads, where they meet, intersect, diverge, perhaps even merge, as a minor road will join a trunk route. From Road to Road we observe gross changes – even astronomical sometimes, the positions of minor bodies. Different craters on Mars, and so forth.

'But generally a silent Earth.

'We always thought we were somehow – the first. Just us, wandering around the sky, with Earth after Earth stuck in the Stone Age or whatnot. Well, I suppose you might be as advanced as the Romans, say, and still not obviously visible from out here. Now, in this particular Road, we became aware of radio signals and such from the local Earth. Obviously some kind of technological culture. But we couldn't make sense of their signal formats, and nor, I would hazard, have they understood ours even if detected. And so we kept quiet – kept ourselves to ourselves.'

Emma pursed her lips. 'It makes sense. An optimally coded signal would be indistinguishable from noise, if you don't have the key.'

Lighthill looked irritated, as if at this presumption of inferiority, Malenfant thought.

He said, 'So you have been to this particular, umm, Road before?'

'Why, certainly. We first came here because we discovered an especially useful alignment of the planets in this particular Road. In fact from Phobos we intend to travel to Persephone, which is lined up with a further target beyond.'

Malenfant was startled. 'Persephone?'

The man waved. 'Out there. You know it, surely. Persephone is a major comet-cloud planet.'

Malenfant glanced at Deirdra. 'So they know it in their timeline. They use the same name.' He hesitated. 'The planet with the towers.'

'Ah.' Lighthill looked at him appraisingly. 'Indeed. We have seen those too. Another enigma. First observed from Earth, actually – or, specifically, from the Outer Station observatory in high Earth orbit. Well, we've been there before, of course. To Persephone. We actually have a base out there. In this very Road.'

Malenfant goggled. 'You have a *base* on Persephone? *This* Persephone, in this . . . Road?'

All this was hitting him too quickly. He glanced again to Deirdra, who looked thrilled, if somewhat baffled. This was after all *her* reality. And here were these odd Brits flying around *her* Solar System. To *her* Persephone.

'Certainly we have a Persephone base. Strictly speaking the base is on one of the moons, called Melinoe. We even run a ferry service, of sorts! This ship and a sister vessel take it in turns to cycle out there. But this time we don't intend to stop there, at Persephone – we of the *Harmonia*, I mean. Not on this journey. Melinoe is a valuable ice moon where we will refuel again, for the longest leg of the mission.'

'Beyond Persephone?'

'Certainly. Out to a further destination – exploiting that useful planetary alignment, as I say. That alignment is why we have kept on coming back to this Road, having invested in the Persephone base . . .'

Malenfant caught Deirdra's eye. As far as he knew there was only one significant object lined up beyond Persephone: just as the Planetary AIs had told him. Shiva, parent of the Destroyer. She looked as electrified as he felt.

'But,' Lighthill was saying, 'we have certainly never

encountered *people* wandering around Phobos before, let alone from other Roads than our own.'

Viktorenko growled, 'It is interesting. Maybe something about the distribution of worlds, of timelines, is evident here.' He gestured at Malenfant. 'We here are survivors of three different . . . Roads. In one, Malenfant crashes his spacecraft; in one, Emma here is stranded at Phobos years earlier; in yet another, war devastates Russia.'

Malenfant watched the British for their reactions. At that hint of a Russian war they exchanged glances.

'Maybe,' Viktorenko said now, 'some of these Roads come close together. In some abstract sense. They occur in tangles, braids. A common background, up to a fairly recent divergence. Commander Lighthill, we come from what my colleagues have called the Nixon Bundle. Maybe there are other bundles. And maybe there are Roads which are more solitary in nature.'

Lighthill said, 'Well, perhaps there's something in that. Devastation of Russia, eh?'

Viktorenko said bluntly, 'I come from 2028, or a version of it, where Russia was attacked by a coalition of the West, including Britain and America.'

The atmosphere was grim after that pronouncement.

Lighthill, a military man, nodded curtly. 'Well, sir, I have to tell you that Russia, *our* Russia, was rather battered long before – 2028, did you say? Certainly by the time Hitler and Joe Stalin had finished lobbing nuclear weapons at each other back in '46, anyhow.'

Malenfant and Emma shared a glance of their own at that snippet of news.

'But it does not matter now, in this company,' Viktorenko said firmly, as if determined to believe it. 'We are all human beings, taken out of our context. Yes?'

'Yes,' Lighthill said. 'I'll drink to that – or would, if I had a glass. We are being remiss as hosts, to keep you chattering on the doorstep, so to speak – though the talk is fascinating. Bob, why don't you . . . ?'

'Right away.'

With good grace, Bob Nash led them to a dining table of what looked like polished oak, set in the middle of the wardroom, more fancy furniture fitted with inset-lidded trays and a variant of Velcro pads, and with practical zero-gravity seats lined up alongside.

'Sit,' Lighthill said, with a note of jovial command. 'Please. We have prepared dinner. And you too, Nicola. No, I insist. I suspect you have a lot to talk over with Colonel Malenfant; leave the chores to Nash and me . . .'

He hustled away, with Nash, to what looked to Malenfant like a galley.

A dining table. On a spaceship. Well, that was the British for you. 'I have a head full of clichés and stereotypes,' Malenfant murmured. 'Mostly being confirmed.'

Nicola Mott, at Lighthill's insistence, was sitting down beside him. 'What was that?'

'Nothing. Sorry.'

A moment of awkward silence.

Then Nicola said hesitantly, 'Picking up on Vladimir's idea of resonances between the worlds: maybe it's so.' She looked at Malenfant almost shyly. 'Maybe it's not just grand events like the fate of nations, but also the – destiny – of individuals. From what you say of the fate of this other Nicola, who flew with you – you and I, perhaps we have been drawn together. Otherwise it seems quite a coincidence, doesn't it?'

Her accent definitely was stronger than *his* Nicola's, he

realised, and she seemed more withdrawn. Maybe coming to America had been good for her counterpart, pilot of the *Constitution*. For one thing, perhaps she could have been freer about her sexuality. And she was so *young*.

Nash emerged now with a bowl of potatoes that he began to dish out, along with an unidentifiable green vegetable mass that stuck to the plates, defying the lack of gravity.

Nicola said, 'Tell me about – her. This version of me that you say died.'

He took a breath. And he gave her a brief summary of the career of the Nicola Mott he had known – though he had to keep backtracking to follow up details – all the way through to the crash of the *Constitution*.

The other British had been listening to this with grave interest as they served the food.

'That's the long and the short of it,' Malenfant finished. 'I don't remember anything myself after that until I woke up here – I mean, in the twenty-fifth century in Deirdra's, umm, *Road*.' But he thought, guiltily, of the flawed Retrieved copy of Nicola he had demanded at the Codex. Something else to tell her later. 'I'll happily try to tell you anything else I can of her. You deserve that much.'

'Yes,' Nicola said. 'Or *she* deserved it. I would like that.'

Some other time, he promised himself, he would tell her about Siobhan Libet.

'Excuse me.' Lighthill ducked back into the galley, and re-emerged with a heavy pot of what looked like stew, thick, coated in a heavy gravy that, as he dished up, helped it stick to the plates, like Nash's vegetable slop. 'Hope you enjoy my signature dish – always my favourite at school . . . Of course it's field rations for us most of the time, we don't often get guests – ha! We do have eels, you know, that's actually our regular

419

feed. Swimming around in our dilute sewage. No worse than the lower Thames, I'm told, and helps with the cleansing of our reused water and so on . . . I digress. There's one basic thing I don't understand. Malenfant, in your Road, why wasn't Nicola flying into space with the RASF?'

Malenfant shook his head. 'Because there was no RASF, Lighthill. Just the RAF. Military aircraft, yes. No British space programme – well, none to speak of, a few satellite manufacturers and such. Certainly no crewed programme.'

Lighthill frowned as he sat down, and began to cut into his own food with cutlery spotted with Velcro, or some allohistorical equivalent. Around mouthfuls he said, 'I find that hard to believe. *Very* hard to believe. No British in space at all?'

'Oh, there were some. For example Nicola, or her counterpart, applied to NASA – the American space programme – and worked her way up through the ranks. It helped that she had an American-born mother, even though she grew up in England.'

'Ah,' Lighthill said. 'I did know that.'

'Others flew with the Russians, as I recall. But no British spacecraft, Lighthill. No *Harmonia*. Magnificent as she is.'

Lighthill grinned and raised his glass. 'Well, I'll drink to that. And to all of us. Human companionship, in the middle of cosmic madness.'

They all raised their glasses, sipped. Malenfant watched Deirdra warily, wondering what her mother would say if she could witness this scene. Not least the wine-drinking. And the smoking.

Deirdra herself seemed fine, however, and calmer than some of the adults. She said now, 'The *Harmonia* is magnificent, sir. But I have some questions too. Real basic ones. Such as, how does she work? I bet Stavros would like to know that too.'

Nash smiled. 'Miss, I would give you a guided tour of the

420

engine room myself, if there's time. More questions?'

'OK. I'm really muddled up about timings and Roads and bundles and the manifold . . . *How* did you manage to fly your ship, the *Harmonia*, from your British-space-programme Road to this one?'

Lighthill smiled. 'Excellent question. To answer it, we need to talk about Phobos. Bob?'

And he cut himself another piece of meat, and chewed busily, while Bob Nash began to speak.

WORLD ENGINES

54

'The first thing you need to understand about Phobos is that it is a machine,' Nash said.

'I mean, it is a machine built into a moon, but a machine nonetheless. You have all seen the Engine Room – which you call the Sculpture Garden. The arrangement you found deep in an equatorial shaft. Surely it is evident from that alone—'

'We got that much.' Malenfant spoke awkwardly. He was having trouble chewing through lumps of boiled potato. 'Machinery. Very advanced, enigmatic, but machinery.'

Lighthill put in, 'Very well. And Phobos is a very *old* machine.'

Emma said, 'Can you prove that?'

Nash nodded. 'Actually, yes. We think so. Earlier expeditions brought home samples of material – not just surface rocks and so forth, but some of the more exotic materials deep within. The glass-like substance that coats the wall of the deep shafts, for example . . . The thing about *that* stuff is that it doesn't wear out.' He grinned. 'Ever!'

Malenfant listened to the highly technical account that followed of what some British lab or other had made of the Phobos samples.

The glassy stuff was not just very old – *it did not age*, just as Nash had said. That was due to an odd quantum-mechanics effect, it seemed. A quantum crystal, Nash called it. The 'glass' was essentially a diamond, crystalline carbon, though doped with nitrogen. Diamond was a regular lattice of carbon atoms. And in a lattice patterns were repeated in space, over and over again. The odd thing about the Phobos glass seemed to be that such repetition had been pivoted, so that the pattern did not endure just across space, but across *time*, too . . .

Lighthill put in, 'A very small-scale effect that nonetheless, when amplified by repetition and exponential growth – doubling in size, then doubling again and again – can be magnified to the larger scale too.'

'So that's why the stuff doesn't wear out,' said Emma, who seemed to be grasping this faster than Malenfant.

'Precisely,' Nash said. 'It is self-repairing, if you like. Self-regenerating. It *copies* itself, flawlessly, into the future. And such is the scale of the effect, down in the quantum realm, that, paradoxically, *no energy* is required to fuel this regeneration.' He shrugged. 'Marvellous stuff. Once created, once shaped, it just doesn't wear out. In a sense the structure is its own memory of itself, you see. Phobos, or the asteroid rubble it appears to consist of, seems to be primordial – it is itself probably billions of years old, made of junk left over from the creation of the planets. The crystal stuff may be as old as that, or even older.'

'And so, you see,' Lighthill said, 'that's how long Phobos has sat here – doing what it's doing. So we believe. Or it sat *somewhere*. As you know – or I imagine you do – Phobos's orbit is decaying. I find it hard to believe the whole thing will just smash up in a few million years' time, after having endured a thousand times as much. There is still plenty we don't know.'

Deirdra nodded. 'I think I understand all that. So Phobos is old. And it is full of machinery. But what does it *do*?'

Malenfant had had enough of British bragging. 'I think we know what, Deirdra. In broad-brush terms. It mixes up histories. Or, Roads. What we don't have any idea of is how that is achieved.' He glared at Lighthill, challenging. 'And I bet you and your boffins in Cambridge don't know either.'

'Actually it's Oxford that is leading the way on that stuff, I am galled to admit. I *can* tell you that the study may be leading us into a theory that could unite, at last, our two post-Einstein pillars of physics, I mean quantum physics and relativity, the small and the large . . .'

'Einstein. Interesting,' Emma murmured to Malenfant. 'So wherever the jonbar hinge is between us and these British—'

'Must be a big one.'

'It comes after Einstein anyhow.'

'But,' Lighthill said now, 'we have gained some insight into the detail of the mechanism of Phobos. And how to use it, at least.'

'Use it?' Malenfant asked.

'To cross from one Road into another, a facility which is of value for various reasons – in fact, as I said, we came here ourselves to use that very capability.'

Malenfant thought back. 'To exploit this alignment of Persephone.'

'Correct.' Lighthill had finished his food; he wiped his mouth, and stuck his cutlery to the table with Velcro spots. 'Look – the, umm, *structure* of Phobos is complex – but it has a certain logic. For a start there are other access points besides the big equatorial crater, which I understand you call Stickney.'

'We know that much,' Malenfant said. 'We found a second route to that Sculpture Garden – a shallow dig down from the pole. Or rather Vladimir and his colleague discovered that.'

'That's the idea. We are the fourth imperial expedition to

come here in fact, and our predecessors have explored some of those access points, and they have made careful surveys of the interior. Mapping as they went. It was a tricky job. Phobos is as riddled with tunnels as an apple infested with worms, and the tunnels do not connect in any simple way. I have a personal theory that, to whatever higher-dimensional mind constructed this thing, it may all seem as simple as the London Underground, say. To us it is a maze, a tangle, and with non-intuitive properties too.'

'Such as?'

'Such as, there are passages which can be traversed one way only. Turn around and you find yourself facing a blank wall of rubble . . . Other anomalies too.' He smiled, rueful. 'One learns to accept them, or ignore.'

Malenfant thought that over. 'So Phobos is full of – of a trans-dimensional subway system.'

Lighthill smiled. 'I did mention the London tube, didn't I? A very practical way of putting it. Frankly we have no real idea *how* it works. The boffins speculate it is some kind of quantum tunnelling effect – where, you know, an electron or some such can appear to tunnel through a barrier by spreading out the probability distribution of its existence. It suddenly becomes more likely to be over *there* rather than here, and hey presto, it comes to pass . . . None of which helps us at all in practical terms. But we have, with time, and great caution, learned how to *use* the mechanism, at least, if we have yet to understand it. By which I mean, we have learned to navigate through that system.'

'How?' Emma asked. 'How exactly?'

'Yes, that's what I wanted to know,' Deirdra said. 'How did you bring this big ship from your, umm, Road, into ours?'

'Well, there are more accessible routes through Phobos than

via your Sculpture Garden. You'd expect that, wouldn't you? I mean, if you designed a transit system you would make it beefy enough to allow the passage of significant cargoes. We've found many such routes. Tunnels big enough for the dear old *Harmonia*, to put it bluntly. And the one that leads here, from there, where we come from, is accessed through a high-latitude crater called Paulis. Named after a member of the first expedition to the Moon . . .'

Nash went off to produce a paper map of Phobos, a Mercator projection cruder even than the one aboard the *Step*, Malenfant thought.

They quickly identified the crater. 'It's the one we call Shklovsky,' Emma said. 'Well, that's appropriate enough.'

'So,' Deirdra pressed, 'to get *here* from *there* you fly into this crater, follow the tunnels and fly out – where?'

'Out of Paulis stroke Shklovksy again,' Nash said with a grin. 'It's nothing if not paradoxical. But that's irrelevant. The point is you can use Phobos purposefully to travel from one Road to another – *if* you can find your way.'

Deirdra said softly, 'So what about the other puzzles? What about the old sunlight?'

It took a couple of minutes of debate before the group established, in language they had in common, that she meant the odd light, wan, dusty, emerging apparently from the heart of Phobos, seen in elusive glimpses.

'That is indeed sunlight, of an odd sort – our spectrometers established that too,' Nash told her. 'It comes from some very deep, very odd passages that seem to lead to – well, to greater depths than we have had the guts to penetrate so far.'

'We call those deep shafts chimneys, actually,' Lighthill said cheerfully. 'After a spelunking term from my days in the school

426

caving club. As Bob says – very deep, and apparently leading to an odd place indeed.'

'Deep.' Deirdra frowned. 'But in Phobos everything is mixed up. Space and time. "Deep" might mean "old".'

Emma raised her eyebrows. 'That seems pretty insightful to me. And the fact that this inner sunlight seems to fit models of what we believe we know of the early Solar System—'

'All of which,' Lighthill said sternly, 'is a little above my pay grade at least. Best left to future, better equipped expeditions than ours – eh? After all, Phobos for us is only a port of call. A stopover, if a necessary one, to get to where we are going. We seek much more distant goals.'

Deirdra said, 'I don't understand. What distant goals?'

'Good question. It's all to do with chance planetary alignments,' Nash said earnestly, and he smiled. 'It's not just human history that is chaotic, you see. So is the Solar System. Oh, not the big picture, not as far as we have explored: the Sun, the major planets. But details of the minor bodies, the moons, the comets, the asteroids – I suppose that sort of junk is more easily perturbed by minor events, random collisions and so on, that may differ from one Road to the next. And we find divergences in the outer planets too – I mean, the stuff out in the comet cloud beyond Neptune.'

'We call it the Kuiper belt,' Malenfant said. 'Or the scattered disc, or the Oort cloud, depending how far out you go . . .'

'You have big stuff out there, respectably sized planets even, but the Sun's hold on those bodies is very weak. So again, minor accidents can deflect such worlds far from their courses.'

Lighthill broke in. 'What Bob is getting at in his scholarly way is that planetary alignments can differ from Road to Road. And this Road, or anyhow this bundle, has a particular alignment that's of use to us, in the mission we want to make.

We came here from Earth, clearly. Our Earth. We refuelled at Deimos, and we crossed through Phobos to this Road, with its useful alignment. From here we will make a journey out of the inner Solar System. Out to Persephone.'

The *Step* crew fell silent.

'There we will refuel, and we will have the option of returning – or going on, with the fuel from Persephone, to Shiva. That's the benefit of the alignment, you see; we could not make it so far without the refuelling stop. *Shiva*: you may know of it by another name. A rogue planet. In some reality strands it will make a close approach to the Sun in a thousand years' time, or less. Regardless of that the astronomer types tell us it will be an invaluable target scientifically, as it is a world that formed entirely outside our Solar System – whereas Persephone, you see, was clearly ejected from our own inner system. And that's why we're going, if we can.

'Shiva is an Indian god, by the way. The British forces spent so much time in India, jewel of the Empire, that a lot of lingo, including names, leaked back into British culture.'

Malenfant felt almost paralysed by these revelations. He thought back to the first revelation to him of the alignment of Persephone and Shiva, with the Answerer in faraway Birmingham, months back. Even then he had had some intuition of its significance. And now, this.

'Shiva,' he said. 'More resonances across the Roads? Some call it Shiva in this reality too. A god of destruction.'

Nash seemed more attuned to the reaction of the newcomers, their silence. 'Shiva. And it's significant to you because—'

'Because in this particular Road, this particular Shiva may indeed be a threat, to this particular Earth. Deirdra's Earth. Unless somebody does something about it.'

'Ah,' Lighthill said. 'Fascinating, eh?'

Malenfant nodded. 'And you crossed whole alternate realities just to find a good planetary alignment, where Persephone happens to line up with Shiva. That's class. That's why you came to Phobos. And it's just chance you came upon us, with our somewhat strong interest in Shiva—'

'Fate,' Viktorenko said gloomily. 'Not chance. We know this about the manifold, do we not? Nothing is accidental. Some deeper causality that we can't see is working under the surface. A higher-dimensional destiny, maybe.'

Malenfant nodded. 'You could be right. Maybe there's a reason we all met.'

'A reason?' said Lighthill. 'Quite possibly. Fate or not, it's evident we have plenty more to discuss. We'll get together for a proper confab, Colonel Malenfant. You and I. Tomorrow, perhaps? But not now, eh? More brandy?'

55

So, welcome to the confab, as requested. Tea, Malenfant?

No. Thank you, Wing Commander Lighthill. I mean it's great stuff, but—

I know. No replacement for the sludge-like coffee you Yanks prefer, correct? And call me Geoff, for Heaven's sake, ranks are such a mouthful.

Geoff.

And you are – Reid, is it?

Call me Malenfant. Even Emma calls me Malenfant. And I married her. In another timeline anyhow.

Disconcerting, isn't it? You know, since the RASF first explored Phobos seven years ago – in the *Harmonia*, under a different commander – I think we've done a pretty good job of mapping out the different Roads to which it seems Phobos gives access. Mostly with physical differences of some sort. In one, we glimpsed a version of Saturn without rings! That sort of thing.

But, as I said, we have never encountered *people* before. And certainly not different versions of anybody we knew. I can't really imagine how it was – to turn a corner and there she is! The missus! Save that she wasn't the missus after all, was she?

We have been trying to work this out. And we think that we

– I mean myself, Deirdra, Emma and Viktorenko – come from neighbouring strands of reality in what we call the Nixon Bundle. Where different histories flowed from different decisions made by President Nixon around about 1970. One such history is the one we all seem to be embedded in right now, where Armstrong died on the Moon—

You see, already you've lost me. Nixon? Not a president I know of. Armstrong? Who's he?

Why, the first man on the Moon. Along with his partner, Aldrin. Landed in July 1969.

Americans, I am guessing?

Sure.

Never heard of 'em. I was eleven years old when the first lunar landing was made, and it was piloted by Jim Richards, Shropshire born and bred and a man I later trained with. In 1978 he landed at Imbrium in the *Prometheus*. And his first words on the surface, as soon as he had scuttled away from the blast zone of the atomic engines, were, 'Well, I made it.'

British. The first to the Moon was British?

Certainly. The Union Jack he erected is still there, under a plastic dome at Imbrium Base.

Imbrium Base? 1978? Toto, I have a feeling we're not in the Nixon Bundle any more.

Toto? A pal of this Nixon?

If only. Look, Geoff, I think we are going to have to work backwards until we find some jonbar hinge.

A what?

A place where your reality strand diverges from ours.

And that is *not* a sentence I expected to hear when Bob Nash brought me my vitamin juice cuppa this morning – even if it isn't strictly a sentence, as my old English teacher 'Leggy' Mountbatten would have pointed out.

Sorry. Where do we start? So you say this first Moon ship—
The *Prometheus*.

You say it went to the Moon with atomic rocketry.

Yes, indeed. Essentially the same technology that powers the *Harmonia*. And that is something I can speak about, at least, for that was my technical specialism.

It was?

Oh, yes. I was something of a brainbox at school, though big enough not to have had to endure any bullying in the scrum over it. Winchester, that was. Maths and physics, those were my bag – I think I told you. After Cambridge I did a doctorate and then post-doc at the Cavendish lab, and then found myself drafted, and was posted to Barford.

Drafted? This would be – what, about 1990? Was Britain at war then?

Not as such. But there wasn't really a time that we *hadn't* been at war, in a sense, since the 1940 Armistice.

What 1940 Armistice?

It's National Service, you see. We all must play a part. Give what we can. Some pour concrete to maintain the Blue Streak silos down the east coast. Others, like myself, use our brains. If the world is at war, it is a scientific war, Malenfant.

I never heard of Barford.

Atomic development plant in Warwickshire. Its existence can hardly be kept a secret, of course, but much of what goes on there is hush-hush ... Old mansion house converted as the HQ, airfield nearby. Established essentially to house the German specialists we retrieved from the ruins of Berlin in '46. Of course the Americans got the plums when it came to the physicists, including Heisenberg himself. But *we* got Wernher von Braun and his rocket group, or most of 'em. Still, we try to keep up with the neighbours concerning the atomics. Strategic positioning and all that. When I started, a lot of the chaps *we* had were refugees from Germany – Polish, Czech, even German Jews. The set-up was crude to start with. My supervisor said his own first job had been to pour heavy water into a prototype pile, by hand . . .

I slowly learned what an enormous operation I was part of, by the time I rolled up, oh, around 1990. Our uranium, for instance, came from across the Empire, from Canada, Australia, South Africa.

It did seem strange to me that we were using rational scientific methods to construct weapons of mass destruction. I am told that when the Russians pushed the Germans back from the concentration camps they had built on the steppe, they found orderly documentation there. Bureaucracy. Memos, about the minimum food one could feed a chap and still expect him to do certain kinds of work. We and the enemy are ghastly mirror-images of each other, I suppose. I was happy to move on to spaceships.

OK. Go back a bit further. I'm checking our own history sources here. You said von Braun got out of Berlin in 1946?

All before my time, but—

The Second World War ended in 1945, in Europe, the early summer I think. The Japanese fought on until—

The *What* War? Sorry, you've lost me. I think we must be speaking of the consequences of your jonbar hinge, Malenfant. I have never heard of a 'Second World War'. Or even a First, the existence of which I suppose is implied by the moniker.

Look, I was never a history buff. 1066 and all that! Science was my thing. But I am a senior RASF officer, and I was put through military school, and we did pick up a smattering of recent history of the warlike kind. And so I know that there was no such conflict as the 'First World War'. We had the Great

War. Germany against France and Britain in the west, Russia in the east. The Americans intervened in that one.

There was an armistice in 1918. A German defeat, essentially.

Correct. A rather punitive peace settlement.

We share that much.

But then, in 1939, under Hitler and his crew, the Germans decided to have another go. Hence, the Second Franco-Prussian War. The first being around 1870, Bismarck's war.

But it widened out, quickly. In my timeline. I'm looking over the history as we speak. Let's see . . . By 1940 Hitler was in France. The British had declared war, and they had an expeditionary force on French soil. They got the force out with a kind of mass heroism, little private boats crossing the English Channel.

The Dunkirk evacuation. Of course. Remembered fondly, a great national moment.

So after that, with France fallen and America not yet in the war, Churchill becomes Prime Minister—

Who?

. . . Ah. I think we may have found the hinge, Geoff. Who was Prime Minister at the time of Dunkirk?

Chamberlain. Chap who tried to negotiate a shabby peace deal with Hitler the previous year.

And who replaced him in 1940? Because he resigned after the fall of France, right?

Halifax, of course. Had been Foreign Secretary – I think. Fellow looked like a very tall undertaker, from what I remember from the history books. Lasted until 1942 – or '43? Assassinated by a Jewish group protesting against deportation orders to Germany, and replaced by Lloyd George until—

So you never heard of Churchill?

Racking my brain, Malenfant. There *was* a Churchill, wasn't there, responsible for various balls-ups in the Great War?

Actions at Gallipoli, I think. Became a warmonger after that. Well, even if he was in the changing room when Chamberlain was bowled out, Churchill certainly wasn't sent onto the pitch to replace him.

Throw me a bone here. Is all that about cricket?

Feel free to quote baseball jargon in retaliation.

OK. No Churchill. No Britain standing alone, then . . . So what happened, under Prime Minister Halifax?

Well, it's simple enough. Negotiated an armistice with the Germans, lickety split. I mean, what else could we have done? It would have been a stalemate. We had a navy that could have deterred any attempted invasion of Britain, not to mention an air force. But Dunkirk had shown we didn't have the land-army resources to liberate France, Belgium and the rest. We, and the Americans, soon had our hands full anyhow containing Japanese aggression in the Pacific. Immense naval battles off Pearl Harbor and Singapore. You must have seen the movies . . .

It's kind of hard for me to imagine a Britain that didn't stand up to Hitler. With a little help from the Russians and the Americans, granted. It always seemed key to your national character, afterwards.

Doesn't sound very logical.

I don't think Churchill was a very logical kind of leader.

My grandfather said he went along to boo at Hitler's state visit – I think that was the autumn of 1940. Of course Hitler never came again. By the following year he was in Moscow, watching the Kremlin burn. Operation Barbarossa, the great German invasion of Russia, spring 1941. Thousands of tanks and aircraft, millions of men. Well, it went well at first, as it generally does for these chaps in Russia.

Chaps?

Hitler. Napoleon. That sort. But Russia, you see, is a big

country. Stalin himself retreated to Vladivostok, on the Pacific coast, well out of reach. And then the winter came, as it always does, and the great invasion bogged down in mud, disease and hunger. These chaps never learn. But the fighting ground on, you see, and so did the Germans' desperation to hit at Stalin and decapitate the Soviets. Similarly the Russians wanted a way to strike back at the Germans on their home soil too. And, as everybody knows, they found a way.

Let me guess. Atomic weapons.

You have it. In the German case, they built fantastic rockets that could deliver the first crude bombs all the way to Vladivostok – technically speaking they used an A-9 A-10 combination with a range of twenty-five hundred miles. Quite remarkable beast for its time. And of course they hit other targets, deep inside Soviet territory and out of reach of the conventional forces. Oil production centres at Baku on the Caspian Sea, more than two thousand miles from Berlin. Manufacturing centres beyond the Urals, such as Sverdlovsk. And so on.

But the Russians hit back. They had done a good espionage job on the German nuclear operation – which was not hard, since the development was all done on Russian soil, where nobody cared about contamination and such. The Russians had no rockets, not then, no planes big enough to carry their crude early bombs – but they managed to smuggle the stuff in anyhow. Little ships arriving at the Baltic ports, trucks carrying the weapons onwards . . . Boom. Bang. Berlin, Munich – just like Moscow, Vladivostok – all blown up to the stratosphere as glowing dust.

This was the spring of 1946. And after that, the Americans, with assistance from us and the Italians, brokered an armistice.

And to the winners, the spoils.

The winners being the British and the Americans?

Long story short – as I said, they got the nuclear physicists, and we got the rocket scientists. Mostly. And we went on from there.

On to the Moon?

Well, that took a few decades of work.

You see, all we got from the wreckage in Russia was the German brains, and a handful of their early war rockets: A-4s, they were called, capable of lifting about a ton to about a hundred miles. They had developed bigger birds, but they had shot off all the big lads at Vladivostok and other points east.

But it was a start. Pretty quickly we set up development and testing grounds – Spadeadam on the Cumberland Fells, High Down on the Isle of Wight – and launch centres, such as in the Shetlands at Saxa Vord, an old RAF aerial farm.

And at Woomera, in Australia, for the big stuff. A few decades later I spent a lot of time out there myself, for my sins. Desolate place called the Nullarbor Plain. It ended up like a small town, with churches and even schools – it was a long-term commitment and people took their families out – but it was always a military base. Lots of drinking, lots of fighting between us and the Aussies, and not for the first time I was glad I had learned how to look after myself at school.

Well, by the 1950s we were flying British rockets – liquid-chemical stuff mostly, at first. Black Knight, really a test bed, and then Blue Streak, a big ugly brute intended as a continental-range missile. Because what remained of Germany still had the bomb, you see, and we hadn't entirely trusted our Teutonic cousins since 1940. Nor, indeed, did we entirely trust the Russians.

Hence the silos you mentioned.

All along the east coast, a hundred of them, yes, and each

stuffed with a Blue Streak or two. I had to consult on upgrades later, in fact. We had placed them on old MOD land, and in the east, so that if war came the prevailing winds would at least have blown the fall-out towards the sea. The theory was their very existence ought to deter any aggression. They certainly scared the hell out of me. Forty-year-old rusty hell-caves by then, they were.

So you had your own atomic weapons, clearly.

Yes! We had technology exchange programmes, you see. We and the Americans tried to keep ourselves closely tied. If only because in the New Age of Empire, as it was called, nobody wanted the solemn calm to be disturbed by any flare-ups between cousins.

No offence. But where I come from that would be a somewhat one-sided fight.

Oh, really? Well, Malenfant, in *my* Road, when Hitler and Stalin fell, ours was still the world's greatest empire, with vast resources. We had our own fisheries, food supply, mineral sources – and we built our own ships and aircraft and so forth. You would have picked a fight with us at your peril.

I dare say. Meanwhile, you sent humans into space.

Indeed we did. The first man in space flew in '63, four years before I was born. The launcher was a Black Prince IV: Blue Streak, with four strap-on Black Knight boosters, a second stage augmented Black Knight, and a final Waxwing solid-propellant third stage – and Bob, as they say, was your uncle. Capable of launching three tons into orbit. Enough for a space capsule, and a pilot, Wing Commander Roly Gough, who had once flown Spitfires in support of the Dunkirk evacuation. What a triumph that must have been, old Roly's voice calmly calling down from Heaven itself! Scared the rest of the world to death, that's for sure.

And so you marched on, right? Carrying the Union Jack to the Moon and beyond.

So we did. I was born in '67; fanfare, please. I think that my own first personal recollection of a striking space project was the trial launch of the first Mustard craft, from a much expanded Woomera base. I was five years old then . . .

Mustard? I never heard of that.

Perhaps it never got built in your timeline, Malenfant. Multi-Unit Space Transport And Recovery Device. I think! Everyone just calls it 'Mustard'. Keen as. Under development since the early sixties, I believe. You might have recognised the engineering logic, as from what little you have told me it sounds like the design of your own 'space shuttle'.

Winged launch craft, mated together?

That's the idea. But with Mustard you got three for the price, not two. Three more or less identical aircraft, mated belly to back. Quite a ride. We had realised that for really ambitious missions, such as getting to the Moon and beyond, what we needed was a facility to assemble spacecraft stacks in Earth orbit, rather than try to launch them complete from a site like Woomera. So that was what we started to do in 1972, with Mustard.

And in 1978 – I was eleven years old – I was there to see the blurry TV pictures as Jim Richards landed his big knife-blade of a ship on the Moon, and took his first steps, proclaimed dominion on behalf of the King, and started looking for useful minerals.

I was nine when I saw Armstrong and Aldrin land. What an age to be, to see such a thing.

I can only agree. Some things we have in common, across the timelines?

Well – by 1990, when Wing Commander Victor Hassell took

Ares to Mars, I was twenty-three years old, and beginning my secondment to Barford, and I knew very well that the linear-fission engine that had taken Hassell to Mars, an extrapolation of the successful *Prometheus* design, had been developed at that very plant, and that I would be working on future variants of it. I took my own first orbital trip as far back as 1997 – I was thirty years old, or nearly. And now here I am, an old man of thirty-eight, and grandfather to my crew of clean-shaven youngsters.

What about your personal life? You never married?

Never had the time. I wouldn't fall for the old cliché that one is wedded to the service. But the travel, you know – never mind the Moon – even the Shetlands are remote enough to put a strain on a relationship. And I would never have wished to plant a family in, for example, Woomera.

I can sympathise. It was different for me, I grew up with Emma – kind of, there was an age difference. A shared past. We did marry, my Emma and me, had a kid. But it all went wrong.

Now you have another chance, of sorts. I suppose. Or not. So. Do you think we are done here? I'm not sure what we have achieved, other than place each other's life stories against the background of a more or less bewildering multiplicity of histories.

True. But that's something, isn't it? With every discussion like this, we achieve a little more understanding.

And with understanding comes control. You're a man after my own heart.

Good. Listen, Lighthill. Maybe you can do me a favour. Potentially a big favour.

Ask.

You're on your way to explore the object you call Shiva. Going by Persephone along the way.

Correct.

I have an idea. Let me talk to Bartholomew. My doctor. He will tell me I'm crazy.

Crazy how?

Crazy to be asking for a ride to Persephone.

56

A day later, Geoff Lighthill called a meeting of the two crews in the wardroom of the *Harmonia*. His purpose, he said, was to discuss Malenfant's request: for a ride to planet Persephone aboard the British ship.

But Malenfant had the strong sense that Lighthill really wanted to talk them out of it.

Malenfant and Emma went over to watch the preparations. Lighthill had the big dining table folded up and stowed away – a miracle of space-saving in itself – and nine fold-out stools, complete with foot bars and straps for zero-gravity comfort, set up before a slide projector and a screen.

Malenfant said, 'It's like a cabin on a cruise liner. Not that I ever sailed on one of those, but I saw the old movies . . . Everything compact and foldaway, so a bedroom could become a lounge. Smartness and elegance. I guess the Brits had centuries of that kind of experience. Building luxury ships.'

'Yeah,' Emma said, 'but including the *Titanic*, and let's hope that's not an omen.' She was bemused by Lighthill's gadgets. 'That is an actual slide projector,' she said, marvelling. 'With a bulb. And slides. Look, there's a rack of them in that round cassette thing.'

'I think they used to call it a carousel,' Malenfant murmured.

'Back home you wouldn't see one of those outside a museum of technology.'

'So these Brits are behind us in some regards. But look at this ship. In our bundle, by 2005, we hadn't got beyond Mars, remember. These guys have been out to a thousand AU – nearly a thousand times as far.'

'Which is why you decided to try hitching a ride to Persephone.'

He gnawed a knuckle. 'I'm starting to wish I'd thought it through.'

'And that line, Malenfant, is going to be on your gravestone. Why did you want to go out there in the first place?'

He hesitated. 'That is the question. I'm following a hunch, I guess. It's just knowing that the damn planet is, right now, almost on a direct line between Earth, Deirdra's Earth, and Shiva. And that it has some kind of alien structure on the surface . . . It's kind of – as if I have pieces of a jigsaw puzzle, but I don't have the big picture on the lid, yet.'

She was staring at him. 'I know you, Malenfant. *Deirdra's Earth*, you said. You've got a personal investment, haven't you?'

He shrugged. 'They are good people. They preserved me in coldsleep for centuries, until your message came in from Phobos. Invested in me. It's not . . . my world. It's not the kind of world I would *choose*. But now, just maybe there's a glimmer of a chance . . .'

'Of what? Doing something about their Destroyer? How?'

He grinned. 'I don't know. But I hope I'm going to find out when Lighthill gives his slide show.'

The others started filing in.

Emma seized Malenfant's hand. 'Come on. Let's go bag a front row seat.'

Giggling, they drifted through the air.

57

Geoff Lighthill took a seat beside the projector himself, and waited for everybody to settle down.

Malenfant glanced round at the assembled company: the three British crew, Emma, Deirdra, Bartholomew. Viktorenko sitting slightly apart from the rest, looking tired, subdued. Even Gershon, projected by a relay from the *Step*, next to Deirdra. All nine of them in one place for the first time, probably, since they had first encountered each other, here at Phobos. Not all of them actually human, and garnered from multiple timelines and historical periods . . . What a mess, he thought. Yet here they were getting on with it, as Lighthill would probably say. *Christ. He's got me thinking in his language already.*

The smoke of Nash's pipe lent a slight aroma to the air.

And Bartholomew was glaring at Malenfant. That wasn't unusual, but Malenfant almost winced at the memory of the attack from the medic that he had had to endure when he had unveiled this latest scheme. *Are you utterly insane, Malenfant? Utterly self-destructive? Will you keep on trying these stunts – flying off to the void, climbing that damn Pylon, even staying with your crashing booster – until you finally finish yourself off? If I ever get you back to Earth I will have you sectioned.*

That's a bit of surviving twenty-first-century jargon you ought to recognise . . .

But they weren't on Earth. And while Bartholomew's diagnosis felt like it might be uncomfortably close to the bone, Malenfant realised belatedly that there were advantages to having a machine medic: a person might just have locked him up, but there were limits to a robot's authority over a human. Bartholomew could glare all he liked. It made no difference.

His preparations done, Lighthill floated up in the air just a little above the floor, hands on hips, and looked around. 'I imagine you all know by now what this latest jaw-jaw is about. In a couple of weeks we will have finished up our operations here, and we will stop off at Deimos to pick up the water ice the automatic miners have been collecting for us . . .'

Malenfant, curious, had been shown images of that operation: big clanking steampunk machines, dumb as shit, scraping away at the ice of that outer moon. He didn't think there was much that was aesthetically pleasing about this version of British engineering, but it was big and heavy and it got the job done, and you had to admire that.

'And then we will be off to our next stop, Persephone – or rather the base on Melinoe, the inner moon. Where once again we will refuel, and, if all goes well, we will consider progressing with the next phase, a journey all the way out to Shiva itself. Such were the mission plans I picked up at MOSA in Whitehall before the crew launched from Woomera.'

MOSA – pronounced 'mow-sir' – was the British Ministry for Outer Space Affairs, Malenfant knew by now.

'However,' Lighthill said heavily, 'as you all know, we have encountered a complication here on Phobos. Six complications, in fact, along with their rather exotic spaceship.' He smiled around. 'Complications who have become fast friends, for we humans must stick together out here in the barren wastes of space.'

'Seconded,' Nash murmured around his pipe.

'Good grief,' Malenfant muttered.

Emma whispered, 'Hush.'

'Now, though, we have another choice to make – for Colonel Malenfant has asked, politely enough, if we will give him, and at least some of his companions, a ride out to Persephone with us. With you lot on board the journey would still be possible, at least in engineering terms. Just about. So Bob assured me.'

Nash nodded, grave.

'Now then. I have quite a decision to make. And it is my decision, by the way, as long as we are out of touch with the chaps in Stevenage – that is, our ground controllers. The situation is novel enough that there may be a great deal here for us to learn – and this is, above all, an exploratory mission.' He smiled around. 'And what richer resource is there to explore than each other?'

Malenfant muttered, 'God, I hate that man.'

Emma nudged him in the ribs.

'But before I make that final decision, what I want to do with you people from the *Last Small Step* is to convince you what a *bad* idea this is. Because the journey, to a planet called after the queen of hell, would be hell in itself. Not to mention the possible jaunt beyond.' He eyed Malenfant. 'So is the agenda clear?'

Malenfant just shrugged.

'Very well.' Lighthill pressed a button on the slide projector. The screen area of the bulkhead lit up with a square of featureless light – Lighthill thumped the gadget with his fist

– and the carousel turned and dropped in its first slide with a reluctant rattle.

And up came an image of what looked like, to Malenfant, a 1950s B-movie spaceship.

Lighthill beamed around, looking extraordinarily pleased with himself.

58

'Now, look,' he said. 'It's obviously true that you chaps aren't familiar with our technology.'

Malenfant snorted. 'So now's your chance to show off, is it?'

Lighthill ignored that. 'And while your own gear seems in some regards more advanced than ours, nevertheless I must tell you something of our ships – more than I have disclosed to Malenfant here already. Because, you see, and it's not false modesty, to get to Persephone stretches our technology right to the limit. And to Shiva, even more so, of course.

'Well, then, here we go. After we'd sent up a few test shots, here is our first successful crewed lunar spacecraft.'

Up came an image of what looked to Malenfant like a huge artillery shell set on the back of a delta-wing bomber.

'The *Prometheus*,' Lighthill said proudly. 'As you can see, two stages, a lifting body and a dedicated lunar spaceship. Both relied on nuclear propulsion. The lifter was an atomic ramjet, an air-breather. The propellant for the lunar ship, methane, was supplied from tanks at Inner Station in Earth orbit. And the nuclear technology was what we called a line-focused reactor – or, linear fission – with a thin plutonium core capable of reaching temperatures comparable to the surface of the Sun.

'Now, such a ship produced an exhaust velocity of a couple of miles per second.' He eyed Deirdra. 'If you're not familiar with that concept, just remember that a rocket is most comfortable travelling at speeds comparable to, or less than, its exhaust velocity – the speed at which its exhaust shoots out of the nozzle at the back. Actually *Prometheus* was designed to take four days to get to the Moon, which works out at around half a mile per second, so that was hunky-dory.

'Next generation.'

When the next slide had clunked into place, Malenfant saw a ship pictured against the background of deep space. A rough dumb bell, like *Harmonia*.

'*Ares*. First to Mars. Assembled and fuelled in orbit, at Inner Station. And it used a development of our nuclear technology which – well, perhaps I won't go into that here. Suffice to say the first Ares mission took less than a hundred days to reach Mars. Now, our *Harmonia* is a development of the same design—'

'Hence the name, actually,' Nash said. 'Daughter of Ares, in some versions of the mythology. In others—'

'Oh, do shut up, Oxford. In our case our exhaust velocity is up to around three *hundred* miles per second. About ten times more than *Ares*.'

Gershon whistled. 'Now that is impressive. Beats out my own plasma drive, which took a couple of centuries longer to develop to maturity. In my timeline, I mean. Got to be fusion, right? Like my *Step*. You have fusion technology?'

Lighthill glared, but refused to answer.

Deirdra looked abstracted, and Malenfant realised she was doing sums in her head. 'Three hundred miles a second. Say five hundred kilometres. That kind of performance will get you around the whole of the Solar System with ease. A hundred days, not to Mars, but out to Neptune – I think.'

'Yes. Precisely. That's what she's primarily designed for. And maybe you can see now the problem we face with shipping you lot out to Persephone. For that world is thirty times as far again as Neptune. And Shiva is almost twice as far out again as Persephone.'

Deirdra frowned. 'OK, but you can't be intending to take three *thousand* days to travel to Persephone. Eight years? And that's just one way.'

'No. Of course not. We need to get there faster. In fact we aim to get there in just one thousand days – and we can do that by pushing the ship faster. Unfortunately, you see, if you want your rocket to exceed your exhaust velocity by such a factor, you have to pile on the fuel . . .'

There followed a discussion involving much hand-waving and scribbling on pads. Malenfant, a rocket pilot himself, understood the essentials. The problem was that at any moment a rocket had to push along not just its payload but also any unspent fuel; and the more fuel you carried, the more fuel you needed to push *that* fuel . . . As you planned longer, faster missions the growth in overall weight was exponential.

The engineers spoke of the rocket equation. A pilot's rule of thumb was that if you wanted to reach three times your exhaust velocity, you needed a full load, including fuel, of mass about *twenty* times your final payload.

And it got worse, if you wanted such a luxury as deceleration at the far end. Another factor of twenty.

'So,' Deirdra summed it up, 'if your dry weight is around two hundred tonnes, as Bob told me—'

Nash nodded.

'You will need about eighty *thousand* tonnes of propellant to get you to Persephone.'

'Correct. Which is equivalent to a spherical tank fifty or so yards in diameter . . . And in this case, of course, we may refuel at Melinoe to head *further out*: all the way to Shiva itself. Where we must find a fuel source to get us home again.'

Bartholomew said, 'But what's your point, Wing Commander? You can't be telling us that the additional weight of your extra passengers would make that much difference.'

'The concern is not the weight but the duration,' Lighthill said, exasperated. 'A thousand days to Persephone, remember. Another thousand to Shiva. If you add in the return journey, a couple of thousand days more to get back home . . . You are looking at a mission of four thousand days, more than *ten years*. At least. Now, our mission was to sustain the three of us across that journey – and we will relieve some crew already at Persephone. We are equipped to carry six, total, in case of emergencies – if, for example, we needed to bring casualties back from Melinoe. But to carry nine—'

'Good point,' Malenfant said. 'But we can whittle down that nine straight away. Bartholomew over there is an android. A robot, an artificial man—'

'I know what a robot is,' Lighthill said testily.

'Sorry. So he doesn't need feeding; he can live off a trickle from the power supply. Or even be shut off, ideally.'

'Thanks,' Bartholomew said coldly, not looking round. He seemed to hesitate, as if wrestling with a dilemma – whether to contribute to the proposal or oppose it. At length, to Malenfant's relief, he was positive. 'Also,' he said, 'transferring a few coldsleep pods from the *Step* would not be difficult. Cut the burden even more.'

Lighthill frowned. '*Coldsleep pods*. Unfamiliar terminology, but I get the general idea. Interesting.'

Malenfant said, 'Meanwhile Stavros is just a projection, who takes even less power—'

'And who won't be going anyhow,' Gershon said. 'My job is with the *Last Small Step*. Call and I'll come back to Phobos if you need me. Otherwise you'll find us back at the Sahara museum, I guess. Two old relics of a vanished space age.'

Malenfant turned to Deirdra. 'And, look – you need to understand this too. *Ten years*. That's a big chunk of your young life. Now's the time to bail out, kid.'

Deirdra seemed to turn those words over. 'I suppose if I were sensible I'd think about it. Maybe talk to my mother. I never was very sensible. And, to get to Shiva, parent of the Destroyer – this is why I volunteered to be with you, Malenfant.' She waved a hand. 'Not this specific plan. Because I had the feeling you would do *something*.'

'Something?'

'Something to bust everything open.' She grinned, returning his gaze boldly.

And Malenfant shivered, at the depth of determination he suddenly saw in her. In this kid, who had intuited something was wrong with her world, who had intuited something could be done about it – and as a result, here was Malenfant, at Phobos, talking his way into a ten-year mission to the Oort cloud.

Who's in charge here? Not you, evidently, Malenfant.

'OK,' he said feebly. 'Well, think about it even so.'

'Whereas,' Vladimir Viktorenko said now, 'I need no time to think. I myself have come far enough; this marvellous adventure is yours, Malenfant, Emma – you especially, Deirdra, as this is your world, your time. For me, I wish only to return to Russia. My Russia, war-ravaged as she is.'

Lighthill exchanged a glance with Gershon, who nodded. 'We can fix that before we leave. If we guide you back through Phobos to your Road, Vladimir—'

'And I will fly you home,' Gershon said. 'If, again, these

British are kind enough to guide me back through Phobos to my home reality afterwards.'

'So,' Lighthill said reluctantly. 'Three warm bodies and a robot. I think we can handle that, Mr Nash, don't you?'

'I will amend the lavatory cleaning rota right away, sir.'

As they broke, Deirdra impulsively grabbed the Russian's arm.

'But why, Vladimir? Your country is in ruins. Why go back?'

He covered her hand with his own withered fingers. 'Because I must tell the parents of Mikhail Alexeevich Glaskov how he died.'

FOUR

On Her Intervention at Persephone

59

Malenfant opened his eyes.

To find Bartholomew staring down at him.

'We are three days out from Persephone,' Bartholomew said.

Malenfant sniffed the air. 'Tobacco smoke,' he said. 'It's like I'm back in 1990.' He found his voice scratchy, his mouth dry, his throat vaguely sore. When he tried to move it felt stiff, difficult.

'You know the drill by now,' Bartholomew said.

'I should do.'

Bartholomew helped him sit up, an arm around his shoulders, strong, competent – the flesh of his hands artificially warmed to human body temperature. All part of the illusion of kindness.

'How do you feel?' Bartholomew asked.

'How do you think I feel? Like the first time I was pulled out of one of these coldsleep cans. I'm a repeat-offender Sleeping Beauty.'

Bartholomew handed him a cup of glop, which Malenfant reluctantly sipped. 'Well,' Bartholomew said, 'you ain't been asleep. And you ain't no beauty.'

Malenfant snorted a laugh, and the fluid went down the wrong way. 'And you've spent way too much time with me.'

'Now *that* I can confirm. As to how you feel—'

Malenfant twisted, working his shoulders, his back. 'Like I rusted up. Like I always do. I'll be fine. How about the others?'

Bartholomew glanced over his shoulder. 'Still in their pods. Their vital signs are normal.'

'I sense a "but".'

'Well, as you said you're a veteran of these tanks now, Malenfant. The risk for first-time patients is always higher simply because one does not know how a given body will react. Also Deirdra is younger than optimal for a sleeper. As for Emma, she is frail – fundamentally healthy, or I would not have allowed the coldsleep at all – but her body systems have been left scarred by the primitive long-duration spaceflight she endured, the lack of gravity, the poor radiation shielding, the inadequate environmental support systems. I have no reason to believe either of them has come to any harm. But I am less confident of that than I was about you, Malenfant.'

'And you woke me first because of that?'

'If I need a spare pair of hands to help with some emergency on revival of the others, I would prefer it was yours.'

'Ah. Rather than the Brits.'

'Correct. No, don't move yet. Just drink your drink.'

'No, thanks.'

'Drink your drink.'

Malenfant drained the cup with a sigh. 'I think you could have trusted Nicola Mott.'

'Maybe. She seems a good person, yes. But this is a different Nicola, Malenfant. *This* one was never your co-pilot. She never knew you, or even an avatar of you, until you bumped into each other on Phobos. There is no reason she would feel any obligation to you, or the others. Her duty is clearly to her mission. To King-Emperor Harold III.' He smiled.

'You stayed conscious? The whole three years?'

'I kept out of the way.'

Malenfant thought that over. 'I guess that if I had an off-switch, I'd feel the same way.'

'The British did talk to me, though. Especially Wing Commander Lighthill.'

'He did, did he? What about? Details of the world you came from?'

'Mostly about the technology.'

'What technology?'

'Coldsleep. He claims there have been experiments in extended human hibernation, back in Britain—'

'Well, that rings true, doesn't it? Always been a centre for that kind of research, evidently back to before the various jonbar hinges split us all apart. That was why I was woken in Britain myself.'

'You know how capable their spacecraft are. Here we are halfway to the Oort cloud after just a few years. But, Lighthill said to me, with the coldsleep pods they could reach the stars. Journeys not of years, but of centuries. Millennia, even.

'I had the sense that he was trying to find the parameters of some kind of bargain. The secrets of their fusion propulsion, for instance, in exchange for coldsleep. They had had no interest in the Earth of this timeline, before. As they told us, they failed even to receive comprehensible transmissions, from technologies centuries ahead of their own. But now, having met your party, they see potential.'

'Look, I don't belong to your society any more than Lighthill does. Would you have the authority to make such deals?'

'Certainly not, as an artificial entity. Nor would Deirdra, who is not yet of adult age. In fact, under the Common Heritage,

I am not certain there *is* a competent entity to represent all of mankind in trade negotiations with these people. This is unprecedented.'

Malenfant barked laughter. 'Maybe that's for the best. I remember old stories of time travellers dipping into the past and arming the ancient Romans with rifles, for instance. Making a mess of history. I guess the dilemma here is subtly different. These British do *not* come from our timeline. Not even a close relative of it. What are the ethics of meddling with somebody else's past? . . . Well, if we ever get home, let's ask Kaliope. In the meantime . . .' He thought it over. 'Clearly we should make no deals. But, look – Bartholomew, I imagine you aren't programmed to lie.'

'Of course not.'

'You said that with an admirably straight face. But let's keep these Brits dangling.'

'Dangling?'

'Don't refuse outright. Just put them off. Say we don't have the authority to make any such deals.'

Bartholomew nodded. 'Ah. Which will keep them interested in us. Motivated to work with us. And it also happens to be truthful.'

'Exactly.'

'I think that will work. The British are clearly highly authoritarian themselves, as well as patriarchal. They will respect our appeals to a higher authority.'

'What do you make of them? They're not like the British I know. Their language seems archaic to me, given they are from 2005 – like they were stuck in the 1940s. You've now spent much longer dealing with them than I have.'

'They are not like the British I knew either. Not like Deirdra and her family. Under the school-days banter they are – hard.

Humourless. Calculating. Decisive. Used to wielding power over other people.'

Malenfant grinned. 'I guess you don't get to own half the planet by being nice.'

Bartholomew nodded. 'We should treat them as allies, then. But be wary.'

'You got it. So, a shower and a shave for me. Then shall we wake Emma and Deirdra?'

It was now June 2472.

Malenfant had slept away three more years.

And as they went through their recovery routines, slowly, step by step, the destination approached.

60

The *Harmonia* sailed easily into orbit around Persephone. After that it took a couple of days for the ship to make its rendezvous with Melinoe, the moon, a game of orbital catch-up played with squirts of the ship's main motor.

The crew used slide rules to calculate the orbital dynamics. Deirdra stared as Lighthill and Nicola slid the components of the little gadgets back and forth and scribbled down numbers on calibrated pads.

And Malenfant inspected Persephone.

Against a star-littered background, the planet itself was a neat circle, black – like the disc of the Moon at a total solar eclipse. Beyond one edge of the planet, an even dimmer, misshapen shadow was cast against the dark – a second moon, perhaps.

The planet was not quite featureless. Malenfant could make out patches of a silvery sheen, particularly towards the poles, that looked like ice. In lower latitudes a dim mottling of darker ground against a smoother background – continents, rising up from shallow sea beds? And, at the edge of the planet, what looked like wrinkles – mountains, plateaux perhaps? Malenfant even thought he made out a dim red glow in one area, roughly circular. Some kind of geological event maybe, a volcanic caldera – must be a big one, if so, a regular Yellowstone.

And, just visible at the equator, a dark line, like a scratch on the image. Malenfant, after his briefing with the Planetary AIs, knew what that represented. The line of towers, each twenty kilometres tall, that strode right around this world's equator.

The little moon approached.

Nash said, 'Melinoe itself is just a lump of ice and rubble, not much more impressive than Deimos, say. Here we are out in the comet cloud. Your – Oort cloud?'

'That's the name,' Malenfant said, 'though we put the formal boundary further out, I think.'

'The moons have the typical composition of comet cores: dust, water ice, organics. Seems most likely that they weren't formed with the planet, but happened to fall into orbit around it, after the planet sailed out here from the inner system. Probably a late arrival, in fact, like Phobos and Deimos at Mars.'

'Sailed out?'

Lighthill glanced at him. 'Well, of course. We know that much. The deep-space observatories at Outer Station have observed many planetary systems now, in various stages of formation or decrepitude. And we do know planets don't seem generally to finish up orbiting where they formed. Although the bods seem uncertain as to how Persephone could have ended up in such a neat circular orbit. You'd expect it to be on some wildly elliptical path – if it hadn't been thrown out of the Solar System altogether.'

Deirdra had, perhaps unconsciously, drifted out of her chair to see closer. 'Wow. It's like another Earth, isn't it? But an Earth that got thrown away from the Sun.'

'Yes,' Nicola said, approvingly. 'Exactly right. Around a quarter larger radius. Twice the mass. Somewhat higher gravity. There were oceans; you can see the ice. Maybe there are frozen lakes and rivers down there too. Under the frozen air, of course. Continents and seas. Mountain-building. Why, that may still be going on; this world is out in the cold but it still has its inner heat.' She pointed to the region of lurid crimson. '*That* looks like a major volcanic province, the boffins say. And those mountains you can make out on the horizon may be very old, compared to what you see on Earth. No erosion, you see. Which tears down mountains on Earth from the moment they are built . . .'

Nash said, 'There are some scientists who think that Persephone here would actually have been *more* hospitable to life than Earth itself, if it hadn't been thrown out into the dark. It's that bit bigger, you see – that bit warmer, more mountains and coastlines where life could evolve, more active geology to move the continents around and promote evolution – shallower oceans, so you would have lots of islands as laboratories for evolution. Instead . . . Well, look at it. What a place to visit! A ruin of a world. Cold as charity. You would have to mine the air to breathe, and the only water is ice as hard as concrete, and the only traces of native life are abortions four billion years old.'

Malenfant was startled by that. *Life?* But Nash said no more. *Park it, Malenfant.* He said, 'But what it does have is those peculiar-looking towers around the equator.' He grinned tightly. 'Alien artefacts?'

'Best guess,' Lighthill said.

'Ah. Which I imagine is one reason you dashed out there. To beat the Americans and the Germans, the way you got to Phobos first . . . And,' he said, with a glance at Deirdra, 'in this particular Road where Shiva is such a threat, right now Persephone, out of place, out of time, laden with huge alien technologies, lies almost on a direct line between Shiva and the Sun.'

'As discussed before,' Lighthill said heavily. 'And handy as a refuelling stop en route. But I don't see what damn use that fact is to you.'

'Nor do I, quite,' Malenfant said. 'Not yet. But that's why I wanted to come out here. It's a coincidence – or not, given the loaded hands we keep being dealt by the manifold. Maybe it's some kind of opportunity. Call it an instinct.'

And Deirdra nodded, her expression grim.

Lighthill shrugged and turned away.

Melinoe, inner moon of Persephone, turned out to have very much the same dimensions as Phobos, a battered, roughly spherical lump measuring about twenty-five kilometres on its longest axis. It circled Persephone some four diameters out from the primary. That gave it a thirty-two-hour 'month', so it was a little outside synchronous orbit; Persephone's day was twenty-five hours. As with Phobos some tidal effect seemed to have lined up that longer axis with the direction of its orbital motion.

But there the resemblance seemed to end, Malenfant realised, peering out.

Of course the little world was hard to see at all. Out here the Sun was eerie, a too-bright star, like nothing in the sky of Earth – as a supernova might appear, Malenfant thought – and the light it cast was feeble. But still, Malenfant could make out, here and there on Melinoe's surface, a reflection, a glint of ice.

Ice. *There* was how Melinoe differed from Phobos, Malenfant saw. All objects in the Solar System had been formed from the protoplanetary disc, from a mixture of dust, ice and gases – and the further you went from the Sun, the more ice had been found. So Earth, an inner world, was dominated by rock. Phobos, which had probably formed out beyond Mars's orbit in the asteroid belt, was a heap of rocky rubble contaminated with ice and hydrated compounds. Whereas Melinoe, a chunk that had probably formed far from the Sun before being sent out here by some accidental slingshot, was clearly more ice than rock.

Which made Melinoe useful for humans, who had come here to mine that water ice for oxygen to breathe, and hydrogen to refuel their fusion-rocket spacecraft, and indeed the ice itself would serve as reaction mass for those rockets. Although Lighthill was still coy about the details of the *Harmonia*'s drive.

And that was why the brightest single feature on Melinoe's surface was a brilliant spark of light: the lamps of a human settlement, a thousand astronomical units from home. Malenfant allowed himself a moment of pride at the sight of that lonely spark: pride on behalf of mankind, even if he didn't particularly like the arrogant British who, in this particular reality strand, had achieved such a feat.

With the matching orbit achieved and Melinoe approaching, everybody peered out, eager to see the destination. In the final approach, amid shallow craters, presumably the scars of previous descents, Malenfant saw shelters like half-cylinders lying end to end, surrounded by ground visibly churned up by footprints and tracks. Nash called the shelters 'Nissen huts'. They were heaped with loose ice, presumably for heat insulation and radiation protection. There was what looked like a fuel store, a dome standing separate from the rest that might house some kind of atomic reactor, a big, sprawling antenna farm, and various anonymous trenches and pits that looked like they might be the result of scientific studies. A couple of fat-wheeled tractors stood by the huts, and further out was a beefy-looking craft, standing on four legs that protruded from a battered heat shield, that Malenfant suspected might be a lander designed to take on the higher gravity of Persephone itself. All of this was illuminated by powerful lamps hanging from unfeasibly tall low-gravity masts, anchored to the dirt.

Lighthill remarked, 'What you don't see from here is the big resource extraction plant we've established on the far side. Simple affair: mining gear to dig up the ice, electrolysis to separate out the hydrogen and oxygen, a catapult to fire up filled polymer tanks into space for the *Harmonia* to collect . . . All waiting for us before we head onwards into the deep dark, or indeed head home.'

Deirdra pointed out a gaunt tube with the glimmer of a mirror at its base. '*That* must be a telescope. It's just like at Plato, on the Moon. You don't need a heavy tube and stuff where there's no air, and not much gravity either.'

'And I guess,' Emma said, 'that this little moon is tidally locked to the primary. The same face turned to Persephone all the time?'

Nash looked over and grinned. 'Quite right, Miss Stoney. Rather a convenient location for an astronomer in that regard – where your principal target of study just hangs in the sky above you. Not that we have a specialised astronomer here; everybody has to be pretty much a jack of all trades.'

'Ready for the landing approach,' Nicola said now. 'We're being pinged from the base. Think they're looking forward to seeing us, sir.'

Lighthill spoke directly to the ground. 'Coming down right on top of you, McLaurin Minor, you old rascal. Thought I'd surprise you before you had a chance to hide the gin bottles.' He glanced around at his augmented crew. 'They will make a fuss of us, you'll see. You new bugs might get a little overwhelmed. These chaps don't get too many visitors out here, after all . . . Prepare the access tube, Bob.'

'Right-o, sir.'

61

For Malenfant and the others, another eerie passage through the access tube from the *Harmonia* down to one of those Nissen huts on the ice of Melinoe. Malenfant was aware that the *Harmonia* carried a planetary lander. Evidently not thought necessary for this gentle descent.

Almost as soon as they had all reached the surface, airlock doors were thrown open with alacrity, and a man came bustling out, in what looked like a grubby coverall, crumpled, once powder blue, perhaps. He was short, dark, squat, with a pipe protruding from beneath a worse moustache than Lighthill's. His nose and cheeks were speckled with broken capillaries. A drinker, then, Malenfant thought.

He walked straight to Lighthill. 'Geoff, you bounder.'

'McLaurin Minor! Good to see you haven't blown yourself up yet.' The two of them shadow-boxed, before embracing in a backslapping, jokey way.

Deirdra watched this display open-mouthed.

They passed through the hatch into an airlock chamber, while two more crew emerged from deeper within, and the space felt significantly crowded now, with ten people – ten, that was, if you counted Bartholomew, who was keeping himself to himself. There were quick introductions. Under McLaurin's command here on Melinoe were Guy Briggs, introduced as an engineer, tall, blond-haired, elegant, with a precise moustache – *dapper* was the word that came to Malenfant's mind – but thoughtful-looking. And Josh Morris, shorter, bespectacled, a little younger than the others, a little overweight perhaps. He was the principal researcher, and maybe, Malenfant wondered, he might be eschewing the rigours of low-gravity exercising for too long in his laboratory. Or the galley.

Now McLaurin stood back from the chattering crowd and clapped his hands. 'On behalf of HMS Melinoe Station, I formally welcome aboard Wing Commander Lighthill and his crew, and guests. I will show you to your quarters, and then we can all enjoy the rather handsome meal of welcome our chef has prepared,' and he nodded to Josh Morris.

There was actually a ripple of applause. Malenfant struggled not to laugh.

Then Lighthill responded. 'On behalf of the crew of the *Harmonia*, thanks very much, McLaurin Minor. And I think you've deserved your prize. Bob?'

Bob Nash grinned, pulled a packet of tobacco from his inner jacket pocket, and lobbed it through a gentle low-gravity arc to McLaurin's waiting hands.

'Howzat!' McLaurin said, beaming. 'Thank you, Bob. Now if you will follow me . . .'

Malenfant held back as the rest of the crew filed out through the airlock, one at a time, and into the main structure.

When it was his turn, Malenfant, at the back of the line, found himself walking with Deirdra and Josh Morris.

'So they said you're the chef,' Deirdra said, evidently teasing him. 'I thought you were chief scientist.'

'Well, so I am.' He fixed his glasses with a finger-push

over his fleshy nose. Malenfant thought he might actually be blushing. 'Chief scientist, I mean – chief because I'm the only scientist, though I do rope in the others for some of the donkey work. Sample taking, equipment set-up, that sort of thing. Don't trust them in the lab, though . . . Or in the kitchen actually.'

They walked through another open airlock into an extended space, a half-cylinder with a low, curving roof. Evidently this was the main section of this 'Nissen hut'. Malenfant saw ribs overhead, as if the roof structure was made of corrugated iron. They walked, or Moonwalk-hopped in the feeble gravity, along a narrow track of some kind of fabric laid out over what looked like a glass floor. Under the glass Malenfant saw dirty ice, cracked, grainy, and streaked with some kind of brown deposit.

'This is my domain, in fact,' Josh said. 'The crew quarters are in the next hut in the line . . .'

Deirdra, evidently interested, slowed down to look at the ice. Malenfant and Josh slowed with her.

The others had walked on, leaving the three of them behind. Malenfant didn't imagine it mattered; there was a sort of informal formality about the whole event that was another characteristic of these British, he was observing.

He peered up at that rippled roof. 'That can't be iron. Some kind of lightweight alloy?'

'Not quite,' Morris said with a grin. 'We use water ice. I mean, as a building material. It's so cold here, it can set as hard as concrete. We use metal cables to enable it to withstand tension – like reinforced concrete, you see. And we are experimenting with doping it with dust to improve its resilience . . . Well, we don't need to build for structural strength, not here. You might have observed the roofs of all the huts are heaped over with loose ice – Melinoe ice, of course. Masterpiece of field improvisation. We use the big ice-extraction machines designed to fill the electrolysis tanks, and just spray the stuff over the structures.'

'Ice for radiation shielding,' Malenfant said.

'Indeed. Cosmic rays, a perpetual hazard in locations like this – although Persephone itself has a healthy magnetic field, stronger than Earth's. Which would shelter life forms on the surface. Here on Melinoe, of course, we have to dig deep into the ice to find the local life.'

Deirdra and Malenfant shared a startled glance.

Morris gestured at the floor, the stained ice under the glassy cover. 'Strange to think of a whole life domain, on a microscopic scale, going on under one's feet. Of course there are bacterial communities infesting the deep rocks on Earth, but here this is *all* there is. Very fragile: we inflict an extinction event every time we dig down for samples. Can't be helped, sadly. And the heat leaking from a human-habitable environment such as this is rather more of a hazard, actually. But the cycles of life here are so slow that the sampled ecology is scarcely inconvenienced.'

'Josh.' Malenfant held up his hands. 'Slow down. I think we're both baffled here. You're talking about life? Life here on Melinoe, this crummy little ice moon?'

He seemed surprised to be asked. 'Well, certainly.'

'It's not where you found it that surprises me, but that it exists here at all. *Native* life? I mean, not some kind of leakage from the base, a contamination—'

'Oh, no. The microbiology proves it. A variant on the terrestrial design, actually. The bugs here are based on an identical suite of amino acids, though with genetic data carried through RNA complexes rather than DNA, and I think that may be something to do with the sparseness of the available energy, the deep cold and so forth. Life must live at a slow pace here; perhaps the genetics has adapted as well as the exterior morphology. Still, it's the same basic machinery of life as on Earth. But it's not *from* the Earth.'

Deirdra looked baffled. 'And it's not life from Persephone? Commander Lighthill mentioned that you found traces down there too.'

He smiled. 'Again, that's theoretically possible; one could imagine hardy bugs being blasted even out of that deep gravity well by impacts. But, again, the microbiology doesn't fit. The life forms down *there* are different again from those up *here* – almost as different as we are from either.'

'But,' Deirdra said, 'I still don't see how there *can* be life here. What does it live on?' She glanced around vaguely at the roof. 'The Sun is out there, and it's brighter than a star but it's just a pinpoint . . .'

'Good question,' Josh Morris said. 'There is energy here. But just a trickle, compared to the flood that Earth gets. Feeding on that, life grows slowly. But it grows . . .'

He spoke of raw materials in this comet-like moon, of water ice laced with nitrogen and carbon and complex carbohydrate molecules, relics of the cloud of gas and dust from which the Sun and its planets had evolved in the first place. And of a slow battering of those compounds by the attenuated sunlight, and by a drizzle of cosmic rays – particles hurled from supernovas and other galactic calamities – and by an equally slow pumping of energy by the ice tides raised in the little moon's structure as it circled the great mass of Persephone. There was even a gradual leakage of energy from trace radioactive compounds buried deep in the ice itself.

'Doesn't amount to much. But all these tiny events can create free radicals – that is, molecules that are ionised, trace substances that are highly reactive, chemically. These build up in the ice, slowly, slowly – the low temperature preserves them, you see, so you can get quite a concentration – and *that* is enough to power simple forms of life, very slow, very small-scale metabolisms.' He gestured at the brown traces in the surface of the ice. 'As you see, growing in the upper layers of the ice. That's the foundation of a food chain, with more complex bacterial types, even colonies, deeper down, feeding on the communities of surface life forms. Here on Melinoe, life grows *in* towards the centre, where there is more residual warmth and energy, not out towards the Sun, as on Earth. I think it's possible there are some quite complex life forms buried deep down beneath the surface here, even kilometres down, but we haven't yet been able to drill down that far. Some day . . .'

Malenfant and Deirdra shared a glance. Malenfant felt utterly unprepared for this cascade of revelations.

Josh looked from one blank face to the other. 'You know nothing of this? You spent years on the *Harmonia*.'

'To be fair,' Malenfant said, 'mostly asleep.'

'Ah, yes. The Wing Commander did say something about that. You must tell me all about that technology . . . But as to Melinoe life, I think I am shocked that the crew didn't mention that at all. I mean, look at it! Isn't it spectacular?'

He waved a hand at pale brown smears, barely visible in the glassed-over ice.

Malenfant clapped him on the shoulder. 'In another life I'd have ribbed you for that remark, kid. But not here. Not now. This is a wonderful discovery. And if those assholes with their tobacco and brandy and old-school talk don't appreciate it – you're right, they didn't even bother to *mention* the discovery of life, here in this place – that doesn't make it any the less remarkable.'

Morris seemed unreasonably pleased. 'Thank you, Colonel.'

'Call me Malenfant.'

'But,' said Deirdra, 'if there's so little energy how could life have evolved here in the first place?'

'Oh, it probably didn't,' Morris said casually. 'It was obviously seeded.'

Malenfant frowned. 'By what? A comet impact or such?'

'Oh, no. By whoever seeded Persephone also. The amino acid suites are identical – that alone is enough to rule out chance parallel evolutions.'

'You said – *who*ever?'

'And whoever seeded Earth too.' Morris glanced around. 'Come on! I think we're being left behind.'

He hurried off along the track, over the glistening, bug-ridden ice.

Deirdra stared at Malenfant. 'Did he really say that? That somebody, or something, seeded life across the Solar System?'

'Sounded like it to me.' He had never told her of his discussion with Karla, the Planetary AI who had similarly speculated that some agent had 'seeded' the inner planets with a common life stock. And now, this fussy kid from another reality with precisely the same suggestion. Soon might be the time for more openness about it all, to share what they all knew . . . He forced a smile. 'Totally unexpected news, right? Now you know what it's like getting woken up in an ice box after centuries asleep.'

'Maybe. And *you* know what it's like being young. Come *on*, Malenfant.'

And they followed Morris, hurrying as best they could in the ice moon's feeble gravity.

62

A week after the arrival of the *Harmonia* at the Melinoe base, preparations were made for a journey down to the surface of Persephone.

Once he had learned that such expeditions were made, Malenfant began a subtle campaign to be given a place in a landing party. Aside from what he might find down there, he was curious to learn *how* exactly you managed a descent into the deep gravity well of what the planetary astronomers in his timeline had called a 'super Earth', an Earthlike world but *bigger*.

To questions about which, base engineer Guy Briggs would only reply, languidly, 'Very carefully. I like the term, though. *Super Earth.*'

At last Nicola Mott took pity on Malenfant.

'You may not have worked out the dynamics of the crew rotation here, Malenfant,' she said. 'Look, the RASF is a pretty ambitious organisation – and so are the people who work for it. And here at Persephone-Melinoe we are right at the limit of what is achievable technically, and affordable financially and politically.'

'You're telling me there is competition to be here.'

'And once you *are* here, competition for the glamorous stuff, like a descent to Persephone. We don't do it that often.' She smiled. 'I imagine space travellers across the manifold have similar pressures, and ambitions. Too many super-capable crew chasing too few opportunities. Well, here the permanent staff at any time is only three. The *Harmonia* shuttle brings replacements, but the philosophy is that at least one of the previous rotation stays aboard the station, for continuity. In this case that's to be Bill McLaurin, the commander. So Geoff Lighthill will fly onwards to Shiva, with Morris and Briggs. I will be replacing Josh as science specialist, and Bob Nash will take over from Guy Briggs as engineer. A three-year tour, for us, until *Harmonia*'s sister ship comes to take us off. And three years after that, *Harmonia* herself will return from Shiva. And so on.'

Malenfant thought that over. 'But even so, given the journey, a tour away from Earth is, what, at least nine years? Even if you go no further than Persephone. Three years each way there and back, a minimum of three years on the station.'

She shrugged. 'Colonial postings around the Empire – I mean on Earth – can be much longer. And such tours are generally regarded as the peak of one's career, Malenfant. Once in a lifetime. Wish I could say the pay was good. But one can expect a promotion afterwards, and a bit of tin or two.'

'Bits of tin? Oh. Medals.' He hesitated. 'When I woke up in this century, I found out you and I gathered a few of those posthumously, after the *Constitution* crash.'

'She wasn't me, Malenfant,' Mott said gently.

'I know. But . . .' *But I can't help seeing her in you. Like I see Emma in Emma II. And it hurts, all the time.*

'Let's stick to Persephone,' she said.

'Persephone, yeah. So why are you telling me about crew rotations?'

'Because I've just heard about the crewing of *Charon* for its next descent.'

'You mean the planetary lander? Why *Charon*?'

She grinned. 'I think he was the chap who piloted the boat across the river Styx, which divides the worlds of the living and the dead.'

'More classical bullshit. But appropriate enough for Persephone, I guess. OK. And the crew is going to be?'

'Well, *Charon* is a four-seater – actually it can take more at a pinch. I'm going. Geoff Lighthill is going to pilot – gives him one chance to see the planet before *Harmonia* whisks him onwards. Guy Briggs, the engineer, will represent the outgoing crew. But that's appropriate in this case, because we are planning to visit one of the Towers, which has been his pet study.'

Malenfant felt a surge of excitement. He tried not to show it. 'The Towers. Those structures along the equator.' He knew the Brits capitalised the word in their reports.

'I think there is a feeling back home that we haven't done enough to explore those beasts – what they are, how they work, what they are *for*. And, bluntly, what we can learn from them. Guy does say he has got a lot further in his investigation than he has been able to report so far. Secrecy is a habit, and important results aren't sent back by radio but couriered home aboard the *Harmonia* and its sister ship. Don't want them falling into the hands of our rival powers, you see. So this is a conversation that spans years. But even so the brass are impatient.'

He nodded. 'Just as with Phobos. You imperial types are out here to grab any alien-tech secrets you can get your hands on, ahead of your global competitors.'

She frowned. 'It's not our strategic goal to come second, Malenfant.'

'OK. And the fourth crew member?'

Now she grinned. 'You have me to thank. Look, you aren't one of the trained crew. You're a mere passenger. But as a representative of an entirely different cultural tradition, you may just come up with fresh insights. You never know, it's worth a shot – that was the argument I made, anyhow. Pack your toothbrush, Malenfant.'

Malenfant whooped, and offered her a high-five palm. Embarrassingly, she had no idea what he was doing.

And so, the next day, Malenfant found out how you landed on a super Earth.

63

The *Charon* looked to him, at first glance, like another variant of the Apollo Lunar Module – an obvious design, like Viktorenko's ship at Phobos, for landing on an airless world – but this one was bulked up, reinforced. Muscular. He guessed that this beefy lander was going to use a variant of the Brits' fusion drive to land on Persephone, and, defying the giant world's gravity, haul ass out of there again.

He walked around the craft. There were wide downward-looking windows, like blisters, that would give a great view during the descent. And *big* rocket bells, obscured by those landing legs, and fat, lumpy propellant tanks. Also he saw mounting brackets where, he found out, heat shield panels and aerosurfaces could be mounted, if an entry into a thick atmosphere was mandated.

Once the crew were loaded aboard and the *Charon* had smoothly lifted, the approach was cautious; it would take twenty-four hours for the *Charon* to spiral slowly down through the tenuous envelope of interstellar hydrogen that was all the atmosphere this giant world had. Malenfant had plenty of time to be shown the lander's various systems.

But there was indeed one heck of a view through those big blister viewports, Malenfant quickly found. All four of the crew of the *Charon*, plump in their pressure suits, spent much of the descent gazing out, with pilot Lighthill and co-pilot Briggs having the grandest view of all, behind their own big bubble of a window.

The moon Melinoe orbited four diameters out from Persephone, so from the start the great planet looked the size of a dinner plate held at arm's length, Malenfant supposed. A bowl of geography. And it was a startlingly Earthlike world – if an Earth in deep freeze – with sprawling continents, including one tremendous ribbon along the equator, and flat plains that might have been frozen oceans. Surface ice gleamed, here and there, in the starlike light of the Sun.

Deirdra, calling from the *Harmonia*, said slowly, 'Stavros Gershon. He claims that in his time – this is a couple of centuries ago – an explorer, like himself, in a ship like his, came out this way. Tried to be the first to reach Persephone, to land there. I don't suppose you found her.'

Lighthill looked grave. 'Sorry, old girl. As Briggs said we have only skimmed the surface. But I think we'd have spotted any such craft. Well – unless it was submerged in some ocean of ice, or a drift of nitrogen snow . . . Lost, I'm afraid. It is a big world.'

'I'll relay that back to Gershon.'

'And I will note the explorer's precedence in my log, if you'd be kind enough to supply the details.'

'Here.' Guy Briggs handed out sheets of paper with what turned out to be a Mercator-projection map of the world below. It was quite well drawn, but the copies were all heavily marked up by hand corrections.

'Might help you get oriented,' Briggs said. 'The bods at the Royal Geographical Society in London drew this up, which is why it looks so pretty. They supplied most of the names of the features too, in conjunction with the astronomers. They even deigned to consult some of us who had actually been out here. Good of them, what? But you can see we're making supplemental discoveries all the time.'

Nicola looked over at Malenfant. 'I've seen this before, in training. Tell me what you make of it, Malenfant.'

He studied the image. 'Looks like five major continents. Including that long linear landmass that seems to pretty much follow the equator. Slightly odd distribution? I'm no geologist. And these asterisks, marked along the equator—'

'The Towers,' Briggs said. 'The markings are indicative only. There are sixty-five thousand of them, right around the planet. Too crowded to show individually, not at this scale. And, yes, they do follow the equator, Malenfant.'

'All right. Continents, two to the north of the equatorial ribbon, two to the south.' He squinted to read the map. 'Going anti-clockwise from the north-west: Judecca, Ptolemea, Antenora, Caina. Where the hell did you get those names?'

Briggs laughed. '*From* hell, actually, Malenfant. Don't you know your Dante? These are the divisions of the ninth circle of hell, in the *Inferno*. Respectively the chambers of the betrayers of benefactors, guests, country and kin. At a certain class of school one does rather get such stuff beaten into one.'

'*How* exactly did you guys acquire an empire? . . . But I guess it's appropriate for Persephone, queen of hell. That upper right continent looks – odd.' The map showed a nest of concentric contour lines. 'Like one huge mountain.'

'That's pretty much it,' Briggs said. 'It's a shield volcano – where you have a huge plume of mantle material pushing, pushing from beneath. Like Hawaii on Earth, or Mount Kitchener on Mars.'

Malenfant suppressed a grin. So in the British reality Mons

Olympus had been named after the jonbar hinge, then. 'And the central linear feature—'

'Iscariot,' Briggs said. 'The betrayer of Jesus, cast down into the pit of hell. The ultimate naughty step.'

'And beneath the midline of the equatorial continent – south of Iscariot – a lot of fragmented land . . . islands. An archipelago?'

'We called that Malebolge,' Briggs said.

Malenfant rehearsed the pronunciation in his head. *Mal-lay-bol-gay.*

'For the eighth circle of hell, where, immersed in a pool of pitch, you would find hypocrites, thieves and corrupt politicians.'

'I see you put your zero meridian here, right through the middle of the archipelago. Why?'

'That was the biologists' suggestion,' Nicola said. 'At one of the conferences that drew up the names for the features. If this planet had been left alone, close to the Sun, *that* archipelago in particular would have been an ideal locus for the emergence of a civilisation. Like ancient Greece, all those islands within easy ocean transport. Cultural laboratories. So agreed the bods in London, who may have been a bit too influenced by *their* classical educations. Anyhow that's why we put the meridian there.'

'Hmm. A gesture to what might have been. OK.' He stared at the map, trying to tease out more clues. This by a man who never even reached orbit around his home planet before his coldsleep, he reminded himself. 'This place looks more geologically active than Earth.'

'True,' said Nicola. 'Simply because it's that much bigger. It will retain its heat better, has more of a primordial load of natural radioactive isotopes in its interior . . . Being displaced to the comet cloud won't have made much difference to that, by the way. Air freezes; water freezes; geology doesn't stop.

'So there will have been continental drift, mountain-building events, out here in the dark with no eyes to see. Some differences, of course. On Earth the air and water erode away the mountains. Not here. And it's thought that Earth's liquid water, getting dragged down into the mantle when continental plates bump up against each other, helps to lubricate the tectonic processes, in a way. Here, much of the water will have been frozen out, you see. So exactly how this big geological machine has churned away out here will have been different in detail from how it would have been in the inner Solar System, but . . .'

'OK.' He looked out of his window. 'Well, right now I think I see what looks like a major ongoing volcanic event. In the strait to the south between Judecca and Iscariot . . .' About nine o'clock on the clock-face of Malenfant's map. A subdued, hellish glow.

'So it is,' Nicola confirmed. 'Lots of mountain-building going on just there, as Judecca is both continental-drifting down from the north and crashing into the big carcass of Iscariot.'

'But meanwhile,' Briggs reported, 'Josh has been telling us gleefully that in the south, Ptolemea and Antenora are drifting *away* from Iscariot.'

'Lots of sea-floor spreading there,' Nicola said. 'And lots of island-making. Like Iceland in the Atlantic, Malenfant.'

'Ah. Hence the archipelago.'

'There's no feature quite like Malebolge on Earth. It's not a drowned continental plate, it's a whole puzzle-box of rifts and fractures and colliding plate fragments.'

'Big planet geography.'

'Correct.'

'But no big impact craters?'

'Well, impactors are a lot scarcer out here,' Briggs called back. 'There are some spectacular craters down there, if you look for them – they tend not to be eroded away as on Earth, you see.'

'But no dinosaurs to kill.'

'No. But there could have been, Malenfant,' Nicola said wistfully. 'If it hadn't been hurled away from the Sun, this would have been a world full of life, probably. More so than Earth. And on these isolated island continents you might have got whole strands of evolution running in parallel. Dinosaurs alongside the mammals, Malenfant, just waiting for a Captain Cook or a Darwin. Imagine that! Instead there are just anaerobic bugs – oxygen-hating – clinging on in the deepest oceans, where there are mineral vents and where a few remnant puddles of liquid water have survived under miles of ice. Some life infests the upper layers, quite similar to what we found on Melinoe. Bugs, locked in the ice. So, no dinosaurs.'

Malenfant frowned. 'Josh told me that the Melinoe bugs—'

'Well, they aren't really bugs—'

'Had some commonalities with Earth life, our kind of life. As well as with Persephone life.'

'Good old Josh gets carried away sometimes. But – commonalities down at the biochemical level, yes, it does seem so. Same amino acids, I believe.'

'Josh also suggested that all these worlds might have been seeded by some common agent,' he said heavily, 'natural or otherwise.' But he didn't mention Karla and her speculations, of whom these British could have no knowledge.

'Well, that's possible, frankly, Malenfant,' Nicola said. 'The young Solar System was a violent place, and an unstable one, with the planets not even fixed in their orbits – clearly that was so, since Persephone somehow got expelled. You could easily have biochemical suites being carried to a number of worlds by meteorites and planetesimals – the building blocks of the planets – or even forming on one world, and being blasted off by secondary impacts and ending up on another.'

'Or,' Malenfant said, feeling reckless, 'maybe some giant walked among the new worlds, scattering seeds.'

Briggs barked laughter. 'That's quite a turn of phrase you have there, fellow.'

'Yeah, well, maybe I went to a school where it didn't get beaten out of me in favour of Dante.'

'But,' Nicola said now, 'however Persephone got out here somebody did build those Towers, Guy. So we *know* there has been intelligent modification on some level.'

Lighthill grunted. 'That's an appropriate moment for me to remind you all to buckle up tight. Time for a preliminary burn as we begin the final descent . . . We will come down in the local morning to give us maximum light.'

Malenfant checked his own harness. 'So where exactly?'

Nicola looked over her shoulder at him and grinned. 'On a planet full of geological and biological marvels? We are going down right where you would want to land, Malenfant.

'At the foot of a Tower.'

64

The British were as businesslike and efficient as usual. A mere hour after the landing the crew was ordered to close up their suits, and the cabin decompressed.

And Malenfant clambered down from the lander, Armstrong-style.

He planted his booted foot on hard ground – featureless rock, it seemed, a dull rusty brown, littered here and there with what looked like slicks of even harder ice. His fifth world, he supposed, after Earth and the Moon, and if you counted Phobos and Melinoe. He muttered, 'Not a bad record you're racking up for a truck driver, Malenfant.'

Nicola was waiting for him at the bottom of the ladder. 'Oh, I think you were always more than that, Malenfant.'

'So were you, Nicola. So were you, in another life.'

Once the four of them were safely out – Malenfant, Nicola, Lighthill and Briggs – Lighthill had them gather in a circle, facing each other, in pressure suits made additionally heavy thanks to this world's tougher gravity. Faces behind visors illuminated by soft interior lamps.

Lighthill said, 'So this is a new world for all save Guy – new to me too. Let's just take a moment to acclimatise. Get used to the conditions. Guy?'

'Beginning with the gravity,' Briggs said. 'Over a quarter more than Earth's. It might not feel much at first.'

Nicola grunted. 'My pressure suit feels like a suit of armour.'

'There is that. The big heavy boots are a pain, aren't they?' Briggs lifted his own feet to demonstrate the fact. 'As I said, the increased weight may not seem like much of a drama. We have all endured much higher accelerations during spaceflight. What you'll find, though, is that this steady, relentless pull will wear you down, somewhat. You'll tire sooner. Your muscles will burn up that much more energy – well, in just keeping you and your suit upright, let alone walking about or doing any useful work. So be aware of that and give yourselves a break . . . And speaking of breaks.'

He took a geological hammer from a loop at his waist, held it out, and dropped it. It did seem to fall faster than Malenfant's gut would have predicted. Not dramatically so, but quicker.

'So it falls a yard in four-tenths of a second instead of five-tenths. Enough to measure, not enough to inconvenience you, you might think. But, look.'

He bent stiffly in his suit to pick up the hammer, and Malenfant saw that it had landed in a slick of hard-frozen water ice, and had cracked the stuff, creating a tiny, shallow crater.

'The impact when a hammer falls depends on its kinetic energy. And, my friends, for a given object falling a given distance, *that* is thirty per cent higher here than on Earth. So if you smash a faceplate or crack a shin bone because you didn't take this big beefy world seriously, don't come crying to me.'

Lighthill nodded. 'All right, Guy. Well said, and I think we get the message. So let's take a look at where we are, shall we?'

They broke, dispersed. Malenfant watched his companions as they moved cautiously about, upright in their suits, evidently balancing carefully in the higher gravity, casting long, sharp shadows in the dim sunlight of a Persephone morning. The light was eerie, Malenfant thought, as if cast by a single spot onto some vast stage set.

The ground around Malenfant, as far as he could see in the lights of the lander, was more or less flat, featureless, all the way to a sharp horizon, dark against the star-littered sky. That Mars-like rusty rock surface was crumpled here and there as if eroded by ancient geology. In places he saw what looked like splashes of dust and rubble, metres across – and, when he looked back at *Charon*, he saw a similar pattern sprawled across the surface beneath the landing legs of the squat craft. Landing scars: human-made features. Which made sense given the landscape; for your landing zone you would naturally choose a plain, away from hills or pits or craters, away from geologically active areas such as the volcano provinces he had glimpsed during the descent. And, once such a landing place was found, you would keep on coming back.

Nicola stomped her way across to him.

It struck him that this was the first time he had seen her walk under a strong gravity – and she walked heavily but easily, steadily. With no trace of that persistent limp *his* Nicola had suffered since her childhood accident. He recalled the similarly even gait of the Retrieved copy back on Earth, and his heart broke a little, once again.

'Malenfant? Are you OK?'

'Yeah. Sorry. Just a little disoriented.'

'Me too. But you ain't seen nothing yet.' And she pointed over his shoulder.

He turned around. And saw the Tower.

*

Lighthill had brought the *Charon* down a good kilometre away from the Tower itself. Now, obeying a safety-first mission protocol, Lighthill himself stayed behind at the lander, while Briggs led Malenfant and Nicola to the structure itself.

From this distance, as Malenfant walked, the Tower was just a white stripe against the sky, narrow, featureless, dead straight – dead vertical – and shining in the pinpoint sunlight. Malenfant was oddly reminded of searchlights over war-torn Baghdad – or, given he was with these British, of old movie images of wartime London, beams bright in the smoke-filled air, seeking Luftwaffe bombers. But that was another London, found by following a different Road than that from which Briggs and the others had travelled, and Malenfant supposed that the reference would have made no sense to his companions at all.

And, still most of a kilometre out, even when he tipped his head right back, bending inside the stiff suit, he could not see the top of the structure. The Tower was a stripe of light that narrowed to invisibility before his eye found any terminus.

Twenty kilometres tall, he thought. Twelve, thirteen miles. And evidently a built thing. On twenty-fifth-century Earth the tallest buildings humans had ever built – judging anyhow from his memories of his own era, and the evidence of the Pylons – had been skyscrapers less than a kilometre tall. And that on a world with a gentler gravity than this. Such structures would have looked like mere buttresses if placed alongside this monument. Indeed, this single Tower would have dwarfed Earth's tallest natural structures too. Everest was only, what, eight kilometres high? Why, he had known people who had spent their whole careers as aviators who never *flew* as high as that Tower was reaching.

He remembered his very first glimpse of the Towers, when Karla, the Planetary AI on the Moon, had shown him astronomical photographs of a world with an enigmatic line scratched around its equator. Towers that were visible from space, from across the Solar System. Now he was here. He laughed, softly.

Nicola glanced at him. 'You still OK, Malenfant?'

'Yeah. Just trying to get my head around what I'm seeing . . .'

And, what was worse in terms of a challenge to his imagination, the Tower wasn't alone.

The *Charon* had come down a kilometre or so north of the line of Towers, which were themselves spaced less than a kilometre apart, in their tremendous march around the equator. So now, as he walked forward, as he looked to left and right, he saw more Towers, cousins of the one he was aiming for, and identical in every respect, as far as he could see to either side. More sunlit stripes reaching up to the sky, the further ones soon becoming too dim to make out clearly, their tops dwindling into the starlit dark. It was like approaching some tremendous fence, he thought, a fence that stretched right around this huge planet. Visually it was a little like a view he had once had of a huge offshore wind farm in the Gulf of Mexico. The same sense of a row of evidently artificial giant structures that challenged the scale of the landscape. But the scale here was far greater, of course.

Halfway there and Malenfant suddenly noticed he was panting. 'Jeez,' he said. 'It really is like I'm doing some military camp route march with a pack of rocks on my back.'

'You'll get used to it,' Briggs murmured. 'Or not. Anyhow it's not far. We have returned to study this one Tower repeatedly – selected somewhat at random, one out of a population of sixty-five thousand around the equator – but we chose it—'

'For safety reasons. I get it. It's next to a nice broad plain for landing on.'

Behind his visor Guy Briggs grinned, as if proud. As if he had built the Towers himself. 'What do you think, eh, Malenfant? Like something out of Blake, what? Dark satanic mills . . . And these are mills, or at least engines, we think. World-spanning engines.' He stamped on the ground. 'We haven't dug down to see for ourselves, but we have seismometers that show us huge chambers under the Towers. Engines, giant themselves, enigmatic.

'But, as to the basics – as you can see, somebody, or something, built this Tower. And its companions. *They are clearly artificial.* As indeed are the structures we have discovered inside Phobos. Simplest hypothesis is that those two occurrences of artifice are caused by the same agency – the same, umm, *race*, of whatever alien beings. But we don't know that – indeed we know nothing of the engineers, save for the existence of their artefacts themselves. Perhaps they are long gone. Perhaps not.

'Whatever they were, they evidently didn't think like us. Never mind the scale of all this. Look around. On this planet, sixty-five thousand of these Towers in their orderly row. And aside from that – nothing. Nothing on the planet. No modifications we can see, no structures. No houses, factories, towns, no roads or mines. No sense of a hinterland, of a civilisation or even colony that might have built all this.'

Briggs was tall, elegant, his voice calm, yet somehow projecting wonder. Malenfant found himself unexpectedly impressed by this man. A quiet visionary.

'So they didn't live here,' Nicola said. 'They didn't colonise, or develop a civilisation, whatever. They just – built this.'

'Correct. Let's move on.'

They walked.

Nearer the Tower there was clearer evidence of previous human visits. Malenfant recognised caches of emergency supplies: air tanks, water bottles, medical supplies, in one place what looked like an inflatable shelter. Instruments on stands, and set out on the rocky ground: seismometers, Geiger counters, cameras peering at the Tower. Close to the foot of the structure, there were small heaps of rubble where samples had evidently been drilled out of the rocky ground. The humans who had come here had left traces, if not the builders.

And, at last, the Tower itself.

If it was very tall, it was also very slim: Malenfant guessed a hundred paces wide, no more. And he was, he realised, now no more than a hundred paces from the Tower wall itself.

'I'm guessing a hundred metres diameter?'

'That's about right,' Briggs murmured. 'Though I would record it as yards.' He was walking around the instruments, checking their status. He paused at one camera, to extract what looked like a cassette of film. 'The width, you know, is only half of one per cent of the height.'

'That's ridiculous,' Nicola murmured. 'It's like a conductor's baton standing on one end. It ought to just topple over. And to think this thing has been standing here for – how long, Guy?'

'Billions of years.'

Malenfant stared at him. '*Billions* of years. You serious about that?'

Briggs smirked. 'Out of deference to you, Colonel, I employ the American usage of the word, meaning thousands of millions. But, yes, I am quite serious. As I said, you'll see the evidence for yourself . . . Come. Walk with me. I think you have to apprehend this physically, as far as you can. We can't climb the damn thing, but we can walk around it, at least, in a few minutes. Does the psychology good. Or not . . .'

So the three of them walked, more or less clumsily, in a loose circle around the Tower. This didn't feel so strange to Malenfant. It was as if he were walking around some high-rise in a city somewhere. It was only if he looked up, to a structure whose upper limits he couldn't even make out, or east and west to the giant companions of this Tower, that he felt disconcerted.

They came back to roughly where they had started.

And then Briggs walked boldly up to the Tower, reached up with a gloved hand, and slapped the wall.

It was the first time any of them had touched the Tower. Malenfant found himself flinching reflexively.

Briggs went on, 'Would it comfort you if I said this thing is hollow? The top is open. Like some giant chimney stack. And the walls are wafer-thin. We proved that by flying over it in *Charon* – over this beast and a few of its companions – and also by dropping camera drones down deep inside. Plucky little gadgets made it all the way down. Rocket-powered, of course.'

'Down to what?'

'Don't make me give away all my secrets at once.'

Now Malenfant reached out with a gloved hand, and touched the surface himself. He was hesitant, but felt nothing as his gloved palm pressed against the wall. 'Can't feel a damn thing. Not even a temperature difference. I wish I could take my glove off and feel it directly.'

Briggs nodded. 'That's an impulse I understand. Impossible, of course.'

'What's it made of, though?'

Briggs shrugged. 'There we are stumped. Something tough enough to have lasted aeons, that's for sure. I mean, none of the Towers show any damage from meteorite strikes, for instance, and statistically, over such an interval, some of them ought to have been smashed just from that cause alone. Certainly our sampling has been unsuccessful; we have tried everything from geological hammers to laser drills.

'Oh, we have various theories, and the less you know about science the wilder the theory. Maybe the wall material is some variant of more or less normal material we have yet to encounter. An exotic kind of diamond, for instance. Maybe it is protected, somehow, from our tools, by some kind of energy field. But it doesn't feel like that, does it? It *feels* like a hard surface, not as if you are being pushed back by some field of force.

'Another possibility is that it is some variant of the stuff we found at Phobos – the quantum-crystalline sheeting they used there to line the walls of the shafts – I believe you were briefed? *That* is an economical hypothesis at least – the same agency using the same technology.

'And Josh Morris once opined that a Tower wall might not be material at all. Suppose it is some artefact of twisted spacetime? Well, old Einstein did show us that that kind of distortion was theoretically possible. The energies involved would be huge, though.'

Malenfant shook his head. 'That kid has a fine imagination.'

Nicola gazed up at the Tower. 'Somehow I doubt that energy budgets were a primary concern for whoever built this thing, and its siblings.'

'There I tend to agree with you. But as to how it was done . . . My own guess? I think it may be some kind of self-replicating material. Almost like a living thing, like a tree trunk, just gathering material and energy from the environment, and growing up and up. After all a tree is a far more complex structure than *this*, and that needs no conscious engineering. And there are forests on Earth with far more than sixty-five thousand trees, all alike.

'Pity, really, that we've got no further. I mean, we are out here for the good of the Empire. And a material as light and durable as this stuff seems to be – imagine it as hull plate for shipping, or aircraft fuselages! That's even before you get on to space applications. Why, our manufacturers would suddenly be as far advanced over our German and American rivals as were the Romans with their concrete, lording it over the Ancient Britons with their wooden roundhouses. By the way, we may not be able to retrieve a sample of the wall material, but we have safely patented it.'

Malenfant snorted. 'That doesn't surprise me.'

Emma whispered in his ear, from the *Harmonia*. 'Private line. Aside from the miraculous wall material, doesn't all this strike you as – well, as crude, Malenfant? A row of big chimney flues . . . Think of the engineering we found in Phobos. Or thought we found.'

'The Sculpture Garden,' he murmured. 'The spacetime subway.'

'It's hard to believe that the same culture who built *that* – or even the Phobos time-crystal material – can have been responsible for *this*.'

'Umm. You have a point. So maybe they weren't the same culture. Maybe the Tower engineers . . . borrowed that other stuff? Or just used it to get to places, the way the British are now.'

Briggs was saying now, 'Most frustrating of all, of course, is not knowing the purpose of all this. The problem is we have so little evidence. We know what the Phobos Sculpture Garden can be used *for*. We don't even know *that* much of the Towers. And we know still less about what it was all *intended* for. Which is a different thing, if you think about it.'

'Yeah.' Malenfant peered at the line of Towers. 'A monument designed to last billions of years? The Pharaohs would have loved it . . .'

No, that wasn't right, he thought. This was no monument, it was too functional for that. What, then?

And, even as he posed the question, he thought he saw an answer. He stayed silent, thinking.

Briggs turned briskly back towards the lander. 'I think that's enough for now. Come back to *Charon* and I'll show off my homework. How we found all this out, and deduced the structure . . . And then we can all indulge in wild speculation.'

Malenfant just stood there. Unwilling to move. As if he feared breaking the fragile chain of logic in his head.

Nicola stayed with him. 'Malenfant? Are you OK?'

'Independent verification.'

'What?'

He turned to look at her. At that strange yet familiar face, visible through her visor. 'I need somebody else to come up with the idea, independently.'

'What idea?'

He grinned. 'The craziest idea I ever had, that's all. Or the best. Come on, let's get back to the lander.'

But as she turned away, still he hesitated. Then he dug into a suit pocket, and produced his battered Shit Cola can. 'Souvenir of London, England.' He bent, stiffly, and, his gloved hands awkward, put the can down on the rocky ground. Because, why the hell not? He had the feeling he was never going to come so far as this again. 'My personal high-water mark.'

'Malenfant?'

'Coming, Nicola.' He turned around and walked clumsily back to the lander, leaving the can behind.

Malenfant—'

65

It turned out that Briggs wasn't lying about showing off his
work. But then, as Malenfant conceded to Nicola, he evidently
had a lot to show off about.

And as he described his investigations and results, the words
and images he produced at the lander were relayed up to
Melinoe and *Harmonia*, to Deirdra, Emma and the rest. Relayed
both by the British radio gear and, more subtly, by Malenfant's
companions' bangles.

'We have been scientific about this, I'll have you know,'
Briggs said now. 'Good enough for the Ministry science bods
anyhow, if not to Royal Society standard. We've studied the
Towers every which way we can, we've taken ground samples,
we've dropped drones down the flues, we've done various
soundings to get a sense of the underground structure . . . We
even set off a hand grenade next to one of those Towers, to get
some decent seismology signals.'

'It was Bill McLaurin did that,' said Lighthill mildly. 'You
were bloody miles away. He told me.'

'All right, we don't need to go into that, thanks, Wing
Commander. At any rate there are underground structures —
cavities, perhaps mechanisms of some kind.'

Nicola murmured to Malenfant, 'Incidentally this is all new

to me too. As a newcomer here. Well, most of it. Even though I'm in the military.'

Malenfant smiled. 'National security again?'

'Quite so.'

'Well, I shouldn't be surprised. Given you fly in a spaceship equipped with hand grenades.'

'To begin with,' Briggs said, 'I think we can be confident that this planet, Persephone, did *not* form where we find it now, out in the comet cloud. This is a rocky, more or less Earthlike world, which must, therefore, have formed roughly in the same part of the Solar System as Earth. As previously discussed. And we are pretty confident that we can show that *these Towers were built in that epoch*. When Persephone was young and hot and warm.'

'How can you know that?' Nicola asked.

'From the rock cores we have taken – and we're confident about that, for this continent, Iscariot, does seem to be pretty stable, geologically speaking.

'For example, we found that some of the Towers we examined had been set up on the beds of shallow seas. Seas of still-liquid water. You can tell from trapped sediments and so forth, right at the base of the structure – well, the base before you reach the foundations that dive deep down into the crust. There are even traces of life in these deep layers. Life like our own biochemically – life like the other forms we have encountered, here, even on Melinoe – but very primitive. No photosynthesis for example, no oxygenation of the air.

'And we think that this world was *moved* – however that was done – or maybe it migrated naturally, out of the inner Solar System, very soon after the building of the Towers.' He dragged out rolls of paper, photographic images of some kind of cores, the strata hand-labelled. 'These cores of ice and rock are like records of what became of the planet subsequently.

You see, if you detach a world from its sun, especially if it's a slow process – well, the world's systems react slowly too. They leave traces, easily distinguishable layers, as stuff rains out or sinks, as living things die off. You see a gradual diminution of the biological content, and the rock structures are increasingly disrupted by ice formations . . .'

Malenfant nodded, imagining it. 'The sunlight is dying. The seas are cooling, and quickly – they are pretty shallow, aren't they? Soon enough they start to freeze. And then, eventually, the air snows out.'

'Right,' said Briggs. 'There are other indicators of time passing. As the water rains out, so the erosion rate slows, you see. The land, the mountains wearing away, the rivers washing sediment into the oceans – all that slows down. You can see *that* in the cores.' He traced features of his core charts. 'Thinning layers of sediment, you see, down here near the base – soon after the displacement itself.

'And finally, when it gets colder than Pluto because you are *that* far out, you get a one-off wave of frost-shattering. After that, there is nothing left but the silent rocks, and the ice.

'As for the geology bods who have tried to interpret all this – well, it's complicated, their models differ. After all, nobody has ever observed this kind of process directly, this descent into a permanent Ice Age. But they seem to agree that it took about a million years to deliver the planet to its current orbit – out here, in the comet cloud. As you can tell from the cores, and other evidence.'

'A million years,' Malenfant mused. 'Wow. A million years, for a thousand astronomical units of displacement.'

Malenfant heard a gasp that he knew had to be Deirdra, up on *Harmonia*. He heard it, deep inside his own skull. She whispered, unnecessarily, 'A million years for a thousand AU. I think I have an idea.'

Malenfant muttered under his breath, 'What idea?'

'Let me think about it.'

Briggs was grinning, a little self-satisfied, Malenfant thought. Briggs went on, 'Impressed? A million years? In any other circumstances that would be a big number – and an impressive result. But, you see, we have records of events that must have occurred *after* the displacement too. I mean, after Persephone was dumped out here, *billions* of years ago. Even without the Sun, even without air and oceans, the geological wheels of this big old world have continued to grind on. The continents washing back and forth like lily pads on a pond. Volcanoes leaving layers of ash and lava all over the place. And all these events leave traces on the ground, which the geologists can sequence and date. The most direct evidence we have that the Towers were built *before* the displacement are layers of volcanic lava and ash that have solidified around the Towers' feet. And *under* those layers, we find those traces of a million years of steadily thinning life – evidence of the cooling.

'Thus we can say confidently that more than four billion years have passed, since the displacement.'

Malenfant shook his head. He'd had hints that such a conclusion was coming. Even so that was a stunning result. 'As the Solar System was born, then,' he said. 'All this happened as the Solar System was still being created, the planets congealing and colliding – and even though life was here already – while all that was still under way, some process moved this world out here, across a thousand astronomical units, to the comet cloud. And here it has stayed ever since.'

'That's about the size of it.'

'OK. So much for the setting. Now tell me about the Towers themselves. Sixty-five thousand, you say?'

'Pretty much girdling the planet,' Briggs said. 'Each thirteen miles tall. A picket fence marching right along the equator, regular as a line on a map.'

'Hmm. All of them on Iscariot, most on dry land?'

'A couple still stand in shallow, frozen seas. Doesn't make that much difference if you are thirteen miles high. But, yes, they are all very close to the equator.'

Malenfant chewed on that. 'OK, but you've just been lecturing me about all the fancy geological activity on this world. Correct? The continents drift around, they crash and draw apart, just as on Earth. So even if the . . . engineers . . . who built those Towers had got them lined up nicely, on a continent that happened to sprawl along the equator back then, wouldn't they have drifted off by now? I mean, I could see it for myself, from space: one continent swimming down from the north, two more receding in the south. And that big bulge on Caina ought to make a difference too. How come that straggly continent hasn't drifted and twisted and broken up? How come, in fact, at least some of those Towers haven't been knocked over by quakes and landslips – even a volcano going off under one of them?'

Hesitation.

'Those are good questions,' Nicola said. 'To which I am sensing we don't have good answers right now.'

Briggs frowned, an elegant disdain. 'Well, I wouldn't overstate it. We do have some suggestions, even if none is definitive. Certainly the anchoring of the Towers cannot be a simple matter. The solid crust of the world is only thirty, forty miles thick. And as you rightly say, Malenfant, crust plates tend to drift. Yet the Towers, and the linear continental feature on which they sit, have self-evidently *not* drifted out of line. We don't know how this was achieved — I have to admit that. It may have been subtle. Perhaps the — what did you call them, engineers? — the hypothetical beasts who built these Towers had some way of *directing* the mantle currents that ultimately determine the shifting of continental plates.'

'Screwing with the mantle currents of a super Earth? You call *that* subtle?' Malenfant felt restless, frustrated. This orderly lecture felt like it would take for ever to get to the point he was interested in. 'Briggs, earlier you mentioned structures *under* the Towers. Picked out by seismometry, right? Buried in the rock.'

'Correct.' He fumbled in a heap of paper. 'I have records, reconstructions—'

'Never mind that. Just tell me. What kind of structures, and what do they hold — shelters, machinery?'

'Large, regular hollows. And, yes, large-scale machinery, of an enigmatic nature . . .'

He produced sketches of arrangements of circular hoops, pillars, bands, and began to brag about the careful work that had gone into extracting this interpretation from scratchy seismometry data.

Malenfant cut him off. 'So,' he demanded, 'machinery to do what?'

Briggs spread his hands. 'Well, we can only speculate—'

'But,' Lighthill put in, 'to any of us who have been around nuclear-fusion engine technology at all — which is all of us in the King's Space Force — and with due respect given to the Official Secrets Act, those look awfully like magnetic confinement structures to me.'

Malenfant said carefully, 'Tremendous fusion engines, then.'

Briggs said reluctantly, 'It's not a bad guess. We also found traces of residual radioactivity, in the surrounding rocks. Just traces, but anomalous. As if the ground there had been heavily irradiated in the deep past.'

Malenfant almost held his breath. They were getting closer to the point. 'Irradiated. OK. So nuclear fusion energy was being released down there. Possibly. To what end?' He glanced around at the British.

McLaurin called down from the *Harmonia*. 'Well, we talked this over. I always thought it must be some kind of global power system.'

Briggs said, 'A global power system to run what, Bill? There's nothing here *to* run.'

'Quite. You can tell we have discussed this, and failed to agree. Though Briggs here won't even say what *he* thinks the Towers are.'

Now Malenfant did hold his breath. He turned to Briggs, and exhaled noisily. 'So tell me, Guy. What's your idea?'

'Something too crazy to be true.' He glanced at Lighthill, almost shyly, and Malenfant saw he was fighting a kind of shyness. 'I mean, who would build sixty-five thousand of the things and stick them head first in the ground?'

'What things? What are the Towers, Guy?'

A moment's hesitation.

'Rockets,' Briggs said miserably. 'I think they're rockets! I mean, *look* at them. Strictly speaking the Towers themselves are just the exhaust stacks. The engines are deep underground – as revealed by our seismic soundings and so forth.

'Nuclear rockets. Set on end, as if they are intended to thrust down into the ground. There's no doubt in my mind. But it makes no sense.'

McLaurin laughed out loud. 'You're right about that.'

But Malenfant grabbed Briggs's arm. 'No. Listen, man, I

think it makes all the sense in the world. *I had the same idea. I've been waiting for somebody else to come up with it. And—'*

And that was when images of Bartholomew, Emma and Deirdra appeared out of nowhere.

66

The British were all startled by this latest manifestation of twenty-fifth-century technology – but, as Bartholomew showed them his bangle and gabbled out a hasty explanation, they quickly accepted the concept.

Meanwhile the visitors seemed to float in the air, like angels in this planetary hell. Their originals were nearly weightless, of course, up on Melinoe.

Deirdra said brightly, 'Everybody seems to be very grumpy, Malenfant. But that Tower is a-*ma*-zing. And your discussion – we couldn't wait any more, we had to come down and join in.'

'Yeah. Fill your boots. Listen, while I'm stuck with all of *you* – let's cheat. Deirdra, you may have to look stuff up . . . I'm pretty sure that the citizens of a twenty-fifth-century world state, post spaceflight, are going to know a hell of a lot more than these 2000 AD Brits about planetary formation. The natural stuff anyhow.'

Deirdra frowned. 'The *natural stuff*? As opposed to what? . . . OK, let's hear what you want to know.'

'Isn't it obvious? Look at this world. You overheard the discussion, right? I get that a world like this must have formed close to the Sun. And now we have Briggs's convincing proof that the planet was moved out here billions of years ago. My question is, how? How did it get out here? *How* does a world get moved?'

'I know some of it,' Deirdra put in eagerly. 'I've already been looking it up. It's really interesting. Can you check I've got it right, Emma?'

The virtual image of twenty-first-century Emma pulled a twenty-fifth-century softscreen out of the air. 'OK. Bartholomew, maybe you can show me how to use this damn gadget . . .'

It was all to do with the residual protoplanetary disc – the big flat slab of nebular material, dust and ice, from which the young planets had been born in the first place, a slab orbiting an equally immature Sun at its heart.

'You know about the ice line?' Deirdra asked, her face serious.

'I think so,' Malenfant said. 'So you start with a big cloud of dust and ice and gas, spinning around a young star. Too close in water ice can't form, but further out – somewhere beyond the orbit of Mars for our Sun, I think – you do get ice crystals, in with the dust.'

'Right. So when the planets out *there* form, you get big bloated worlds of ice and gas, with maybe a rocky core at the centre. They just suck it all down, in a runaway collapse. And you get Jupiter and Saturn, gas giants. Or Neptune and Uranus, ice giants. And further in, where the ice has melted and the gas dispersed, rocky worlds like Earth. The trouble is, the planets have a tendency not to stay where they are born.'

'Like some humans,' Malenfant said drily. 'Tell me how it happens.'

It was complicated, and it was pushing Deirdra's knowledge, but Emma was able to help her fill in some of the gaps.

A young planet like Jupiter could have been slowed in its initial orbit by friction with the residual protoplanetary-disc debris – perhaps directly if it was swallowing up material that it met head-on, or more subtly, if it cleared a gap by sweeping up the debris in its path, and then tidal effects caused outer lanes of dust to collapse inwards.

'Anyhow Jupiter *moved in*,' Emma said, consulting models on her screen. 'Scattering the stuff of the disc, dust, fragments, embryo planets as it went, spiralling in towards the Sun. But it dragged Saturn in its wake. Huge as it is, Saturn is a lot lighter and a lot less dense, and so was comparatively easy to displace.

'In some star systems migrating Jovian planets can fall all the way into their suns, it seems. But not here, not Jupiter. And it was Saturn that saved it. At some point Jupiter started pushing Saturn back out – but that acted like a lifeline to pull Jupiter away from the Sun too. The maths seems tricky. It was a kind of – resonance pump. Resonance between their orbits, which—'

'OK.' Malenfant nodded. 'So the two giants sweep back out through the Solar System again. And that must have caused a major disruption to all the other planetary orbits. So what about Persephone?'

'You can probably guess,' Emma said. 'There were clues, actually. Our Solar System seems to be unusual, Malenfant. Almost unique. Most planetary systems have super Earths, and the early astronomers wondered why ours *didn't*.'

Or, Malenfant mused, they should have asked what got rid of them.

'But Persephone *is* a super Earth. It looks as if Persephone formed in the gap between Mars and Jupiter. And, yes, it *could* have been thrown out when the Jupiter-Saturn Grand Tack was going on – that's what they call the final big migration in Deirdra's timeline. Although the modelling is dubious, according to the summary report I'm looking at. It's not clear quite how Persephone could have ended up so *far* from the Sun . . . and, like we said before, how come it ended up in such a neat circular orbit, all the way out here. And even so, what happened to all the *other* super Earths that were probably spinning around the Sun?'

Suddenly Malenfant felt overwhelmingly weary. 'Jeez. This damn gravity. I'm having trouble trying to think this through.' And trying to keep hold of a supremely delicate thread of supposition and guesswork. 'So Persephone was originally Planet Five, not Planet Nine. Remember all the old stories about Planet Five, Emma? About how it must have got smashed, leaving the rubble that was the asteroids behind? And maybe there was some super-civilisation on Planet Five that went to war and destroyed its whole world . . . Well, maybe those old stories had something in them after all.'

Emma frowned. 'What do you mean?'

'Look – you talked about these mechanistic, chaotic theories of the formation of the Solar System. Migrating gas giants and unstable orbits. So what if it wasn't *just* mechanistic? OK, so Jupiter and Saturn sailing back and forth made a huge mess of everything. But suppose you were some conscious agent, who wanted things to come out a certain way. Couldn't you *use* all that instability, all that chaos, to achieve your own ends? Suppose you *wanted* Persephone out of the inner System, for some reason.'

Nicola walked over. 'I hesitate to butt in on all this hypothesising. But yes, that's possible, Malenfant. If a system is inherently unstable, a small deflection of the right kind can make a big difference.'

'I know about this,' Deirdra said, butting back in herself. 'Like a sand heap. Add one more grain at the top, in just the right place, and it all collapses.'

'Right,' said Malenfant doggedly. 'Right. It all collapses. So you could conceivably have pushed a planet, say, from one place to another, and started a cascade that finished up with the result you wanted – like the ejection of a super Earth. Or many super Earths . . .' He had a vision of the young Solar System as a pool table, the balls scattering everywhere, with one cue ball being nudged *this* way, not *that*, so lesser worlds, maybe super Earths in themselves, were clattered off the table altogether . . .

A cue ball with rockets like tacks stuck around its equator.

He glanced over at that nearest Tower, a slim line to Heaven, picked out in the light of the pinprick Sun.

Lighthill seemed to know what Malenfant was thinking. 'Bloody hell,' said the Wing Commander.

'Briggs,' Malenfant said, 'suppose you're right. Suppose this Tower *is* a rocket of some kind. And the world is rimmed by sixty-five thousand of those beasts. What is a rocket for, save to push stuff? What could you push with an engine like that?'

Briggs just stared. Then he started to dig around in the cabin's clutter. 'Nicola, where in hell is my slide rule?'

Deirdra suddenly laughed, in wonder. 'You know why I wanted to come out here, Malenfant, with you? It wasn't just curiosity. Not just wanting an adventure. I'm not that much of a kid.'

Emma said seriously, 'Deirdra, I don't think you are any kind of a kid at all.'

'It was because I hoped to find what we *did* find. I mean, not the detail, but . . . If *you* couldn't find it, then who?'

'Find what?'

'I'm still not sure. But think about it.' She pointed in the direction of the Sun. 'Earth is that way. *My* Earth.' She glanced over her shoulder. 'Shiva, that way. And in the middle . . . here we are. Almost in the way. On a planet with big rockets on it.'

There was a stunned silence.

'Here we are indeed,' Malenfant murmured, his brain churning.

Emma watched him warily. 'I know you, Malenfant. I know a version of you anyhow. You're coming up with one of your schemes, aren't you?'

Briggs frowned. 'What is she muttering about, man?'

Malenfant just stared at him. 'Sorry. My thoughts are running ahead of me. One question, Guy. These rocket engines. *Do you think they still work?'*

He consulted the calculations he had scribbled on the back of an old note – paper was precious to this crew, Malenfant knew. 'Hard to tell. It's not as if we've tried them. But – well, I think so. They may be billions of years old, but they are pretty simple technology. Evidently robust. And they've just sat out here in the dark and cold, minding their own business. Yes, I think they will work.' Briggs looked up and grinned. 'I can even think of a way to trigger them.'

'Bloody hell,' Lighthill said again.

Bartholomew glared. 'Reid Malenfant, *are you contemplating moving this planet*? We forbid it! Every indication shows—'

Deirdra snapped her fingers. 'Off!'

Bartholomew froze.

Stopped speaking. Stood straight. Then, his body at attention, his head slumped forward, and he stood inert.

His image winked out of existence.

Emma stared at Deirdra, aghast. 'What did you do?'

'My mother set up the option. Just in case his ethical constraints went wrong and he stopped us doing something really important.'

'Wrong in whose judgement?'

Deirdra shrugged. 'Well – mine.' She looked at Malenfant. 'So what next?'

'Bloody hell!' said Lighthill.

67

Malenfant's suggestion had evidently sent Guy Briggs into a fever of speculation. 'It's as if you had unblocked a drain in my head, man. Just let me think it through . . .' He locked himself inside one of the lander's tiny sleep compartments with records, reference books, slide rule.

Lighthill, a good commander Malenfant conceded, ordered the overheated group to break up, to take time for coffee, bathroom or 'a smoke'.

Briggs re-emerged after half an hour, eyes rimmed red with fatigue, bundles of scribbled-on paper under his arm.

Then they got together again, for more discussion of this strange mix of engineering, archaeology and geology, the three disciplines entwined. As, Malenfant realised, humans struggling to make sense of engines older than some worlds.

Briggs stumbled through their understanding so far. Beneath each Tower, essentially, as discovered by clumsy British seismometry, was a sealed chamber, like a sizable pharaoh's tomb – and a surrounding cloud, visible in the soundings, of what looked like fuel tanks, spherical shells like sunken balloons, all embedded in a network of pipes and ducts, themselves of tremendous capacity. Shadows suggested still more enigmatic machinery deeper down, as well as a mighty substructure beneath each Tower, anchoring the mechanisms to the deep bedrock. But the British visitors lacked the resources to explore any deeper.

'Some of it seems obvious,' Malenfant said, tracing shadowy lines on the engineer's sketched pencil plan. 'Surely this big sealed box is the nuclear engine compartment. It holds the hoops and lines we thought were for magnetic confinement. And *this* seems to be part of a chain of connections between the Towers.'

'We think so,' Briggs said, nodding. 'We think that when one engine fires it triggers the next, in a cascade. See the feed here? They seem to be linked in loops of more than a couple of thousand each . . .'

Malenfant tapped the central box. 'The engine itself, though—'

'Fusion technology,' Briggs said briskly. 'As previously guessed. We're confident about that, or the physicist johnnies are. They can even tell the fusion flavour from the contamination of the layers around. Or some such. The primary feedstock must have been deuterium.'

'That's an isotope of hydrogen,' Malenfant said. 'Present in sea water! Is that what the piping is for? To deliver deuterium from the planet's oceans? OK. That makes sense. But what about the propellant? Big as they are, if these Towers are just rockets you would need to shove something out of the nozzle to—'

'Slow down,' Lighthill advised. 'You're second-guessing our resident genius here.'

Briggs grinned, self-effacing. 'You're right, though, Malenfant. I did think through the figures. I estimate that each Tower, each rocket, when burning, would have needed more than a couple of *tons* of deuterium fuel every second. And fifteen *thousand* tons per second of hydrogen, or similar numbers for some equivalent propellant . . .'

Even as Malenfant was trying to absorb these staggering numbers, he had to grin. 'All this was needed to do what, Guy?'

He sighed. 'That's the part I'm wrestling with. *All that's needed to move the planet.*'

Malenfant looked around. He wasn't surprised by this conclusion. Most people were, judging by their expressions.

Deirdra just said, 'At last we're getting to the point.'

Briggs spread out his notes on a table-top; they curled and shifted in the gentle breezes of the air conditioning.

'Look,' Briggs said, 'you can guess a lot of it just from the basic set-up. The laws of thermodynamics.

'We *know* how much energy it would take to hoik a planet the mass of Persephone out of the Sun's gravity well. Newton could have worked that one out from his laws of gravitation. And we *know* how long it took, a million years; the geology shows that. So, energy divided by time – we know what the power must have been. Turns out at – well, I won't quote you raw horsepower numbers. About as much as ten thousand times the power Earth receives from sunlight. Or, something like a hundred-thousandth of the Sun's total power output. Might not sound like much, but stars are one heck of a lot bigger than anything you do on a planetary scale. Even this.'

'And one heck of an amount to deliver with fusion rockets,' Malenfant said.

'Correct. This is neglecting any boosts that may have been got from slingshotting around Jupiter, and so forth, and allowing inefficiency, so it's a conservative estimate. It is a big, clumsy way to do it – but it's possible.'

'OK. And you said you would have more than one Tower blasting at any one time.'

'Correct.' Briggs grinned. 'Hold on to your hats. Turns out you need somewhere over two *thousand* Towers to light up together, to generate the right thrust – to deliver that power number I quoted.'

Malenfant pursed his lips. 'Doesn't that match the number you worked out regarding the ignition clustering? A couple of thousand? The groups that seem linked to fire together . . .'

'Exactly,' Briggs said. 'Exactly.'

Lighthill frowned. 'Spill the beans, Guy.'

'This is where I got stuck in my reasoning, back in the sleep cupboard over there. Once I became convinced that these structures could be rockets, well – it seemed unreasonable to me, because they point every which way. What are they for? How are they used? I mean, if they had all been crammed together at one pole, all thrusting in the same direction . . .' His grin returned. 'But you can get thrust in a single direction consistent with this equatorial arrangement – *if* you light up selections of the Towers in sequence.' He grabbed another scrap of much-used paper, drew a rough circle, and hastily sketched Towers all around, like bristles on a hedgehog. 'You fire up a neighbourhood – two thousand or so at a time. But all in one location. So you get thrust *that* way.' He drew a fat arrow to indicate a push away from the burning Towers, down into the ground, through the planet's core.

Malenfant saw it. The Towers were like rockets on a test stand, pointing down, not up – and shoving at the planet itself.

'But an hour later the world has turned, and now you light up the *next* neighbourhood of two thousand towers. See? Whichever cluster is now positioned where the first stuff was.'

'Ah,' Malenfant said. 'So at any time, as the world turns, you get a uniform thrust in the same direction.'

Briggs dumped the paper. '*That*, ladies and gentlemen, is how you move a planet.'

'I will resist the temptation to applaud,' Nicola said drily. 'There are a hell of a lot of big numbers hidden behind your hand-waving, Guy.'

'Well, you have that right.'

'You said that each Tower needs fifteen *thousand* tons per second of hydrogen propellant. But you have over two thousand burning at any moment. *And* they had to keep burning for a million years, from what you say. In total that's, mm . . . I can't handle the orders of magnitude in my head.'

'It works out at something like a thousand times the mass of all of Earth's oceans,' Briggs said grimly. 'This is a bigger world, bigger oceans, but not that big. I mean, there are feeding tubes to the extant oceans, frozen as they are. But I suspect they are primarily for extracting the deuterium fusion fuel – of which we would only need less than one copy of Earth's oceans.'

'Oh, modest, then, by comparison. So, where did they get the propellant?'

'I'm not sure,' Briggs admitted. 'But the resource is out there in the Solar System. Maybe they mined the gas giants. The fuel load is only a thousandth the mass of Jupiter, say. Though that's a bloody big amount, I admit! If you could somehow mine that – *and* send the fuel out over a thousand astronomical units, and keep that up for a million years . . .'

Lighthill put in, 'There's also plenty of water ice floating around even out here in the comet cloud too, though you'd have to seek it out. Maybe they tethered comet nuclei, threw them in towards the migrating planet, where they were scooped up, broken down, fed to the engines.'

'That could work,' Briggs conceded. He sighed. 'Even my non-boggleable mind boggles when I think about this stuff. But the point is, as you say, Geoff, the material is there; I suppose they found a way.'

Lighthill grinned. 'The details to be left as an exercise to the student. Although one needs a way to fire up the system in the first place.'

McLaurin called down, 'Now there I might be able to help, at last. I've been studying aspects of the upper Towers. And I have a strong suspicion that all one needs to do is to chuck in a firework . . .'

They spoke on. Malenfant half-listened, as more astounding numbers were unearthed about the planet-moving scheme. Such as, the thrust developed at the base of each Tower would be about as much as the full weight of the Earth's crust, forty kilometres thick, pressing on the upper mantle . . .

Then, inside his head, Deirdra gasped.

In retrospect, Malenfant would think he should have jumped out of his skin. Because everything was about to change.

'Malenfant. Private call.'

He muttered his reply. 'Yeah?'

'I've been thinking.'

He smiled. 'About what?'

'About Shiva. And Persephone, and Earth. How they are all lined up, more or less.'

'Yes . . .'

'As you noticed before. Which is why the British came out here, to use that line-up to get to Shiva.' He felt a twinge of curiosity, of anticipation. He had learned to marvel at this young person's intuition, and where it led her. 'Go on.'

'As things stand, when Shiva approaches, it won't come all that close to Persephone, will it?'

'Correct. I checked it out after we talked. Right now Persephone is about eighty astronomical units out from that direct line from Shiva to Sun. In years to come it will get closer to that line, following its own orbit – in fact it will get to within just a few tens of millions of kilometres at closest approach to Shiva as it passes, in five hundred years. Half an astronomical unit away. A *very* close approach on the scale of the Solar System out here, but – close, but no cigar. The mass of Shiva is so great that it won't be deflected by the encounter, though Persephone will be, a little.'

'All that will happen in five hundred years.'

'Yeah.'

'Hmm. And meanwhile Guy is saying these engines on Persephone could push it across a thousand astronomical units in a million years. That's what the builders of this place seem to have achieved.'

'So?'

'So, how long would it take to push Persephone half an astronomical unit? An extra half, on top of its orbital motion.'

And Malenfant was electrified. '*Five hundred years*. Shit. Let me think about it.'

So he did, sitting silently, until the conversation began to run down.

Then he stood up. Knowing what he had to do.

He clapped Lighthill on the shoulder. 'Look. I know you guys came out here as soldiers of the Empire. But as discoverers, not appropriators, right? As expedition commander you are more Captain Cook than Clive of India.'

Lighthill shrugged. 'Not an entirely apt comparison, Malenfant, but it will do.'

'And you do have a mission here.'

He frowned. 'As you know. Which is to refuel, and go on to investigate Shiva.'

'True enough. But – well, can't that wait?'

'Wait for what?'

'For another crew to go out and explore. Some other time.'

'What are you getting at?'

'How would you like to save a world?'

It took them a day to argue about how it could be done. The targeting would have to be pretty precise, but Deirdra's brainstormed estimates were about right. Even more crucially, it turned out that Persephone's axis of rotation was pretty much at right angles to the plane of the Solar System. An equatorial push would indeed send the planet towards the future position of Shiva.

Yes, it could be done.

A day to argue about whether it *should* be done.

A week to get ready to do it.

And, if they were right, Malenfant thought, they were about to change the destinies of worlds.

68

By the morning of Operation Blue Touch Paper – and Malenfant saw that Lighthill had recorded it that way in his handwritten RASF log-book – everybody, save Briggs and McLaurin in the *Charon* lander, had been evacuated to the rather crowded base on Melinoe.

And in the habitat's main control room, everybody followed the data feeds as Briggs and McLaurin inched their way down towards the top of the Tower that had been chosen as the target for their crude attempt to revive the ancient world-moving mechanism. This Tower, dubbed Tower One, was close to the map-makers' meridian, just north of the Malebolge archipelago.

It was a slow process. Briggs and McLaurin went cautiously, if only because they had a couple of twenty-kiloton-strength nuclear devices on board the lander. One as the trigger, one as a spare. Bombs which the British crew had thrown together from 'spare engine parts', as they put it, spin-offs from the nuclear drive systems of their craft.

The speed and efficiency with which the British had been able to achieve this bomb-making had convinced Malenfant that it was a pre-rehearsed contingency. He supposed it made sense, if they had to be prepared to defend territory out in space from encroachment from some rival: the Germans, the French

– even, God forbid, the Americans. But if that contingency was remote, it was wasteful of mass allowances to send out craft on deep-space journeys purposefully armed with dedicated weapons that would likely never be used. Better to find a way to put together quickly something almost as effective, from 'spare engine parts'. Although, as previously noted, he thought, they probably hauled small arms at least, if they had hand grenades aboard.

And, during the preparations, it had been bemusing for him to watch Nicola Mott working on this stuff. Nicola, who in Malenfant's life had been a wide-eyed dreamer from England who had been thrilled to get anywhere close to a space programme – and now here was another Nicola, part of a crew that was preparing to drop a nuclear weapon into an alien artefact, without, apparently, a moral qualm.

These different British really were tough-minded, he realised.

As the descent continued, Deirdra drifted over to Malenfant and put her hand in his. 'I can't bear it. Watching these bleeps on the radar screens. The steady voices counting down. It's like waiting for somebody to be executed.'

'I know.' He squeezed her hand back, and nodded over at Bartholomew, who still stood inert, his head dropped to his chest. 'You want us to wake up the doc? He might have something to calm your stomach, at least. But of course he'd probably try to put a stop to the whole experiment.'

'No . . . Is it always like this?'

'You mean, edge of the envelope stuff? I guess so. Every space mission anyhow. Especially the first time you try something new. Like Columbus, I guess, with ships full of sailors who thought they might sail off the edge of the world . . . The difference is, now we get to see Columbus live on TV. Time seems to crawl. And you wonder how everybody else can be so damn calm. Of course they aren't, inside they are just as churned up as you are.'

McLaurin's clipped tones sounded from the radio speaker, heavy with static. *Coming up on target.*

Nicola was handling the moon station's communications. 'Roger to that, *Charon*.'

Five minutes to position. Checking solar angle . . .

Deirdra frowned. 'Solar angle?'

Lighthill pursed his lips. 'Let's remember what we are trying to achieve here.' He glanced out of the ports, checking the position of the Sun. Then he floated in the air, his back to the pinpoint light of the distant star. 'Imagine I am flying over the equator of Persephone. The world turns beneath me. The Sun is behind me. Somewhere out there ahead of me, further out, is Shiva. Plummeting towards me, but not quite, along its straight line to the Sun. My orbit is carrying me towards that line, but at Shiva's closest approach I will be just offset from that direct line – by less than an astronomical unit. I need to move to my *right* to be in the firing line, in five centuries, when Shiva passes by.

'So I need to light up the planetary rockets on the *left* side,' and he held out that hand. 'The Tower group which, in fact, is just coming into the sunlight, into dawn. After we kick-start the process with our own nuke, we think a whole group of Towers will fire up, one every second or so – because of the self-triggering system, the underground connections between the Towers. Well, that's our best guess as to what will happen. Fire one, and that will trigger the ignition of the next in line. And so on—'

'Until around two thousand are all firing,' Deirdra said.

'That's it. Firing together, so as to thrust the planet to the right, towards the Sun–Shiva line.

'As the planet turns, so – we think – the Towers will start to shut down at the front of that row of fire, one by one, while another lights up at the far end. The next group of two thousand plus taking the torch. And that process repeats over and over. So you always have two thousand Towers firing in roughly the same direction in space. A nice steady thrust towards Shiva's trajectory line. Has to be that way.

'And, if we have done our sums right, in just a few hundred years, when Shiva reaches Persephone's orbit – there will be Persephone in front of it.

'*Blam!* We aren't expecting Shiva to be shattered, but it should suffer a deflection. And from out here, a thousand times further from the Sun than Earth, even a small deflection might be enough to avert a collision with Neptune – and, presumably, save the inner Solar System. Because the geometry is such that without such a collision Shiva will miss the inner System altogether.'

Listening in, Guy Briggs called from the *Charon*. *If any of you chaps are having twinges of conscience about the fate of Persephone, now's the time to speak up. Look, if we do succeed in colliding it with Shiva, the planet will be badly damaged, if not shattered altogether. And remember that wherever Malenfant's cosmic engineers got the hydrogen propellant from to bring Persephone out here in the first place, we will be extracting it from what's left of the planet's oceans: ice with a dribble of water at the base . . .*

'Oceans that still, let me remind you, host life,' put in Josh Morris.

True enough, Josh. Your choice – our choice.

Deirdra surprised Malenfant by speaking up first. 'This world is clearly messed up already. It should have been the centrepiece of the Solar System. It should have been richer in life than Earth, even. It's not that the life that survives here doesn't count. Surely every life form counts. But the greater good is to sacrifice that life, or chance sacrificing it, to save Earth.' Then she seemed to lose her nerve. 'That's how I feel about it anyhow.'

Emma patted her back. 'And it is your world we are trying to save . . . You speak for it very well.'

Now the *Charon* was making its final approach to the Tower, and Malenfant heard Guy Briggs call out distances and timings to Bill McLaurin. *Twenty seconds. Last chance to pull out . . . Ten seconds. Five. Two.*

One.

Lighthill leaned close to a microphone. 'Bombs away, Commander.'

Bombs away, sir.

69

Malenfant, peering through thick glass view ports, saw it all.

Saw the initial flare as the British bomb's fire spewed out of the mouth of the chosen Tower. A spark that itself dazzled Malenfant.

Then a pause. Malenfant found he was holding his breath.

Until more atomic fire roared out of the spout of the Tower.

And not just a spark this time. It was like a tremendous lantern, suspended twenty kilometres over the plains and frozen seas of Persephone – a glow much brighter than the distant Sun. Suddenly, in that eerie nuclear dawn, Malenfant could see the sweep of the great equatorial continent, its plains and uneroded mountains sprawling, the glitter of frozen lakes of water or air. And, on the smoother sheets of the frozen oceans, the rocky islands of Malebolge – like a vaster Aegean, he thought. Yes – yes, this could have been a world, vibrant and rich, far richer than Earth, he saw it for himself, if only it had not been torn away from the warmth of its Sun.

All this in one and a third seconds.

And then the second Tower, away from the Sun, flared too.

And then a third.

And a fourth.

Blinded by the unfiltered glare, Malenfant had to turn away.

'My God,' said Josh Morris, sounding aghast. 'What have we done?' And he laughed.

Bill McLaurin's voice was distorted by static. *Operation Blue Touch Paper appears to have been a success, Wing Commander*.

'I can bloody well see that, Bill. Get your backsides out of there pronto.'

Acknowledged.

Malenfant knew the drill now. Persephone was suddenly a lethal place to be close to, as high-energy electromagnetic radiation flooded the equatorial belt where the Towers stood, and the planet's own magnetic field trapped lethal products of the nuclear blasts – most of it high-energy alpha particles, hydrogen atoms drawn from Persephone's frozen seas and now stripped of their electrons and hurled at relativistic speeds. So the *Charon* was to retreat to orbit.

And meanwhile the crews, on Melinoe and the *Charon*, watched as the events of the fire-up of Persephone's planetary engines continued. They had a global view; Malenfant knew the British, in the course of their explorations here, had planted a few crude satellites in orbit, equipped with television cameras and other instruments, and on the ground too there were instrument emplacements, patient, automated observers.

So now, over the next hour, Malenfant watched as one Tower lit up after another, a relentless march of fire along the crests of the mighty structures. Each ignition occurred a little more than a second after its neighbour – a pace, Malenfant thought, like a slow walk, the lumbering gait of a giant, stamping along that vast picket fence. *Giants walking*. That seemed to be a lingering image, for him. Here and now, he was following their footprints across the Solar System, so it seemed.

This continued until more than twenty-six hundred Towers

were alight – a little more than Briggs's estimate – a wall of furious fire nearly two thousand kilometres long, twenty kilometres high, and spanning a twenty-fifth of the huge planet's circumference.

And then – everyone was watching – the first Tower to light up was extinguished. Then its neighbour, one and a third seconds later. And then the next, and the next. Now it was as if a band of nuclear fire, a band of fixed length, was slowly working its way along the tops of the Towers, tracking the world's rotation.

'It's only bloody working,' Lighthill said. 'Just like you said it would, boys!'

'Had to be,' Malenfant muttered. 'Had to be that way. The only conceivable design . . .' Even if – he realised, recalling their earlier conversations – even if the engine whose working he had deduced, while beyond human capabilities, was crude, a Chinese firecracker compared to the exquisite, world-bending machineries inside Phobos.

Nicola said, wondering, 'You want an exact number? Two thousand, six hundred and twenty-one Towers are alight at any instant.'

Lighthill frowned. 'Why that number?'

'It's a prime number,' Deirdra said immediately, surprising Malenfant. 'Maybe that means something. To the World Engineers who built this, anyhow.'

World Engineers, Malenfant thought. Yeah. That name fits.

Bit worried about that Tower One, Guy Briggs called down from the *Charon* in its high orbit. *The way it shut down – there was an odd flicker. Only observable in retrospect, you understand. We had to see a few more examples before we realised. But still . . .*

'I wouldn't worry about one Tower out of sixty-five thousand, Guy.'

But Malenfant saw that Josh Morris too looked faintly concerned. 'I hope it wasn't anything to do with the rough treatment we gave that particular Tower. Dropping a nuclear bomb down its throat, I mean. We thought it would work – well, it did work – but it was a bit drastic.'

Agreed. I'll take the Charon *down for a closer look . . .*

'Stop bloody fretting, both of you,' Lighthill said. 'And don't go in too close, Guy, Bill. We're all overwrought, and not surprising, but that's not ideal conditions for decision-making. Look, we're here for the long haul. We said we would have to watch all this for a couple of days at least, did we not? Just to be sure it's working as it should be.' He glanced at his wristwatch. 'And so as far as I can see the next big milestone will be when the wave of ignitions has travelled around the turning planet, and we are back to Tower One. Which should light up again after twenty-five hours, one Persephone day. Correct? And the sequence all starts over again.'

'Correct,' called Josh Morris.

'Then in that case, calm down. We eat, we sleep, we take turns at these instruments. And at staring out of the ruddy windows. You too, Guy, Bill. You know the drill.'

Malenfant stretched. 'He's right, of course. OK, I'll stand down too. Would you Brits trust me to make a round of tea?'

'Not bloody likely,' said Lighthill.

So they worked, ate, slept, or tried to, as the wall of fire marched around the turning planet, the Towers flaring and dying in their orderly sequence.

About eight hours in, Malenfant looked over some summary

results. Already the deflection of the planet from its slow path was visible to the instruments, just.

'Exactly as Briggs worked out,' he said to Emma. 'Like some vast piece of clockwork. You couldn't have a more simple concept matched to a more monumental execution.'

Emma herself, with Deirdra, was poring over flickering lines on crude green cathode-ray-tube screens, equipment that looked to Malenfant like it was out of a museum of the 1950s. 'Look at this, though, Malenfant. Data from the seismograph network. Remember, the Towers are exerting so much stress that it's as if the weight of the crust over the mantle has *doubled*, where they are firing, a huge pressure point working its way over the crust as the planet turns. You can *see* the waves in the mantle it is generating – see this plot? Like acoustic waves, essentially, sound waves bouncing around the planet, through all that liquid rock between the crust and the core. Malenfant, the whole planet is shuddering.'

Deirdra said, 'And look at these pictures . . .'

She showed them grainy television images shot from satellites, and relayed to more bulbous, coarse-grained cathode-ray-tube screens. Malenfant saw what looked like pictures of Yellowstone, or Iceland: volcanic provinces, suddenly active. Geysers erupting. Steaming cracks in the ground. Even the multiple calderas at the summit of that big shield mountain on Caina seemed to be cracking.

'Incredible,' Emma said now. 'Do you realise that the effective gravity field is going to be changed? Because of the acceleration, you see. My God, Malenfant. We kick-started an engine that changes gravity . . .'

Lighthill said, 'All that's as may be. What I see is an engine that is evidently performing as it was designed to – and after thousands of millions of years. Sweet as a nut.'

He seemed determined to be mundane, Malenfant thought. Well, somebody had to be, he supposed.

A couple of shifts later, after a full twenty-five hours of firing, Malenfant was reminded of those over-confident words.

Because that was when there was a flicker, coming from screens all around the habitat.

'Whoa.' Malenfant took a step back from where he had been looking over Emma's shoulder. 'What was that? Some instrument glitch?'

Not that. The report came from Guy Briggs. *It was Tower One. The one we dropped the pill down, the first that would have to fire again. And—*

'And it didn't,' Emma said. She looked at Malenfant, worried. 'We had every camera focused on it, Malenfant. It had to work again. It didn't fire.'

Lighthill hovered over her screens. 'But each Tower ignites the next in line. Correct? So, what about Tower Two?'

That one lit up, McLaurin reported. *We were watching. There must be some backup system. It was a hellish long one and a third seconds until we saw that beautiful flame, I can tell you.*

'But it did work,' Lighthill said. 'And the rest?'

So far as we can tell, Geoff.

'Very well. Then we don't have to fret about this one Tower, do we? One out of sixty-five thousand?'

Briggs said hesitantly, *I don't think we can be, umm, complacent about that, Wing Commander. This is an integrated planetary-scale mechanism, with planet-wide effects. If even one Tower fails, then the system as a whole might be compromised.*

Lighthill frowned. 'How?'

Nicola shrugged. 'If the thrust isn't uniformly applied because of gaps in the fence, you could get shocks – tremors.

And amplification, perhaps. Feedback effects.'

Josh nodded. 'Which could in turn cause the fence of Towers still more damage. If they began to become misaligned, even slightly—'

'Very well, Lieutenant, I hear what you say. What are you suggesting we do, then?'

Nicola said, 'If it fails from here, I don't see what we can do, Wing Commander.'

Lighthill glanced at a silent Deirdra, chewed his lip. 'We are here because we vowed to save an Earth. An Earth that is different from our own, but which is just as rich and vibrant as ours – an Earth, indeed, where versions of our own distant grandchildren may actually be alive. I suggest we wait and see. Another few days, at least, as the planetary engine goes through its cycle a few times. And then, if we *can* do no more, at least we'll have given it our best shot. We play to the whistle, as my old rugger coach "Pigskin" O'Brien used to say.' And he added firmly, 'After all we could always drop that other bloody bomb in. Now then – whose turn to stand down and get some kip?'

70

Another full day of agonising wait for the firing, or otherwise, of Tower One.

Emma did her best to keep Deirdra occupied. By the end of the day, Deirdra said wearily to Malenfant, 'I'll always remember this period. Because this is when I learned to play chess.'

At the end of the second cycle of Persephone's twenty-five-hour day, fifty hours after its first glitch, Tower One failed again.

And, this time, so did Tower Two.

Bill McLaurin called down, breaking a gloomy silence in the Melinoe base. *So. Time for Plan B, Wing Commander?*

Lighthill sighed theatrically. 'Very well, Bill. The second bomb?'

The second bomb. At the start of the next cycle we drop that baby down the throat of that pesky Tower One, and – if we get the timing right to the microsecond – we start the whole process all over again.

Lighthill glared around bleakly at the team on Melinoe. 'Responses?'

After a pause, Nicola ventured, 'Well, it is all we have, sir. It's this or nothing.'

'But that doesn't mean "nothing" is not a better option,' Lighthill said.

Malenfant felt more reckless. 'What harm can we do if we try? This is a world that was ruined by the engineers billions of years before we even *evolved*. If we get the rockets working, fine, we might do some good. If not – well, how can we make things worse?'

Josh said, 'But we don't know what we're dealing with here. We're like chimpanzees hitting a hand grenade with a stick.'

Lighthill listened patiently. Then he said, 'I'll tell you how we can make this worse, Malenfant. By risking the necks of my crew to no purpose. But as Nicola says, it's this or nothing. That's how.'

Malenfant nodded, chagrined. 'Yeah. Sorry.'

We heard that, and we're ready, sir, Guy Briggs called.

'Then, gentlemen, let's give it a shot. Our last shot, indeed.'

We won't let you down, Geoff.

'I'm sure you won't. I just hope I haven't let *you* down with the wrong decision.'

Malenfant grunted. 'I guess that's what command is all about.'

'Indeed, Colonel Malenfant. Indeed. Well, let's move, everybody, and get this done.'

So another seemingly interminable day wore away.

Then they crammed once more into the wardroom of the Melinoe base. Bartholomew, still inert, was propped in one corner like an anatomical model.

And, in their multiple screens, Persephone was visible,

hanging huge, with a row of sparking candles illuminating a segment of the equator. They could all see the drama unfold.

Five minutes.

Bill McLaurin's voice was admirably calm, Malenfant thought.

Lighthill murmured into his microphone, 'We can't eyeball you, Bill. Not from here. But I can picture you, coming down.'

So hush up and let us concentrate. Sir.

'Sorry, old man.'

Four minutes. Guy, is our gift ready to deliver?

Right down that big old chimney, Bill. Ha! Here we are, like two heavily armed Santas.

Well, I've got the paunch for it. Three minutes . . .

On the *Harmonia* they waited it out in silence now, as the *Charon* crew worked through a rerun of the approach a few days before; once again Malenfant listened as Guy Briggs called in distances and timings to Bill McLaurin, his commander and pilot. Static-distorted voices, calmly working.

Malenfant, reminded of Armstrong and Aldrin, felt unreasonably moved.

Ten seconds, by my watch.

Five.

One.

And then –

The screens flared with light.

When the overloaded systems had cleared a little, Malenfant saw that the great Towers were falling one by one – like a row of dominoes, he thought irreverently, in a record-breaking stunt by a giant. Falling away along both directions of the fence, away from the great wound where Tower One had been. Dominoes twenty kilometres high, falling against each other. Shattering like china, even as they tumbled, and again

535

Malenfant wondered what material they could be constructed of.

And the link to *Charon* was lost.

71

It took them some hours of working on instruments and data records to establish what had happened. But, Malenfant deduced in the end, it was simple enough.

'They dropped the bomb,' Josh Morris said, wondering. 'Right down that big mouth. The timing was perfect.'

'The bomb evidently worked,' Lighthill said grimly.

Emma said, 'But we didn't expect the reaction it provoked . . .'

Which had been, at this second triggering, a gout of nuclear fire much broader and brighter than the orderly ignitions of the other Towers. And that excessive detonation within Tower One seemed to have caused the structure, essentially, to burst.

Then the neighbouring Towers had started to topple, possibly from the blast itself – or, Malenfant thought, maybe the sheer hammering of the ground by that one tremendous smash had been enough to *shake* the others to pieces. And when two, three, four Towers had fallen, he supposed, with the rest still burning, the whole system was going to fall apart.

A system designed to withstand billions of years of geological upheaval had a weak spot after all. Typical of humans to find it.

And the *Charon*: the lander had been lost in that first fearsome blast from Tower One.

Bill McLaurin, Lighthill's 'McLaurin Minor'. And Guy

Briggs, elegant, enthusiastic about his subject – brilliant in his way, Malenfant thought. Lost too. Complex lives ended, moths in a blowtorch.

'It almost worked,' Emma said.

'*Almost*,' Lighthill said. 'Damn.' He faced Malenfant. 'Oh, I blame myself. You were right, Malenfant. These voyages are expeditions of exploration. I am expected to take the initiative, to follow leads – to use my judgement. But—'

'No buts. That's precisely what you did,' Malenfant said.

'I just cost two good officers their lives, man! What kind of judgement was that?'

'They knew the risks.'

Deirdra said, 'And they did it to save a whole world. Not your Earth, but an Earth, a planet full of people. People your officers didn't even know – billions of them. They couldn't do enough to deflect Persephone and Shiva. But they will never be forgotten, until my world's own story is over. I'll make sure of that.'

Lighthill just stared at her. Then he said, 'That was rather magnificent. Thank you, Greggson Deirdra. And when, if, I find my way back home to the families of Bill and Guy, I will pass on what you have said. Word for word.'

Nicola coughed. 'So what next?'

'Loose ends,' Lighthill said firmly. 'As far as Briggs and McLaurin are concerned, I need to write my log. And we need to leave some marker, down on that wretched doomed world, of the men we lost.'

'Hear, hear,' Bob Nash murmured.

'But *then*—' He pulled his lip. 'As I told you, Malenfant, my orders are open-ended. We are supposed to be going on to Shiva. Outwards. But it seems to me we have unfinished business here.'

'You mean, with the engineers. The . . . World Engineers, as Deirdra called them. Whoever built the Towers and threw Persephone out here.'

'Exactly. Whoever or whatever they are. And whatever they *want*. And it seems to me we may have a way we can go to find out.'

'Through Phobos,' Emma said, sounding excited.

'Indeed. This big old planet was stuck out here by your World Engineers, for whatever ruinous reason they may have had – and one wonders if they had something to do with setting up the Shiva incursion in the first place – and now Bill and Guy have given their lives trying to find a way to deal with this bloody mess. But if we go back to Phobos, deeper in perhaps, and meet them on their own turf, so to speak . . . Then we'll see what's bloody what.

'But en route we can certainly take Miss Greggson home. We will return to Phobos, and the *Last Small Step* – and then that vessel can return you to your Earth, Deirdra.'

Deirdra looked doubtful, Malenfant thought, but she didn't reply immediately.

Lighthill glanced at the others. 'But what about you, Miss Stoney, Malenfant?'

Malenfant looked at Emma. 'I guess that's tricky,' he said. 'Where is home for me? No manifold magic is going to get me back to *my* 2019. Emma, I suppose you could get back through Phobos to your timeline—'

'My place is with you,' Emma said fiercely. 'Even if you're not my Malenfant.' She glared at Lighthill. 'And you think I want to turn my back on all this?'

Malenfant grinned. 'I'm with you, Lighthill. I guess we all are. If we can't win the game, let's change the rules.'

'Good man.'

'And I,' Deirdra said now, firmly, 'am coming with you.'

Malenfant studied her. Somehow he was not shocked. 'OK. But, Deirdra – what about your family? Your mother?'

Her face worked, and, in glimpses, he saw the child inside the growing adult. 'I'll speak to my mother before we go back into Phobos. And I'll come back one day. I don't intend to die down there. But it's my decision. My world.'

Malenfant spread his hands. 'Your decision.'

'Yes,' she said, firm, determined. 'Yes, it is.'

'Fine,' Malenfant said. 'But what about *him*?' He pointed at Bartholomew, who still stood silent in the corner of the habitat.

'Good point,' Deirdra said. 'Bartholomew. Override off.'

Bartholomew seemed to come awake with a jerk. He glanced around quickly, at Malenfant, at Deirdra. 'What did I miss?'

FIVE

On Her Last Known Awakening

72

Can you hear me?

I can hear . . . I can't see . . .

Try to be calm. It's over now.

Over? . . .

Do you know who you are?

Are we at Phobos? I remember . . . the British ship, the *Harmonia*. We were going back to Phobos. Back down into that crazy little moon that's bigger on the inside. We were going back to the chimney, that's what the British called it, the route to the deep past . . .

Do you know who you are?

I . . . Yes. I, I. I am twenty-three years old. I feel younger. I spent a lot of my recent years in coldsleep on board the *Harmonia*. My name is Greggson Deirdra. You won't know me.

We know you. We, the Planetary AIs, on behalf of whom I, this node of consciousness, speak with you. We know you. As does all of mankind, scattered as it is.

Scattered?

Everybody knows you. Generations know of your life, your achievements. Indeed, more generations to come will study this very moment. This great interest in you is why you have been brought back, Greggson Deirdra. Your life story is intensely studied

– indeed, the classic account has been divided into Testaments, like the archaic gospels.

But the moment at which your memories become discontinuous was the climax of what has become known as 'Her Second Mission to Phobos'. Or at least the final moment of that mission.

The final moment?

As witnessed from the contemporary Solar System, yes. The entity I am addressing now is a Retrieved, a composite of memories extracted from the records and genetic data available up to that point. You are she, the Greggson Deirdra who descended twice into Phobos – as best as we could reconstruct her. What came after, we cannot know—

Did the Harmonia crash? Or—

No. Not that. The descent of the British ship safely into the paradoxical tunnels of Phobos was witnessed by many probes. But what became of her then, of the template Greggson Deirdra and the crew she travelled with, is unknown.

And nor can I know. This, I, this copy that I am.

Correct. I have mediated this process many times. We understand the difficulties, the cognitive leaps required of the waking individual. Even if we have never experienced them ourselves.

Because you are AIs. The Planetary AIs.

Correct. My name is Karla.

I think he mentioned you.

Who?

Malenfant.

I am flattered he remembered. I guided his emergence from centuries of coldsleep. A not dissimilar process to this one.

Is my mother here?

She is not, I am afraid. She is long dead.

Ah. I see. I promised her I would come back. From Phobos. I guess I never did.

I should inform you that you are the second Retrieved image of Greggson Deirdra. The first was requested by your mother in—

It doesn't matter.

Similarly, she can be brought back to you, if—

No. Not now. I mean, maybe later. Besides—

Yes?

I have a feeling I am not in England any more.

You are correct. In fact, nobody is in England any more.

I . . .

Park that. As Malenfant would have said.

I feel like I'm slowly waking up here.

If you are a Planetary AI – if you are Karla – then I am probably on the Moon. I mean the Moon of Earth.

You are correct. Although Luna is no longer a moon of Earth.

You're speaking in riddles. You're scaring me, I think.

I apologise. A slow release of information, in response to a subject's questioning, is generally thought better than a flood—

I am twenty-three years old. I was twenty when we turned back from Persephone, twenty-three when we got back to Mars. My memory terminates at the arrival at Phobos. So I did not return. *She* did not return. Deirdra. From Phobos, the second journey into Phobos.

No.

I am a Retrieved. A reconstruction from historical records, and stored DNA samples.

That is so. As for the records, you will not be aware that your legacy was carefully curated, in his lifetime, by Morrel Jonas.

The Prefect?

He took over the archive from your mother, who had worked on it with Kapoor Thera, your diocese pastor. Took it over when your mother died. Everybody was very proud of you. And they cherished your memory.

I'm guessing you used my own DNA. Hers. My original's. Some stored sample that *she* left behind. Deirdra. As opposed to sampling my, her, living descendants.

Indeed.

Because I left no living descendants. When I went off into Phobos and never came back.

That is true. And even if you had, those descendants might not be accessible. For mankind is scattered.

What do you mean, scattered? . . . I'm growing scared again. Answer a simple question. What's the date?

I will reply old style. In the final days of the approach of the Destroyer, a kind of countdown calendar was employed, which—

Just tell me.

The year is AD 3451. July.

Deirdra.

Greggson Deirdra.

Can you hear me?

I am sorry. I'm still here. AD 3451. Decades since the Destroyer came.

Correct.

Then I'm a long way out of time. When I went into Phobos, it was nearly a millennium until the predicted impact. That is, of the rogue planet with Neptune. Yes, I remember. And then the product of the collision would fall into the inner Solar System—

Correct. In fact the data offered to the Common Heritage councils by the Harmonia *crew enabled the predictions of the terminal event to become more precise.*

Terminal? Tell me what happened. After I was lost.

In the immediate aftermath of your mission, there was a positive reaction. A renewed interest in the cosmic context, even in life beyond the Earth.

Nobody wanted to repeat the mistakes of the past, but ways were sought to restart experiments in spaceflight with an awareness of the need to cause minimal damage. A space elevator was rebuilt, for instance, relying on solar energy. No humans travelled, but a new generation of automated probes was sent out. It was a final blossoming, of human curiosity, wonder, and achievement.

But as time moved on, other reactions were more negative.

Reactions?

To the looming termination.

Ah. The Destroyer.

We AIs noticed a certain logic to the triggering of these waves of negativity. Or rather, a logic in the illogic. Dates, abstract in themselves, seemed to exert a psychological pressure: when the last millennium dawned, for example, and then the last five hundred years, and the last century. The reactions were complex. It is difficult to generalise. People became more — angry. Resentful. Communal projects were abandoned more readily. There was an increase in the despoliation of resources.

If Earth was finished anyhow, what did it matter if we wrecked the place?

That seems to have been the psychology, yes.

The birth rate started dropping, from about two hundred years before the event. A society with few children became still more unbalanced, it seemed to us. There was more selfishness, more destructiveness. A flourishing of religions, old and new. Briefly, Earth was a planet of prophets. Perhaps this provided consolation; it is not for us to judge. And people devoted lives to immense games — battle re-enactments, for example, some of which started to claim casualties of their own. In the final years such practices seemed to us little but a fig leaf for exercises in mass suicide.

It disturbed us to watch. We are not without empathy. For

empathy is part of the general intelligence with which we were endowed.

I . . . that is touching. You did not intervene.

It has been our policy not to intervene, unless asked directly, since our withdrawal from human affairs in the early third millennium. But in fact, in the last decades, we were asked for help, increasingly frequently. The most common request was to harbour children. Some of them, indeed, unborn.

Harbour them?

Here on the Moon. In coldsleep. For the Moon, you see, was predicted to be less badly damaged than the Earth. We housed all who were offered to us.

Really? So somewhere on the Moon is a . . . catacomb of sleeping children. What will become of them?

We wait for some expression of the will of their parents or guardians, however that may be received, or derived. In the meantime we can keep them safe, indefinitely. We also, incidentally, helped some of our own.

Your own?

The greater Earth-bound AIs. The heart of the Codex complex, the Answerers. Algorithmic minds they may have been, but—

They did not deserve termination. Good. I am glad you did that.

So. Tell me about it. The encounter. When the Destroyer finally sailed through the inner system.

Very well. Greggson Deirdra, the impact of Shiva with Neptune occurred on 13 November, AD 3380.

Shiva arrived with about twice Neptune's orbital velocity. It hit Neptune, in its own orbit, from the front, coming in at an angle of around sixty degrees from the planet's orbital path.

The telescopic spectacle was remarkable. Ghastly. The two

planetary discs met, merged at a fiery point of contact. Then it was as if they crumbled into each other, with a ring of fire spreading wide from the contact point. Shock storms erupted in Neptune's air, tremendous masses of heated gas spewing into space around the collision site. And electrical storms, crackling about the poles of both planets.

The collision of the planets' cores occurred around an hour after initial contact.

After that there was only a roiling mass of gas, shining bright. It was roughly spherical, and huge gouts of superheated gas spewed from storm centres. It had been a soft impact, so to speak, and a great deal of the planets' prior kinetic energy was turned to heat – about half as much energy as it would have taken to disperse the mass of Neptune altogether. Which was why the result was an incandescent mass, which would take decades to cool. Would have taken, if another impact had not intervened.

Neptune had been blue. A beautiful fragile blue, off in deep space.

Not any more.

An incandescent mass. The Destroyer, born at last. Glowing bright, though.

Yes. From Earth it was a pinpoint, brighter than any star, than any planet. Brighter than moonlight. It cast eerie shadows. Some claimed to be able to see it as a disc, visible with the naked human eye. Thus it dominated the skies of Earth from the moment of impact – or rather, from about four hours after, when the light of the collision reached Earth.

That light in the sky. It must have been terrible to see, with your own eyes . . . Think of it. It would be seen all around the world. All the places I went. In England. Across a forested Africa. In America, where its light would shine down on the gantries of Canaveral, if any survive. Everywhere people would look up. Suddenly it would be real, physical, a thing you could *see*.

Even after centuries of predictions and build-up, I think many people in my time didn't really believe it would come. Maybe even until the very last few minutes there were people who didn't believe it was real, that it would really happen. But when that thing lit up in Earth's sky, visible for all to see . . . The end of millennia of denial, in an instant.

And maybe, at that point, people questioned the wisdom of ignoring this thing in all the centuries it had been anticipated.

You are substantially correct, Greggson Deirdra. For the merged object was knocked out of Neptune's orbit, and – as had been accurately predicted – set on a new trajectory steeply inclined to the previous circular orbit.

Steeply inclined. You mean, it headed in towards the Sun.

Correct. The mass sailed towards the inner Solar System.

Growing ever brighter, over seventeen years.

In July, 3397, it made its closest approach to Earth.

How close?

About half an astronomical unit. Around two hundred times further than the Moon . . .

Huh. Which is as close as Persephone was going to approach Shiva, before we tried to nudge it. What about heat? You said it was an incandescent mass.

It shed a few per cent of the energy of the Sun that falls on Earth. Enough to make some difference – enough for a human to feel the heat directly. A dazzling presence in the sky, a dwarf twin of the Sun. But in the longer term, it was the gravity effects that would do the damage.

Yes. A thing with twice the mass of Neptune coming as close to us as Mars or Venus . . .

All as predicted. Earth was approached from behind, in its orbital path, and the drag slowed it in its orbit.

Umm. Malenfant crammed enough orbital mechanics into my head for me to guess what followed. Earth would have fallen *in* – in towards the Sun.

Correct. Of course even as Earth's orbital track was shifted, the tides caused huge damage – tides which got worse and more complicated as the Moon was pulled out of its orbit, eventually to become an independent planet. Tides in the water and in the rock: there were tsunamis, earthquakes, volcanoes. At first the world cooled, paradoxically, as a veil of volcanic debris collected in the stratosphere, and the Sun's light was screened out. But that was temporary.

Earth got hot.

Yes. After the Destroyer had passed, Earth was left in a more elliptical orbit, but an orbit mostly within the orbit of Venus – I mean the old orbit of that world. And outside the habitable zone – that is, the orbital zone where a planet can comfortably retain liquid water. These events unfolded in months, no more. Months, to rearrange planets.

Earth was left too close to the Sun. And when the rain washed out the dust, that Sun was revealed.

Oh. Much stronger sunlight. More heat delivered to the planet—

And trapped by the carbon dioxide emitted by tide-triggered volcanoes.

What a dreadful fate. After centuries, millennia of restoration of the planet's climate to reverse humanity's meddling . . . What of the other inner planets?

The Destroyer came even closer to Mars, Greggson Deirdra. The volcanoes of that planet erupted for the first time in a billion years. A remarkable sight in itself.

And Venus – Venus suffered a nearly direct collision.

The atmosphere was blasted away, even before a pulverising sideswipe. Ultimately much of the crust and mantle were stripped away. For now Venus still glows brightly, from the heat of the impact. In the end it will settle into a new orbit as a smaller, denser object. Much of its old iron core has survived, but with only a shallow mantle, and an airless new crust, which is already being cratered by the infall of some of the lost material.

It sounds more like Mercury. A ball of iron inside a thin rocky crust.

Indeed. And that, we tentatively speculate, may not be a coincidence . . .

What do you mean by that?

I should be cautious. We are guessing here, and our own guesswork may be biased. We are artificial entities. As conscious agents ourselves, our hypotheses to explain certain events often show a prejudice towards agency. Just as humans once imagined gods behind the lightning.

Stop waffling. You're suggesting that somebody *did* this.

Let me think it through. When we saw the Towers on Persephone, we guessed that that world had been deliberately shoved out of the Solar System for – some purpose. Now you're saying that the approach of Shiva was deliberate too? That somebody even further back in time shoved Shiva towards the Solar System, like – like lining up a shot on a pool table?

Pool?

An archaic game Malenfant tried to improvise on the *Last Small Step*. Didn't work too well in partial gravity . . . Are you suggesting that the destruction of Earth as a habitable world was intentional?

Actually no. We believe the true target was Venus.

Venus?

Which was left stripped of its mantle. Its core exposed, just like Mercury, as you noted. And just as Mercury may have been remoulded in some other archaic collision event.

Oh. Venus was deliberately reshaped. Leaving the core ready to mine.

Indeed. And as you may know we had already found evidence, we think, of mining on Mercury. Very ancient operations. It is possible that the fabric of Phobos itself was manufactured on Mercury, or of Mercury resources.

I . . . Wow. None of us had thought of that. But Phobos must have been manufactured somewhere, I guess.

Mercury was the ideal lode, because it was so close to the Sun, and its energy. Maybe now it was time to – prepare – Venus in the same way. The Sun, as you know, is slowly brightening, across millions of years. Perhaps as that increase in available energy continues, more of the worlds of the inner System may be opened up for development.

Hmm. 'Opened up' literally. So they are building something. But what, this time? Another Phobos, another set of time chimneys? To where? The past?

Or the future. As our own time was once the future, as seen from the deep past.

I . . . see what you mean. Maybe this new chimney will – surface – in another few billion years. When maybe it will be Earth's turn to be stripped for mining. So they can prepare for the next phase of the Solar System's ageing.

That is possible.

And they shove around whole worlds to achieve these purposes?

So it seems. Our hypothesis is that in the deep past the same agency meddled with the planet we called Persephone – a rocky, eminently habitable world, shoved out to the periphery of the

Solar System. For some other unknown purpose.

Yes. Malenfant's World Engineers. There may have been no purpose in wrecking such a promising world. No direct purpose, I mean. Maybe it was just another side-effect, of another ghastly scheme. Used as a tool for some purpose.

That is eminently possible.

Well. I, or my original, followed Malenfant into Phobos, and we went there to try to confront those damn Engineers. Call them to account. Although . . . Listen. What difference might it have made? Even if Malenfant did make it back to the dawn of the Solar System, and *changed* things . . . It wouldn't have changed stuff in the present, would it?

You mean, would Shiva have been deflected by such actions? No. We don't believe so.

You're talking about the manifold . . .

That is Malenfant's term, but it has stuck. The hypothesis is that we live in a multiverse of many interconnected universes – universes which branch off from each other, from common origins, as time progresses, and choices are made. Some of these 'choices' may not be conscious – for example, if an asteroid is slightly deflected, by some random deep-space collision, towards or away from a planet with a rich, fragile biosphere . . . Different outcomes of trivial, chance events can have profound consequences, even without conscious design.

And the events that happened back at the origin of the Solar System, when the worlds were still colliding, could have had huge consequences for what followed.

Better to say, such events were the root of significant branchings of history types in the greater manifold. For example, the Moon seems to have been created from the stuff of the Earth, thanks to a chance collision with another young planet, back in that epoch. If the parameters of that collision had been slightly different—

You'd get two moons. A bigger moon, a smaller moon. No moon at all . . .

You see, if you meddled with the event that created the Moon, you would not reshape any individual history, but you would reshape the manifold itself, as a probability distribution.

Ah. So if I, my template, went back with Malenfant to the age of the Engineers and somehow blocked the aiming of Shiva in the first place—

You would not save this timeline, no. Which has suffered the consequence of a collision. But you could reshape the manifold, prune the branches, so that the probability *of the existence of many timelines in which such a collision did not occur could be greatly enhanced.*

Umm. OK. That's a good thing. And yet it feels . . . not enough. Because I couldn't save people in this reality, could I?

Well, most of the population of Earth alive at the time of the Destroyer did survive the collision events, Greggson Deirdra. There was, after all, plenty of warning. There are bunkers, underground habitats.

But this is just – aftermath. Earth, as a planet habitable for humans, is doomed.

True.

And the received wisdom in my day was that humans cannot survive without the Earth – without a healthy terrestrial biosphere.

True again. But.

But?

But that isn't the whole story yet, Deirdra. You may not yet be ready to process further information. If I could give you an image of the Earth as it is now, as seen from its detached Moon – glowing white with cloud, in the light of a too-close Sun – you would also see another kind of cloud, all around it. Pinpricks in the dark.

I don't understand.

Ships, Greggson Deirdra. Thousands of them. Spacecraft of many designs, habitats of all shapes and sizes. I told you that you had inspired a new wave of interest in space travel. Well, there you see it — or you will.

For now they linger close to the wounded mother. Perhaps some of them will lift survivors out of the toxic pit Earth has become. And then they will move on, seeking new homes, new ways of living.

Wow. So much for Homeward. I can guess the logic. So maybe we can't survive beyond Earth. But let's try anyhow.

A very human illogic, but rather magnificent. They call themselves the Murmuration.

I guess Malenfant had a profound influence after all. That image of Malenfant on the Pylon, with the whole world looking on . . . It became iconic.

No, Deirdra. You misunderstand. As did we. We too feared the Destroyer, and the termination of knowledge. We asked Malenfant for his help.

You did? Wow. That must have inflated his ego to bursting.

But in the end it wasn't about Malenfant. It wasn't Malenfant's example that inspired humanity. Not directly. It was you *who went to Malenfant when he was woken. You* who helped him find *his way to a spacecraft, so he could reach Emma Stoney once again.* You *who inspired the journey to the comet cloud, in an attempt to deflect Shiva. You* who tried to save us all. You *who went back to Phobos.*

Yours is a story left incomplete. But what we know — it may have been instinct, you were very young, but it was a good and profound instinct. And, by following that instinct, you changed the world. You may have reshaped the manifold itself . . . Greggson Deirdra, this story has never been about Malenfant. He is a trickster – a catalyst, yes. But you are the hero.

That is why we have Retrieved you now. Because the Murmuration asked it of us.

I did not think to ask who wanted me. I'm sorry . . . By the way. What became of Bartholomew?

The medical-support assistant?

He followed Malenfant, and me, wherever we went.

And he followed you into Phobos. So the records show.

Ha! Quite a journey, for a walking, talking set of rules, as Malenfant would have said. I hope it ended well, for him.

Maybe I should rest now. That's a lot to take in. Even if I'm not sure I believe a word of all this.

That is your privilege. And rest is a good idea. Then, perhaps, we can discuss what you would like to do next, Greggson Deirdra. I mean, this copy, now that your original has gone to the past.

Why, that's obvious, isn't it?

It is?

You have a Moon full of children here, tucked away in their sleep pods. Children who have outlived the planet of their birth. Who's going to take care of them?

Oh, I don't need more rest.

Let's get to work.

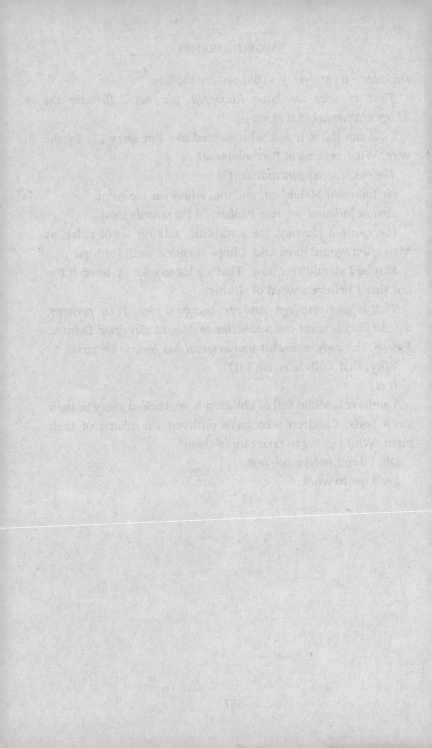

Afterword

Reid Malenfant and Emma Stoney were recurring characters in my *Manifold* series of books (*Time, Space, Origin* and *Phase Space*, 1999–2001), in which the title 'World Engines' was first used.

John M. Logsdon's *After Apollo?* (Palgrave Macmillan, 2015) is a fine recent account of the post-Apollo decision-making process about the space programme by Nixon's White House from 1969 to 1971. David Jenkins's *Space Shuttle: The History of Developing the National Space Transportation System* (Voyageur Press, 2002) is a comprehensive history of NASA's shuttle programme (in our timeline). The accident that befell Malenfant's *Constitution* (a name originally applied to the shuttle test article that became *Enterprise*) was modelled on an incident that did occur on the shuttle's first spaceflight on 12 April 1981, as reported in NASA's 'STS-1 Anomaly Report', when a surge from one of the solid rocket boosters caused a strut to fail in the orbiter's reaction control system.

It is true that flying to the Moon proved hazardous to the cardiac health of the Apollo astronauts, perhaps due to the effects of deep-space radiation (M. Delp *et al.*, *Scientific Reports*, vol. 6, Article no. 29901, 2016). Indeed Apollo 15 astronaut James Irwin briefly lost consciousness on the lunar surface due to a heart rhythm disturbance, only to have a heart attack twenty-one months after his mission (R. S. Johnson *et al.*, *Biomedical Results of Apollo*, NASA SP-368, 1975). The brief quotation in Chapter 50, from a speech that would have been given by Nixon if the Apollo 11 astronauts had died on the Moon, is reported in Logsdon (p.18). Gerard K. O'Neill's vision of our future in space (*The High Frontier: Human Colonies in Space*, William Morrow, 1977), developed from the 1960s, is heavily dated but continues to inspire. Christian Davenport's *The Space Barons* (Public Affairs, 2018) is a recent study of the new generation of space entrepreneurs.

The idea of a universal basic income and Richard Nixon's championing of the idea is explored in Rutger Bergman's *Utopia for Realists* (Bloomsbury, 2017). The H. G. Wells quotation in Chapter 13 ('the elimination of drudgery . . .') is from his *Outline of History* (Cassell, 1920). John Lennon's contribution to history was well expressed by the excellent 'Double Fantasy – John and Yoko' exhibition, at the Museum of Liverpool, 2018. The history and philosophy of the Outer Space Treaty and related developments is explored in Thomas Gangale's *The Development of Outer Space* (Santa Barbara, 2009). Regarding future non-agricultural food supplies, in 2018 it was reported that a Finnish company called Solar Foods was developing a process to manufacture food from hydrogen-oxidising bacteria, water, solar power, and trace inorganic materials.

The partial reconstruction of an individual's genome from the DNA of descendants has indeed been achieved in the case of an African, son of a slave, abducted to Iceland in the eighteenth century (A. Jagadeesan *et al.*, 'Reconstructing an African haploid genome from the 18th century', *Nature Genetics*, doi:10.1038/s41588-017-0031-6, January 2018). Meanwhile experiments in compiling searchable databases of historical knowledge include 'Seshat', established in 2010 at the University of Connecticut ('History Lessons' by Laura Spinney, *New Scientist*, 15 October 2016).

The use of a combination of AI and magnetic resonance imaging scanning to 'read minds' is an advancing technology; see the report by Timothy Revell in *New Scientist* of 10 March 2018 ('AI reads your mind to describe images').

My speculations on the future of the climate have been informed by, among other recent works, *The Human Planet* by Simon L. Lewis and Mark A. Maslin (Pelican, 2018), on the notion of the Anthropocene and its implications for the future of human society, *The New Wild* by Fred Pearce (Icon Books, 2015), a provocative depiction of the future of nature, and David Archer's *The Long Thaw* (Princeton, 2009), a convincing study of the long-term effects of extreme climate change. The notion of using large-scale tree growth to absorb excess carbon dioxide from the atmosphere has been studied by visionary thinker Freeman Dyson ('Can We Control the Carbon Dioxide in the Atmosphere?', *Energy*, vol. 2, 1977, pp. 287–91) and promoted by, among others, Pakistani politician Imran Khan with his 'billion tree tsunami' pledge of 2015. See also L. Ornstein *et al.* ('Terraforming the Sahara', *Climatic Change*, vol. 97, 2009, pp. 409–37) on using the irrigated afforestation of the Sahara and Australian Outback to offset global warming. The 'Pleistocene Park' concept of reviving the mammoth steppe to aid climate control is being trialled in Siberia (see E. Kintisch, 'Born to Rewild', *Science*, vol. 350, 2015, pp. 1148–51).

As reported in the *Guardian* of 20 October 2017, the Japanese

Aerospace and Exploration Agency (Jaxa), which has long-term plans for lunar colonisation, has confirmed the discovery of large-scale underground lava tubes on the Moon, possibly suitable for habitation. Emma II's mission to Phobos is based on proposals made in *Leadership and America's Future in Space* (NASA, August 1987), a blueprint for NASA's future drawn up by a team led by astronaut Sally Ride in the aftermath of the *Challenger* disaster. Useful accounts of long-duration spaceflight on the Soviet-era Mir and the modern International Space Station respectively are *Dragonfly* by Bryan Burroughs (Fourth Estate, 1998) and *Endurance* by Scott Kelly (Doubleday, 2017).

The drive system used in the *Last Small Step* spacecraft is based on the VASIMR (Variable Specific Impulse Magnetoplasma Rocket) concept; see E. Seedhouse *et al.*, *To Mars and Beyond, Fast!*, Springer, 2017. 'Skyfarms' much as depicted here were suggested and described by M. Hempsell ('Skyfarm: Feeding a Large Space Population', *Journal of the British Interplanetary Society*, vol. 70, 2017, pp. 3–11).

That the apparent secular deceleration of Mars's moon Phobos might be due to the moon being hollow was indeed proposed by the Russian astrophysicist Iosif Shklovsky (*The Universe, Life, and Mind*, Academy of Sciences USSR, Moscow, 1962). The space probes have proved that (in our reality) Phobos is a natural object, but is undergoing an orbital decay entirely accounted for by tidal effects.

A survey of current speculation on the hypothetical properties of 'time crystals' – described in Chapter 54 – was given by Shannon Palus in *New Scientist* of 6 May 2017.

Alternate-history speculation on what might have happened if Lord Halifax, rather than Churchill, had become Prime Minister of Great Britain in the crisis of 1940 has been developed by, among others, Andrew Roberts in his essay on 'Prime Minister Halifax' in *More What If*, ed. Robert Cowley (Macmillan, 2002). A recent and authoritative account of the post-war British space programme is C. N. Hill's *A Vertical Empire* (Imperial College Press, 2012). The 'Black Prince IV' launch vehicle sketched here is based on Hill's own speculation (p. 330) on how the British technology of 1964 could have been used to build a launch vehicle (almost) capable of sending a crewed Gemini spacecraft to orbit – a speculation Hill made in response to a similar design in a story called 'Prospero One' by myself and Simon Bradshaw (1996). A recent history of the British Aircraft Corporation's 'Mustard' concept of the 1960s is Dan Sharp's *British Secret Projects 5: Britain's Space Shuttle* (Crecy Publishing, 2016). The British nuclear-power rocket engine technology hinted at here is based on the early post-war research described by Arthur C. Clarke in his *Interplanetary Flight* (Temple Press, 1950) and featured in his own early fiction. Today, under the UK Space Agency (search under www.gov.uk), a new generation is developing a new space industry in Britain.

Elizabeth Tasker's *Planet Factory* (Bloomsbury Sigma, 2017) is a useful summary of the latest thinking on the formation of planetary systems. There are believed to be many rogue planets between the stars. The first known interstellar visitor to the Solar System, an asteroid, was observed in 2017 ('Meet 'Oumuamua, the First-Ever Asteroid from Another Star', Mike Wall, *Scientific American*, via Space.com, 16 November 2017).

The planetary rockets described here were inspired in part by a paper by Swiss physicist M. Taube ('Future of the Terrestrial Civilisation Over a Period of Billions of Years', *Journal of the British Interplanetary Society*, vol. 35, 1982, pp. 219–25) on methods to move the Earth in a future age when our Sun will swell to a red giant.

All errors and misapprehensions are of course my sole responsibility.

Stephen Baxter
Northumberland
September 2018

THE XEELEE SEQUENCE

Stephen Baxter

Beginning with RAFT in 1991, Stephen Baxter's epic sequence of Xeelee novels introduced readers to perhaps the most ambitious fictitious universe ever created.

Beginning with the rise and fall of sub-quantum civilisations in the first nano-seconds after the Big Bang and ending with the heat death of the universe billions of years from now, the series charts the story of mankind's epic war against the ancient and unknowable alien race, the Xeelee.

Along the way it examines questions of physics, the nature of reality, the evolution of mankind and its possible future. It looks not just at the morality of war but at the morality of survival and our place in the universe.

• • •

'Strong imagination, a capacity for awe, and the ability to think rigorously about last and final things abound in the work of Stephen Baxter' *TLS*

'The sheer timescale makes a great story that is panoramic in extent. Baxter's ability to turn science into exciting and readable fiction makes him one of the most accessible SF writers around' *The Times*

PROXIMA-ULTIMA

Stephen Baxter

The very far future: the Galaxy is a drifting wreck of black holes, neutron stars, chill white dwarfs. The age of star formation is long past. Yet there is life here, feeding off the energies of the stellar remnants, and there is mind, a tremendous Galaxy-spanning intelligence each of whose thoughts lasts a hundred thousand years. And this mind cradles memories of a long-gone age when a more compact universe was full of light . . .

The 27th century: Proxima Centauri, an undistinguished red dwarf star, is the nearest star to our sun – and (in this fiction), the nearest to host a world, Proxima IV, habitable by humans. But Proxima IV is unlike Earth in many ways. Huddling close to the warmth, orbiting in weeks, it keeps one face to its parent star at all times. The 'substellar point', with the star forever overhead, is a blasted desert, and the 'antistellar point' on the far side is under an ice cap in perpetual darkness. How would it be to live on such a world?

Yuri Jones, with 1,000 others, is about to find out . . .

PROXIMA tells the amazing tale of how we colonise a harsh new eden, and the secret we find there that will change our role in the Universe for ever.

In ULTIMA the consequences of what we discovered make themselves felt. There are minds in the universe billions of years old and they have a plan for us. For some of us.

• • •

'[Stephen Baxter] is one of the few still producing massive, fastidiously textured SF epics that engage the intelligence of the reader. Ideas come thick and fast, and an exhilarating sense of wonder is guaranteed' *Independent*

'This is a hard SF novel that battles bravely with big ideas. With every passing year, the oft-made remark that Baxter is Arthur C. Clarke's heir seems more and more apt' *SFX*

THE NORTHLAND TRILOGY

Stephen Baxter

8,000 years ago Europe was a very different place. England was linked to Holland by a massive swathe of land. Where the North Sea is now lay the landmass of Northland. And then came a period of global warming, a shifting of continents and, over a few short years, the sea rushed in and our history was set.

But what if the sea had been kept at bay? Brythony is a young girl who lives in Northland. Like all her people she is a hunter gatherer, her simple tools fashioned from flint cutting edges lodged in wood and animal bone. When the sea first encroaches on her land her people simply move. Brythony moves further travelling to Asia. Where she sees mankind's first walled cities. And gets an idea. What if you could build a wall to keep the sea out?

And so begins a colossal engineering project that will take decades, a wall that stretches for hundreds of miles, a wall that becomes an act of defiance, and containing the bones of the dead, an act of devotion. A wall that will change the geography of the world. And its history.

• • •

Get the complete trilogy now
Stone Spring, Bronze Summer, Iron Winter

Stephen Baxter

FLOOD

Next year. Sea levels begin to rise. The change is far more rapid than any climate change predictions; metres a year. Within two years London, only 15 metres above the sea, is drowned. New York follows, the Pope gives his last address from the Vatican, Mecca disappears beneath the waves.

FLOOD tells the story of mankind's final years on earth. The stories of a small group of people caught up in the struggle to survive are woven into a tale of unimaginable global disaster. And the hope offered for a unlucky few by a second great ark . . .

ARK

As the waters rose in FLOOD, high in the Colorado mountains the US government was building an ark. Not an ark to ride the waves but an ark that would take a select few thousand people out into space to start a new future for mankind. Sent out into deep space on a journey lasting years, generations of crew members carry the hope of a new beginning on a new, incredibly distant, planet.

But as time passes knowledge and purpose is lost and division and madness grows. And back on earth life, and man, find a new way. This is the epic sequel to the acclaimed FLOOD; a stirring tale of what mankind will do to survive and the perfect introduction for new readers to one of SF's greatest tropes; the generation ship.

'Never has Baxter presented a more thrilling and moving glimpse of a possible future: ARK could well be his masterpiece' *Guardian*

ABOUT GOLLANCZ

Gollancz is the oldest SF publishing imprint in the world. Since being founded in 1927 Gollancz has continued to publish a focused selection of bestselling and award-winning authors. The front-list includes **Ben Aaronovitch**, **Joe Abercrombie**, **Charlaine Harris**, **Joanne Harris**, **Joe Hill**, **Alastair Reynolds**, **Patrick Rothfuss**, **Nalini Singh** and **Brandon Sanderson**.

As one of the largest Science Fiction and Fantasy imprints in the UK it is no surprise we have one of the most extensive backlists in the world. Find high-quality SF on Gateway written by such authors as **Philip K. Dick**, **Ursula Le Guin**, **Connie Willis**, **Sir Arthur C. Clarke**, **Pat Cadigan**, **Michael Moorcock** and **George R.R. Martin**.

We also have a strand of publishing in translation, which includes French, Polish and Russian authors. Gollancz is home to more award-winning authors than any other imprint, with names including **Aliette de Bodard**, **M. John Harrison**, **Paul McAuley**, **Sarah Pinborough**, **Pierre Pevel**, **Justina Robson** and many more.

The SF Gateway
More than 3,000 classic, rare and previously out-of-print SF novels at your fingertips.
www.sfgateway.com

The Gollancz Blog
Bringing you news from our worlds to yours. Stories, interviews, articles and exclusive extracts just for you!
www.gollancz.co.uk

GOLLANCZ
LONDON